Hannah's Home

Also by the author

~ * ~

Call Me Lydia
Maple Dale
Favored to Win
Maple Dale Revisited
The Frog, the Wizard, and the Shrew
Ellie's Crows
For the Love of Horses

~ * ~

Soon to be released

Odds on Favorite – A Sequel to *Favored to Win*

Hannah's Home

MaryAnn Myers

Sunrise Horse Farm
11872 Chillicothe Road
Chesterland, Ohio 44026
440-729-0930
www.sunrisehorsefarm.com

First Edition
10 9 8 7 6 5 4 3 2 1

1. Fiction 2.Horses 3. Love Story 4. Ghosts

Formatted to save paper

Hannah's Home is dedicated to every woman who has ever struggled to make it on her own, and to the spirit of horses...

Chapter One

Hannah had either taken leave of her senses or craved yet another monumental failure. The old Brubaker Homestead had been chopped up at least a dozen times since its day, and now sat on a pithy, oddly configured eleven acres of overgrown orchard that had long since given edible fruit. The house was a total wreck and the barn was literally falling down around itself, reasons enough why the place hadn't sold after all these years, not to mention that it looked haunted. Who in their right mind would even think of buying it?

Hannah paid the deposits for the gas and electricity to be turned on and held her breath with that first toilet flush. "Go down, go down," she whispered to the stagnant rusty toilet bowl water. It filled to the rim and took to bubbling and gurgling.

"Oh no!"

Just when it was about to overflow, it started swirling and swirling. Then ultimately with a splash, it disappeared.

"Thank heaven." The fact that it was replaced with water as red as Mississippi mud didn't cause Hannah to bat an eye. The old well was still pumping and now she had proof there was a functional septic system.

"At least the water went somewhere."

She and her two best friends, Lucinda and Colleen, went back into the living room and cracked opened a bottle of wine.

"Cheers!"

"To your new home!"

"To a fresh start!"

"Hear! Hear!"

Hannah wasn't new to farm life; she grew up on a farm. She wasn't new to life period, or hard times either for that matter. She'd be turning fifty-five soon, and had been on her own since her husband Charlie left for work at the sawmill one morning two years ago. He never came home. He e-mailed her from a motel lobby in Fresno later that night before she could really start worrying. He was fine and said she should get on with her life, because that's what he was fixing to do. They'd been married thirty-four years. No children, just lots of dogs and cats and horses and cows and goats and chickens along the way. Charlie hadn't been the same since they lost the farm. The same could be said for Hannah. She blamed Charlie. He blamed her. Blame ate away at them day after day.

"This is never gonna go away," he used to say.

He was right. Hannah was sad for about a month after he left - even sadder when she had to start selling things, like their dining room set for instance, to get the truck fixed. She had her truck; Charlie had his. She stared out the window. His was the newer of the two and probably still running like a top. Charlie always took good care of it.

"What's your plan?" Lucinda asked. She and Colleen looked at her expectantly.

Hannah had two weeks left on her apartment lease. "Well, tomorrow Jim Gaskin's going to come look at the foundation. I guess I'll go from there." It wasn't much of a plan, but a plan nonetheless.

The news from Jim Gaskin the following day was not good. "The foundation is beyond help."

Hannah shook her head. "You're kidding. Are you sure?"

"Positive," he said, showing her. "See right here."

Hannah leaned down to look at the crumbling mortar.

2

"And here. And here. And over there. There too. The whole thing's like this. It's falling apart. Like I said, it's shot. I'm not a betting man, but if I were...." Jim stood up and rubbed his sore back. "I'd say this house won't be standing next year this time. The barn neither."

Hannah glanced away. "Don't cry, don't cry, don't cry," she told herself. "Don't cry." She stared at the barn and found herself counting cracks in the cinder block.

Jim took out a pack of cigarettes and lit one. "Are you all right?"

"Yes." Twenty one, twenty two, twenty three.

"You weren't planning to bring your horse here, were you?"

She nodded, and then shook her head and stopped counting. She'd been hoping to bring him here this week. Billy Bob, named after the actor Billy Bob Thornton because of his square jaw and wide-set eyes, was a big strong Leopard Appaloosa. He was Hannah's only horse now, her only animal, her only companion. She cleaned five stalls a day and fed evenings and weekends at the stable to pay for his board. All those hours working in addition to her full time job at the undertakers....

More than once, she wished she'd kept up her hairdresser's license. But she hadn't, hadn't kept up with styles either. All she was qualified to do was old people's hair. That's how she got the job at the funeral parlor. Small town that it was, on slow hair days, she put on the meals set up in the basement after the services. She knew how to cook; that didn't need updating. Charlie had been a lucky man that way. Even when they grew tired of each other, he still looked forward to her cooking. They'd probably still be together if all they had to do was sit down at the table and eat.

The barn inspection was next. Hannah glanced back over her shoulder at the house. How was she so mistaken, so misguided? She stood there even now blaming Charlie. Wasn't he the one that used to say how a house and barn like this lasts forever. Unlike marriages, she thought.

Jim went through the motions of walking around the outside of the barn, no easy task with all the brambles and overgrowth. The barn walls were splintered and rotting and the north side of the building was literally slipping off the foundation. "I'm sorry, Hannah," he said, holding up his hands. "But I think this place's a big waste of time. You should have checked all this out with me first."

Hannah nodded, as if she agreed, and trailed along after him to look inside the barn. They both had to pull and tug hard to get the doors

3

to open. In its day, this barn housed milk cows and then later on, riding horses, sale horses. Some of the cow stanchions were still standing, barely discernible for all the cobwebs. There were two relatively intact box stalls at the other end of the barn, but no stall doors. Since Billy Bob liked to look out his stall anyway, Hannah had figured she could just use a stall chain, and....

"Do you think the barn leaks?" she asked.

"It'd have to."

Hannah sighed.

"I say tear it all down and start new. Build yourself a cute little barn and get a nice doublewide, and...."

She looked at him. "How would you tear a barn this size down?"

"With a bulldozer. Just have someone come in and flatten it. The house too."

Wonderful. More money she didn't have. "What about the wood then and the siding? Would I be able to save any of it? Use any of it? Sell it?" The rafters creaked overhead.

"Probably not. If you're lucky, it would all end up like matchsticks."

"Then what?"

"I don't know. Have it hauled away, bury it. It's up to you."

The two of them walked out of the barn and into what used to be a pasture many years ago. It was now nothing but brush. Beyond that stood the barren orchard. There was a small paddock to the side of the barn.

"You know I worked here summers as a teenager," Jim said. "They made maple syrup every year."

"Here? You mean here in the barn?"

"No. They had a sugar shack out back."

Hannah's face lit up, a pretty face for her age, with big brown eyes. "Where out back?" She envisioned a quaint rundown little sugar shack with an overhang, running water and....

"They tore it down years ago."

Hannah nodded, thinking, that figures. She thanked Jim for his time and advice and walked him to his van.

"I'm sorry I couldn't be of more help."

"I know."

"You okay?"

She hesitated. "I'll figure out something."

4

Jim smiled sadly. He'd been Charlie's best friend. Charlie had walked out on him too. "Do you hear from him?"

Hannah shook her head. "No."

"Probably just as well, so you can get on with your life."

Hanna smiled, hands tucked in her jeans pockets and shoulders hunched. "Get on with your life." She wished she had a dollar for every time someone said that to her. She'd be rich. It would be like winning the lottery.

"Call me if you need anything," Jim said.

Hannah promised him she would.

"Sara and I'll go with you if you want me to help you pick out a trailer."

"Thanks." Hannah watched him maneuver his van out the drive. It bounced up and down like a yo-yo through the potholes. Then she turned and looked around. The farmhouse had been built in the late 1800's and had such charm, even in its dilapidated state. It wasn't a big house, nothing like the house she grew up in or the one she and Charlie used to have. It was a small saltbox style farmhouse with nice big windows. She walked over and sat down on the front steps and heaved a heavy sigh. What was she to do now?

Buying this farm made sense when she was going to be living here soon. Later, or in a trailer, tearing down the house and barn and rebuilding another one never entered her mind. She didn't have the money for any tear-down and rebuilding. She didn't have any money at all. Why didn't she just tell Jim that? Why? She shook her head. Pride, and God help her, she was still protecting Charlie. She'd never told anyone, not even Colleen and Lucinda, but when Charlie left, he left her without a penny to her name. Not one red cent. To his credit, when he left, he had little more than half a paycheck himself. He'd paid the rent on the apartment, she had about a week's worth of groceries in the fridge, and that was that.

Hannah combed her fingers through her shoulder-length sandy blonde hair. It was lighter than it had ever been, thanks to the salt and pepper graying throughout. She was of sturdy build, a result of farming her whole life, but slight in weight. She still looked good in jeans.

She relived the last two weeks' turn of events. She'd never had to transport a body before, but Jeb, the funeral home driver had come down with the flu. It was a chance to make a little extra money. Her boss Richard told her he'd pay her fifty dollars "under the table" to make the pick up, and would even buy her lunch. Hannah remembered thinking she'd better time the trip so she could eat on the way. Dining on takeout with a corpse in the back of the hearse seemed somehow disrespectful to her.

She didn't notice the "For Sale" sign on the way, but did notice it on the way back. She rarely went down this road, if ever. She couldn't recall seeing this farm before. She turned the hearse around and pulled into the driveway up to the first pothole. She checked to make sure the back of the hearse wasn't hanging out onto the street, edged up a little more, and sat looking at the farmhouse. Once upon a time it might have been brown, it was hard to tell. Either that or the paint had just faded to a wood-brown color. It must have had shutters over the years. There were rectangular patches of a slightly brighter shade of fade flanking each side of the windows. She wondered what color the shutters had been. White? Red? There was nice brickwork up the side of the house to the chimney, probably for a fireplace in the living room. Judging from the flowered curtain that still hung in the window at the back of the house she figured that room had to be the kitchen. Glancing at her watch, she thought about getting out and peeking inside, but with the time, decided against it. "I'll come back," she told herself. She talked to herself a lot these days. "Oh look. There's a barn."

Her traveling companion was a man of eighty-seven years. She preferred not to get to know the deceased too well. She couldn't get them out of her mind if she heard too many details of their life or death. This particular man had died in prison. Try as she might, she couldn't help wonder how long he'd been there, and for what offense.

As luck would have it, she made another trip back to the prison the following day, this time in her pickup truck. The prison warden had forgotten to send along the man's personal effects the day before, specifically his eyeglasses and false teeth. Since it wasn't her error, her boss said he'd pay her an additional twenty-five dollars cash plus gas money. She filled the tank in her truck, first time in a long time.

She rode by the farm again that evening and on the way back, slowed down and once again pulled into the driveway. Her truck sat up higher than the hearse and had 4-wheel drive, so she pulled in all the way and parked to the rear of the house, as if she lived there and was coming home to fix supper.

Through the windowed back door she saw an old, old, very old kitchen. From a side window and standing on her tiptoes, she could see

6

the nice-sized living room from several angles. She pressed her cheek against the window pane. It looked like the fireplace was right around the corner just beyond her view. She could see the corner bricks. She imagined her couch facing the fireplace, a warm crackling fire ablaze, a good book, a cup of chamomile tea. She looked at the floor. It was covered with an old green carpet, so threadbare she could see the grungy padding underneath and in spots, even the wood flooring. She wondered if the house had hardwood floors.

"Ma'am."

She turned and jumped all at once, gasping, and fell into a bush. She struggled to get to her feet. Two thorns of some sort imbedded themselves in her arm just below her elbow. They drew blood, an amazing amount of blood for such tiny thorns.

A little boy about ten years old stood watching her. "Are you okay, lady?"

"Yes," she said, pulling out the thorns and dusting herself off. He was a cute little kid, dressed in obvious hand-me-downs, and had an old baseball cap cocked sideways on his head. His tennis shoes were ancient.

"Have you seen my dog?"

"No, what's he look like?" Hannah asked, wiping the blood off her arm, again and again and spitting on her fingers to wash it away.

"It's big. It's a German Shepherd."

Hannah shook her head. "Sorry. What's his name?"

"He's a she. Her name's Bessie."

"Bessie...?"

"She almost died when she was a puppy. We kept her alive feeding her cow's milk. That's how she got her name."

Hannah nodded. "I see. Who's we? You mean you and your mom and dad?" Hannah inspected her arm and found another thorn. She pulled it out, wincing.

"No. Me'n and Maggie. I gotta go. I gotta go find her."

"Okay. Good luck," Hannah called after him, smiling. He'd disappeared into the brush like the baseball players stepping into the "Field of Dreams" cornfield. It would take at least a week of brush hogging to clear this land, she thought, and that would probably just be a path. She looked in the rest of the windows of the house. No bedroom downstairs. Just the kitchen, living room, bathroom and a tiny utility room. Judging from the number of windows upstairs, she figured there were probably two, maybe three small bedrooms. With a saltbox style house, it was hard to say.

She made her way to the barn, stopped short of entering when she heard a noise in the distance, and listened. It was the little boy calling for his dog.

"Bessie! Come on, Bessie! Come on, girl!"

"Poor little guy. I hope he finds her." She and Charlie had lost their share of pets over the years. One day they were there and the next day they were gone, never to be seen or heard from again.

"One less mouth to feed," Charlie would always say, but he missed them too. She swore she saw him shed a few tears when "Blue" showed up missing.

"How does a dog show up missing?" she remembered asking him, as she cried like a baby. "You either show up or you're missing! All right?"

He'd put his arms around here then and didn't say anything, not for a long time. She hugged him hard. His chest was trembling. "We'll get another one," he finally said, and walked outside. It was time to do chores. It was always time to do chores. He worked so hard. They both did.

"I want to go dancing," she said one day.

"You know I don't dance."

"Yeah, well too bad," she teased. "It's high time you learn. Come on, I'll teach you."

He shook his head. "Nah, I think I'll save my moves for later on tonight."

Hannah laughed and wrapped her arms around his neck. How old were they then? Thirty? Thirty-five? "Come on, please. I really, really want to go dancing. Just once. Just once, and I'll never ask again. I promise."

Charlie gazed into her eyes. "Let me think about it," he said. And he did. Three days later, seemingly out of the blue, he came in after night chores, "battening down the hatches" Hannah called it, watering off the livestock, making sure they all had hay, picking out the manure, closing up the barn. "I'm gonna take a quick shower," he told her. "You want to go dancing?"

"What?" She stared. "Yes, of course. Yes, I do! I'll go get ready!" She threw the dishtowel in the sink and hurried and got dressed in her favorite sweater and jeans. She pulled her hair back with a ribbon tied in a bow and put on mascara and lipstick and perfume.

"Don't you look pretty!" Charlie said, all spiffy-ed up himself. Charlie wasn't drop-dead gorgeous, but he did have a way about him. Hannah loved him in jeans and a cowboy hat. She loved putting a crease in those jeans and would starch his shirts and iron them just so. "I need to get something out of the hayloft," he said, as they walked to the truck. "Come on with me and I'll hand it down."

It was a beautiful, warm summer night. Hannah gazed up at the stars as they walked along. It wasn't often they held hands, but he was holding her hand now. She stood at the bottom of the ladder leading up to the loft, waiting for him. One by one, the cows looked at her. She smiled.

"Hey, Hannah," Charlie said. "Can you come up and help me a second?"

"No, I don't want to get dirty."

"Come on, you won't."

Hannah climbed the ladder and when she got to the top step, stood in awe with her mouth open. Charlie had swept the loose hay back to form a circle on the loft floor and had plugged in some Christmas lights all around. When he turned on the CD player, George Straight started singing her favorite song.

Charlie reached for her hand, helped her up the last step, and then led her onto the dance floor. "I believe this dance is mine," he said. And they danced with the Christmas lights twinkling, both of them smiling, holding on to one another, dancing and dancing, twirling and twirling. They were so much in love, so happy....

"Wait, there's more." Charlie opened the loft doors that looked out over their corn field. "Just for you," he said. There before them, under the stars, lighting up their cornfield, corn that would feed their livestock come winter, corn that was "Knee high by the Fourth of July" were hundreds and hundreds of fireflies sparkling in the night.

"I love you, Hannah," he said. And he did, then.

Hannah wiped her eyes and walked back to her truck.

She still had to deliver the dead prisoner's effects.

She also had to cut the man's hair.

Chapter Two

Hannah personally knew at least half the population in the town of Ridge Creek. Chances are she'd either grown up with the person, was related in some way, or had been their hairdresser or helped them bury a family member or friend. She was respected and loved by all, as the saying goes. As comforting as that was for Hannah, it also brought its share of heartache. At the mere mention of her name, people would always stop what they were doing and sigh. "Damn that Charlie for leaving her. Poor Hannah, she didn't deserve that. She's too nice a person. How could he do that to her? I'll bet he left her for a younger woman." Hannah saw nothing but pity in their eyes, felt it in the air all around them. From a distance and standing facing the wrong or right direction, she would swear she could even smell it in the wind.

This basically was the main reason she'd bought the Brubaker Homestead signed sealed and delivered, without consulting anyone until it was a done deal. She couldn't stand the thought of any more pity, or the well-intended but weighted advice, and those dreadful resounding sighs.

Hannah was a farmer and that's all there was to it. She'd do just about anything to be back on a farm, even with the prospect of losing that farm again. At least she'd have it for a little while. It was that determination that drove her to leap head first. Even now, with all the bad news about the house's foundation, Hannah was excited about moving in. Plus there was something akin to her about the seller's way of thinking. Chopped up the way the parcel was, it wasn't likely that a builder would buy it. Still, the seller, a man or woman unknown to her but for the paperwork, E.J. Riley, had it written into the contract that the remaining acreage was not to be subdivided and that the property had to be sold as a farm. Since it was completely owner-financed, priced right with no money down and right up Hannah's alley, she signed on the dotted line in a flash.

Money. Hannah looked around her apartment living room. There wasn't much left. She had the couch and loveseat, coffee table and the one end table, a lamp, and a throw rug. The other end table was the first thing she sold. It had been Charlie's. The man who bought it didn't mind the coffee ring at all. He said he'd probably be adding a few more to it. It had been pretty challenging having a garage sale at a twelve-unit apartment building without any garages.

Hannah didn't want to call it a yard sale. If it rained, no one would come. She and Colleen put an ad in the newspaper announcing, "Rain or Shine." Hannah needed the money badly. She remembered pretending to be so happy to be rid of each item of hers that sold. "Another memory bites the dust," she'd say. That part was true. Some held bad memories for her, but a lot held good ones too. That's why she never sold the bedroom set.

It had been her idea to sell baked goods at the garage sale, and that turned out to be a huge success. She made more money on her sweet potato and boysenberry pies than she did on the book shelf and tea cart. No one cared that the furniture was solid oak. No one knew how long Hannah had saved money to buy the pieces. Oak or veneer, it didn't matter. Twenty dollars each was all the money the only woman seriously interested in buying them would pay. Hannah dusted both pieces of furniture one last time while considering the price and then gave them up. She even helped load them into the woman's beat-up mini-van.

She wished she had them back now. She wished she had a lot of things back now. How was she going to furnish her new house? She picked up a magazine she'd brought up with her from the laundry room of the apartment building and leafed through it. Comfort was all Charlie ever wanted. Hannah liked comfort too, but she also wanted it to look nice. When they still had cable TV, her favorite channel was the Decorating Channel. Charlie came in from the barn one day and found her sitting cross-legged on the kitchen table, mesmerized by one of those 24-hour decorating turnarounds.

"Look, Charlie! Isn't that pretty?"

"Yeah," he said, running cold water over a cut on his hand. He'd been out fixing fences. "Gretta's due to drop."

"I know," Hannah said. She had a lap full of clean towels, all set to go. She tore her eyes away from the television screen. "What'd you do?"

"Nothing," he said. "It's nothing." His hands were large and callused, with scars everywhere. Chances are this cut would scar too. Hannah knew better than to suggest they go to the emergency room for stitches. With them not having hospitalization or any money to spare, Charlie always just "toughed it up." Hannah dried off his hand, dusted some gringo powder on the cut and bandaged it, then dropped a kiss on his fingertip.

Gretta's calf was big, almost too big. It was her third. Over the years they'd helped one hundred and seven calves come into this world and only lost two. Hannah didn't particularly like calving, didn't like the pulling. She shuddered at the thought. She always wished the calves could stay with their mothers longer too, but one day was all they had. It was the dairy way.

Hannah thumbed through the rest of the magazine and sat back. She would have loved to have taken a nap at the moment, but didn't have time. She and Charlie used to always take naps. That too, was the dairy way: up every morning at four-thirty, work until noon or so, eat lunch, take a nap (sometimes they'd make love if so inclined and they had the energy) and then back out to the barn at three until around seven. The night Gretta's third calf was born they were in the barn at her side, sweating and agonizing right along with her until well past midnight. It was a male calf, and he bayed as loud as they come.

Hannah was meeting Lucinda and Colleen at the Honky Tonk for some chili and dollar beer in about a half hour, and decided to use that time to do a little more packing. Being forced to downsize and sell practically everything she owned over the past couple of years had its advantages. There wasn't much to pack. Hannah took the drinking glasses down off the shelf and wrapped them in newspaper. She wrapped the dishes too, and then laughed at herself. Without dishes and a glass to drink from, what sense would leaving silverware make? She ended up packing everything in the kitchen: pots and pans, trivets, the spices, staples, all of it, even the few items that were in the fridge.

This was the new Hannah. She was getting good at making snap decisions. She and Charlie used to debate and deliberate decisions for hours. When she arrived at the Honky Tonk later than expected, Lucinda and Colleen were in their usual booth waiting for her and on the verge of getting concerned.

"Your beer's warm," Lucinda said.

Hannah drank it anyway. "I've decided I'm moving tonight."

"What? Where will you sleep?"

"I've got my bed in the back of the pickup."

"You're kidding."

"Nope." Hannah shook her head.

"But what about the foundation?"

12

Hannah shrugged and waved for another round of drinks. "When Jim said the house probably wouldn't be standing next year this time, he didn't say anything about tonight."

The three of them laughed and were laughing again at Hannah's account of how she loaded the mattress and box spring off the balcony herself and down into her pickup parked on the grass, when Dave, the bartender with a crush on Hannah, put their beers down in front of them. "You're looking pretty," he said to Hannah.

"Thank you."

Dave wasn't her type. Actually, there weren't very many men her type or that even got a second look, unless they resembled Charlie is some way. The way they talked, the way they smiled. The way they walked. A certain sparkle in their eyes. Dave had none of these traits.

"What're you girls up to tonight?" he asked.

"We're moving Hannah into her new house," Lucinda said.

Hannah gave her a look.

Oops.

"Not really," Hannah said. "I'm just taking a few things over."

"Do you need some help?" Dave asked.

"No, no thank you." Hannah smiled. "When I do though, I'll let you know."

Dave nodded in anticipation and walked away.

"Lucinda!" Hannah hissed.

"Sorry." Lucinda sipped the foam off her beer. "I just thought it wouldn't hurt to have a little manpower on the job." Lucinda was forever trying to get Hannah to take Dave up on a date; to go out and kick up her heels, get on with her life.

"This *is* my life," Hannah would always say, and promptly change the subject. "Oh, and I pulled up the carpet in the living room today and the floor actually isn't too bad. I'm excited. Eat!"

A big bowl of chili and crackers for each and they were on their way. The three had been friends since grade school and there were times, even though they were all in their mid-fifties that they still felt like teenagers, or at least twenty-somethings. Lucinda had been married twice and was ready to tie the knot again. It was just a matter of time. Colleen was married to Lucinda's brother. Lucinda had two children, grown and on their own, and one grandchild. Colleen had three grown children and two grandchildren. All of their combined children and their families lived out of town or in another state. There was a saying in

Ridge Creek that even if you loved your kids and they loved you, it wasn't enough to keep them around. No sooner had they come of age, they were gone from this farming ghost town.

The hardwood floor in the living room wasn't what most people would consider a hardwood floor. This was more like the hardwood planking that would go under the hardwood flooring, but Hannah like it. It looked sturdy, and with the house falling down around her, the sturdiness of this floor was just what the doctor ordered to remedy a case of the doubts. She'd swept and mopped the floor earlier in the day and now it almost had a shine to it. She'd also scrubbed the old kitchen table and chairs that the previous owner had left too. It cleaned up nice.

"Oh my God!" Colleen gasped.

"What?" Hannah and Lucinda turned, followed Colleen's throat-clutching wide-eyed stare, and watched a big huge brown spider trying to squeeze its way out of Hannah's upright sweeper. Head and two legs, three legs, four....

"Quick!" Hannah screeched. "Open the door!"

Lucinda scrambled to unlock the latch, Hannah grabbed the sweeper, and out the front door it went. Five legs, six.... No sooner had the spider made its break, than it was gone, down over the side of the porch.

"I have never, I mean never *ever* seen a spider that big before!" Colleen said.

"I know." Hannah agreed. "I sucked up three of them that size today, not to mention a gazillion that looked just like them only smaller." Hannah didn't like spiders, but from all the time she'd spent in a barn, was accustomed to them being around. "I should have emptied the bag. I'll go do it now."

"Did you run the sweeper in all the rooms?" Lucinda asked.

"No, just downstairs."

"I'm not going up there," Colleen said.

"I'll run it when I come back. I don't want any more to sneak out."

Hannah dragged the sweeper down the front steps and through the thicket over to the woods. It was there; she heard voices calling and stopped dead in her tracks. Children's voices? No, a child's and an adult, a woman. No, a child and an older woman, elderly. And the name, "Bessie." Were they *still* looking for that dog?

Hannah turned with a start when something brushed against her thigh. The porch lamp offered very little in the way of light this far from the house. She looked down and there stood a German Shepherd. "Bessie," she said, hoping this was indeed Bessie and that Bessie was of a friendly sort. "Hey, girl. How are you doing?"

Bessie wagged her tail and then with a bound, jumped up and started licking her in the face. "That's a good girl. She's over here!" Hannah shouted. "Bessie's over here!"

Nothing. No response.

"Your dog's over here!" she shouted again. "Over by the Brubaker House. I mean my house. We're over here!"

"Hannah?" Lucinda and Colleen stood on the porch, calling to her. "Are you okay?"

"Yes, I'm fine. I found that little boy's dog?"

"What little boy?"

"The little boy! Over here, little boy. Your dog's over here!"

"What kind of dog?" Lucinda asked.

"A German Shepherd."

"You'd better watch. They can be mean."

"Not this one." Hannah laughed. "Little boy, do you hear me? Little boy! Misses!"

Nothing, no response. Just the sound of Lucinda and Colleen, down off the porch and making their way toward them. "Where are you?"

"Over here?" Hannah said, and just then the dog jumped down, took off, and ran into the woods. "Oh no! Come back! Bessie, come back!"

Lucinda and Colleen were at her side. "Where'd it go?"

"In the woods. Right there."

"Wish we had a flashlight."

"Or a candle."

The three stood there calling to Bessie again and again as they listened for voices or barking. All they heard were crickets and frogs and the sound of the breeze rustling through the trees. Finally, Hannah dumped the sweeper, and they went back inside.

"Well, at least we know she's okay." Hannah washed her hands in the kitchen sink and then rinsed her face. Her shirt was streaked with dirt and wet blades of grass. She brushed it off over the waste basket and was just about to lug the sweeper upstairs when the three of them heard a noise on the second floor. A loud scratching noise.

"Oh, Hannah, you can't stay here tonight. It's probably a raccoon." Lucinda said, shuddering. She hated raccoons. It was a well-known fact. Ever since some coons tore up her attic and peed down through the ceiling and....

"I didn't see any sign of coon up there." Hannah had been upstairs several times that day. "I didn't see any signs of any animal anywhere."

"Then it's probably rats in the rafters," Lucinda insisted.

"Oh wonderful."

They heard the scratching sound again.

"It sounds like it's on the roof."

"Bats. Probably bats in your chimney," Lucinda said, ducking, as if they were right overhead.

Hannah laughed. Perhaps under different circumstances she'd be rather frightened too, but with a belly full of Honky Tonk chili and those couple of beers, she was feeling rather mellow and in total charge of her circumstances. "I'll go shut the doors and just put my bed up down here for tonight."

Lucinda and Colleen nodded. That sounded like a good plan. "Do you want us to come with you?"

"No, I'm fine," Hannah said. They followed her up the stairs in a tight clump anyway. It reminded Hannah of the time when they were in High School and the three of them snuck into.... They closed all the doors for the three bedrooms and one bathroom, and hurried back downstairs.

"There. All better."

Lucinda set her sights on the kitchen, wiping out all the cabinets for a second time before putting all the kitchen items away. Colleen and Hannah hauled the bed inside, and set it up. Hannah had lots of pillows since Charlie hadn't taken his, and when they got the bed all made up with the sheets and pillow cases and shams, and then pushed it up against the wall, it looked like a daybed, queen size. Against the wall was the only way Hannah could sleep. She'd even take her chances with a creepy-crawling spider or two, rather than try to fall asleep without a sense of security and belonging at her back.

"Are you sure you're going to be okay by yourself?"

"Yes," Hannah said, thanking them for the umpteenth time for all their help.

"What about your bathroom? Do you want us to help you clean it?"

"No, I'll do it," Hannah said, and gave them both a hug. "Go home. You've done enough. Thank you."

She locked the door and watched them pull out the driveway. Lucinda was driving and flashed her lights. Hannah smiled, very happy and content for the moment as she waved, blessed to have such good friends and a home of her own. Then all she saw was darkness and a feeling of sadness washed over her. She'd never felt so alone in her life. What was she thinking, moving in here like this in the dead of night? She hugged her arms to her sides.

Drapes. First thing tomorrow, she'd have to find drapes. Perhaps at Annie's Consignment Store; maybe she'd have some. Hannah glanced into the bathroom. It definitely needed a good cleaning. All she'd done earlier was wipe down the toilet and de-cobweb the cubby around it. She drew a deep breath and sighed. Not tonight. She was simply too tired, too mellow. She sat down on the bed to take off her shoes and socks and turned out the overhead light, then crawled under the covers and slid out of her jeans, just in case someone was looking in the windows. Within minutes, she was sound asleep.

Chapter Three

Hannah woke with a start to the sound of someone or some-thing tapping on the window just above her head. At first she thought she was dreaming. But no, this was very real. Tap! Tap! ... Tap! Tap! "Hey, lady!"

She recognized the little boy's voice. She wrapped the blanket around her waist, secured it with her belt, turned on the light, and glanced at her clock. Two-thirty-two. What on earth...? She opened the door. "What's the matter?"

"Nothing," the little boy said. "I'm looking for my dog."

"I saw her earlier," Hannah said, wiping the sleep from her eyes. "Shouldn't you be home? Don't you have school tomorrow? I mean today."

"I have to find my dog." He looked close to tears.

"Listen, I'll tell you what. She seems real friendly, so next time I see her; I'll tie her up, okay? And then I'll call you. What's your phone number?"

The little boy shook his head. "We don't have one. I'll just come back. Sorry I woke you, lady." He scurried off the porch.

"My name's Hannah," she called after him. "What's yours?"

No answer. He was gone.

Hannah locked the door and sat down on the bed. Where were this kid's parents? And why did they let him out this time of night? Why weren't they watching him? Did they even know? She turned off the light, unwrapped herself and spread the blanket and got back under the covers and made herself comfortable. With the day facing her, she relished a few more hours sleep. Trailering Billy Bob home today was not going to be fun. He was the worst horse in the world to load in a trailer, that's if he would load at all. She'd missed many a trail ride with friends from the barn when he just flat refused to load no matter what. They tried everything. They even had a self proclaimed "Horse Whisperer" at the barn once who tried, only to give up after two hours. Running out of daylight, he said he wanted to come back and shoulder hobble Billy Bob and drop him down, make him submissive, become the herd leader.

Hannah said that wasn't necessary and promptly gave Billy Bob his "bow" cue. A tap on the back of his left elbow and down Billy Bob went, first onto his knees, and then down onto his side, happy as could be. Hannah could sleep on him, sit on him. She could do whatever she wanted with him. He was totally submissive. When she tugged on his halter to get him to stand, the horse whisperer motioned for her to try loading him now, and Billy Bob promptly planted his feet. He wasn't going to advance one inch toward that trailer.

Hannah drifted off to sleep, recalling that night, and hoped beyond hope that today he'd walk right up the ramp. There were times he would. She crossed her fingers and then her toes. When she woke a little over three hours later all her "wish crosses" were still in place and she had muscle cramps everywhere.

Her neighbor at the apartment promised to help her load up her living room furniture at nine o'clock and was ready and waiting when she pulled in. "Hannah, I'm going to miss you," he said, grinning. "You know, you and me could have made some beautiful music together."

Hannah laughed. He and his wife were so nice. She was going to miss them too, and promised to visit them often and have them over for dinner as soon as she got settled.

It wasn't long before they had her furniture loaded and she was on her way. Unlike the day she and Charlie drove out of the farm driveway for the last time with Hannah in tears and looking over her shoulder, today she never looked back.

Against what most people would consider better judgment, "Putting the cart before the horse," as Charlie would say, Hannah decided to put off rigging up a paddock for Billy Bob until tomorrow. Today being Saturday, last day of the week not to mention the last day of the month, if she stayed another day at the boarding stable she'd either have to pay for the day, which she didn't have the extra money to do, or work it off doing another day of barn chores, which took at least four hours – time she had very little of as well.

She stopped at the feed store and bought a fifty pound bag of grain, five bales of hay, and three bags of sawdust. She loaded them onto the tailgate of her truck behind all the furniture and tied them down nice and snug with a bungee cord. No sooner had she arrived at the farm, it started to rain. Hannah stared at her windshield in disbelief. It wasn't supposed to rain. Plastic. Did she have any plastic? As she sat there behind the wheel, mind scrambling, it started to rain harder. Her furniture would be soaked in minutes at this rate. She put the hood up on her parka, climbed down out of the truck, and stood glancing around frantically. No shed, no garage, no lean-to. The barn. She ran down and around the rear side of the barn, pulled the doors open, no easy task, and ran back to the truck.

"Come on, baby," she said, dropping the truck into four-wheel drive. The truck sat in place, tires spinning for a few seconds, then down over the hill and around to the back of the barn Hannah went. She fought the urge to yell "Yee Ha!" She didn't want to jinx herself, knowing if she got the truck stuck she'd have to ask for help, pay for help, beg for help. The truck bounced and veered and fishtailed in the slick tall grass. Another big bounce and she hit her head on the roof. "Damn!" she said. "Don't stop now!" Bounce! Bounce! Bounce!

"Oh shit!" With clear aim for the open doorway, she worried the furniture might not clear the height. "Shit! Shit! Shit!" If she stopped, she'd get stuck for sure! She plowed ahead, scrunching down in her seat, as if lowering herself would somehow lower the truck bed. She imagined her living room furniture tossed like sacks of potatoes into the field on impact. She imagined the barn falling down on top of her. She imagined Billy Bob being sold at an auction to pay for her funeral.

The truck cleared without a hitch. "Yes!" But, stopping it proved a challenge. When she hit the brakes, the wheels locked and the truck slid sideways clear to the other side of the barn before coming to a rest.

Trembling, shaking, Hannah turned off the ignition, laid her head on the steering wheel and drew a deep breath and sighed.

"Good job," she heard someone say. She raised her head and looked around. The barn was empty; truck off, radio off. The voice sounded like Charlie's. She must have imagined that too. It was just like her to want his approval for a job well done. "Go away," she said. "You left. You're gone. Go away."

She got out of the truck and checked her furniture. It was wet, but not soaked, not ruined. She'd loaded the sawdust bags over the hay and feed, so chances are they'd be fine too. She debated getting back into the truck to wait out the storm. There was no electricity in the barn and it was too dark inside to take on bedding the stall. What if it rained for hours? What a waste of time. "I could turn the truck around," she told herself, "and shine the headlights on the stall." It took a little maneuvering because she was afraid of hitting a beam.

She bed the stall nice and deep, of the strong opinion that one actually uses less bedding that way and it was better for the horse. Since this was an old cow barn, the floors were concrete. Some day she hoped to be able to acquire some rubber mats for the stall. Until then, heavy bedding would have to do. She hung the stall chains. Billy Bob's feed tub and buckets were still at the boarding stable, so those would be coming with him. Once those were hung, it would be home sweet home.

Her heart sank. Who was she kidding? There was no way he'd load in the rain. It would only add to an already challenging situation, and if it started to lightning and thunder, forget it. She'd end up having to pay for another day of board, not to mention no trailer for tomorrow because of the horse show taking place in Springfield. She tried putting all of this out of her mind. Positive thinking, she told herself, positive thinking, and went and looked out one of the broken glass windows. Pouring! Pouring! Pouring! It couldn't rain harder if it tried.

She walked around the inside of the barn for a while, looking closer at different aspects she'd only glanced at before; the rafters being one, the old cow stanchions. There was still a cow smell in the barn, and leaks everywhere. She walked down to Billy Bob's stall, noting three leaks in the back, and one right where he'd be standing looking out his

20

stall. There was also a really big leak where she'd planned to stack her hay. Good thing she saw that now.

She decided she'd better start the truck and let it run for awhile to recharge the battery, and was getting chilly anyway. She climbed back in, turned the engine on, and after a few minutes, turned on the heat and then the radio. She turned it up loud and was singing along with Brooks & Dunne when someone yanked open her door and startled her.

"Oh my God, Hannah! Are you trying to kill yourself?"

Hannah laughed at Lucinda and Colleen and turned down the radio. "Come on. As drafty as this barn is, I'd have run out of gas first. Wow, it stopped raining."

"Yes. Now turn off your truck. You're scaring me to death."

Hannah turned off the ignition. "How did you know I was in the barn?"

"We heard the music from way up at the house and then we saw your tracks."

Hannah chuckled. Charlie used to tell her she was hard of hearing. Maybe he was right. "Hop in," she said, motioning them around to the other side.

"Oh no. No way." Lucinda and Colleen backed up shaking their heads.

"Come on. You're a lot safer inside the truck than in my way."

On second thought. Both women agreed and piled in. "Just don't do anything stupid," Lucinda cautioned.

"Yeah, right. Like wreck my truck and trash my furniture?"

"I'm serious," Lucinda said, holding onto the security bar for dear life. "Maybe we should put on our seatbelts."

Hannah laughed and reached behind the seat for her cowboy hat, in the same mood as when she was a kid competing in barrel racing - same determination, same look in her eyes. She glanced in the mirror and adjusted the brim of her hat down nice and low.

"I'm scared," Colleen said.

"Of what?" Hannah looked at her.

"I don't know. Getting stuck, maybe flipping over, hitting a tree, peeing my pants."

"Fear not." Hannah backed the truck up as far as it would go so she could turn it around. "Bo and Luke Duke have nothing on me. Daisy neither." Now facing outside, Hannah revved the truck engine for effect and gripped the steering wheel. "Hold on!" she warned. And off they went, downhill first. It was a dangerously narrow and slippery path. At the bottom Hannah picked up a little more speed. Not too much, she kept telling herself. Otherwise she'd just sit and spin the in mud; just give it enough to try to build some traction. The truck started to bog itself down, but only for a second or two. Then it started climbing up and around the side of the barn, throwing mud everywhere in its wake.

First bump, the women laughed! Second bump, more laughing! Then smack dab in their path stood Dave, the guy from the bar who had a crush on Hannah.

"Oh no!" Hannah screamed. "Move!"

He seemed paralyzed, stunned, unable to move, deer in the headlights! Hannah swerved at the last second and took off into what used to be the orchard.

"Oh my god! Oh my god!" Colleen kept saying.

And Lucinda, "Stop! Stop! STOP!"

"I can't!" Hannah said, searching for the best spot to turn. "We'll get stuck!" She recalled seeing a flat area just beyond the pear trees. If she could get that far without getting stuck, she could maybe turn around and come back using the same path the truck was forging now. They hit a big bump and all three women bounced out of their seat.

Hannah laughed! This was so ridiculous it was pathetic. "Hold on! Hold on! There it is!" The turnaround area wasn't as big as she'd thought. If she tried to turn around slow, she'd get stuck for sure. It was designed for a tractor, not a truck. She turned the wheel and hit the gas, which spun the truck completely around and when she let up a little on the accelerator; the truck made another half turn and headed back in the right direction.

"Yee ha!" she shouted. And then her pat, "Hold on!" They barreled through the fruit trees, fishtailing and slipping and sliding, hit another big bump, and all of a sudden, were going sideways. "Oh shit!" Hannah stared ahead, no easy feat, with bouncing and going in circles now. "Hold on!" She turned the wheel hard the opposite way, and the truck glided over the mud path as if it were on skis...slide, slide, grip, grip, grab, grab, slide. Suddenly they were straightened, but headed right for the house. Hannah turned the wheel as little as she possibly could. Unable to stop, she just wanted to miss it, and did, but then was staring at a large protrusion in the grass. Was it an old foundation? An old shed? She slid right past it too, then up the side yard around to the front of the house. The truck came to a rest as if by divine intervention, right alongside the porch steps. A few more inches and she'd have taken them out.

"Wow!" she said, turning off the engine and leaning back. "Did you see that? I mean, was that amazing or what?"

Lucinda and Colleen both just stared at her, white-knuckled and wide-eyed. By this time Dave had made his way back up to the house and was standing by his truck.

"Wait a minute, what's he doing here anyway?"

"He came to help," Colleen said, opening her door with trembling hands.

"See, now that's the kind of help I don't need," Hannah said.

Colleen flipped her off. "You're crazy, Hannah! I love you, but you're crazy."

Hannah climbed down out of the truck, checked out her tires, and laughed at all the mud. The furniture was unscathed, clean, and now practically dry. "God, I wish I had me a cigar. I'd smoke it!"

Dave laughed, as did Colleen and Lucinda. Hannah gave up smoking years ago, and never smoked a cigar in her life.

She glanced at her watch. "Oh no, we have to hurry! Jackie's probably already at the barn waiting for me."

Chapter Four

Billy Bob was all worked up by the time Hannah, Lucinda and Colleen arrived at the barn. Jackie thought she could actually load him on her own, secretly wanted to prove that she could, but succeeded only in turning the horse into an angry, agitated, sweating, bordering-on-mean, wild mustang from hell.

"I'm sorry," Jackie said. "I kept thinking if I just...."

"It's okay," Hannah said, taking the lead rope from her and wanting to cry. The words of the song, "Impossible Dream" ran through her mind. She stroked Billy Bob's wet forehead. He pulled away. "It's okay," she told him. "You load this once and I promise you, you will never have to load in a trailer again."

Billy Bob set his jaw tight, a definitive no.

"I just need to get you home. I promise." She urged him toward the trailer ramp, tugged at the lead rope, tugged again, and then made a few more promises; green grass forever, ripe apples galore, carrots, carrot cake. Everyone stood around quietly. They'd all been through this before with Billy Bob. One time someone sneezed, and that was that. Apparently Billy Bob took that as a sign of bad things to come and flat refused to budge another inch forward that day.

When coaxing and promises didn't work, Hannah went through her usual try-to-get-him-to-load tactics, pick up one leg, turn him from side to side, swish a broom at his back legs, grab an ear, lock hands behind him. At one time or another, any one of these methods might work. The downside was there were times when absolutely nothing would. Once, Hannah threatened to turn him around and "back" him into the trailer and would have, had it been one with a ramp and not a step-up. Today's trailer was perfect for bad loaders. It was a stock trailer, big and wide, with a nice sturdy ramp. It would be just like walking into a stall.

No way.

Jackie had already tried bribing him with grain. It obviously hadn't worked, but Hannah figured she'd give it another try. Maybe if it came from her. Billy Bob stretched his neck as far as he could when she shook the feed can, but kept his feet firmly planted a good ten feet from the trailer. It hadn't been that long since feeding time. He evidently wasn't all that hungry. The look on his face said he'd rather starve to death than surrender.

Hannah sighed. How many times had they done this? Too many to count. She glanced up at the sky. Charlie used to marvel how she could tell time at just a glance. "Jackie, go ahead and go."

"Are you sure? I've got a tranquilizer in the tack trunk. Maybe if...?"

"No, that's okay. Thank you." Hannah smiled. "We've already taken up too much of your time. Go." She started toward the barn, and of course, approving that direction, Billy Bob turned and trailed right along after her, obedient as can be. Lucinda and Colleen followed.

"Are you going to try tomorrow?" Lucinda asked. "What are you going to do?"

Hannah put Billy Bob in the crossties instead of his stall and went to get her tack.

"You're going to ride!?" Colleen asked.

"Yep," Hannah said. "I'm going to ride him home."

"What?"

"I have to. I can't afford another night," Hannah said, tossing saddle pad and then the saddle onto Billy Bob's back.

"But it's TWENTY miles!"

"No, it's not, it's nine," Hannah said, tightening the girth. "I've driven it several times and clocked it."

"So you're just going to ride down the side of the road all that way?"

"Yes, unless you have a better idea," Hannah said, going into the tack room and coming back with the bridle.

Lucinda and Colleen stood speechless for a moment. "How long does it take to go nine miles?" Colleen asked.

"I don't know. I don't know how fast a horse walks. How fast does a person walk?"

Both women shrugged. "I can walk four miles in a little under an hour," Lucinda said.

"Okay, so you walk four miles an hour," Hannah said, pressing against the bottom of Billy Bob's jaw with her finger to get him to open his mouth and take the bit.

"Is that what that means?" Lucinda said. "Wow, I never made that connection before. So it means how far you can go in an hour?"

"Oh my God," Colleen said. "Now I know where your brother gets his smarts. It runs in the family."

The three women laughed, then fell silent. "I'm not sure this is safe, Hannah," Lucinda said, watching as Hannah picked out Billy Bob's hooves. "It's rush hour."

Hannah straightened up and looked at her. "We don't have a rush hour in Ridge Creek. Who you kidding? The only rush hour around here is the race to get to the Honky Tonk on Friday nights!" They all laughed again.

Hannah glanced inside Billy Bob's stall. She'd cleaned it this morning, but it needed to be mucked out again. "Here." She handed the reins to Colleen, hurried to get the muck basket and cleaned the stall as fast as she could, but thoroughly. Lucinda loaded Billy Bob's brushes and blankets into the truck, feed tub and water buckets.

"We'll follow you," Colleen suggested. "I'll drive your truck."

"Okay, just don't follow too close," Hannah said. "I don't trust my brakes."

"What?"

"Just kidding," Hannah said. "They only stick a little." She threw the reins up over Billy Bob's head, mounted, and with one leg propped over the front of the saddle, tightened the girth another notch. All set. "Okay, with a little luck, we'll get there before dark. Clock him."

Billy Bob walked along at a pretty good clip. He varied from three miles per hour to five, and would break into a handy trot now and then, which took them up to ten miles per hour. "Wow," Colleen said, yelling the results out the window. "At this rate, we'll be there in no time."

Hannah glanced over her shoulder and smiled. Billy Bob was probably the worst horse on earth to load into a trailer, but when it came to trail riding or taking to the roads like today, he was as carefree as they came. He didn't even mind when people drove by and honked, and a lot did, which made no sense. They only had one four-lane main street in town, which was coming up soon. The rest were all two lane roads with big berms and grass shoulders. As they approached town, they encountered more traffic and all concrete. Hannah reined Billy Bob to a walk. She glanced around. She loved this town.

"Hey, Hannah!" The butcher yelled to her from his door. "Where you been?"

Hannah waved. "I'll be coming by! You got fresh sausage?"

"You betcha! I just made up a batch this morning. How's Billy Bob?"

"He's doing good!" The horse was strutting his stuff. "Don't you be looking at him like that!" Meat!

The butcher laughed.

As they walked past the library, two small children ran down the steps to the sidewalk for a closer look. "Is that an Indian pony, lady?"

"Nope, Hon, he's a Leopard Appaloosa. He looks a little like an Indian horse though, don't you think?"

Billy Bob eyeballed the little children as they came closer and as if in slow motion, gently lowered his head.

"Can we pet him?"

Their mother caught up with them. When she smiled her approval, Hannah stopped Billy Bob and let the children say hello. He snorted in the littlest one's hair and the children laughed.

"He's so pretty!"

"Thank you. We've got to go now. Nice seeing ya!"

The little girls and their mother waved, and then waved to Colleen and Lucinda, tagging along behind. They both waved back. "I feel like I'm in a parade," Lucinda yelled, and started waving to everyone they passed.

Hannah turned in the saddle, saw them waving, and chuckled. "She thinks she's Princess Di or something!" Colleen shouted.

Hannah laughed. Three miles to go.

The funeral parlor was on the outskirts of town. The parking lot was full. Hannah wondered who had died and why she wasn't called to do his or her hair. "Probably a bald guy," she said to herself. The driver of an approaching car turned on its blinker then waited for her pass, and she glanced into the back seat where a large German Shepherd lay. She looked at the driver; an old man with tears in his eyes. She pressed her hand instinctively over her heart. "I'm sorry," her actions said.

The old man nodded; one tear and then another trickling down his grief stricken face. The dog looked up at her with eyes equally as sad.

She recalled the day her mother died as she turned to watch the old man pull into the funeral parlor parking lot. It was empty that day, not another car there. She hadn't talked to her mother for years before her death. She talked to her all the time now.

A little over a mile out of town, Billy Bob had to pee and stopped. Hannah stood in her stirrups and leaned forward to take the pressure off his kidneys. A car passed right at this moment. Lucinda and Colleen waved to the driver. Then here came a truckload of teenagers. They all shouted and whistled. Colleen flipped them off. "Brats!"

When they were back on a road with a wide berm, Hannah urged Billy Bob into a slow trot. "Seven miles per hour," Lucinda shouted.

Good, Hannah thought. Judging from the sun, they only had about fifteen minutes of fading daylight. She didn't want to lead Billy Bob into a dark barn, particularly a barn he'd never been inside before. Even a horse as rock-solid as he was would probably become unnerved. It would be different if there was another horse in the barn. She'd given thought before to how he'd fare, alone, since horses are herd animals. She felt pretty confident that he'd do all right. Prior to the barn she'd just left, she had him at a friend's place where there were no other horses, just cows. He seemed perfectly happy there. It was a short-lived residence. Her friend's family also lost their farm and ended up moving to Detroit.

Hannah looked ahead. The roof line of her house lay on the horizon. The sight of it brought tears to her eyes. "You're almost home, Billy Bob," she said, and bit at her trembling bottom lip. "It's just you and me now, you know." Sometimes she wondered if he missed Charlie too. In the beginning he used to look at her oddly when she came to the barn, as if she was only half there. That's how she'd felt too.

She glanced behind her to check for traffic and crossed the road. Lucinda and Colleen turned into the drive a safe distance behind her and parked. "I told you she was crying," Colleen said when Hannah dismounted.

"Don't say anything."

"What? Like, gee, are you scared? Are you tired? Are you worried? For Pete's sake, she's my best friend. I know all that."

"She's *our* best friend. Shhh." Lucinda gestured toward Hannah. She was wiping her eyes with her sleeve and trying to put on a happy face. She turned toward Lucinda and Colleen and shook her head. She'd put off crying for too long. The tears came in torrents. She leaned against Billy Bob.

Lucinda and Colleen walked over and put their arms around her. "It's okay. It's okay," they kept saying, all three of them crying now. "It's okay."

Billy Bob shifted his weight and heaved a big sigh, which struck them all as funny, and soon they were laughing and wiping their tears. "All right, boy, we're going." Hannah led him down and around to the back of the barn. It was almost dark, the last of the natural light but a sliver through the window. Hannah put him in his stall and un-tacked him. He went right for a mouthful of hay and then walked around his stall checking things out. The three women watched as he sniffed and snorted, pawed at the one corner, and then promptly pooped.

They laughed. "Just like a man," Colleen said. Billy Bob looked right proud. He was settling in. "All he needs now is a remote and a can of beer and he'd be in heaven."

"Speaking of beer...."

"I'll go get some," Lucinda said. "Should I buy some cheese too?"

Hannah nodded and reached into her pocket. She had two five dollar bills and gave her one. Lucinda knew better than to not take it. "I've got some salsa left. Get some corn chips." Hannah and Colleen unloaded the truck and hung the feed tub and then the water bucket and filled it. The water was running crystal clear now. Hannah rubbed Billy

Bob's back with a towel. He'd hardly broken a sweat, but was a little wet from under the saddle. Using a flashlight to see, the two were still in the barn when Lucinda returned. Billy Bob seemed perfectly content, so they all walked up to the house.

The living room looked a little strange but cozy with the bed all made up and the living room furniture placed all around it. There was hardly room to walk. It looked like a stop and hop into bed arrangement. "Gee, if you were younger, you could set up business here," Colleen suggested, making herself comfortable on the bed.

Hannah laughed. "No thank you. I'd have to give them change."

"Yeah, right," Lucinda said. "Have you looked at yourself in the mirror? You look fantastic."

"Oh no," Hannah said, hiding her eyes behind her beer. "This isn't going to lead into one of those get-on-with-my-life talks, is it?"

"Okay, okay, I'm sorry," Lucinda said. "It's just...."

"Good. Pass the chips."

When they heard a scurrying noise overhead, Lucinda and Colleen stared at Hannah. "Did you check it out?"

"I didn't have time," Hannah said, yawning. "I'll do it tomorrow."

"Oh, great! A raccoon's going to come down here and chew off half your foot while you're sleeping."

"As long as it doesn't wake me in the process," Hannah said. She told them about the little boy's visit last night. "What kind of parent lets their kid out in the middle of the night like that?"

"One that probably doesn't know," Lucinda said. She could write a book about it.

Colleen glanced at her watch. They had to leave. "Go," Hannah told them. "I'm going to go check on Billy Bob and then go to bed."

"Do you want us to come with you?"

"Are you going to come with me every night?"

"Good point."

When they pulled out the drive, Hannah headed down over the hill with her flashlight.

Chapter Five

Billy Bob lay in his stall; all curled up and half asleep, his bottom lip relaxed and sagging. Hannah crawled in next to him and rested her head on his shoulder. He sighed contentedly as she breathed in his scent. Was there anything better than the smell of a horse? Their sweat, the sun, the earth; the grass they ate. It was all in their skin. She thought about the day. She thought about tomorrow. She thought about Charlie.

"Come see this horse," he'd said. They were at the auction.

"What's wrong with him?" Hannah asked, wanting to prepare herself. Charlie liked big, rough, tough horses; and if they had an attitude, all the better.

Billy Bob wasn't rough and tough, and didn't have an attitude either. At least not until after they bought him and tried to load him. He'd been tranquilized and it was starting to wear off. Charlie put on a horse-loading clinic that day. Hannah smiled, recalling the crowd reaction.

Their friend Jim loved to tell the story. Billy Bob was barely two at the time and hadn't been gelded yet. "There's only two things on a stud colt's mind," Charlie said. "Eating and screwing. I've been there."

Hannah laughed.

Charlie offered the colt a handful of grain. Every time he got his mouth close enough to Charlie's hand to eat, Charlie would nudge him with a knee to his underbelly. The horse didn't like that; it was too close to his "business area." After a couple of missed mouthfuls of grain and dodging Charlie's knee he got aggravated and started reaching more aggressively. Charlie nudged him a little harder. The colt went up the ramp and into the trailer sideways to try to prevent Charlie from touching his underbelly again, and all the while reaching for grain.

That was the one and only time that method of loading Billy Bob worked. He was gelded the following week. "Most people would think that frigging colt would kick or bite," Jim said. "But not Charlie. He grabbed the bull by the horn. Did you ever see Charlie ride a bull? It's like poetry. I tell you, pure poetry."

Hannah gave Billy Bob a hug and walked back up to the house. It had been a long day and she was beyond exhausted. She hoped the little boy had found his dog and that he wouldn't wake her again in the middle of the night. She glanced ahead and stopped dead in her tracks.

There was an old man sitting on her back stoop. She blinked her eyes and glanced around, unsure what to do. He looked pretty feeble. She figured she could outrun him if need be.

"Sir...?" she said, shining her flashlight on him.

He looked up.

That's it. He just looked up and then he was gone.

"Holy shit!" Hannah gasped. She felt a cold chill. "I didn't see him. I didn't see him. I didn't see him," she kept muttering out loud. "I didn't see him. I didn't see him."

She hurried around to the front door and inside, bolted the latch behind her. The man looked familiar. It was the man she'd seen in the car outside the funeral home, the very same man. She turned on the radio. She wanted noise, lots of noise. She turned up the volume.

Patsy Cline was belting out the tune, "Crazy."

"Yeah, I'm crazy," Hannah said. "I'm crazy for feeling sooo blue." She sang along. "Worry, why do I let myself worry? Wondering...."

There was a knock at the door. Hannah stared at the latch. The door vibrated against it. "Lady? Hey, lady!" The little boy jiggled the handle. "Lady, are you home?"

No, Hannah thought. I'm not home. I'm in the Twilight Zone. She remembered an episode where a woman put her hand under the bed and was sucked through the wall of her home to another dimension. She recalled the movie where the little boy said he could "see dead people."

"I see dead people."

"I see dead people."

"Lady?"

She opened the door. "Yes?"

"I wanted to let you know I found Bessie."

"Oh good," Hannah said. "Is she all right?"

"Yes. I'm sorry if'n I scared you?"

Hannah looked at him. "You mean just now, or...?"

The little boy nodded, not much of an answer. "She was in your root cellar."

"My root cellar?"

"Yes," he said. "I bolted the door. She won't get back in. Bye."

"Wait!" Hannah called after him. "Do you mind if I shake your hand?"

The little boy looked at her. "Tomorrow, maybe," he said. "I gotta get back now or I'm gonna be in trouble."

Hannah watched him disappear into the darkness and started to close the door, but then quickly opened it back up. "Wait! Where is my root cellar?"

"Out behind the well," the little boy called from a distance.

Hannah hesitated. The well wasn't too far, maybe if she went to look now before…. She closed the door and locked it. It was pitch black out. "No thank you," she said to herself. The old man could stay a figment of her imagination until tomorrow. And if he's sleeping in the root cellar, so be it.

She made herself a cup of green tea and sat on the couch. Though it wasn't windy out, the house creaked and groaned and even shivered now and then. She pressed her hand gently against the wall. "One would think you'd be settled by now after all this time," she said, talking to the house, to herself. "Oh look who's talking." She laughed.

She fell asleep curled up on the couch and woke a little after eleven. When she looked out the front window into the night, her reflection gazed back at her and told stories. With her hair mussed and sleep clouding her eyes, she appeared younger, happier.

"You're beautiful, Hannah," she heard Charlie say, remembering. It was the night after she'd lost the baby. She'd been crying. "Come on, let's go out to eat." This was Charlie's way, a farmer's way. She'd cried enough, he said. "We'll try again."

Hannah feared deep down they'd never have children. "I just know it," she said, and cried some more. She touched the window pane. It was frosted, but within seconds the ice melted under her fingertip. "I miss you, Charlie," she said. "After all you did to me, I still miss you."

She closed her eyes and could swear she heard him say, "I miss you too." No sooner said, she heard other voices, the ones that kept insisting she get on with her life. She slept like a baby that night and woke to a phone ringing.

"Wait a minute," she said, sitting up and looking around groggily. "I don't have a phone." She hadn't called yet to have it transferred. It rang again. She looked out the window. "What the hell?"

Just beyond the porch was an old man on a very old bicycle, ringing its bell.

"I *am* in the Twilight Zone," Hannah said, scrambling to get dressed at the old man's persistence. "Okay, okay!" She opened the door. "Hello."

"Your horse is out," he said.

"Billy Bob?"

The old man shrugged. "Don't know his name, but he's out."

Hannah grabbed her shoes and hobbled into them on the way down the porch steps.

"You oughta be takin' better care," the old man said.

Hannah glanced at him, mumbled, "Thank you," in an exasperated tone, and took off in search of her horse. He was just outside the back of the barn and from the looks of the path of eaten grass, he'd been out quite a while.

"Don't go anywhere," she told him, and hurried into the barn for his halter and lead rope. As soon as she returned and got close to him, he trotted away. "Good thing you're used to grass," she said. She expected to find the old man watching, but he was nowhere to be seen. "Don't move," Hannah said softly to Billy Bob, and laughed at herself. "Because I am the 'horse whisperer' and I have spoken."

Billy Bob trotted further away.

"Now cut it out." She decided rather than try to catch him she'd make an attempt to herd him back into the barn. She circled up and around, clicking to him, and he jogged right past her, tossing his head in a playful way.

"Well, damn you too, you silly ass!" She leaned down and tore off a big fat handful of grass and started waving it at him. It got his attention. He turned and looked at her. She grabbed some more and held it behind her back as she walked toward the barn, glancing over her shoulder at him and still shaking the grass. Billy Bob followed her inside, reaching for it every step of the way. Acres and acres of grass to graze, and here he was, baited by an already-picked handful. She walked into his stall with him trailing after her and fed it to him.

"Good boy," she said, gently, secretly wanting to scream.

She put his halter and lead rope on him, tied him over by his feed tub, then fed him his grain and topped off his water bucket. He took a good long drink, another indication of his having been out for quite a while.

"That'll teach me to sleep so soundly." It had been years since she'd had to listen for night sounds from a barn. She examined the stall chains. Billy Bob had popped the screw-eyes right out of the wood. Something must have spooked him, she decided, and went to get her hammer and a screwdriver to put the screw eyes back in. She placed them lower this time and thought about a young bull they had once that kept getting out. "Bulldozer Bad Ass," Charlie called him. Hannah chuckled and then saddened. When *will* I get on with my life? Why does it always come back to Charlie?

She untied Billy Bob and gave him hay and mucked his stall. He was easy to clean up after, particularly with his being out for so long. She was going to have to rig up some sort of turnout for him today, but first....

"Behave," she told him, and took off in search of the root cellar. She'd all but forgotten about the old man. Remembering now, she wondered where he lived, where he'd gone. Was there one man or two? Was it the same old man she saw last night? This farm had been vacant for a long time, maybe he was in the habit of just hanging out here. She wondered if there was a park bench anywhere on the property, and then wondered why she wondered that.

"I'm losing it," she said. "No wonder Charlie left me." She rolled her eyes. "Oh, God, there I go again, thinking of Charlie. Enough already; give it up." She pushed her way through the tall grass and thistle, climbed down a little ridge, then up the other side. And, there was the well. It didn't make much sense to her for someone to dig it this far from the house. What were they thinking? She looked around. The little boy said the root cellar was just behind the well.

"Humph." She started tamping the ground with her foot, thinking she'd uncover a door. She searched everywhere behind it, then starting exploring to the left of it, and then the right. Nothing. She was just about to give up, since all of a sudden she needed to go to the bathroom, when she came upon a door embedded in the ground. Why she didn't see it before made no sense, because there was clearly a path leading right to it.

"That's because you were looking behind the well, silly, and not in front of it." Why would the little boy say it was behind the well? Of course, it's because he probably lives next door. Duh. She unlatched the bolt, held shut with a Hickory stick, and pulled the door open. The entryway was riddled with cobwebs. She wished she had a flashlight. It was darker than night inside. She started down the steps, figuring to just take a peek, used her hands to brace herself down the rickety stairs and touched what felt like a light switch.

Sure enough. When she flipped the switch, the root cellar lit up. White Christmas lights hanging everywhere twinkled and sparkled. She smiled as she peered inside; her hand in front of her face to fend off the spider webs.

"Oh my," she said. There was a chair in the middle of the room with a small table next to it where an open book lay alongside a cup. Shelves behind it were filled with jars of peaches and green beans, corn and apple butter, all looking perfectly edible but for the telltale thick layer of dust and rusted lids.

"Such a shame," she said, and turned when she heard a noise behind her. Octopus-like roots clung to the wall by the doorway; petrified potato knots hanging like anchors that swayed back and forth with the breeze. They looked like fingers, hands, arms. She swallowed hard. "I'm outta here," she said, and ran up the steps two at a time. The old man sat on his bike at the top, waiting for her.

"I'm worried about this land," he said, his eyes a silvery blue and cheeks sunken.

He motioned to all the skid marks from her truck the other day. "You must be a city girl."

"I'll have you know that I'm not."

He looked at her long and hard. "You can't even keep your horse in the barn."

"What?" She glanced past him. "Is he out again?"

"No. Once is enough." He motioned over her shoulder. "What are you going to do about the trees?"

"I don't know yet. Why?"

"Why?" He shook his head again. "Because it's fall and they need tended to."

She agreed. "I plan to do something once I get settled in."

The old man nodded and gazed up at the sky, his skin transparent in the morning sun. "We're going to have a storm, a bad one."

"Yeah, well thank you for letting me know," Hannah said, edging past him. "Now if you'll excuse me." Her bladder was speaking louder than anything this old man had to say. "Have a nice day."

"Don't say I didn't warn you."

She waved.

Chapter Six

Hannah had a quick breakfast of toast and jam along with some strong black coffee, then got dressed and started working on a turnout for Billy Bob. She'd have to check in with the funeral parlor before noon to see if she had work, but until then....

The fence posts and rails still standing were rickety at best, but they would have to do. She figured she had enough salvageable stall boards from inside to replace the rails that were rotted and splintered. She spent about an hour sorting through them and disturbed an army of mealy bugs. "Sorry," she kept saying, with a shudder. She preferred spiders over mealy bugs any day. At least spiders run away. The mealy bugs just turned onto their backs, looking scared to death, disoriented and sad. They had "Oh no!" written all over them. She knew the feeling. She righted the ones that looked in a panic and eventually had enough wood stacked to pen in the small paddock behind the barn.

She'd been saving the baling twine from the boarding stable for over a week to use for this repair. She notched each fence post in two places. Fearing the fence rails would only split if the tried to nail them to the fence; she tied the rails to the posts using the notches as an anchor point and wound the twine round and round in a triangular pattern. Once a Girl Scout always a Girl Scout; she'd tethered the rails in perfect arrowhead-tomahawk formations. She stepped back to admire her handiwork; Charlie would be proud.

"Forget Charlie," she told herself.

The gate proved more of a challenge. The female side of the hinge still held tight, but the male side needed help. She laughed. "Who's tougher now?" The wood was split behind the screws. This would never work. She headed back into the barn to see what she could find. Billy Bob nickered at her. She smiled. She was having fun, the first real fun she'd had in a long time. "That's our ground you're standing on," she said, pointing at his feet. "Does it feel like home?"

The horse put his head down and grabbed a mouthful of hay.

"As good an answer as any," she said. She searched through an old tin bucket of ancient hinges and screws, and then a pile of corroded angle iron; nothing. She surveyed the old cow stanchions and was trying to figure out how she might fashion some hinges out of the broken anchor pieces, when her eyes fell upon four rusty but seemingly

36

sturdy hay hooks. "Ah ha!" She scratched her head and then quickly brought her hand down. Charlie would always stand and scratch his head when contemplating a situation such as this.

She crossed her arms and looked tough, mean...strong. "It'll work," she said. Billy Bob looked at her and heaved a sigh. That sigh of his made her laugh again. "Just you wait and see, Mister. And you had better not go through it." She cocked two hay hooks in each hand pistol style. "Because you don't want to mess with me."

"Oh really?" Dave said, standing in the doorway. "You don't say?"

Hannah chuckled, blushing. "What are you doing here?"

"I came to see if you needed any help?"

Hannah shook her head and started past him. "Thanks, but I'm okay."

"I can see that," he said, following her with his eyes. "But I'm not. I have the whole day with nothing to do."

Hannah looked at him, a thousand thoughts running through her mind. He was such a nice guy. Good looking. Honest. "I have to go to work at noon," she said, and glanced at the sun. "Holy shit. I'm late."

Dave looked at his watch. "Yes, you are. It's a quarter after. He motioned to the hay hooks. "What are you going to do with those?"

"I'm going to rig the gate with them," she said, and laughed again. "I'm sorry." She shook her head, feeling silly, childish, no...childlike. "I'm just having so much fun."

"You sure you don't need some help?" he asked, watching her turn the hay hooks every which way.

She shook her head.

Dave smiled. "Do you want to get something to eat later? I can swing back by?"

"No, um...." She leaned down and looked up into the hinge blocks. "Lucinda and Colleen are coming by for dinner."

Dave studied her. "Are George and Jason coming?"

"Yes, why?" Hannah looked at him.

He shrugged.

Hannah hesitated. There was something about the way he.... "Do you want to come? It's nothing fancy, I'm just going to make stew. Lucinda's bringing bread, Colleen's bringing dessert."

"How about I bring some beer?"

"Okay, sure."

He nodded, and started to walk away, not wanting to push his luck. This is the closest thing to a date, or even a hint of a date, that they'd ever had. "What time?" he asked, glancing back.

"Six-thirty."

He smiled. "Are you sure you don't need any help with those?" he asked, pointing to the hay hooks.

"Yep," she said. "Positive." Though she had an idea how to make the hay hooks work, it would have to wait. She needed to leave and check in at work about her schedule. .

When she arrived, her boss Richard had on his "Mortician's Face" as Hannah called it. "I can't stay in business if no one dies," he said.

Hannah chuckled. Morbid as it sounded, it was true. The lack of business affected her too. "Didn't you have a family yesterday?"

He shook his head.

"And none coming up?"

"Nope."

Hannah sat down. "There was an old man driving in here yesterday when I went by with my horse."

Richard nodded, smiling. "I heard about that. You caused quite a stir."

"What, with all ten people in town?"

He laughed. "You could have tried to scare one or two of them to death. That would have been nice."

Hannah shook her head and fell quiet. "Well, uh…."

"Sorry," he said, knowing she needed the work. "I wish I could predict how the rest of the week will go. Maybe we'll get lucky."

Hannah nodded, chuckling again. For as much as this man joked about the dead, he took very good care of "the departed" once they arrived, and their families too. "Are you sure there wasn't…?" She hesitated. "An old man, maybe here for a pre-arrange?"

"Nope."

"Alrighty then," Hannah said, smacking her thighs and standing up. "I'll have my phone in on Friday. I'll stop by until then."

Her boss looked at her. "Do you need an advance? I can…."

"No, thank you. That's okay. I'm okay."

Her next stop was the grocery store. She picked up a small chuck roast, some potatoes, carrots, peas, an onion, and celery to make beef stew. She thought about buying something for an appetizer, but decided against it. If she had the stew ready for when everyone arrived, they wouldn't need one, and it would save her the money. That was the plan. For the first time in a long time, she also gave thought to what she was going to wear.

Chapter Seven

Hannah learned how to cook from her mom and also how to stretch a meal if need be. Hannah's mother loved cooking, loved feeding people, and so did Hannah. As she added a little flour mixture to the stew to thicken it, she could almost feel Charlie's presence. He'd have just come in from doing chores and would lean over her shoulder and smell the aroma of the bubbling pot. "When are we eating?" he'd always ask. And she'd always say, "Whenever you're ready." Then he'd kiss her on the cheek and would wash up at the kitchen sink. She'd hand him a towel.

Hannah sighed. She'd never actually kissed anyone but Charlie. He was her High School Sweetheart. "Surely I must have kissed someone else," she said, adding a little more pepper to the stew.

"Taste and add, taste and add," she could hear her mother say. "It's what makes a good cook." Her mom may well have been the person who coined the phrase, "Season to taste." And if not, it didn't matter, she took credit for it. "There's nothing worse than following a recipe to the letter."

Hannah turned the stew on low and covered it with an "open lid;" another of her mother's favorite expressions. "If you're going to eat it right away, turn it off and put the lid on tight. If not, open the lid a little and have the heat on low."

Hannah stared out the window, wondering. What if Dave tries to kiss me? What'll I do? Kiss him back? And if I did, will I really be feeling it, or faking it? She tried to force these thoughts way into the back of her mind and went about setting the table; six plates, six bowls, six knives, six forks, six spoons, six, six, six. Three couples. Couples! If she sat at the one end of the table, did that mean that Dave should or would sit at the other end? Oh Christ! She already felt as if she was cheating on Charlie. Why did I invite Dave? What was I thinking? Maybe we should just sit in the living room. Yeah, right, in there with the bed.

When a knock sounded at the front door, it startled her. She clutched her chest and almost yelled, "Who is it?" But shouted, "Come on in," instead.

It was the old man. He opened the door, but then just stood there on the porch. "I was walking by," he said, "and smelled something good."

"It's beef stew," Hannah smiled. "Would you like some?"

The old man shrugged, glancing past her into the kitchen. "Maybe just a cup."

"Do you want to come in?"

He gazed down at the doorstep, not budging.

"I'll be right back," Hannah said. "Would you like something to drink?"

He shook his head.

When Hannah returned with the soup, he'd made a seat for himself on the edge of the steps with his back against the railing post. She looked for his bike; he must have walked. "Thank you," he said.

"I'm having a dinner party." Hannah made an attempt at idle conversation as she sat down next to him. "Just some friends."

"Where's your husband?"

"I don't have one," Hannah said. "Not technically at least."

He blew on a spoonful of soup. "What happened to him? He die?"

"No, worse," she said, heaving a sigh. "He left me."

The old man looked at her and nodded. He didn't say anything, he just nodded.

"Well, I'd better go change," she said. "Take your time."

"This is good."

"Thank you." Ordinarily, Hannah didn't wear makeup, so it took her by surprise when the thought crossed her mind. She felt silly, and told herself that if she did put makeup on, she'd feel even sillier once Lucinda and Colleen noticed. This is not a date. This is not a date. This is not a date.

The old man left two quarters for the soup. Hannah smiled and put it in her pocket. She decided she had enough time to check on Billy Bob and the new paddock before everyone arrived, and walked down over the hill. Her horse was in his stall, munching hay lazily. She checked the gate hinges she'd made out of the hay hooks and marveled at her ingenuity. They worked. Or at least they'd work for a while. She hoped to be able to buy some woven wire fence before winter and a sturdy metal gate.

She checked Billy Bob's water bucket, thankful that the spigot in the barn worked, and threw him some more hay. She was happy that he didn't seem to mind being in the barn alone. She wished she could afford another horse, but....

"Hey, Hannah!"

She turned. "Speaking of a herd," she said. They must have all arrived together. Why Lucinda chose to give her a greeting hug, made no sense. She felt obligated to give everyone a hug then, even Dave.

Lucinda's fiancé, George, was last and smelled like garlic. He always smelled like garlic. "How do you stand it?" Colleen had asked her one day.

"I close my eyes and imagine he's Andrea Bocelli! Sing, sweetheart!"

Hannah remembered the three of them laughing.

"How's Billy Bob doing?" Jason asked.

"Fine," Hannah said, still feeling somewhat awkward just standing there after all the hugging. "He seems to like it here."

Dave walked over to inspect Hannah's gate-hinge handiwork. He did not seem impressed. He didn't say so, but she could see it in his eyes. He was obviously itching to fix it himself. She didn't know much about Dave's home life, other than his wife died several years back and he lived on a farm the other side of town and had some sheep.

"I hope everybody's hungry," Hannah said, nudging them along. "Come on, the stew's nice and hot." Billy Bob picked his head up and watched them walk out of the barn. Hannah secured the wood rail she'd rigged up earlier that would keep him inside the barn if he broke his stall chain again. She glanced back at him. He looked so innocent. Who me?

"It's all about impulsion," she pictured Charlie saying when she set it up. "He won't be able to build up steam in here, so he's not going to break it. Secure it from the inside and rest easy."

Jason wrapped his arm around Hannah's shoulder as they started up the hill. "I'd better hold on to you. You lose any more weight and it won't take a storm to blow you away."

Hannah thought about the old man's warning of a storm. She'd forgotten. "Are we really supposed to get a storm?"

"Tomorrow," Colleen said, wrapped in Jason's other arm. "Tomorrow night. They're calling for thunderstorms, some possibly severe."

Hannah looked to the west; nothing but blue skies. This was the first time the three men had been in the house, so with beers in hand, they scoped out the utility room, the kitchen, bathroom, and the living room. Hannah had rearranged the couch and loveseat to the one side of the room, L-shaped, put down the throw rug under the coffee table and had placed the end table and lamp on the one side and the television over between the fireplace and one of the windows. It looked crowded but cozy. The bed, dresser and chest of drawers were on the other side of the room. "Love the bed," George said, bouncing on it.

"Get off," Lucinda said. "You big, rough, tough men need to go upstairs and scare the raccoon."

"Raccoon?" all three said.

"No, come on," Hannah insisted. "Let's eat. There's no coon up there, I cooked him for dinner. Watch out for the bones."

They all laughed and sat down at the kitchen table. There was never a lack of conversation between the three women, or between Jason, George, and Dave either for that matter, since they saw a lot of one another at the Honky Tonk. But again, there was awkwardness among them today. It didn't feel right with Charlie not being there and Dave in his place. Even Dave felt it. When he reached for bread, his hand trembled slightly.

Hannah passed the butter. She could hear her mother's voice in her head. "Make your company feel at home."

"I stopped by the funeral parlor today," she said. "And get this, there were no dead people."

Everyone laughed, easing the tension at the table. "I still don't know how you do dead people's hair, Hannah," Jason said. "That would give me the creeps."

Hannah looked at him. "Gutting a deer would give me the creeps."

They all laughed again. "Touché."

"This stew's delicious," George said, and everyone echoed the sentiments, even Hannah.

"It's a good batch." Wanting to keep the somewhat casual momentum going, she told them about the old man. She still had the two quarters in her jeans' pocket and showed them. George motioned for her to hand them to him. They were worn practically smooth. He had to look hard. One quarter was dated 1956, the other 1948.

George handed them back.

"I've seen him a couple times now, him and this little boy. I don't know if they're related, but they both live nearby somewhere. And this dog, this big German Shepherd named Bessie."

"Speaking of dogs," Colleen said. "The Smiths up on Parkman have a sign out for some free pups, says they're Bassett Hound and Lab mixes."

"Wonder how that happened?" Dave said.

"Someone had a ladder," George suggested, which had them all laughing again. Talk then went to the bread, good and crusty, and second helpings of stew.

"Did you ever think of selling stew like this, Hannah?" Jason asked. "You could sell it by the container and make a fortune. You'd have 'em standing in line."

Hannah shrugged. "I'd thought about selling pies once. We did really well at the garage sale with them, but you have to charge so much to make any money at it, and then you have to buy the ingredients up front. It would be fun though. I'd never have to leave the farm. Maybe next year, when I get the trees turned around."

By then, everyone was on their second or third beer and much more relaxed. Charlie's presence or lack thereof was all but a distant memory. "What do you plan to do with them?"

"Well, the first thing I'm going to do is prune them back, drastically. One book I read said that 'If you are kind when pruning, you are out of your mind.' It says that you have to be almost brutal. That's going to be hard. I've never farmed fruit trees before."

"I'll tell you what," Dave said. "I'd pay ten dollars for a real homemade apple pie tomorrow."

"Hmmm, I'll have to think about that," Hannah said. "Anyone want coffee?"

The men shook their head. Lucinda and Colleen nodded. When Hannah got up to brew a pot, Lucinda and Colleen cleared the bread plates and bowls. "Hey, hey," Jason said, reaching for the last of the bread. Lucinda and Colleen glanced at one another. The bread could have been breakfast for Hannah. They'd both looked in the fridge when they'd arrived and saw that there was still hardly anything in it.

43

"Are you sure you don't want to save room for cake?" Colleen asked, trying to wrestle it from him.

"I always have room for cake, don't you worry about me," he said, stuffing his mouth full of bread and patting his stomach. "Bring it on."

"Do we want to go into the living room?" Lucinda asked of Hannah softly.

"No, there's more chairs in here," she said, giving her the evil eye.

The cake was butter pecan. Lucinda had brought vanilla ice cream to go with it. "This is delicious," Hannah said, licking the knife when everyone had a slice.

"The rest is for you," Colleen said. "Maybe your old man will come back and like some."

"Do you mean Charlie?" Jason said, well on his way to getting buzzed.

"No." Colleen jabbed him with her elbow.

"What?" he asked, innocently. "Who else would you be talking about?"

"The old man that stops by from time to time," Hannah said. "The quarters, remember? Come on, eat your cake. I really do want you guys to go upstairs when you're done and see if there are any raccoon and bats up there and scare them away."

There were no raccoon or bats. If there were, they'd be scattering to the heavens and the hills. The men jumped up and down, war-whooping and hollering. They inspected all the nooks and cracks and corners, beating on them. They closed all the bedroom doors again. Bang, bang, bang. They flushed the toilet. Swoosh!

"Get out of the way, I've got to take a piss," George said.

"Don't!" Hannah shouted. The three women huddled at the bottom of the stairs.

"Why not?" George asked, unzipping.

"Because it leaks," Hannah yelled up to them. "It's leaking! Oh no!"

Colleen and Lucinda laughed. Hannah was making that up.

"Shhh, shhh. That's going to be *my* bathroom," Hannah whispered. "No men peeing all over the toilet and leaving the lid up." She raised her voice. "There's water everywhere! Hurry!"

The men came running down the stairs like a stampede. "Where's the leak?" And "What leak?" turned into "Who's on first? What color?" Then, "Who wants another beer?" From there they all went outside and sat around on the side of the porch. It was a beautiful night, everyone talking. It was as if they were all sitting outside on the deck at the Honky Tonk. All that was missing was the sound of cars passing by and the jukebox inside.

"This is nice here, Hannah," Dave said. "A person could get used to this."

"Great pickup line, Dave," George said, laughing. "Where were you when I was trying to get lucky with Lucinda?"

Dave laughed. That's not what he'd meant, but....

"I'm going to go tuck Billy Bob in for the night," Hannah said.

Everyone decided to tag along. "I want to see this root cellar you told us about," Jason said, going to his truck for a flashlight. "Wait up." Dave and George grabbed their flashlights as well, and off they went. Hannah led them right to it.

"Slowly I walk, step by step," Dave said.

They all laughed.

Hannah unlatched the door and opened it, all four flashlights shining. The resident spiders had been busy. Intricately-laced web upon web adorned the entrance. Hannah turned on the Christmas lights.

"What the shit!" George said, batting cobwebs away. "This could be a bomb shelter. Look at all this food."

As Dave and Jason inspected the shelves where old rusty tools lay, George dusted off a jar of peaches, pried it open, and coiled at the overpowering stench. He put the lid back on as fast as he could.

"I wonder how old this cellar is?" Dave asked.

"Probably as old as the house," Hannah suggested. Her eyes had been drawn to the table; the cup was missing, the book gone. Probably the old man, she figured, and then instantly she thought of Charlie.

"You okay?" Lucinda asked, creeping down next to her.

Hannah nodded. "Fine," she said, thinking, "just fine." I'm getting on with my life. Yeah, right. "Okay, next stop," she said, in the voice of an English tour guide. "It's on to the stables." She stole one last glance inside the root cellar before turning out the light and latched the door behind them.

Billy Bob eyed the men warily when they all entered the barn wielding flashlights, then promptly snorted and turned his backside to them. "He's a woman's horse," Hannah said, though he did like Charlie. Quit, quit, quit! she told herself. Quit! Enough! Send everyone home but Dave, and jump his bones for Christ sake! She laughed.

45

"What's so funny?" they asked all at once.

"Nothing," Hannah said, with another laugh. "I guess I've had one too many beers."

"You only had three," Dave said, and blushed. "Not that I was counting."

They all laughed again, one joke or jab following another. Hannah felt as if they were old teenagers. She glanced at each one of them. They'd all grown up together, Charlie too. When tears filled her eyes, she pretended that it was from laughing. She fooled all of them except for Lucinda. As they walked back up to the house, Lucinda drew her close.

"It's still too soon, isn't it?" she whispered.

Hannah nodded. "God, I miss him."

"I know."

"Why'd he leave me, Luce? Why?"

"Because he's crazy, that's why. Who knows?" Lucinda hugged her tight, and they both wiped their eyes. "I hate him."

"Me too," Hannah said, and they both laughed.

"Was that lightning?"

"Nah, probably just our flashlights," George said.

The gathering broke up then, with hugs and kisses all around. Within minutes, they were all gone.

Hannah wondered; did I say anything to Dave? She remembered thanking him for the beer, but beyond that.... She stood on the porch, watching the trucks and car vanish from sight. She wrapped her arms around her sides and shivered in spite of the warm night air. "Charlie, wherever you are," she said. "I want you to know I still love you. I love you, and I always will."

Chapter Eight

Hannah stepped out onto the porch, barefoot, first thing the next morning, and gazed up at the threatening dark clouds in the sky. She'd have to hurry if she was going to get to the store and back in time to get any baking done. The more she'd thought about it in her waking moments at night; she decided to make two pies and try to sell the second one as well. Her boss at the funeral parlor loved her pies. "Who wouldn't?" she could hear Charlie say.

"Shut up." She dressed quickly and went down to feed Billy Bob. Thankfully, he was in his stall, waiting for his breakfast. She threw him some hay, dumped his water bucket and filled it with fresh, and then picked out his stall and gave him some grain. "I'll bring you an apple," she told him, and headed for the store as the clouds grew darker and darker.

Apples were on sale; it was a good year. She bought a bag of locally grown, some unbleached flour, and hurried home. She had to fiddle with the pilot to get the oven to light, and dug through a box of cooking items for an oven thermometer. The last thing she needed was burnt pies. When she got them made and in the oven, she took Billy Bob his promised apple. He was out of his stall and standing at the back door leaning over the rail of wood she'd rigged up to keep him inside.

"Well, at least this worked," she said. She put his apple in his feed tub rather than just feed it to him. She didn't want him thinking he was getting a reward for breaking out of his stall again. She examined the stall chains. He'd popped both screw eyes on the right side. Something had to be spooking him again, was all she could figure. She led him outside and into the paddock, marveled once more at how well her makeshift gate hinges worked, and headed back to check on the pies. The sky had actually brightened and far off in the distance there was a sliver of sun shining through.

The pungent smell of cinnamon and apples filled the house. She opened the oven door and took a peek. "Another five minutes," she said, tapping the crust lightly with her fingertips. She'd made a decorative "S" in the middle of the pie to let off steam. "S" for Shaw; it was her and Charlie's last name. She'd made so many pies over the years using that same flamboyant "S" insignia; she couldn't imagine making a pie any other way.

She glanced out the window. The postman was putting mail in her mailbox. She hurried out the front door and tried waving him down. Surely the mail was intended for the old owners. He never looked back.

"Humph." She opened the rusty mailbox and looked at the envelopes. They were both addressed to her. One was an ad from the phone company for the phone that hadn't even been installed yet. "Have you thought about bundling?"

"All the time," she said. "I don't sleep nights for wondering." The second letter was from the Courthouse. The sight of the return address brought back memories of all the letters she and Charlie had received when their farm went into foreclosure. "Wonder what this is about." She hesitated. "I'll open it later." She hurried back into the house, threw the mail onto the kitchen counter, and took the pies out of the oven. "Perfect."

"Hello."

Hannah turned, thinking it might be the old man, but it didn't sound like him. This man sounded younger. "I'm from the phone company," the man said, through the screen.

"Oh! Come on in." Hannah opened the door and stepped back. This man had to be at least seven feet tall and three hundred pounds.

"My name's Hank."

"Nice to meet you," she said.

As the man went to work installing the phone, Hannah boxed up the two pies and headed out to put them in the truck. "How long are you going to be?" she asked, in passing.

"Not long," he said, and motioned to the pies with a screwdriver. "Boy, those smell good."

"Well, I'd offer you a piece," she said, blushing instantly when she realized how that sounded. "But these are for sale." Worse….

The man nodded. His hands were as big as meat cleavers.

"What do you sell them for?"

"Well." Hannah hesitated. "Since these are the first two I'm selling, I'm thinking ten dollars a pie. I doubt anyone would pay more than that."

"Sold," he said. "I'll take them both."

"Wow." Hannah stood holding them. "Um, would you take just one? One of them is spoken for."

The man nodded. "Good enough."

Hannah put the one pie back on the counter, and took the one for Dave out to her truck. Her phone was installed and activated shortly thereafter. The man paid her for his pie, and took a big sniff of the pie mixture oozing out the big "S".

"My mom used to make pies like this."

"Mine too," Hannah said.

Another sniff. "Do you have a plastic fork I could have?"

"It's hot," Hannah cautioned, after finding him one. "You don't want to eat it yet."

"I know," he said, and stuck the fork in it anyway. "I just want a taste." He blew on a forkful and brought it to his mouth.

48

Hannah waited for his reaction. "Oh my Lord," he said, rolling his eyes in a good way.

Hannah smiled.

"How often you gonna make these?"

"Um...."

"I'm out this way early every Friday. I'll take two each week. I'll be here before eight."

"Okay." Hannah looked up at him. "For ten dollars each?"

"Yep."

"Deal."

The man gave her his phone number and left, but not before having two more forkfuls of pie as he sat in his truck. Hannah checked on Billy Bob and headed to the other side of town to drop off Dave's pie. The sky was as blue as it could be. As she pulled into his driveway, she caught a glimpse of him out behind his barn herding his sheep.

"Beep, beep, beep...beep," he kept saying.

She laughed. "Hello!"

"Hey." He smiled and picked up one of the lambs. It was limping. Hannah watched him as he tucked it gently under his arm. "Coyote this spring," he said.

Hannah nodded. When all the sheep were in the pen, which was as solid as Fort Knox, Dave washed his hands in the barn and walked with Hannah to her truck. "Are you ready for the storm?"

Hannah laughed. "You're kidding, right?"

"No, it's about an hour away, I guess. Do you want to come in for some coffee?"

"Thanks, but...." Hannah glanced at the sky, still blue. She stood for a moment, silent.

Dave studied her profile, smitten written all over his face.

"I'd better get going," she said. "How bad is it supposed to be?"

"Well, there's a tornado warning," Dave said. "But you know how that goes."

Hannah glanced over her shoulder. The direction of the wind was changing. "Here's your pie," she said, handing it to him. When he took a couple of deep, prolonged sniffs, she chuckled. "I'll see you later. Thanks." As she hopped into her truck, he reached for his wallet and fished out a ten dollar bill. She thanked him again.

"Hannah" he said, as she started to back out.

She looked at him. "What?"

"Nothing." He shrugged. "I just wanted to thank you again for last night."

"It was fun," she said, and pointed to the sky, which all of sudden had started to darken. "I gotta go. We'll see you at the Honky Tonk tomorrow night."

Dave waved.

There was no activity at the funeral parlor. "Good thing," she said, hurrying to get home. "I'll call." After all, she had a phone now. A few minutes and she'd be there. She looked ahead and marveled at the site of the old man pedaling his bicycle on the other side of the road, coming the opposite way.

When she waved, he shook his head. "Yeah, yeah, I know," she said to herself. "It's the storm you told me about." When she glanced into her rearview mirror, he was gone.

As she turned into her driveway, the approaching clouds were swirling very nearly overhead, and pitch black. She glanced at the house, then the barn, and steered the truck down over the hill. She parked just outside the barn, where hopefully it would be out of the wind, and ducked under the board inside.

Billy Bob was wide-eyed and pacing his stall. A lightning bolt sliced through the sky, one, two, three, four, five, six, seven seconds…a boom of thunder rattled the barn.

Hannah stood frozen in time, panic so close she could almost taste it bubbling in her throat. She could run for the root cellar, and probably make it. Billy Bob whinnied and screamed and pawed. Another bolt of lightning!

She wondered if she could get him down the steps into the root cellar. Not hardly. "He probably would think it was a horse trailer." She stuck her head out the barn door into a gust of wind that nearly sucked her outside. There was no way she'd be able to pull the barn doors closed. No way….

Billy Bob squealed, pawing and pawing. Another bolt of lightning had him charging his stall chains. "Stop! Stop!" she cried. "Stop!" She grabbed a bale a hay, and then another, and stacked them in front of his stall. The next bolt of lightning brought thunder in six seconds. If she ran now, she might still be able to get to the root cellar.

"I don't know what to do! I don't know what to do!" she kept saying, and stacked another bale. There was only one left. She piled it to the side of the others and scrunched down between them. "It's okay, it's okay," she kept telling Billy Bob. "It's okay...." She reached up and touched his face. "It's okay."

The roaring sound of a freight train barreled down on them. She couldn't hear the rain. She couldn't hear the thunder. She couldn't hear her own voice.

"It's okay.... It's okay...."

Billy Bob screamed; the sound so distant, so far away.

"It's okay...." Bile burned her throat, tears and mucus, choking. "It's okay...." Horrible sounds, glass shattering, wood snapping, metal being pried apart, screeching wind. Then the silence.

Chapter Nine

Hannah raised her head and opened her eyes. Everything was a blur. She wiped her eyes and nose on her sleeve. Billy Bob nuzzled her face. More tears. She looked up at him. He seemed to be smiling at her, thanking her. "Thank you for staying with me. Thank you."

She stood on wobbly legs and stroked his forehead. He grabbed a mouthful of hay. "Yes, life goes on," she said, and chuckled nervously. "I'm fine and you're fine, thank God." She and Charlie had once weathered a storm that sounded just like this one. It proved to be more bark than bite. She hoped....

She turned and looked at her truck. There it sat, wet from the rain and covered with leaves and twigs, but aside from that, seemingly unscathed. Even the little yellow smiley-face ball on the radio antenna was still intact; a good sign indeed. She walked to the barn doorway and leaned out. The paddock fence was still there, the hay-hook hinges steadfast. She smiled.

"We're okay, Billy Bob," she said, and he snorted. She ducked under the rail meant to keep her horse in and shielded her eyes from the blinding sun. Was she seeing the old man far in the distance or was it the little boy? She blinked sun spots from her eyes. When she could focus, she swallowed hard.

"Oh my God."

Debris and wood and trees lay everywhere, piled like matchsticks.

"Oh no, the house," she said, biting at her trembling bottom lip. "Not the house. Oh please...."

She climbed over several stacks of wood and rounded the corner of the barn. There stood the house, apparently unscathed as well. Before she could even wonder where all the scattered wood had come from, it dawned on her that she shouldn't have been able to see the house this soon. She would have had to climb further up the hill to see past the barn. She turned quickly.

"Oh my God, no."

All four walls of the upper level of the barn had been blown to smithereens. It was all gone; every beam, every board, every slat, every old barn tool. There wasn't even a blade of old hay or straw left. It was as if someone has gone up there and swept it clean.

"I need this barn," she said, and looked up at the sky. "Why are you doing this to me? Why? What did I do to deserve this? All I want to do is farm. Is that too much to ask?"

She wiped snot off her face with her sleeve again and took a good long look around. "Oh no...." She stared. "Not the fruit trees."

The old overgrown orchard looked like desert tumbleweed.

She knelt down to the wet ground and just sat there, big tears welling up in her eyes and trickling down her cheeks. "Don't you see, Hannah, we've got nothing," she could hear Charlie say. "We've got nothing left. They took it all."

"I hurt," she said. "I hurt so bad."

"Where?" she heard someone say, and looked up. It was the old man. "Oh God." She shook her head. "If you don't mind," she said, holding up her hand. "I really need to be alone right now."

The old man nodded. "I knew you weren't no country girl, I told you that."

Hannah sighed. "Are you even real? Do you even exist? Go away." She pulled herself to her feet and started back down over the hill.

"You need to look on the bright side," the old man said.

"Oh yeah?! And where is it? Where is the bright side?" Hannah held her arms out. "Where? Show me where!"

"Well." The frail old man pointed over her shoulder. "Pruning's been made easier."

Hannah laughed. She couldn't help herself. She didn't mean to be disrespectful. She just couldn't help herself. She laughed until her body ached, then drew a deep breath and raked her fingers through her hair. "I wonder if I could sell my hair," she said, and sighed.

The old man walked away.

She turned and called after him. "I don't need you coming around pointing out my mistakes all the time," she said. "You hear me?"

He looked at her and nodded.

"I'm doing just fine," she said. "I don't need anyone." She watched him walk away and when he was almost out of sight, whispered to herself. "I'm sorry. I didn't mean that."

The old man turned slowly and smiled. "You'd better stop acting like a city girl."

Hannah folded her hands on top of her head and just stood there, watching him as he vanished beyond the thicket of trees. Then she walked back down to check the paddock more thoroughly. There wasn't even a sliver of a board in it, no tree branches, no glass. The angle of the storm's path completely missed it *and* the truck. For some sense of normalcy, she decided to turn Billy Bob out and filled and hung his water bucket on one of the fence posts. After that she took a walk up to the house, marveling again that it was still standing like a rock. There wasn't even a broken window. She wondered where all the glass strewn about came from.

Off in the distance, she heard sirens. She wondered how hard the town was hit. She went inside and using her phone for the first time, called Lucinda.

"It's bad, Hannah. So bad. A lot of homes were leveled. They're saying on the news that it was an F-3 tornado. Colleen and Jason's place is okay. Are you okay?"

"I'm fine. The hayloft of the barn is gone, but everything else seems okay. What about you?"

"The garage has some damage and we lost some trees. The house next to us is totally gone. I can't believe we still have power."

No sooner said, than they lost their connection. Hannah checked to make sure she still had a dial tone. She did. She tried phoning Lucinda back, but her phone was busy. She decided to try again later, and went back out to get a closer look at the damage to the fruit trees. She first checked the door on the root cellar. It was shut up tight, the piece of hickory still in the latch. She startled a bunny and smiled. Two bunnies, three bunnies. Life.

Of the sixty trees, at least a third of them were uprooted. The ones still standing had all suffered wind sheer damage; some were cut off clear down to the trunk. Hannah weaved her way through the branches and turned when she heard a noise from up at the barn. It was Billy Bob. He could see her. She called to him. "You're okay. I'm here."

Charlie was always one for burning brush. He'd saw up what they could use in the fireplace and the rest got turned into a huge bonfire. She looked around for a good place to start, and went back to the house to get her gloves. She stripped off her wet jeans and stood in the kitchen in her underwear, eating the rest of the cake from last night. She washed it down with a cold beer, another leftover from last night.

"Hannah! Hannah, are you home?"

It was a man's voice, one she didn't recognize at first.

"Hannah!"

It was her boss from the funeral parlor.

"Richard? Wait! I'll be right there." She glanced around the kitchen for something to wear. She'd left her wet jeans in the bathroom, the path in clear view of the front door. She cleared the table off and wrapped the tablecloth around her waist. "How nice." The colors almost matched her shirt. She pushed her hair back off her face, drew a deep breath, and walked to the front door as if she always dressed this way.

"Hey, did you come to see the house?" she asked.

He smiled and shook his head.

"Come on in. Can I get you anything?"

"No." He had on his Mortician's Face, but that was normal for him. She wondered for a second how he looked at home, how he looked brushing his teeth or kicking up his heels. The only times they'd ever spent together, usually death was involved. Her smile faded from the look in his eyes.

"I didn't know if you'd gotten your phone in yet."

She nodded.

"We've got work," he said. "Four bodies. They're there already. You'll need to come today. Two are Jewish and need to be buried before sundown."

"All right." Hannah nodded, sadness welling up in her heart. "I'll be right there."

Richard turned and started out the door but then just stood there for a moment. "One of them is a little girl, Hannah." His voice cracked. "I wanted you to know ahead of time."

"Thank you."

Chapter Ten

Hannah's time-worn defense system failed her again and again throughout the day. Working alone had its advantages. She could cry at will. She talked to the two men and woman as she washed and styled their hair. Family members had brought photos, which was customary. Hannah tried hard to keep their hair style consistent to how they looked alive. In her opinion, there was nothing worse than going to a funeral and hardly recognizing the person. She applied makeup with the same consideration.

Richard checked in with her from time to time. The bodies had been prepared otherwise and he was mentally and physically exhausted. One of the women had been a good friend of his family's.

The little girl was last, her tiny body misshapen and broken. Deep, now sutured cuts and torn flesh raked her arms and legs. She'd been sucked out of her house and found lying next to her swing set. Her grandmother, now in the next room ready for the calling hour, was found lying ten feet away from her.

Hannah washed the little girl's hair gently. It was a honey shade of brown, shoulder length, with bangs. There was a deep purple bruise on the side of her face. With her hair dried and curled slightly at the bottom, Hannah covered the bruise completely. "Such a pretty little girl."

"Is she done?" Richard asked from the doorway.

Hannah nodded.

"Good," he stepped aside. "Her parents are here."

Hannah didn't like mingling with the families. She looked for a back door, a way out, knowing there wasn't one, but looking anyway - a miracle perhaps.

"I'm sorry," Richard said. "They won't wait any longer."

Hannah stepped back as the little girl's mother and father entered the room, backing further and further until she was pressed hard against the wall. The mother screamed and wailed. The father held her up, so she wouldn't fall, crumble.

"Why, God? Why? Why!"

Hannah stood, tiny brush and comb in hand.

"Why?"

Hannah lowered her eyes, willing herself far, far away.

"Please," she heard. "May I have those?"

Hannah looked up. There were strands of the little girl's hair entwined in the brush and comb. "Yes."

When the woman walked back to the little girl's side, Hannah quietly left the room. Richard was standing in the hall. "The food arrived," he whispered.

Hannah nodded. "Give me a moment." She went downstairs to the employee rest room. Once inside, she leaned over the sink and took deep breaths to try to regain her composure. Her hands shook; her heart raced.

Being alone with the deceased was one thing. She tended to them lovingly; she treated them with respect. Always, always, always, she said the less she knew about them, the better. This was her first child, her first family of a child.

She looked at her image in the mirror. "What were you thinking taking this job?"

Someone tapped on the door.

Hannah tore off a paper towel, soaked it with cold water, and dampened her face and neck.

Another tap on the door. "Hannah."

She shook her head. It was Richard. "What the....?" She leaned over the sink, nauseated, fearful she might become ill.

Richard cracked the door open. "I'm sorry. The child's mother wants to see you."

Hannah looked up. "Why?"

"She won't say."

"Tell her I'm busy. Tell her I'm cooking. Tell her...."

Richard just stood there. He knew Hannah better than this.

She shook her head and sighed. "All right. Give me a minute."

Richard nodded. "She's in my office."

The woman sat in a chair holding her daughter's picture. She stood when Hannah entered the room. "I want to thank you," she said, her voice choked, "for making her look so pretty."

Hannah walked over and put her arms around her, and just held the woman as she wept, deep sobs wracking her body. "It's one thing to lose my mother, but my little girl too. What will I do without them?"

Hannah struggled with what to say. The old woman and the little girl were together when the storm hit, and when it ended. "Your little girl did not suffer," Hannah said.

"I hope not. I couldn't bear that."

"She didn't."

The woman lifted her head, wiping her tears. "How do you know?"

Hannah smiled. "I just do."

The woman's husband and Richard entered the room then.

"I'll be back," Hannah said, when the woman's husband wrapped her in his arms.

"The service is at five," Richard mouthed anxiously.

Hannah nodded. "I know. I'll be back."

Hannah passed the room where the little girl lay and went to stand by the grandmother's coffin for a moment. "Your daughter loves you," she said. "Take good care of her little girl."

Chapter Eleven

Hannah rushed home to check on Billy Bob, fed him, took a quick shower, and was back on the job in less than an hour. She prepared the meal to specification, served the sustenance to the grieving family, and cleaned the dining area and kitchen "Spic-n-Span," as her mother would say. Richard, back from the actual burials, sat clutching a cup of coffee at the counter.

She looked at him. Reverend Beasley was due any minute to discuss the arrangements for the remaining two deceased that were to be buried on Tuesday. They were unrelated but had both attended the same church.

"I'll have to call you with my phone number," Hannah said. "I can't remember it."

Richard nodded. "Thanks, Hannah."

She smiled. Time to leave; she didn't want to get stuck.... Too late. Reverend Beasley came down the stairs, humming softly. The man was always humming. "It keeps me sane," he often said.

Hannah gave him a hug.

"Any word from Charlie?" he asked.

"No." She and Charlie had ruined his track record. Of all the marriages he'd performed, not one had failed before. "I'll let you know when I do."

Richard poured the man a cup of coffee.

"Reverend, do you ever feel guilty?" Hannah asked. "You know, getting paid to do this, like me. I guess I'm asking more for me than anything. I don't know how to feel on days like today."

Reverend Beasley smiled. "If we didn't get paid, we wouldn't be able to do it, because we'd have to be doing something else. I look at it as getting paid for doing what I love. I would hate to not be able to do this. This is what I do."

Hannah planted a kiss on his cheek. "Thank you. And you," she said, looking at Richard. "Don't you dare go soft on me ever again or I swear I will find something else to do."

Richard laughed. "Go home. I'm tired of looking at you."

As soon as Hannah stepped outside, her thoughts immediately gravitated toward her situation at home - the barn, half a barn actually, the orchard, the mess. She stopped at the store and bought a potato. One lone potato. "Dinner," she said, plopping it down on the seat next to her in the truck. She had a taste for shoestring fries. With a little luck, she might have just enough oil to fry them. And ketchup; she hoped she had enough ketchup.

The path the tornado took was an odd one. It spared one house and trashed the next. She shook her head at the sight of a corn field, flattened, too early to harvest. She glanced ahead. Dave's pickup was in the driveway and he was standing next to it.

"What?" she said. "The pie wasn't any good?"

He smiled. "No, it was great, delicious. I was just stopping by on my way to work to check on you."

"Well, thank you. That was nice of you, I guess," she teased.

"What are you going to do with the barn?"

Hannah shook her head. "I don't know. I guess I'll have to give it some thought."

Dave laughed. "I don't understand you, Hannah. I've never known a woman like you."

"Like me? How's that?"

Dave shrugged.

"What was your wife like?"

Dave hesitated. "Well, she was independent in ways. But...."

Hannah walked to the porch and sat down. He didn't seem in a hurry.

"Did you have a good marriage?"

He nodded and smiled self-consciously.

"I wish I'd met her. I don't know how I never did."

"She liked staying home," Dave said. "Well, I'd better get to work. Let me know what you need, and I'll do it."

Hannah smiled. "I'll see you tomorrow."

She lucked out, just enough oil, just enough ketchup. She filled her plate, drew a tall glass of water, and made her way down over the hill to eat with Billy Bob. It was almost sundown. She sat on a bale of hay next to his stall, and as Charlie would say, "Chowed down."

It felt like paradise inside the barn. "We are in our own little cocoon," she said, "safe from the world, safe from harm."

Billy Bob looked at her and sighed.

"What? I'm just making conversation."

Her horse heaved another sigh.

When she finished eating, she bedded him down for the night. Hay, water bucket topped off, stall picked. He was all set. "Stay put," she told him. As she started up the hill, she glanced ahead and moaned. There was a big long Cadillac in her driveway. Who on earth could this be? And this late? It was almost nine.

"Hello!"

Hannah picked up a piece of wood and pretended to use it to aid her climbing the hill. "What can I do for you?"

"Well," the middle-aged-looking cowboy said, "I'm wanting to know what you're planning to do with all this here barn siding?"

Hannah almost laughed. "Is it against the law to burn it?"

"Yup," he said, grinning from ear to ear. "Because I'm thinking I'd like to buy it."

Hannah looked at him.

"Why, Missy, you don't know who I am, do you?"

Hannah shook her head.

"I'm Cal Able – to put you in a car today! Don't you recognize my Cadillac?"

Hannah stared at it. "No, can't say that I do. But if you're wanting to buy the barn siding, give me your number, and I'll...."

"Is your husband home? Maybe we can talk price now."

"No, actually he's not. But...."

Cal Able - to put you in a car today, fished inside his lapel pocket and handed her his card. "How many miles you got on that?" he asked, looking at her truck.

"Too many," she said. "But it's a good fit."

"I hear ya, sweetheart! I hear ya!" With that he tipped his hat and honked his horn as he pulled away. No sooner had he left, in pulled Jim and his wife Sara.

"You okay?"

Hannah nodded.

"We were going to town and just wanted to make sure."

"Thank you. I'm fine! Thanks for checking on me! Is everything okay at your place?"

"Yes."

"Good." Hannah waved.

"I told you that barn would fall apart," Jim said. "We need to get you outta here, Hannah."

"Thank you!" Hannah waved again. "Bye-bye." She smiled and through that smile, said to herself, "Please leave now."

She went inside and locked the door behind her. "Stay away, all of you," she said. "You too, old man." She put her dish in the sink, went into the bathroom to change into her night shirt, Charlie's shirt, and crawled into bed.

Chapter Twelve

Hannah heard a disturbing noise from out on the porch and for a second just lay there listening. It sounded more animal-like than human. She glanced at the clock radio next to her bed. Six thirty-two. She tried falling back to sleep, but the noise persisted.

Grumbling, she propped herself on her elbow and looked out. When two eyes stared back in at her, she screamed.

"Hannah, I'm sorry. It's me!" It was Colleen.

"Jesus!" Hannah gasped. "What are you doing?"

"I didn't want to wake you. I brought you breakfast."

Hannah reached over and unlocked the door. "If you didn't want to wake me, why did you make so much noise?"

"Well," Colleen walked in past her and headed straight for the kitchen, "actually I did want to wake you. I just didn't want you to think I was trying to wake you. You are really a sound sleeper by the way."

Hannah trudged into the bathroom, grumbling all the more.

Colleen had a pot of coffee brewing and a breakfast of scones, clotted cream, and marmalade set out on the table when Hannah emerged.

"Everything's all set; it was left over. I've gotta run." She gave Hannah a hug, and playfully messed up her hair.

"The phone's in," Hannah called after her.

"I know. Lucinda told me. I'll see you tonight."

"Thanks," Hannah said with a mouthful. "Ooh, this is good!"

The first thing Hannah wanted to do after breakfast and feeding Billy Bob, was to start stacking the barn planks. Charlie had an old friend at the sawmill that she knew fairly well. She figured she'd phone him to get an idea what old barn siding like this was worth. Since she had originally planned on burning it, just about anything would be a bargain. Plus it would save her the work of hauling it out back to the burn pile.

"Anywhere from three to five dollars a square foot," the man said. "Maybe even a little more depending on the condition."

"Thank you. Did you get any damage last night?"

"No, we were spared."

"Good."

"Do you hear anything from Charlie?"

"No," Hannah said.

"That's a shame. He loved you, Hannah. I know that."

"Me too," Hannah said. "Thanks again." She hung up before he could start up on how she should get on with her life. "'Cause that's exactly what I'm doing." She surprised herself by chuckling at that. "Wind me up and watch me go."

Billy Bob nickered as she made her way down over the hill. It was such a pleasant greeting, such a welcome sound. But then there he was leaning out over the board at the back of the barn. She shook her head. "Bad Billy Bob," she said, ignoring him as she ducked under the board and past him. "I'm not talking to you. I'm mad at you."

He turned and followed her, his head hovering over her shoulder as she inspected the screw eyes on his stall chains. When he nudged her, she ignored him still.

She decided to feed him outside in his paddock, got him all set up out there with grain and water. He followed her back and forth inside the barn. She made him wait. "Think twice next time, big man." When she led him out, he went right for his grain. She watched him eating.

For an Appy, he was big, 15.3. She'd counted his leopard spots once. He had ninety-four of them. Her favorite was the heart-shaped one on his hip. When he'd finished his grain and started grazing, Hannah went back into the barn and stood debating what to do for a stall gate.

After only a moment's deliberation she laughed at herself, at her set of circumstances; an entire yard full of lumber and probably not one board let alone two or three or four that would do. She decided to worry about a stall gate later. Right now she wanted to get started on stacking the barn siding. "Good thing this wasn't our old barn." Though that one was huge, this barn wasn't small, by any standards. It was probably 40' X 60'. Size...size, size, SIZE. "What's with everything having a size lately?"

"Behave," she told Billy Bob. "I'll be watching you." She took her gloves out of her back pocket, three of the cloth fingertips were missing on both hands, worn out. But they'd have to do. She drew a deep breath surveying the work laid out in front of her and heaved a heavy sigh. "Let the fun begin."

It made sense to stack the barn siding in the driveway up by the house, since if "Cal Able – to put you in a car today" came through with his offer to buy it, it'd be easy access. She stacked them in length sizes, twenty boards high, for easy counting. She removed any imbedded nails, marveling how few there actually were, and every once in a while stopped and stared at what was left of the barn.

"It's amazing," she said. All four corner poles had been sheared off about a foot from the hayloft floor. If they'd been sheared off any lower, they probably would have taken the barn level with it or have done considerable damage below. The upper level could have caved in on them, crushed them, it could have....

"What did I tell you about could haves, would haves and should haves?" She shrugged. "And the what-ifs too." When she needed a break, she went inside for a glass of water and cooked the apple peels from yesterday. When they were soft enough, she sprinkled on some cinnamon and sugar, grabbed a spoon, and took the pan outside on the front porch. She counted the wood piles while letting the apples cool some.

"Apples hold heat, little girl," her mother used to say. "Potatoes too. Watch yourself." Hannah blew on a spoonful.

Four stacks of an approximate ten foot size. Seven stacks of eight footers. Twelve stacks of six footers. And eleven stacks of four to five footers. She wasn't sure Cal Able – to put you in a car today, would want planks that small, but stacked them anyway just in case.

She took a sip of water and then tested the apples. "Delicious." When she remembered the ice cream from the other night, she hurried inside and came back with the container. There she sat, spooning one into the other, when Dave pulled in.

"I can't stay away," he said.

Hannah laughed.

"Wow, that looks like a healthy lunch."

"Thank you," she said, and didn't offer him any. His comment annoyed her.

"I came to ask again if you need help."

"Well, as you can see," she said, swirling some more apples into the ice cream and raising her spoon. "I don't. I'm doing just fine."

He blushed. "I didn't mean…"

"And neither did I," she said. "I'll see you tonight."

He nodded and got back into his truck. When he waved, Hannah gave him a polite nod.

"He's just being nice," she told herself when he pulled away. "Nice my ass. I'll bet your wife had to ask you for everything." She finished the rest of the apples and ice cream and downed her glass of water. Time to get back to work.

A few hours later, she was down to only thumb digits on her gloves, and they were getting pretty tattered and torn. She sat down on one of the piles of wood and pulled a sliver out of her right palm. "That's not a sliver, it's a shim," she could hear Charlie say. "Here, give me your hand." She studied her lifeline, watched it fill with blood, and wiped in on her jeans.

Three more stacks and she phoned Cal Able. She got his answering machine. "I can put you in a car today. You just wait and see." She left him a message. She'd filled Billy Bob's water bucket several times throughout the afternoon, and now walked down to give him his evening grain and deal with the stall gate situation. She walked aimlessly around the inside of the barn, climbed over piles of rusted pieces of farm equipment, and stood staring at the old cow stanchions.

She smiled. "McIver has nothing on me." She pried a side piece of one of the stanchions from the rest and lugged it over to the stall. "It's like it was made for this," she said. She had to move the screw eyes on the one side, figuring it would be best to open to the right for Billy Bob to come in and out. With the screw eyes in place, she hoisted the stanchion up and tried to slide the pivots down in. The screw eyes were too small. She put the stanchion down, bloody hand again, and went for a hammer. Using the pry bar side, she opened the screw eyes a little. Not enough. She opened them a little more. This time they fit. She swung the stanchion, the new stall gate, back and forth. It screeched and hollered. She'd seen a can of oil somewhere back by the old tractor and went to find it. As she passed the barn door she glanced out at the setting sun.

"Too bad," she said. "So I'll be late."

She oiled the pivots until they no longer squeaked. One squeak near an unsuspecting Billy Bob and there'd be another tornado - him! She used two double-end snaps to secure the new stall gate, brought her horse inside, and bedded him down for the night. "Don't you dare go through this stall gate, you hear me?"

She gave him a hug and walked up to the house. It was almost nine. She was supposed to meet everyone at the Honky Tonk at eight for dinner, but she was exhausted. She was beyond exhausted. A cool shower revived her. She loved cool showers. She didn't always, but learned early on that not only did it save on the gas bill it was good for her skin.

"You're so soft," Charlie would say.

As she was drying her hair, the phone rang. Thinking it had to be either Colleen or Lucinda, since they were the only two people who knew her new number, she picked up the phone saying, "I'll be right there. Hold your horses."

"Okay…" a male voice with a distinct twang said. "Where do you want to meet, darlin'?"

Hannah laughed. It was Cal Able – to put you in a car today. She'd recognize that voice anywhere. "I thought you were someone else. Sorry."

"I have to tell you, I found quite a few other farms with some siding for sale. It may affect the price if I end up with too much on my hands."

Hannah hesitated. Any other mood than the one she was in and she might be grappling. Not today, not tonight. "Okay, thank you. I'll take it elsewhere."

"Wait! Wait! Wait! Now hold on. I didn't say I didn't want it."

Hannah stared at the envelope from the Courthouse lying on the table. She'd all but forgotten about it.

"I'll be over in the morning and we'll talk. How's that?"

"Fine."

Lucinda and Colleen heard about the conversation at the Honky Tonk when Hannah finally arrived. She waited until Jason and George went up to the bar to get another round of drinks.

"Oh, Hannah," Lucinda said. "Maybe you should get one of the guys to be there when he comes, to make sure he doesn't gyp you."

"Who?" Jason said, placing beers down in front of them.

"Cal Able," Colleen said.

Hannah sighed.

"Cal Able? You mean the used car salesman? Did you ever see that man on TV? He's got a Cadillac a mile long. He had it custom-made, and he's got a kickass hemi in it! What'd he want?"

Hannah fudged the conversation. "I saw him the other day somewhere and he looked at my truck, like he wanted to buy it. That's all. I'm not selling it, so...." She took a long swig of beer, and over the top of the bottle gave Lucinda and Colleen the evil eye.

Dave came over to see if anyone wanted to order from the kitchen. They decided to split a couple of platters of nachos and fries. When Dave walked away, Lucinda and Colleen exchanged curious glances. Hannah and Dave hadn't even acknowledged one another.

"Does anyone need to go to the ladies room?" Colleen asked.

Lucinda nodded and tugged at Hannah's arm. "Come on."

The men laughed. "You wanna go to the bathroom with me?" Jason asked.

"In your dreams," George said, and they laughed some more.

Colleen shut the ladies room door and demanded to know, "What happened?"

"I don't know," Hannah said, examining the tiny cut above her eye in the mirror. It was in the shape of an arrow. "I guess I did it cleaning up the yard today."

"Not that," Lucinda said. "You and Dave? You act like he has the plague. Him too."

Hannah looked at them, started to say something, but then just shrugged.

"He really likes you, Hannah."

"Okay, and I like him. End of subject. I thought you had to go to the bathroom."

Colleen shook her head. "I went right before you came."

"Well, then if you'll excuse me." Hannah headed into one of the toilet stalls. "And I'm not talking to you while I'm peeing, okay?"

Colleen laughed. "Okay, but can you just listen. I've been thinking."

Hannah chuckled.

"What about if you tell him you need to take it slow? What about if you say, I'm still hurting, I need time. Can we just be friends?"

Silence....

"Hannah?"

"I'm thinking."

"It's just that I hate to see you lose out on such a nice guy."

"Why? I'm good at losing. It's just the getting over the losing part that's a challenge. Damn it, I said I wasn't going to talk to you through the door. I hate when you do this to me."

Lucinda and Colleen laughed. "All right," Colleen said. "We'll be quiet."

Hannah couldn't stand the quiet. She flushed the toilet to drown out the tinkle- tinkle. When she emerged, her best friends were standing with arms crossed, waiting patiently. "Well?"

Hannah walked past them to the sink and washed her hands. She looked at their reflections in the mirror. "You know what, the bottom line. I wouldn't mind having a relationship, with Dave, with someone...."

"I'll bet Charlie's having one," Colleen said.

Hannah looked at her.

"I'm sorry. But come on, be realistic."

Hannah sighed. "Call me delusional, but I don't think so."

Lucinda nudged Colleen discretely. Don't push it. They followed Hannah back out to the bar area. "Lay Down, Sally," was playing loud on the jukebox. "Come rest here in my arms. Don't you think I want someone to talk to."

The men were already eating the fries and nachos. "We ordered more," Jason said.

"What? We weren't even gone five minutes," Colleen said.

"Lay down, Sally. Don't you ever leave. Lay Down Sally...."

"I hate that song," Hannah said.

"Since when?" Colleen asked.

Hannah laughed. "Since now."

"You come rest here in my arms."

More fries and nachos arrived, and another round of ice cold beer. When a slow song started to play on the jukebox, a few couples got up to dance.

"Hannah?"

She turned. It was Dave. "Would you care to dance?"

She hesitated. "Shouldn't you be at the bar?"

"I took a break," he said, smiling. "And if you turn me down after walking all the way over here, I'll be awful embarrassed."

Hannah chuckled. "I suppose you'll want to lead."

Dave laughed and reached for her hand. "It's the only way I know how." They walked out to the dance floor and as summarized by Hannah to Billy Bob later back home, they assumed the position. "It was a nice dance. He didn't hold me too close. I was happy for that. I didn't want to "make a spectacle," as my Mom would say."

Billy Bob grabbed another mouthful of hay.

"After the dance we ate a little bit more and then I got up to leave."

"It's early, Hannah!" Colleen said. "Don't go yet."

"'I'm beat,' I told them. 'Besides, I haven't lived at the farm long enough yet for the truck to know its way home.'" She stroked Billy Bob's forehead. "And here I am, slightly mellow, slightly happy, slightly...sad." Tears welled up in her eyes. "I have a long day tomorrow, so you behave tonight. Okay?"

She walked up to the house by flashlight, heard the mournful call of an hoot owl far, far away, and fell asleep stretched out on her bed, fully dressed. She didn't even take off her boots.

Chapter Thirteen

"Hannah. Come on, Hannah, wake up." She felt someone smacking her face again and again. "Come on, Hannah, you can do it. Come on, wake up."

She opened her eyes. Colleen and Lucinda were hovered over her. "What the hell?"

"Oh, thank God!" Colleen said. "You have a gas leak in your house. Can't you smell it?"

Hannah shook her head and sat up rubbing her face. "Why were you hitting me?"

"We thought you were dead."

Hannah shook her head, looking at them, and then laughed. "Wait a minute, let me get this straight. You thought I was dead and so you thought it would be nice to...?"

"This is no time to be joking around," Colleen said. "Didn't you hear us? You have a gas leak in the house. It could blow up any minute. I can't believe you don't smell it." They tugged her toward the door.

Hannah sniffed. "That's not gas. What the hell is that?" She walked toward the kitchen, sniff, sniff, sniff. "Go," she told Colleen and Lucinda. "Go out on the porch."

"Not without you."

Hannah stood, staring first at the stove, then.... "Oh my God." There was steam coming out of the freezer compartment of her refrigerator. She turned to alert Lucinda and Colleen and bumped into both of them, glued right behind her. "Is that weird or what?" Both nodded.

Hannah approached the refrigerator with her two best friends in tow. When she was just about to place her hand on the freezer door, she pulled back. "It's hot. How can it be hot? It's a freezer!"

Colleen ran to the phone and called Jason.

"Unplug it," he told her.

"How?" The plug was behind the appliance.

Hannah stood thinking. "Fuse box, fuse box. Where's the fuse box?" She hurried down to the basement, found the fuse box, and unscrewed every one of them. She yelled up the stairs. "Is it still steaming?"

"Yes, but less! Wait, it's stopping!"

Hannah climbed back up out of the basement and stood with Lucinda and Colleen assessing the situation. "Well, that definitely was the smell. It's taking my breath away." No sooner said, the three started opening windows and doors. Hannah propped the front door open with a chair. When they gathered back in the kitchen, Hannah touched the side of the freezer with her fingertip. "How on earth can it get so hot?"

Colleen and Lucinda touched it too.

"Do we want to open it?"

"No," Hannah said. "I don't want the smell worse." She nudged them out of the way.

"What are you going to do?"

"I'm going to get it out of here."

"How?"

Hannah looked at them. "Wait a minute. What are you two doing here anyway?"

"We brought you breakfast."

"Let me guess, leftovers again. What is it today? Tea biscuits and latte`?"

"Close," Lucinda said. "Harvey Ballbanger donuts from Ditz's."

"Wow!" Hannah said, licking her lips. "We're going to need coffee."

"We brought some."

"Awesome." She made a quick stop in the bathroom, then down to the barn to feed Billy Bob. He stood safe in his stall, nickering for his grain. "That's a good boy. Mommy's so proud of you."

Lucinda and Colleen had the kitchen table all set with chairs around it on the front porch when she came back up to the house. Hannah sat down, took a sip of coffee, and then a big bite of a Harvey Ballbanger and leaned back in ecstasy. "Who says this ain't the perfect morning?"

The three of them laughed. There was destruction and rubble all around them, not to mention the steaming hot refrigerator. "How are you going to keep your food cold?"

"What food?" Hannah said, laughing again. "Another one of these Harvey Ballbangers and I'll be good to go for days."

The three women sat eating. "It's like communion," Lucinda said, dipping a piece of Harvey Ballbanger into her coffee. "I wonder what's in these things."

"Flour, yeast, cinnamon, apples, sugar, milk, Hazelnut liqueur…and a secret ingredient Harvey won't disclose," Hannah said.

"Knowing him, it's probably spermies," Colleen said.

Lucinda pretended to gag.

"Actually," Hannah said. "I've given it a lot of thought over the years and I think it's white pepper."

"You're kidding. It doesn't taste peppery," Lucinda said.

"That's the beauty. Taste again."

Lucinda took another bite and chewed and chewed.

69

"See?"

"Oh my gosh, yes. I think you're right. It's very subtle, but it's there."

All three nodded.

"A toast to Ditz!"

"To Ditz!"

"Dirty old man that he is, but one hell of a donut maker!"

"Cheers!"

"So what are your plans today?" Hannah asked.

"We don't have any. We're going to help you."

"You don't have to. Don't you have messes of your own to clean up?"

"Yes, but the men are going to do it. You don't have one, you just have us. No offense."

The three of them laughed. "No offense taken," Hannah said, reaching for another Harvey Ballbanger.

"Not that you couldn't have one really nice one at the moment."

Hannah held up her hand.

When they'd finished eating, topped off with a second cup of coffee, Hannah tackled the refrigerator. It was relatively easy getting it out of the corner. She just kept moving it back and forth followed by a little tug forward. Though it was closer to the back door, she'd then have to get it down four steps that way. The freezer compartment was still warm to the touch, but no longer smelly, now that steam wasn't seeping out all over. With Lucinda and Colleen guiding her, Hannah walked the refrigerator through the living room, step by step, stop and rest, more steps, stop and rest, and onto the front porch. Once outside, Hannah opened the freezer compartment.

"Wow," Colleen said. There was nothing in the freezer but two trays of melted ice cubes. The water was still hot. "I'll bet these little suckers were boiling."

"The smell must have come from back here," Hannah examined the refrigerant apparatus in the back. "Ooh, yes," she said, when she leaned down close; same smell, only stronger. She stood back and shook her head at the sight of this old fridge on the porch next to the table and chairs. "I'll be the envy of the neighborhood with this outdoor kitchen."

The three of them laughed again.

"All right, I'm going to go get my truck." Loading the refrigerator took less than five minutes. "Stand back in case it gets away from me." With the truck backed right up to the porch, clearing the steps, Hannah stood inside the bed and slowly, very slowly, started tilting the refrigerator toward her. When it got to the point where she couldn't support it any longer, she let it go, and it fell into the truck bed with a clang and a thud.

"Cool!" Hannah climbed down and started pushing it the rest of the way in, her feet braced on the porch floor and leaning with all her might. "Okay, you can help now," she said, laughing along with her huffing and puffing. The three women pushed and shoved. "That's good. Stop." Hannah motioned them out of the way, closed the tail gate, and dusted off her hands.

"Wow, Hannah," Colleen said. "Are you sure you're not a guy?" She peeled the top of Hannah's shirt back. "Are those for real?"

Hannah laughed. Too much laughing, she thought, too silly of a start to the day. "I'm going to go turn out Billy Bob."

"What do you want us to do?" Lucinda asked.

Hannah hesitated. Both women had acrylic fingernails. "Well, the more barn siding I get stacked before...."

"Then that's what we'll do," Colleen said. They'd both brought gloves and went to work. Hannah took care of her horse and then drove the truck all around the property picking up pieces of the old asphalt shingling. She stopped up front when the truck bed was overflowing. "I'm going to go drop this stuff off at the dump. I'll be right back. Keep an eye on Billy Bob."

As soon as she pulled out of the driveway, Lucinda and Colleen sat down to take a break. "How does she do it?" Colleen wiped her brow. "Where does she get all her energy?"

"I don't know." Lucinda shook her head. "Same age as us too."

Hannah lucked out at the scrap yard. The man gave her fifteen dollars for the fridge. She stopped at Rickety's Convenience Store and bought a 2-litre bottle of cold ginger ale, a bag of potato chips, a loaf of bread, and a half pound each of turkey breast and sliced cheddar cheese. Everything came to $14.98. She tossed a couple of packets of mayonnaise and mustard in the bag.

"Lunch!" she said, when she returned. With the sun shining in through the basement doorway, Hannah made her way down the steps and turned the power back on. She pulled the cord on the one lone light bulb in the basement, way on the other side, and for a moment just stood there. Had the foundation crumbled more? She touched the wall lightly with her fingertips. The crumbling was fresh.

"Hannah?"

"I'm coming."

The three women washed up and sat at the table on the front porch to eat. Lucinda took off her shoes. Her feet were swollen.

"That's not a good idea," Colleen said. "You'll never get them back on."

"Do you want a pair of boots?" Hannah asked.

Lucinda shrugged. She propped her feet up on the porch rail and wiggled her toes. "I used to have pretty feet. Remember how pretty my feet used to be?"

Hannah and Colleen rolled their eyes.

"Pass me the chips."

They watched a few cars go by. When a van slowed down in passing, Hannah waved.

"Who's that?" Colleen asked.

"I don't know."

"Then why'd you wave."

"I read once where in the inner city that if someone's checking out a place to rob and someone in the house waves to them, the robber will think twice. They'll wonder if it's someone they know. Or that maybe they'll be identified or recognized. It's supposed to work even better when you make eye contact."

"How would anyone know that?" Lucinda asked.

"I don't know, maybe they interviewed the robbers," Hannah said. "Come on, look. Make eye contact."

All three waved at the driver passing by in a van and then laughed. The next car, a big long Cadillac slowed down and pulled into the driveway.

"Good afternoon, ladies!" Cal Able – to put you in a car today, said, climbing out from the behind the wheel and tipping his cowboy hat. "How ya'll doin' today?"

Hannah smiled. "We're doing great. How about you?"

"Good, good. My rheumatism is kicking up a bit, probably from the storm, but aside from that, I'm doing great." He observed the piles of barn siding with a grimace and a glance. He appeared to be not only stiff and in pain, but in some sort of agony. He took out a handkerchief and wiped his brow.

Hannah offered him a seat. "Would you like some ginger ale?" He looked sick enough to die. She imagined the phone call she'd make to her boss if Cal Able – to put you in a car today, dropped dead on her porch. "Yep, I recruited him. He's ours!"

She poured the man a glass of ginger ale and watched as he downed the whole thing while Lucinda struggled to get her shoes back on.

"Are you diabetic?" Hannah asked.

"Why yes, Ma'am, I am. How would you know that?"

"Just a hunch," Hannah said, fixing him a sandwich. "Here. Eat." Appearing to be shooing a fly, Hannah wiped sweat from the side of his face with a napkin. He was wearing makeup. It was dripping. "We'll need something to write on and tally up the wood."

Lucinda hobbled into the house with one shoe on and toes in the other. Colleen followed her. Hannah studied the man's profile and dabbed the side of his face again.

"Don't know how I got so hungry," he said, wolfing down half the sandwich.

"Where have you been? What were you doing?" Hannah asked, glancing at the makeup residue on the napkin.

"A commercial," he said. "I hate 'em."

Hannah smiled. "So that ain't you, huh?"

He shook his head and stuffed the rest of the sandwich into his mouth.

"How old are you? If you don't mind me asking."

"Forty three," he said, out of breath.

"It's okay…shhh…." She patted his wrist, and then leaned back to call through the screen door. "Could we have a glass of water?"

Colleen came out with one. The man drank that down too.

"All right, we're just going to sit here for a few minutes," Hannah said. She studied the man's eyes.

"I'm okay," he insisted. "I'm okay."

"Us too," she said. "Aren't we?"

Colleen and Lucinda nodded from the other side of the screen door. "What's wrong with him?" Lucinda whispered.

Hannah mimicked giving herself an injection.

Colleen's mouth dropped. "Drugs?"

"Sugar," Hannah mouthed. "Diabetic."

"Oh." Colleen clutched her chest. "Is he going to be all right?"

Hannah nodded. "Cal, would you like to go inside and rest a minute."

"Yes," he said, "if you don't mind. I hate being any trouble though."

"No trouble." Hannah helped him to his feet and steered him inside. He tripped on the doorjamb and they both tumbled onto the bed. Hannah sat him up. "And here you two were worried about me getting a man. I just got one flat out in my bed and wasn't even trying."

Lucinda and Colleen laughed. "Are you sure he's going to be all right?"

"Yes," Hannah said, leading him over to the chair. "He's looking much better. Cal, do you have a test kit?"

He nodded. "In my car."

Lucinda went out to get it and came back, wide-eyed. "His car is full of candy and there's a girly magazine on the front seat. The man's a pervert."

"No, I'm not," he said, when all three looked at him. "They were showing me my ad."

"You have an ad in there?" Colleen asked.

He nodded. "I'm going national."

Hannah laughed. "I have a national pervert in my house. Wait till Billy Bob finds out."

"Billy Bob?"

"Keep him talking," Hannah whispered, and pricked his finger. All three stood over the test kit as it ticked off the seconds in countdown. "Cal, your sugar's seventy-nine. What's normal for you?"

"Oh, that's a little low."

"Okay. We'll check it again in a few minutes."

The three women went into the kitchen and busied themselves counting the piles of lumber in the driveway outside the window. All three jumped when Cal Able appeared in the doorway. "How ya'll doin'?" he asked, apparently back to his former self.

"Fine," Hannah said. "What about you?"

He looked puzzled. "I'm not sure. Who are you?"

Hannah laughed. "You came to look at the barn siding. It's stacked out front. Your blood sugar was a little low."

"Really? You don't say."

Hannah nodded. "How about we check it again? It was seventy-nine about fifteen minutes ago."

This time it was a hundred and two. The man gathered up his test kit and glanced around the living room with a baffled expression on his face. "I hope I didn't take up too much of your time. I wouldn't want to be a bother."

"No bother," Hannah said. "Let's go look at the siding."

With every breath the man took, he became more and more the familiar used car salesman, "hemming and hawing," as Charlie would say. "These here look too splintered. Those are too short, them, too long."

"We only stacked what's worth something," Hannah replied. She crossed her arms on her chest and stood her ground.

"How's $375.00?"

Hannah looked at her notes. "How about $523.00?"

"You drive a hard bargain, darlin'."

Hannah smiled. "Are you interested in the beams?"

"No, but I know of someone that might be."

"You'll be picking up the barn siding then?"

Cal Able nodded. "When we settle on a price."

Hannah looked at him. "I thought we already had."

"Which would be?"

"$523.00. I checked on the going price for siding like this. I know you have to make a profit, your share, but I do too. I need the money. I've got to do something about that barn," she said. "I'm not trying to play hardball with you. I'm not in a position to. I'm just asking what's fair for you and fair for me." She paused, Lucinda and Colleen at her side. "So what'll it be?"

"$523.00," he said, and shook her hand. "What kind of work you do, darlin'?"

Hannah smiled. "I work on dead people."

Cal Able tipped his hat. "Don't I know it." He glanced at his watch and took out his wallet and paid her. "My guys will be here sometime this afternoon. I'll take those beams off your hands too." He peeled off another hundred dollar bill. "This okay?"

Hannah shook her head.

He pulled out another hundred dollar bill. "I'm done. This is it," he said.

"Me too," Hannah said, and took the money. The women spent the next few hours gathering up the rest of the asphalt shingles strewn about and tossing them into the bed of Hannah's pickup. The yard was starting to look pretty good.

"All right, let's call it a day," Hannah said. "Go home!" They made plans to meet for dinner at Lucinda's. "I'll bring the salad." As soon as her friends left, Hannah went down to spend a little time with Billy Bob. "Do you want to go for a ride?"

The horse just looked at her. "I knew that you would." She brushed him down, picked his feet, and tacked him up. He snorted at the orchard branches laying on the ground everywhere, the uprooted trees. "Wow, I didn't know we had a creek!"

They walked alongside of it, stopping here and there. "Oh look! Minnows."

Billy Bob lowered his head. When a frog hopped into the water off the bank, he jumped back. "It's just a little frog, silly." She stroked his neck. The tiny frog's eyes were peeping up out of the water. "It's nice to know this water is here if we're ever out of power."

She loosened the reins and let the horse take a drink. He smacked his lips. Hannah glanced at the sun; time to head back. They took a different route, forging their way through the tall grass and weeds. Whenever Billy Bob grabbed a mouthful, Hannah leaned down and yanked it away. He pinned his ears.

"It's for your own good. I don't want you choking on it." When she came to a clearing, which looked oddly as if it had been mowed recently, she let him graze for a little while. Judging from Billy Bob's reaction, the short grass was very tasty. It even had patches of clover in it.

The barn was visible from this vantage point. It had a sturdy yet forlorn look to it. Hannah stretched her arms and turned from side to side to loosen the tightness in her back. "You know what, Billy Bob," she said. "We don't really need a hayloft. We have plenty of room down below. And it certainly is a nicer view without it."

As soon as this matter-of-fact statement came out of her mouth and went out over the land, it turned into a plan. Back at the barn, she untacked Billy Bob, put him in the pasture, and washed up to go run errands. She made another trip to the dump to get rid of the shingles. Then she stopped at the Farm Co-op Store, which happened to be on the way to the grocery store, and inquired about the price for rolls of asphalt roofing. "The barn is 60' x 40'." If Charlie were here, he could tell her the square footage in a flash.

The salesman took out his calculator. "You're going to need twenty-four rolls, which will come to…." Hannah glanced around the store. "$622.34 plus tax."

"I'll need nails and tar too."

At the grocery store, she picked up salad fixings and ingredients to make salad dressing and marveled at her timing. "First time in a long time I can actually buy food and I have nowhere to put it." She bought a dozen brown eggs, a loaf of bread, and a pound of butter. Blueberries were on sale. She couldn't pass them up. The bananas looked good, and the new potatoes. The avocados were perfect. She also bought cilantro and a little bottle of hot sauce, a small Vidalia onion, a red bell pepper, garlic, and tortilla chips. She was famous for her guacamole, and hadn't made it in so long.

Cal Able's men were finishing loading up the barn siding when she got home. "Do you plan to tear the barn down?" one of them asked, as she hauled in the groceries.

"I don't think so. I'm going to have to check with my husband when he gets home to see what he wants to do with it." Saying that surprised her. It's not as if the man looked threatening in any way. Why the pretense to appear as if Charlie would be home any minute? She caught a glimpse of the old man over by the pine trees. She couldn't wave since she had her hands full so she just nodded instead. When she came back out, he was gone and she felt disappointed. She wanted to explain what she was doing and maybe get his grumpy opinion.

She stood looking at the barn for a moment, second guessing herself. Any kind of shingles on a flat roof has disaster written all over it. I'm going to need a lawnmower too.

"Ma'am, we're all done."

"Thank you." She shook the man's hand, real rough and tough like. "Thank you."

"I know your husband, Ma'am," he said. "We used to work together at the sawmill."

Hannah nodded. So much for having anyone think Charlie was coming home for dinner. "What's your name?"

"Houston," he said. "Houston DeLand."

Hannah smiled. "Your mom had a sense of humor."

He laughed. "I reckon she did."

She watched him walk to one of the trucks. "Wait a minute. Does Cal Able own the lumber yard?"

"He does now. He bought it about a month ago."

Hannah nodded. When she turned, the old man was standing right next to her. "Well, hello!" A big German Shepherd sat at his side, wagging its tail. "How are you?"

"I see you're getting things done."

Hannah grinned. "I'm thinking of leaving the barn the as it is. I won't have to worry about it toppling over again if there's another storm that way. It looks pretty sturdy now."

The old man shrugged.

"I bought roofing asphalt. I'm going to put it down tomorrow."

"Humph."

"And then I'll start on the orchard I guess. How's your place? Did you get any damage?"

"A little," he said.

"Do you need some help?"

He shook his head. "You have enough to do here."

Hannah glanced at the antique watch on his wrist. "I've got to go feed my horse."

"That's a nice stall gate," he said.

She smiled. The old man could be rather pleasant when he had a mind to. "What's your dog's name?"

"Bessie," he said.

"Oh, so the little boy is your…?"

The old man just looked at her.

"Hey, Bessie," Hannah said. The dog offered her paw. "Good girl."

"No, she's bad," the old man said. He and Bessie walked on down the driveway with Bessie still wagging her tail and looking back over her shoulder.

Chapter Fourteen

From the time Lucinda and Colleen left and Hannah arrived for dinner, three more people had been invited to dinner; Tom and Raven, friends of theirs, and Dave. Hannah was somewhat disappointed to see his truck in the drive. She had thought at least for this evening, the pressure was off. Not to mention the "socialites."

"George invited him. I'm so sorry," Lucinda whispered at the door, apologizing after one look at Hannah's face. "I am so sorry."

"Me too," Hannah said. She'd been having such a good day. And then there was Raven, Tom's trophy wife - a dressage rider, a woman who oozed money out of her every pore, a know-it-all. Hannah gave everyone hugs, Dave included.

Lucinda put the guacamole and chips on the table out on the back deck and they all gathered around the bowl. Hannah felt badly, there really wasn't enough for eight people. Damn you, George.

"What's in this?" Raven asked. "It's delicious."

"Oh, the usual," Hannah said.

"What's all that in the back of your truck?" Jason asked.

Hannah sighed. "Um…I picked up some rolls of asphalt roofing for the barn."

"I thought the roof blew off."

"It did," Hannah said. "Perfectly. I'm going to roof it flat."

"What?" All four men scoffed. "You've got to be kidding?"

"Nope!" She reached for the beer Colleen handed her and resisted the urge to bite the cap off to shut them up. "This time tomorrow evening it'll all be done."

"That roof's flat."

"Actually it has a little bit of a pitch, thanks to the way it's settled over the years. With age comes wisdom."

"Okay," Raven said. "Was that a dig at me?"

Hannah looked at her and chuckled. "No. Honestly. No."

Raven pressed her hand to her chest. "Thank God, I didn't want this to be another one of those evenings."

"Speaking of which, how is Bianca doing?" Bianca was Raven's Irish Warmblood horse's name.

"Super. Phenomenal. How's John Boy?"

"It's Billy Bob, and he's doing great."

"Riding much?"

"Actually I rode today."

"I heard all about your hack through town."

Hannah smiled. "Yeah, I yelled yee haw at every intersection. It helped my concentration on our half-passes."

Raven laughed. "Don't knock it till you try it, Hannah."

"Oh, did I tell you the new word Ronnie learned today?" Colleen said for a change of subject. "He said, Gammie. He called me Gammie." Out came the latest pictures of her grandson who was just turning two. "I told him he could call me Gammie forever. It sounds much better than Grandma." Next photo. "That's us at the mall."

Hannah had seen them before. "They're darling, Gammie."

Colleen nudged her playfully.

"Are we all ready to eat?" Lucinda asked.

The men were on their feet. The food was set up buffet style, with two tables for eating out on the side porch. The women sat at one table, the men at the other. "Awe, gosh, 'nobody' elbowing me," Lucinda said.

George blew her a kiss. "Just wait."

"Promises, promises."

Dinner was spaghetti with meat balls, salad, hot bread, marinated olives. "Great batch," Colleen said, of the sauce.

All nodded in agreement, food in their mouths. Hannah reached for her napkin and noticed Dave looking at her. "How's that little guy, the little sheep?" she asked.

"Good." He smiled. Everyone smiled. They were talking.

"So, Hannah," Tom said. "What made you decide to take on this roof job by yourself?"

"Necessity."

"I know of a contractor that…."

"Is he free?"

Tom snorted. "No."

An awkward moment of silence followed this. Hannah raised her eyes from her plate. "What concerns me, Tom, is the stairs door in the hayloft. I'm thinking I'll need to support that somehow."

All four men's eyes lit up, forks in mid-air.

"So if you have any ideas about how I might make it secure. I don't imagine I can just nail the door shut. It'll have to be able to take the weight of snow. Plus, I'm wondering if I'll need an overhang on the perimeters." She swirled a fork full of spaghetti and brought it to her mouth.

The men began talking the roof situation over among themselves. It's as if Hannah was no longer even there. She glanced at the women at the table, a unified expression of "well done," written on each face, even Raven's.

"You know you're going to have to tar the seams," Jason said, at one point.

"Yes."

"If you wait until this weekend we can all help."

"I appreciate that, but it's going to rain Wednesday, Thursday and Friday. I don't want to seal in any moisture. I figure by tomorrow it'll be nice and dry. It was mostly dry today."

The male consensus was that the roof wouldn't need an overhang. Even when it had a peaked roof, there was hardly any overhang. "Did rain seep in after the storm?"

"No."

"Then you should be okay."

"The door shouldn't present a problem either. Just nail it shut. It'll be fine. The weight will be spread evenly on the roof. That door won't be singled out. If you want to be safe, get a big piece of sheet metal to nail on top of it."

Hannah smiled. That had the sound of a seal of approval to it, all four men nodding. "Would you pass the olives?"

Conversation turned to other farms and houses that had suffered storm damage. George reached for another slice of bread. "Did you hear they downgraded the tornado to an EF-2?"

"Can they do that?" Lucinda asked. "I thought they said it was a category three."

"Do you have insurance, Hannah?" Jason asked.

Lucinda and Colleen looked at one another.

Hannah hesitated. Charlie had always been very private with their financial affairs, even long before they "went down the tubes," as he put it. "On the house, yes. The barn, no. It was uninsurable."

"Does that mean we can burn the house down for you?"

Hannah laughed. "No. Because I'd probably be in it. I love that old house. It has charm."

Raven turned up her nose. "Tom says it's falling apart."

"That's because Tom's not seeing it with my eyes," Hannah said, flicking an olive at Tom and hitting him square in the forehead.

Everyone laughed, and then laughed again when Tom retrieved the olive off the floor, dusted it off, and ate it. "When opportunity knocks, open your mouth, and answer the door."

"Pride goeth before the fall," Jason said, adding another saying.

"A bird in the hand is worth two in the bush," George said.

Jason came up with another. "Confucius say woman who has blond hair on head, has black hair by…"

"Quit!" Colleen said, laughing. "How about man who open big mouth get foot stuck."

Raven helped herself to more salad. "This is delicious, Hannah. What's in it?"

Hannah stared at her as if she were kidding.

"The dressing, I mean."

"Oh…mayo and vinegar, a little sugar."

"That's it?"

"Some seasonings. Cayenne pepper mainly, a little sea salt."

"It's delicious."

"Thank you."

"Oh, and I want to buy a pie too."

"What?"

"Dave says you're selling pies to make money."

Hannah looked at Dave, who blushed instantly. "They're delicious pies," he said. "What's the harm?"

"No harm," Hannah said, feeling nauseous. Pride goeth before the fall indeed. "It's all right, Charlie," she could hear herself saying in her mind. "I'm not hungry anyway."

"Right," he'd responded, knowing she ate so little so he would have more. "You had no breakfast, hardly any lunch. Eat, goddammit! Eat!"

"Hannah…?" Lucinda touched her arm. "Hannah, you okay?"

She nodded. "What kind of pie do you want, Raven?"

"You mean, you make different kinds?"

Hannah smiled, her bottom lip trembling. "The absolute best pie I make is one I call 'Boysenberry Surprise.'" She could see Charlie tasting it and smiling. "It's different every time."

"Then Boysenberry Surprise it is. When can you make it?"

"Tomorrow."

It wasn't long before Hannah left to go home. She checked on Billy Bob, gave him some hay and topped off his water, then climbed the hill back to the house showing the way with her flashlight. The battery was running low, the light getting dimmer and dimmer. Hannah felt the same way. She sat down on the porch steps for a moment and looked up at the moon, smiling. "You hold a moonbeam in your hand

and the sunshine in your heart," she could hear her mother say. "Tomorrow is yet another day and a brand new start."

Chapter Fifteen

The old man came for breakfast. He said he smelled the eggs frying. He brought an orange. "Can we eat outside?"

"Sure," Hannah hesitated at the door as she watched him walk across the porch to the steps and slowly sit down. She figured he had to be in his late eighties or early nineties. "One egg or two?"

"One."

Hannah returned a few minutes later, breakfast shared evenly, one egg and one slice of toast each on the plates and the orange quartered - both with two halves. "Do you take anything in your coffee?"

"No."

She didn't think so. She came back with two cups of hot black coffee and sat down on the opposite end of the step. "Where's Bessie?"

"I tied her up. I don't like tying up a dog, but she won't stay put. She's always wantin' to run off somewhere."

"That's unusual for a Shepherd."

The old man looked at her for a moment and then just shook his head.

Hannah shrugged. "Well, it is."

"Dogs are dogs, don't matter the breed."

Hannah nodded. Why debate it? She smiled. "I'm starting the roof today."

"That's why I'm here. I wanted to make sure you start up front." He pointed. "The roof slopes a little. You want to overlap the tops of each row from the bottom up."

"Thank you." She wasn't sure she'd have done that, and might have done it wrong. They ate in silence, but for the birds singing and the squirrels and chipmunks chirping and scurrying about. The leaves on the trees whispered softly in the breeze. It was a beautiful morning.

When the old man was done eating, he drank the rest of his coffee and handed her his plate and cup. "Your horse behavin'?"

"Yes," Hannah said. Billy Bob was as snug as a bug in a rug in his stall this morning.

"Good. Thank you for the breakfast."

Hannah resisted asking the old man if he had a wife, if he had a son, sons, or daughters. Who was the little boy? She went inside and washed up the dishes. She'd phone work in a little while, see if any "touch ups" were needed for the two deceased being buried today. But right now....

She put Billy Bob in his pasture and filled up his water bucket. "I'll be watching you," she said. She had a clear view of him from the roof. When she called his name, he swung his head around and then raised his eyes. Hannah laughed. "See! I told you."

The rolls of roofing material were heavier than Hannah anticipated. Fortunately she could back the truck up the old ramp to the hayloft – soon to be roof, and roll them off the tailgate. She first went around and pounded in all the old spikes on the outside of the floor and cut all of the vertical boards flush. Then she laid the first roll of material out and placed the remaining rolls along the way to keep it flat.

"Here we go." She positioned herself facing the downside edge of the floor and started hammering in the roofing nails. Fearing she'd hit her fingers, she'd put the nail in with a tap, and then started pounding. She quickly lost too many nails with that technique when they went flying, fortunately toward the front of the barn and not the back where the horse would walk – so she decided she'd have to hold them in place. She put two fingers under the nail, hit it fairly hard twice, and then removed her fingers and pounded three times. Perfect!

She edged across the roof on her butt, knowing it would kill her knees if she tried to kneel that long, not to mention her back if she stood and bent over too far for any length of time. She had a birthday in a couple of weeks. Age fifty-five was just around the corner. Of the three women, Hannah, Lucinda and Colleen, Hannah was the only one who'd gone through menopause already. She'd welcomed the "change."

First roll of the roofing asphalt went down without a hitch. She used an old broom to apply the tar. The man at the building supply said it wouldn't need to be heated as long as the weather stayed warm. Putting down the second roll went well too. She was getting the hang of it. When she needed a break, she stretched out onto her back, hands behind her head, and closed her eyes to the sun. "Vitamin D, revive me."

Billy Bob nickered.

"I wasn't talking to you!" she yelled. "I'm talking to the sun!"

He started pawing.

Hannah got up and walked over to find the reason for his pawing. He was watching a German Shepherd who was sitting by the pasture gate with its leash on. "Oh, you're going to get in trouble. You'd better go on home. Go on!"

The dog raised her paw at Hannah, and looked as if she wished she could climb through the air to get to her. The front of the barn, being a bank barn, wasn't but five or six feet off the ground now. The back wall had a drop of about twelve feet, and the sides, somewhere in between.

"Go home!"

The dog wagged its tail and took off.

Hannah yawned. "I think I'm going to take a little nap," she told Billy Bob. "How about you?"

He put his head down and went back to grazing. Hannah walked to the other side, sat down, and with her heels hung over the edge of the roof, stretched out and got comfortable. The clouds took shape and form. An elephant floated by, a potbelly pig, its belly getting bigger and bigger, an arrow, a picket fence, a puppy licking her face. I must be dreaming. Another lick.

Hannah opened her eyes, having fallen asleep watching the clouds, and had a puppy at her side. "Where'd you come from, little one?"

The puppy wiggled and squirmed and trickled pee all over her lap. Hannah laughed. "I haven't been kissed this much in years. Quit!" The puppy laid down next to her and turned onto her back to get her belly rubbed.

"Aren't you pretty? You're so pretty! That's a good girl." She looked like a mutt, but could have some Shepherd in her, Hannah decided. She wondered if she was one of Bessie's pups. Maybe that's what the old man meant when he said she was "bad." She'd gotten loose and gotten herself pregnant. "Where's your mommy?" She picked up the puppy and looked over the front side of the barn, then the back. No sign of Bessie.

She hoped someone hadn't dropped the puppy off. It was too young. It couldn't be but five or six weeks old. To prove that point, the puppy started sucking on her finger. She was hungry. Hannah ran through a mental list of what she had in the house to feed her. "Nothing appropriate, that's for sure." Maybe a scrambled egg, she thought. She walked down the ramp and was headed toward the house, puppy in her arms, when she saw the little boy.

"Oh, there she is!" He came running. "Thanks, Miss! Thank you!" He took the puppy from Hannah, the little dog licking him all over his face.

"She's hungry," Hannah said. "Do you have puppy food for her? Is she Bessie's pup?"

"We do the best we can," the little boy said. "She eats what we eat."

"Okay, but if you need anything," Hannah called to his back, "you let me know. Okay?"

"Okay! Bye!"

Hannah walked down to check Billy Bob's water, filled the bucket and went up to the house to change her jeans. As she started through the front door, she heard the phone ringing.

It was her boss Richard. "Hello, is this Hannah?"

She didn't like the sound of his trembling voice. "What's the matter?"

"We have another storm victim. She's the one that had been in a coma. The family just left."

Hannah paused, allowing him to compose himself.

"I've never seen a body in this bad a shape. And they want an open coffin yet."

"What time do you need me?" Hannah was usually the last to work on a body.

"Can you come now?"

Hannah stared. Roof, wet jeans from the puppy, pies to bake.... "Let me shower real quick and I'll be in."

"Thanks, Hannah."

She didn't know how long she'd be gone, so she tied an extra water bucket to the pasture fence for Billy Bob, threw him some hay, though there was plenty of grass, hurried, showered and got dressed. She gathered the items needed for the pies, and stopped at the local grocer for canned boysenberries. Rhubarb was on sale, so she grabbed some of that too.

Richard met her at the door. "Oh good, I'm glad you're here."

Hannah walked past him and down the stairs to the kitchen. Richard followed her. "I think I'm losing it, Hannah."

"Not now," she said, in a joking manner. "Don't you dare!"

"I'm serious."

"Why?" Hannah laid out the groceries on the counter. "What's going on?"

He shook his head. "There's something about this body. I can't explain it."

Hannah drew a deep breath and walked down the hall with him. The woman lay on the prep table, covered in a sheet, but for her face and head.

"I've had accident victims before," Richard said, at her side. "I've seen it all. But this…."

Hannah peeled the sheet back gently, reverently, and shook her head. "Oh you poor thing," she whispered. Practically every inch of this woman's body had been stitched and stapled back together. Almost all of her skin was a dark purple.

"She was thrown through a plate glass window, head first."

Hannah covered the woman up and took a step back. The woman's hair hadn't been washed and had dried blood and drainage caked over each incision.

"The top of her head apparently took the brunt of the impact, leaving her face relatively…."

Hannah held up her hand. She'd heard enough. "I'm going to go make some pies now," she said, shaking her head at how ludicrous she sounded. "If you need me…." Her voice cracked.

Richard nodded. "Hannah?"

She stopped at the door.

"Is there something about her that…?"

"Yes," Hannah said. "She's still here."

Chapter Sixteen

Hannah kept busy in the kitchen at the funeral parlor. It felt like her kitchen anyway; she was comfortable there, and tried not to "think." Instead, she visualized tarring and laying the next roll of roofing material. She pictured each process in her mind, hammer and nails in hand, the sun on her back. She imagined feeding Billy Bob his dinner, filling his water bucket. She even conjured up an image of driving down the road to deliver Raven's boysenberry pie.

The oven timer had just gone off, pies done, when Richard appeared in the doorway, pale and visibly shaken. Calling hours for the two people scheduled to be buried tomorrow was in less than fifteen minutes and there were always "early birds," as he liked to call them. He wasn't in the mood for joking or anything funny today.

"She's ready."

Hannah nodded. She had the coffee set up in the lounge area, not her job usually. She'd turned the music on, straightened the coat hangers, checked the restrooms and organized the calling cards.

People milled about upstairs as she tended to the woman. She first washed the woman's hair, being careful with the stitches. She talked to the woman. She told her what she thought she might want to hear. "You are very pretty. There isn't even a scratch on your face. I'll bet you heard them talking in the hospital while your heart was still beating. They frightened you, didn't they?"

After her hair was completely lathered, Hannah rinsed it gently, being careful not to get water on her face lest it startle her. "You have beautiful hair. It looks as if you took good care of it." Hannah talked in a soft voice, a tender voice. "There." She towel-dried the woman's hair and combed it out. She had blonde highlights framing her face, a perfect haircut. Hannah looked at the photo of her standing with a middle-aged man, her husband perhaps. Her rings had been removed; just as well, as then Hannah would know for sure the woman was leaving someone special behind.

She and Charlie wore matching wedding bands once upon a time. They sold both to help pay the court costs on the farm foreclosure. The impression on her ring finger was still there to this day.

"For richer or for poorer, in sickness and in health, until death do us part? I do."

Hannah used a dryer brush and curling iron on the woman's hair to style it precisely the way it looked in the photo. Theresa. Her name was Theresa. Hannah didn't want to know her name, but knew it anyway.

"Theresa, you are beautiful. Your suffering does not show. When people see you tomorrow, they are going to be very pleased at how pretty you look. Go in peace."

Richard stood in the doorway. "You're underpaid, Hannah."

Hannah shook her head and walked past him. "I'm a beautician who talks to herself. It goes with the job."

"Right," he said. "I just heard from one of the families for tomorrow. They'd like a luncheon here after the burial, forty to forty-five people. Are you up for it?"

88

"Sure."

Richard looked at the woman lying on the table. "You probably should get here around ten or so." He hesitated. "Thanks, Hannah. She's a lot different now."

Hannah glanced back and nodded. "I'll see you tomorrow." She picked up her paycheck in the office, loaded up the pies using the back door, and drove to the bank. Then it was off to deliver Raven's pie. She and Tom lived in an elaborately renovated showcase colonial, five thousand square feet of house for two people.

She greeted Hannah at the front door in workout gear and sweating. "Wonderful! How much?"

"Same as I said last night," Hannah said. "Ten dollars."

"Do you have change?" she asked, retrieving a twenty-dollar bill.

"Nope. Guess you can't have the pie." Hannah turned.

"Hannah! I just did a hundred crunches! I earned that pie!"

Hannah laughed. "Pay me next time, because you *will* want another one of these." She stopped at the corner ice cream store and bought a small vanilla milkshake. If she hurried, it would still be somewhat milk-shaky when she got home and she planned to pour it on a piece of pie for herself.

She pulled into her driveway and smiled, surveying her roof. "It actually doesn't look bad. I did good." It also felt good complimenting herself.

She wasn't one to lock up a house, so it seemed odd to find the front door bolted. And then the back door too. "Well shit," she said, holding the pie in one hand and melting milkshake in the other. "Looks like I'm fixing to have a little *humble pie.*" So much for "riding high," as her mom would say. She walked back to the truck. She was pretty sure she had a plastic spoon and napkins in her glove compartment. "Yes!"

She took the pie, milkshake, and spoon down to the barn and sat on a rock watching Billy Bob she dipped a spoonful of pie at a time into the cold oozy milkshake. "Now this is the life," she told her horse.

He came over to the fence, sniffing.

"Are you getting fat, Billy Bob?"

She broke off a tiny piece of crust and fed it to him. He scarfed it down and stretched his neck, wanting more. "No, no belly aches for you." He'd colicked once at the boarding stable, a traumatic experience for both him and Hannah. She didn't want them to ever go through that again. It was shortly after Charlie had left, her heart still in pieces. Moldy hay was blamed for the colic.

Billy Bob stared intently, begging, then gave up and went back to grazing. When Hannah had her fill, she put the rest of the pie back in her truck and started checking the windows to try to figure out how she was going to get into the house. The porch windows were locked, the kitchen window was locked, the living room side windows, locked. The bathroom window was unlocked, but even as thin as she was; there was no way she could shimmy through. She imagined the spectacle she would become, half in and half out, kicking her legs and squealing like a pig.

She laughed. Last windows to try were the ones in the utility room. "Oh, please, please, please...." Nope, they were locked too. She stood trying to recall if she'd opened any of the windows since moving in and why were they locked now. Yes, just the other day. She heard a bell sound and figured it to be the old man riding his bicycle nearby, but it was her phone ringing. Ringing and ringing and ringing.

She stood with her hands on her hips, staring up at the second floor. She knew positively that the upstairs bedroom window on the right side wasn't locked because the window pane had rotted under the latch and it no longer worked. She ran through a mental list of items in the barn, wondering what she could use to climb up onto the roof. There was a rickety old ladder, but that wouldn't do. No. Too risky.

The saltbox slant of the roof over the utility room ran the width of the back of the house, one story high. All she'd need to climb was about ten feet. She had three bales of hay left. "Maybe if I stack them on the back of the pickup."

She got in the truck, drove down around to the rear of the barn and loaded up the hay. "Don't worry, I'm not taking it anywhere," she told her horse. "I'll be right back with it." She hesitated. "Wait a minute, what if I fall?" She topped off Billy Bob's water buckets and grained him. "Someone would surely have to find me by tomorrow and you'd be okay till then."

She drove up to the house, parked the truck sideways to the back door, and stacked the hay in a step pattern. She climbed onto the first bale, then the next two stacked, and with very little effort, pulled herself up onto the roof. "Almost as easy getting on a horse." She raised her arms to the sky and then took a bow! "Thank you! Thank you! I am woman! Thank you!"

She was laughing as she gave the window a tug and quickly sobered. It was stuck. Back down off the roof she went for a hammer and a chisel. She saw the mailman delivering the mail. She waved, he waved. Then back up onto the roof she climbed. "Careful, careful." The last thing she needed was a broken window. She'd probably have every critter within miles inside the house by morning. She positioned the chisel along the edge and tapped gently all around, then drew a deep breath and gave the window another tug.

Nothing. It didn't even budge.

"Okay." She placed the chisel under the middle of the window and pounded the end with a hammer, once, twice. On the third whack, it popped open. "Yes!" She reached down for a little of the hay to dust away the dead flies and cobwebs, then climbed in and closed the window behind her. The bedroom had a spooky feel to it. With the door closed, she felt trapped, and turned when she heard a rustling noise behind her.

It was a pigeon, and not just any kind of pigeon. It was a carrier pigeon. It had a band around one of its legs.

She glanced at the floor. There were bird droppings everywhere. "How on earth did you get in here?" It looked scared to death. Hannah turned on the light switch and surprisingly, the lone light bulb hanging from the ceiling worked. The flash of light frightened the pigeon even more and it started flapping its wings and skittering around the floor.

"Awe...." It couldn't fly.

When she saw specks of dust falling from the ceiling to the floor, she looked up and saw a small hole in the wall. "Well, that's explains how you got in."

She stood wondering what to do. Carrier pigeons aren't afraid of people, she told herself. They're used to being handled. Act matter-of-fact, approach with purpose. She walked to the pigeon, leaned down and using both hands, picked it up. "There, there," she said. "We'll find out what's wrong with you, don't you worry. We'll fix it."

She held the bird out in front of her and started toward the door; she'd need a free hand to open it. She hesitated, cradled the bird gently to her chest, turned the handle, and down the stairs she went. "First thing we'll do is get you some water and something to eat." She was leery of turning the bird loose for fear it might flap its injured wings and cause more damage. She held onto it, filled a saucer with water, and smiled as the pigeon drank and drank a tiny amount each time. A little bread next, broken into pieces. It ate.

"Sorry, I don't have any seeds."

The pigeon gazed up at her and then ate some more bread, tossing crumbs all over the counter. "Okay, here's the deal, little one," she said. "I have to go to the bathroom." She took the bird with her, put it in the bathtub, washed her hands quickly and went. "Good girl," she said, leaning over so she could see her. "Good girl. If you're a boy, look the other way." Hannah laughed. "I'm bonkers. That's all there is to it!"

The pigeon appeared to like the sound of her laughter and ruffled its feathers. And with that, it flew up out of the tub and landed on the bathroom sink. "Why, you little faker, you! You can fly!" As if to prove the point, the bird flew back across the room and perched on the shower curtain rod. "With the greatest of ease," Hannah said, as it started preening.

"Here." Hannah reached up, cupped it in her hands, and took it outside. "I think you have a job to do, Missy," she said, and let it go. It flew to the top of the oak tree and appeared to be taking a breather. Then it flew to the roof above the utility room and started hopping toward the window.

"Oh no!" Hannah hurried inside, took the stairs as fast as she could, and tripped on the landing. "Now that hurt." By the time she got inside the bedroom the bird was trying to squeeze its way through the hole in the wall. Hannah rushed downstairs to the kitchen, grabbed an old dishrag, and ran back upstairs, slightly slower this time. The pigeon had half its head inside and appeared stuck. "What the heck is wrong with you?" Hannah nudged its little head gently, hoping it would back out, but it pushed against her with all its might and, as if giving a birth of sorts, pulled and pushed its way inside and dropped to the floor.

"Well you goofy thing!"

Hannah blocked the hole with the dishrag, allowing the pigeon time to recuperate from its crash landing. "You're staying right there till I fix that. No more of this, you hear me?"

The bird just looked at her.

"Yeah right, like you understand." Change of plans. Hannah picked the pigeon up, shut the door behind them and hobbled back downstairs, cradling the bird with one hand against her chest and the other gripping the railing. "You're going in the bathroom till I'm done."

She put the bird's water and bread on the edge of the tub and placed the bird down next to them. The pigeon cooed and cooed for a moment and then hopped down into the tub and pooped. Hannah chuckled. "Well, at least your plumbing works. Now stay put."

Hannah went outside and down to the barn for a piece of wood and nails to patch the hole, then limped her way back to the house, onto the bed of her pickup, up over the bales of hay and onto the roof.

"Speaking of pigeon poop." Hannah shook her head. There was a tiny pile of it below the hole in the wall. "It's a little pigeon shit volcano."

Hannah hammered the board over the hole and climbed back down off the roof, off the bed of her pickup, and stood rubbing her injured knee for a moment.

"Listen," she said, to the pigeon when she went back inside. "You're confused. You're slipping on the job. You need to fly home, or wherever you were going."

The bird pecked at her.

"You sure are a pretty little thing," Hannah said. "I'm tempted to keep you around, but the last thing I need is another hungry mouth to feed, even if you do eat like a bird." Hannah laughed at the pun, and outside, turned the bird loose again. "Now, go! Fly away!" The pigeon flew to the top of her pickup truck and just sat there, cooing.

"Nobody's going to believe this," Hannah said. "I wish I had a camera." She had a really nice one a few years back, a 35 mm with a zoom lens. She and Charlie sold it to the same pawn shop owner in Mechannisburg who bought their wedding bands.

The pigeon flew to the stack of hay and eyed the boarded-up hole in the wall. Hannah shook her head. "This is crazy. Come here." When she reached for the bird, it lowered its head in submission. "I don't know what to do with you. I don't want you knocking yourself out." She glanced at the sky; the sun was starting to set. "But I have things to do, you know."

The bird looked around, as if assessing the situation and wiggled its feet. Hannah set it down on the hood of her pickup and stood just looking at it for a moment. When it turned, setting its sights on the boarded-up hole in the wall again, Hannah diverted its attention. "Here, stand still." She wondered if maybe there was an address or some other identification on the band. It appeared as if there was a number on the band at one time, but it was almost entirely rubbed off. "Probably from squeezing yourself in that damned hole. You wore it down, you silly bird."

She drew a deep breath and sighed. "What am I going to do with you? Let's see." She gathered the bird up and went and sat in the driver's seat of her pickup. Maybe there was something relevant in the message inside the band, that's if there *was* a message inside. She opened the band with her fingernail and out fell a tiny piece of paper.

Hannah opened it carefully.

"Forever is a long, long time," it read. "I love you." Tears welled up in her eyes. It was as if it had been written for her, what she had been feeling. It was as if it had been written by Charlie. Hannah gazed at the bird sitting on her lap and sighed as she glanced around the farm. "Oh, if only it were true."

She folded the message gently and on the back wrote her phone number and a note for the intended person. "Bird waylaid. Sorry." She thought of more to say but there was no room. She put the message back in the pigeon's leg band and gave it "a talking to" as her mom would say. "Now listen, there's nothing upstairs for you. This is not your destination. You hear me?"

When she stroked the bird's head, it pressed against her hand. "I'm going to let you go, and you're going to fly where you're supposed to. You're a smart bird, I can tell." Hannah chuckled. That was a stretch, considering how many times the bird had entered that same hole in the wall to no avail. "Okay, you ready?" She stepped down out of the truck and almost went down on her knees. "Come visit any time you want," she said, wincing in pain. "But if I never see you again, that's okay too. I'll feel privileged to have known you now."

The bird looked at her and ruffled its feathers.

"Go" She launched it into the air and watched it circle the farm twice and then fly off toward the setting sun. "Fly straight, fly strong."

She looked at the barn. If she hurried, she might still have time to get at least one more roofing roll down. She took the rest of the pie inside, had a couple more spoonfuls, and wrapped it in a dishtowel for safe keeping.

Billy Bob watched her drive the truck down around the back of the barn and nickered as she started unloading the hay. "You still have plenty of grass," she said. She checked his water, topped off one of the buckets and limped up and around to the front of the barn. "Where's that roofing hammer? I left it right here." She glanced over the edge. There it lay. "Wonderful." She sighed. "At least it didn't walk away."

She trudged down to get it and when something caught her eye off in the distance, waved to the little boy. She squinted. He had the puppy with him; she could see its wagging tail above the tall grass.

Hannah rolled the roofing material out. With only two more rolls after this one, it was getting harder to keep the material flat. She thought about going down to get the hay bales for a weight, but decided against it, figuring she'd hauled it around enough for one day.

When she heard a car pull in the driveway, she smiled. It was Lucinda and Colleen. "Wait, don't tell me! You have more leftovers!"

They both laughed. "No, today it's surplus wine and cheese," Lucinda said.

"Well, bring it on up," Hannah said. "I'm starving." The three women sat on the roof in a circle, food in the middle, and feasted. "You guys are spoiling me."

"You deserve to be spoiled."

Hannah looked from one to the other. "Okay."

They laughed.

"Raven loves her pie."

"I have some left in the house, I'll go get it."

"No, that's okay, leave it. You can have it for later."

"Or we can have it now," Hannah said, up and on her way, limping.

"What'd you do?"

"Long story," Hannah said. "I'll tell you when I get back." She returned with the rest of the pie, cut in three pieces, saucers and forks. "I had a carrier pigeon stuck up in the one bedroom in the house." She told them all about how she discovered it, and about falling up the stairs, and....

"A carrier pigeon?" Colleen asked. "How'd you know it was a carrier pigeon?"

"It had a little band on its leg."

"And it was crawling through this little hole, and...?"

Hannah laughed. "I don't think it was technically crawling."

Lucinda passed the wine. "And now it's gone?"

"I hope so."

"And you fixed the hole?"

"Yep."

Lucinda and Colleen looked at one another.

Hannah read their expressions. "Bonkers. I know." They all laughed. "Oh look, see, there it is," Hannah said.

"Where?"

"Right there, look up in that tree. Don't you see it?"

They shook their heads. "No."

Hannah laughed. "Just kidding."

They both pushed at her and she toppled over. "Ouch, my knee. Ouch, ouch."

"Look how swollen it is."

Hannah compared one to the other. "Oh my God, it is! Holy Crap!"

"Do you have any ice?"

"Noooo...I have no fridge, remember?"

"I'll go get some."

"No, it's fine. I'm running out of daylight. This is more important."

"Can we help?" Lucinda asked.

"Yes. You sit there," Hannah pointed halfway down the roll of roofing material. "And you up here. Watch out for the tar." Once both friends were in place, Hannah stretched her knee out, sat so she could work sideways, and started pounding nails. It was dark when she reached the end of the last roll. "Thank you." She hugged them both. "Thank you."

Chapter Seventeen

An early riser by nature, Hannah surprised herself by sleeping in until past seven. She examined her knee, which was only slightly swollen, and deemed it healed. She made half a pot of coffee and headed down over the hill to feed Billy Bob. One look at his stall and she could see he'd obviously been restless during the night. Not good. The cow-stanchion stall gate sat slightly crooked on the screw eyes. He'd tried to get out.

"What's scaring you?"

Whatever it was, was gone now. The horse ate his grain as if he hadn't a care in the world. Hannah waited until he'd finished then turned him out in the paddock with hay; just in case to keep him happy, and two buckets of fresh water.

"I'll be back around four. Don't get into any trouble." She gave him a pat on the neck and watched as he walked to the far end of the pasture and stood staring into the woods.

"I wonder if it's coyote. That would explain why he's only troubled at night. Or maybe skunk." She and Charlie had a skunk that nested in the barn once, causing all of the cows to be restless. She sniffed. There was no smell of skunk. "Maybe it's a groundhog." She shook her head. "No, I would have seen evidence of it by now."

Hannah arrived at the funeral parlor early and went right to work. She made two pots of coffee, one regular and one decaf. She made iced tea and lemonade. She set the buffet table, put tablecloths on the dining tables, silverware. She left space at both ends of the table in the event friends and family members brought additional food.

The menu today was simple. The main dish was cold cuts, which Hannah arranged on serving trays with leaf lettuce and rose-cut radishes. She carved each one meticulously. With advance notice, Hannah usually made the potato and macaroni salads, the baked beans. Because the meal was a last minute decision, it was bought from the deli. Hannah dressed the salads with parsley, thin slices of red pepper, and finely chopped sprinkles of hardboiled eggs. She always insisted Richard order extra eggs. She doctored up the baked beans by adding a little more onion and brown sugar. Then she put together a big tossed salad and sliced up the desserts.

When she was done, she stood back and smiled. If she weren't standing in the basement of a funeral parlor, one might think this was a holiday buffet, albeit modest.

"This is where the healing begins," she told Richard once, when he insisted she fussed too much. "The last thing people need at the moment is a sad meal. They've cried for days and had no appetite. They've only gone through the motions of eating. Now is the time to eat hardy, tell stories, and laugh."

She sliced lemon in thin wedges and placed them in a bowl next to the beverages, set out pretty bowls of pickles and olives, and scooped mayonnaise and mustard into decorative serving dishes. She arranged the bread and rolls on platters, white, whole wheat, rye, white, whole wheat, rye...and covered them with cloth napkins to stay fresh.

Just before the people were due to arrive, she went into the ladies room to wash up. She never actually served the meals; she was just there in case she was needed. She turned on the lights in the dining area and drew a deep breath. The dinners following the funerals for her parents were held in this very room. They were both in their eighties and had died less than a year apart.

One chair was out of place. Hannah straightened it. "There."

Richard was the first person through the door.

"All set?"

Hannah nodded.

On the way home, she made a quick stop at the year-round flea-market store in town, a rundown establishment filled to the rafters. There were two ancient refrigerators of substantial size. She considered the fifty-dollar one.

"It runs good," Big Jim said, a potbelly kind of guy in coveralls and a ratty old T-shirt. "I plug it in every once in a while to make sure."

Cobwebs covered the cord. "Let me think about it."

"Half price."

Hannah smiled in acknowledgement of the offer and was glancing all around when her eyes came to rest on a small, college-dorm-size refrigerator. "What about that one?"

"Twenty bucks."

Hannah walked over to get a closer look. The outside was beat up and sporting some funky decals, but the inside was relatively clean. "How about half price on this one?"

Big Jim rubbed his jaw. "I don't know, Hannah. What do you want with one that small anyway?"

"Well, it'll be easy to carry," Hannah said, jokingly. "But you know, really, I've always wanted a kitchen desk. The area where a fridge goes would be perfect for one. Do you have any desks?"

"I just got one in. It's on the back of my truck. Come take a look."

Hannah followed him outside and was disappointed. A huge big old steel office desk sat crammed into the back of his pickup bed. "It's way too big." She glanced at the sun. It was nearing five o-clock. "I'll come back another day," she said.

"Wait, what about the little fridge?"

"Ten dollars," Hannah said.

"How's twelve. I ain't had a sale all day."

Hannah loaded up the refrigerator, paid the man, and headed home. Billy Bob nickered when he saw her coming down over the hill. It was as if he was saying, "But you promised to be home by four! Where have you been?"

His water buckets had a few inches of water left in the bottoms. Hannah swished them, dumped them, and filled them both, then decided to grain him outside. No sense his messing the stall yet. Besides, it was too nice a day for him to be inside. He'd eaten what hay she'd left for him, so she gave him some more. He'd grazed down quite a bit of the grass too.

Hannah shook her head. All this lush green grass everywhere, grass she'd certainly have to get to mowing soon. And here was Billy Bob in only a small section of it. If it were all fenced in, he would have plenty enough grass for three seasons out of the year, and something to at least simulate foraging throughout the winter. She'd always felt sorry for him at the boarding stable in the winters. The horses were confined to the sand paddock to save the pastures from ruin. Because they had so many horses there, it made sense to save the dormant grass roots for the growing seasons. Not necessary here.

"It'd be nice to have a round pen," she told Billy Bob. "That way I could just move it every couple of weeks or so." But there was no way she could afford one or a fence either.

Billy Bob looked at her.

"Sorry," she said, and stroked his neck. "I'm going to go get my fridge set up and then you and me are going for a ride."

As she started up the hill, she glanced inside the barn and noticed an old wood door leaning up against the far wall. She'd seen it before, but looked at it now with different eyes. It was a flat door, a sturdy door, and with a little luck, it just might make the perfect desk top.

It was heavier than she thought, solid and hard, which she considered a good thing. But as Charlie would say, "It was going to be a bear to cut." Hannah smiled. Or was that, "A bitch to cut?" She couldn't remember which. Neither made sense. "Where do sayings like that come from?" She walked up to the house to do some measuring. The desk space was four-feet wide.

"Do I start on this now or go out and work on the orchard?" She debated her options out loud. "I need to organize in here. I need to clean out that little fridge. I need to get rid of those 'college dorm' decals. I need to eat. The orchard's not going anywhere. I need to make a list.

Several lists." That became the deciding factor. She wanted to sit down at her kitchen desk and come up with an official overall plan.

She made herself a peanut butter and jelly sandwich, got a nice cool glass of water from the tap, and walked out onto the front porch to eat. "I guess I'll have to check the mail too." Winter was months away. Even so, she pictured herself bundling up and walking out in the snow to see what the mailman had brought. She used to dread the mail. It was always bills.

"I'll wait until tomorrow." She made herself another sandwich. Peanut butter and jelly wasn't much by most people's standards, yet she relished the taste. It surely beat the days she had nothing to eat at all. She licked her fingers and headed back outside. The old man was sitting on the porch steps.

"Hello," she said.

He grunted, then took out an old handkerchief and wiped his brow. "I'd have thought you would have started on the orchard by now."

Hannah looked at him. "I work," she said.

"Where? In the city?"

Hannah shook her head. Not that it was any of his business. "I work at a funeral parlor."

The old man blew his nose and looked at her with a furrowed brow. "What do you do there?"

"Oh, whatever is needed. I mainly do the deceased's hair. But I fill in elsewhere. That's how I saw this farm, I was transporting a body, and…."

The old man held up his hand. "Which one?"

"Which one what?" Body?

"Which funeral parlor?"

Hannah hesitated. There was only one funeral parlor in town. "Davidson."

The old man folded his handkerchief and shoved it into his back pocket. "Humph. I got no use for them Davidsons."

"Why?" Hannah asked.

"It don't matter," he said, holding his bony hand up again. "I wouldn't give them the time of day."

"Well, that's too bad. They're good people."

"Humph."

Hannah started down the steps past him. "You're welcome to stay as long as you like. Right now I need to go and…."

"I'll walk with you to the orchard," the old man said, rising slowly to his feet.

"Well...that's not exactly where I was headed at the moment, but...."

He had a brisk walk for an old man. Hannah followed along. "How's Bessie?"

No comment, at least not about Bessie. "These two trees here were always the best producers. They're Macintosh."

"Good for pies," Hannah said.

"Ah. Good for anything."

Hannah bit her tongue. Crabby old man.

"I suppose you'll be buying fertilizer."

"No."

"They'll need fertilized."

"I'm going to compost horse manure and use that."

"You'll kill them."

"They're practically dead now."

The old man shook his head. "What about spray?"

"Nope, none." She couldn't afford it; she didn't want it.

"Them there are Bartlett pears."

"I've got no use for pears." Hannah pointed over his shoulder. "What about those?"

"Granny Smiths."

Hannah sighed. "Great for eating, but...."

"You looking to farm or make a living?"

"Both," Hannah said.

The peach trees looked worse than any of the others. "I'd take them down if it were me." The old man pointed. They towered over the two healthiest cherry trees.

Hannah stood looking at them.

"How are you going to get the manure back here," the old man asked, as if he'd been thinking about it.

"With a wheelbarrow," Hannah said.

"Even in the winter?"

"Yes." Hannah gauged the distance between the orchard and the barn. "Well, maybe in the winter I'll use a muck basket. I can tie a rope to it and drag it through the snow, and...."

"Farm women don't talk as much as you do."

"Oh really? Well, get used to it."

The old man laughed. "I'll be getting on now," he said, and glanced back over his shoulder. "It'll take years for that manure to break down."

"Not if I put hot ash on it," she said, picking up twigs to start a burn pile.

"Every day?"

"No, I was thinking maybe every other day," she said, being facetious.

When the old man walked away shaking his head, Hannah smiled. Since she was out here, she figured she might as well get started. She gathered and piled twigs for about an hour and then dusted off her hands and headed up to the barn. She counted strides, eighty-seven of them. "Eighty-seven times three equals two hundred and sixty-one feet. That's not bad." She looked at her horse. "What do you think, Billy Bob, would you be up to pulling a sled this winter?"

He put his head down. "Right," Hannah said.

Sawing the old wooden door proved easier than Hannah had expected. She hauled the four-foot length up to the house and came back down to the barn to look for something that could serve as legs. After about an hour of searching and coming up empty, she sawed the rest of the door into three pieces, found some long nails, and back up to the house she went.

She tapped the wall with a hammer to find the studs and attached two of the boards. She could hear the old man criticizing her for using too many nails. "What do you think you're building, Fort Knox?"

"No, just a sturdy desk."

Attaching the third board to the cabinet side proved to be more of a challenge. The cabinet wall wasn't but a half-inch thick. Back down over the hill to the barn she went. She cut another board, same width as the others but shorter, and figured she would just hold it in place inside the cabinet and pound the nails in from the outside board. Not so. Not only did she not have the physical strength left in her after all the hand sawing, having to hold the inside board with the cabinet door in place brought on a pulsing low back pain she hadn't felt in years. Her knee was feeling pretty good, no sense inviting a back ache.

Another trip down to the barn. She lugged the last piece of wood back to the house and braced it against the outside wall board she wanted to hammer in place, crawled halfway into the cabinet, laid on her back, and started hammering.

"Yes!" she yelled, when she felt the nail penetrate the outside board. "Yes!"

She crawled out from inside the cabinet and finished pounding the rest of the nails, then placed the door piece on the ledges and smiled. Her very own kitchen desk, it was even almost level. "Mine, all mine." She pulled up a chair, sat down, and pretended to write a letter. "I'll have to remember to get stamps," she said.

"Dear, Charlie. I'm not well, but I'm getting better. You'll have to excuse me now because I'm going to go for a ride. Billy Bob is fine and it's good having him home. Love, Hannah."

By the time Hannah hauled in the little fridge, cleaned it out, scrubbed and scraped off all the decals and stickers, the sun had gone down. She tacked Billy Bob and the two of them forged a different trail. She was curious to find where the old man lived. Maybe she'd get a glimpse of his farm. Maybe she'd see the little boy. Maybe she'd see Bessie or one of her puppies.

When they flushed out a grouse in the tall weeds, Billy Bob jumped back and snorted. Hannah reined him out and around in case the grouse was nesting and glanced back to see its return landing.

She calmed Billy Bob with her voice. "You and me are going to have to make a path to the orchard for this winter. We'll do it once I get all the branches picked up and the wood stacked."

The sooner she could get the wood split, the better. Some of the downed branches, though old, were still green. They'd need to dry out if she was going to burn them this winter. She wondered how long it had been since the chimney was cleaned. Chimneys were the one thing Charlie hired done. It made sense to her to follow suit. "I'll add that to my list."

When they came to a clearing she urged Billy Bob into a trot. He had a nice smooth trot that was easy to sit. She hummed for a while as they jogged along, and then started singing. "Momma's little baby loves shortnin', shortnin'. Momma's little baby loves shortnin' bread."

When they came to the familiar grassy area that appeared to have been mowed, Hannah reined Billy Bob to a walk and let him lower his head and graze. He went right for the clover. When a honey bee landed on his neck, Hannah swished it away. Her father had been a bee keeper. She'd lived a lifetime swishing bees and couldn't recount how many times she'd been stung.

She searched the horizon for the old man's farm. The nearest house she could see from this vantage point was a modern colonial. "That can't possibly be his." She turned in the saddle and scanned the acreage behind her. There was a pasture far off in the distance with two cows in it. Hannah squinted. No, three cows; two Holsteins and a Guernsey.

Now *that* could be his, she thought. "I wonder what he does with the fresh cream?" Custard pies were another of her specialties. Billy Bob sniffed an area of the grass and then walked around it. "Do you smell coyote?" When he grazed on unconcerned, Hannah petted his shoulder. They'd have to head back soon, it was getting dark.

Sitting there in the saddle, she surveyed the orchard for the umpteenth time. She was looking forward to cleaning it up and getting it back into shape. "Come on, Billy Bob," she said. "We'd best be getting home." She laughed when she heard herself say, "best be." She sounded just like her mother. When they passed the root cellar, she was happy to see the door still latched with the hickory stick, and sang as she rode along. "Readin', 'riting, and 'rithmatic taught to the tune of a hickory stick...when we were just nothing but kids." She was sure those weren't the exact words, or even the right song, but joked with herself that it was close enough. "Besides, who's listening?"

She gave Billy Bob a good rubdown back at the barn, bedded him down for the night, and checked his stall gate to make sure it was secure. Then she headed up to the house surrounded by a star-filled night. She could hear her phone ringing, but by the time she got inside, it had stopped. Whoever it was apparently had given up. It rang again while she was in the shower.

Chapter Eighteen

Mornings had developed into a routine. Hannah woke, made coffee, and would then walk down the barn to feed Billy Bob his breakfast. She could tell this morning he'd had another restless night. At least he was still in his stall, gate holding. He ate his grain and was eager to go outside. Hannah cleaned his stall then went back to the house to wash up.

On the way to work, she swung by what she thought might be the old man's farm. But it wasn't. A young couple owned this land. The wife was pregnant with their first child. They said they'd never seen the old man and were sorry they couldn't be of help. The Guernsey hadn't been freshened. They had plans to breed her in the spring. The two Holsteins were steers being raised for beef.

"Hmmm." Hannah refrained from telling them that Holsteins weren't the best choice for meat. They were going to end up with a lot of hamburger. "Is this your first farm?" she asked, and thought, Oh no, I sound like the old man.

"Yes, we're from Glen Oak," the husband said.

Hannah smiled. "Well, if you need anything, I'm right up the road. I've been a farmer all my life. My name's Hannah."

He shook her hand. "I'm Douglas and this is Patty."

"It's nice to meet you. When are you due?"

"Not long. November fifteenth."

Hannah thought about the young couple on her way into town, their hopes, their dreams. "I should have asked them what kind of pie they like." She laughed at herself. It was all about pies lately. "I'll take them an apple one."

She stopped at the grocery store and picked up what she needed and drove to the second-hand store. Big Jim was surprised to see her back so soon. "Don't tell me that fridge isn't working."

"No, no, it's working fine. I'm here for a desk lamp, a little one. I'd like one of those ones that shine the light down. You know, with a lid-like shade."

"A Student Desk Lamp? It just so happens I have me one." It was on a shelf way in the back and was so dusty; it was hard telling what color the shade might be. "Five bucks."

Hannah hesitated. "All right, I'll take it. Let's plug it in first though to see if it works."

It did not. Big Jim changed the bulb, still no light, and shook it a couple of times. "Damned thing, I know it worked once upon a time."

Hannah inspected the plug. "Maybe it needs a new one." She gave him two dollars. "I'll see if I can get it to work."

From there she drove to Cal Able's car lot. He was sitting at his desk eating Twinkies and Jelly Beans and looked up with a big welcoming grin. "Well hello, darlin'. What can I do for you?"

Hannah smiled. "Oh, nothing. I was just checking in on you to make sure you're okay. I don't want to show up to work one day and find you keeled over and waiting for me." She motioned to his snacks. "Is that breakfast?"

He sat back and nodded.

"I thought so." Hannah shook her head. "You know, you're not going to be thinking straight one day from all that sugar and someone's going to take advantage of you."

Cal Able laughed. "I like you, Hannah! I really do! Come on, what can I do for you? How can I make your day?"

"Well," she said, crossing her arms. "For starters, you can eat some eggs or something else substantial for breakfast."

He laughed again.

"Aside from that, promise me the next time we do business that you'll be up front with me."

"What do you mean?" His face colored.

"You could have told me you owned the lumber mill."

He nodded. "I never told you I was buying your wood for myself."

"Nope, you didn't," Hannah said. "But if we're going to be friends, and you need a friend, Cal, you have to be honest with me. All right?"

"All right."

Hannah smiled. "I'll see you around." She waved over her shoulder and from there, went to the funeral parlor.

Richard greeted her at the door. "You're looking good."

"I know," she said. "I'm happy."

"Why?"

"I don't know. I just am."

Richard faked a big sad frown. "Now you know that's not allowed around here."

Hannah laughed. "Do you have anything for me to do?"

"A pick up and a transport if you want it. Jeb still hasn't shown up. I was hoping it was him when I heard you pull in. He's probably hung over again." Richard had been threatening to fire Jeb for months now.

"Let's give him a few more minutes," Hannah said. She didn't mind transporting bodies. It was easy money, which she could certainly use. But Jeb had a wife and two children and this was his only job. "Then if not...."

Jeb straggled in about half an hour later. A relatively young man, well-groomed and movie-star handsome, he had dark brown eyes and thick black hair. When he got behind the wheel of the hearse, he looked the part. Richard had told Hannah once that Jeb's appearance was precisely why he'd hired him. "He's good for business."

Hannah stopped by Colleen's on the way home from the funeral parlor. Jason had said she could borrow his small chainsaw and had it sitting on his work bench waiting for her, along with the mixed fuel it used and a whole page of instructions and warnings. Hannah glanced at them.

"You know Jason," Colleen said.

Hannah smiled. "I appreciate this. I do."

"Do you need help?"

"No, thank you."

"Do you want to come for dinner? I promise I won't invite Dave."

Hannah paused. "What time?"

"I don't know. Seven maybe, nothing fancy."

"Okay, I'll need a break by then. But listen, if I don't show up, don't worry."

"I won't worry. I'll just come make sure you're okay and ruin dinner for everyone else making them wait. Lucinda and George are supposed to come too."

Hannah gave her a hug. "I'll be here. Can I bring Billy Bob?"

Colleen laughed. "Go. And don't be late."

There was a note taped to Hannah's front door when she arrived home. It was from the young neighbor woman she'd met earlier in the day.

Hannah read it out loud. "I asked around. There is no old man like you mentioned that lives close by. Sorry. It was very nice meeting you. I hope we can be friends. It's awful lonely out here." Signed, "Sincerely, Patty."

Hannah smiled. "Yes, Patty. We can be friends." If she and Charlie had been lucky enough to have a daughter, she would probably be right about Patty's age. "Just don't take offense when I tell you that in addition to those Holsteins not being the best choice for meat, that Guernsey you have is not going to have any more calves. She's too old."

When Hannah heard a rustling sound in the porch rafter, she turned and smiled. "Well, hello there." The carrier pigeon had returned. "Have you been waiting long?" Hannah went inside and brought out a bowl of water and some bread crumbs. "If you keep this up, I am going to have to go buy some birdseed."

After the little pigeon had eaten some of the bread crumbs and drank, it looked at Hannah and turned its tiny head and cooed. Hannah chuckled. "What?" she teased. "Do you have a message for me?" She picked it up and just for the heck of it, checked the message holder. Sure enough.

"Thank you for your post. Please let me know if this rogue bird goes astray again."

Hannah sobered. "And if I do, then what?" She looked at the bird. "Are you going to get in trouble? What do they do with rogue carrier pigeons? Besides, you don't look like a rogue."

The little bird ruffled its feathers.

"A little directionally challenged maybe."

"Coo."

Hannah folded the message neatly and put it back inside the holder. "Listen, I think you ought to just fly on now and go where you're supposed to go. You stopping off here will be just between you and me. Okay? It'll be our little secret."

She went back inside in hopes of encouraging the pigeon to move on, then snuck out the back door and down over the hill to the barn. Billy Bob looked up from grazing. He'd drunk one bucket full of water and half of another. Hannah filled them both, and then headed back up to get the chainsaw out of her truck. She purposely didn't even glance at the porch for fear the pigeon would still be there.

As she walked toward the orchard, chainsaw in one hand, safety glasses and fuel can in the other; she thought she saw the old man and Bessie standing by one of the pear trees. As she drew closer, she decided it must have been a shadow. No old man, no Bessie.

She stood wondering where to start - this end and take down the two dead trees first or the opposite end and work her way back? She looked midway. The pigeon had followed her and sat preening on one of the uprooted apple trees. She shook her head. "You stubborn little rogue, you."

When she started the chainsaw, the pigeon took flight, and after circling the orchard several times, it flew away. Hannah worked from one downed tree to the next, sawing off the largest of the branches, and then doubled back and had just started taking off the side branches when she saw the little boy and one of Bessie's puppies running through the field. She waved. The little boy waved back, as off into the bushes they went.

"I should have brought some water down," she said, when she stopped to take a break. "Humph, what was I thinking?"

At the time, she was thinking of the bird. She glanced around, happy to see that it hadn't returned, and wiped the sweat dripping from her brow with her sleeve. From where she was standing she could make out the young couple's farm. Young Patty was feeding the chickens. "Give farm life a chance," Hannah whispered. "Just give it a chance."

Chapter Nineteen

Colleen wasn't kidding. Hannah had just brought Billy Bob in, taken a shower, and was blow-drying her hair when she heard a familiar voice. "Are you home?"

"I'm in here," Hannah said. "I'm almost ready."

"I needed to run to the store, so...."

Hannah smiled. "You didn't think I'd show, did ya?"

"Well, there is another reason."

Hannah looked at her.

"Jason called Dave and invited him over."

"I thought you said he wasn't coming."

"I know. And that was the truth at the time. That's why I came to tell you. I figured if I called you and told you, you wouldn't come."

"You figured right," Hannah said. "I've got another hour of daylight. I'll just go back out to the orchard now."

Colleen shook her head. "If you don't come, I'm going to let Jason have it and it's going to be a big fight. I don't know what it is with him lately, but it's his way or the highway."

"Oh great. Blame that on me."

"I'm serious," Colleen said. "I told him not to call Dave and he called him anyway. He said, 'I like Dave. I don't know what Hannah's problem is.'"

"Well, that's because I don't have a problem. Aside from an orchard that needs tending to, that is."

"That's another thing. He said you're being stubborn not letting people help and that if he and George and of course DAVE were to come help, the job would be done in no time."

Hannah put the blow dryer down. "So, let me make sure I understand this correctly. His inviting Dave over was a way of....?"

"Having the last word," Colleen said.

"I see." Hannah nodded. "Well, let's let him have it. The last word I mean," she clarified, chuckling.

"You're not mad?"

"No, the man loaned me his chainsaw and I still need it. Let *that* be my last word." The two of them laughed. "Come on, let's get going. We're already late."

Lucinda had dinner ready to serve when they arrived. The men were out back. Hannah looked at Dave and smiled. He reminded her of a school-boy, all shy and fidgeting. He shrugged, as if apologizing for being there, for being invited. Hannah shook her head. He probably had to be "talked into" coming as well.

Hannah walked out and kissed him on the cheek. "Dave," she said. "Jason, George." She motioned inside. "It's time to eat." They all sat down to a meal of roast beef, mashed potatoes, gravy, and corn. Lucinda passed the rolls, Colleen passed the butter.

"Ooh, I almost forgot." Colleen hurried into the kitchen and came back with a cucumber salad. "I'd have hated myself if I looked in the fridge later and realized I'd forgotten this." She sat the bowl down in the middle of the table and everyone helped themselves.

Hannah and Dave reached for the serving spoon at the same time and both pulled their hand back and apologized. "No, you go," Hannah said, and when he didn't, she served them both: two spoonfuls for him, one for her. It was no big deal, her doing this, but at the same time, it gave cause for her to sit back and take a deep breath.

"How are you doing with that orchard?" Jason asked. "Is the chainsaw running okay?"

"Perfect," Hannah said. "It's got a lot of heart. It cuts good."

"Yeah, I like that little saw."

Hannah smiled. "Me too." She glanced at Dave. "Don't you usually work Thursday nights?"

"Yes, I do," he said. "I'm going in late. I couldn't turn down a home-cooked meal. This is delicious, Colleen."

"Thank you."

"I taught her everything she knows," Jason said, chuckling.

"Yeah right." Colleen rolled her eyes.

"Course, the best stuff…" Jason added.

Colleen smacked him and laughed. "Quit! You're so full of shit!"

"Besides, I wouldn't want to miss out on all this fun and entertainment!" Dave said.

Everyone laughed.

"So how much did you get done, Hannah?"

"Quite a bit actually. I'm just cutting up the logs now and 'letting them fall where they may', as Charlie would say," she said, her voice trailing off. She blushed. "I'll stack everything when I'm done. That way I'll get the chainsaw back sooner."

"No hurry," Jason said, studying her. She'd lowered her eyes and looked miles and miles away. He looked at Colleen and shrugged. "Pass the potatoes."

"Please...?"

"Please," he said.

Lucinda talked up a storm the rest of the meal, doing her very best to keep conversation going. "Hannah, are you okay?" she asked, when they finished eating and the guys had gone outside with George so he could have a cigarette.

Hannah was stacking dishes and clearing the table.

"I'm fine. I'm just tired."

"Do you want to go?"

"If you don't mind," she said. "I'll just finish up here, and...."

"No, Hannah, go. Come on, you look exhausted."

Hannah handed the plates over. "I am. Tell everyone I said good-bye. Okay." As she walked to her truck, she heard someone call her name. She turned. It was Dave.

"Hannah, I'm sorry. I shouldn't have come."

"Why? Why not?"

"I know how you feel. You said, let's just be friends, and even that's a strain. Living with Charlie hanging over my head is ridiculous. It would be easier if he'd died for Christ sake."

"Died?" Hannah glared at him, shaking her head. "What, so he could show up at the funeral parlor and I could cut his hair one more time. Why the hell would you say something like that?"

"I'm sorry. I didn't mean literally, now. I mean before, back when he left you."

That did it. Hannah held up her hands and got in her truck.

"Hannah, I'm sorry," he said, as she pulled out the drive. "But I'm not going to wait for you forever like you're waiting for Charlie. You hear?"

She heard. And she kept right on driving. She was still trembling when she got home. "I hate him," she told Billy Bob. "Who does he think he is talking to me like that? Damn him!" She stared out the barn door at the full moon, the Harvest Moon, and breathed deeply.

She had nothing to harvest. "I will next year," she said. "You'd better believe it." She stroked Billy Bob's neck. "I'll be back in a little while." She walked to the orchard not needing a flashlight, and gazed up at the stars. Not a cloud in the sky. She looked back at the barn and could see Billy Bob. He was watching her.

"Oh, if I could only harness the energy of the moon." She looked around at the tree limbs and branches lying everywhere, picked up one twig and then another and another, and before long had one burn pile stacked, then another one, and then another one. The night air felt cool on her face. There was no wind to speak of, just a hint of a breeze. She decided now would be as good a time as any to light one of the brush piles and walked up to the house for matches.

She brought back a rake and a bucket of water. She figured it would be safest to light the smallest of the piles and gathered some dry grass. Charlie loved a fire. Charlie loved life. "This one's for you." She gently fanned the flame, adding a little more dry grass, then a little more. "There…." She sat down on the edge of a log and watched the fire come to life. It crackled and sparked, smoke billowing to the sky. She looked at the barn. Billy Bob was still watching her. "You're fine," she said. "You're fine."

She breathed in the night air, filled with dew and the scent of burning apple wood. She sat, mesmerized with the dancing flames, the sparks. When the fire burned down she added more brush from the pile next in line. When that one burned down, she added branches from the pile beyond that, and then the next one, and finally the last one. The sun came up over the stand of maple trees to the back of the property to find her raking up the last of all of the twigs and small branches.

She surveyed the orchard and smiled. "Now we're getting somewhere." If it weren't for the uprooted stumps lying here and there, it would be almost perfect.

Billy Bob nickered at the sound of her voice. "I'll be up in a minute," she said. She waited until the rest of the twigs had burned and there was nothing but ash, then doused the fire, and walked up the hill with bucket and rake in hand. Billy Bob was as content as could be. He hadn't torn up his stall, no signs of his pacing or fretting. His stall gate hung perfectly.

"Don't think I'm going to stay out with you every night," she said, as she fed him. "I'll come back and turn you out in a little while." She glanced at the smoldering fire as she started up the hill to the house. "I'm starved," she said to herself. And there stood the old man.

"The fire kept the horses away," he said.

"What?"

"The horses. The ones that come out at night."

"Where?"

"Back there." He pointed.

Hannah glanced in that direction. "Where do you live?" she asked.

"Here, right here," he said. If there was any doubt as to what he meant by that, he lifted a foot and stamped the earth at their feet and then disappeared right before her eyes.

Chapter Twenty

Ghosts didn't necessarily bother Hannah. Ghosts, spirits, souls of the newly departed; she encountered them almost every day at work. What bothered her about the old man was that he seemed stuck in time, and apparently on his terms. She tried calling him back, but he was nowhere to be seen. She even checked the orchard and the root cellar looking for him. Then she took off in the direction he'd pointed to in reference to the horses, "Back there."

When she came to the clearing that always looked as if it had been mowed, she examined the area closer. She even got down on her knee and inspected the grass. It did appear as if it had been grazed upon. But that could have been from any number of kinds of animals, she reasoned. She looked for manure piles. There were none. She looked closer for deer droppings. None. She looked for hoof depressions. None but the area where she'd grazed Billy Bob a couple of times. She glanced back toward the barn and was surprised to have such a clear view of it. She could even see inside the barn from this far away. When her stomach growled it startled her. The noise seemed to have come from somewhere else.

She headed back toward the house, checked on the fire, still smoldering, and looked up at the sun. It was probably around seven,

113

maybe seven-fifteen. She decided to clean Billy Bob's stall now, so she put him out in the pasture, and created a makeshift sled with an old canvas and hauled the manure to the corner of the orchard. Figuring she might as well start the composting, she walked back to the barn for a shovel, and spread the hot ash on top of the pile.

By the time she got up to the house she was so hungry she was shaking. The shaking had never happened to her before because of not eating, and it was disconcerting. She could virtually go days without eating. What was this all about? She gulped down a big glass of water and then another and went into the living room and sat down and rested her head back against the couch cushion. You need to eat, she kept telling herself. You *need* to eat. She wondered what happened to people who just didn't eat anymore, for whatever the reason. Is this how they felt?

She thought about the old man. How long had it been since he'd eaten? "Wait a minute, he's not a ghost. He had breakfast with me last week. I saw him eat." She closed her eyes for a moment. "I wonder if I'm hallucinating. I've never hallucinated before. Maybe I'm dreaming." She opened her eyes and looked at her hands, dirty with soot. "No, I'm not dreaming. And if I am, don't let it be about the orchard." She stood up and staggered through the kitchen and looked out the back window. The fire was still smoldering. "Okay, then you just need to eat."

She sat down at the kitchen table to gather her energies. There were bananas on the counter. They seemed miles away. As she sat staring at them, willing them to come to her, she heard Billy Bob whinny. He wasn't one to whinny at just anything; something had to have gotten his attention. She tried to stand and had to sit right back down. The room was spinning. She'd only been drunk a few times in her life, once on her and Charlie's honeymoon and once when she thought she could down a Long Island Iced Tea like it was water. The room spinning brought back both of those memories.

"Charlie, I don't feel so good."

She remembered him steadying her and chuckling. "You don't look so good either, Babe. Come on, let's get you home."

Home. Hannah looked at her kitchen desk.

Billy Bob whinnied again, this time a little louder. "Go check on him," she told herself. But she was too lightheaded to move. She couldn't move. She laid her head down on the table and tried calming herself. Who would take care of him if something happened to me? Lucinda and Colleen don't know anything about horses. Would Charlie come get him? How would anyone get a hold of him? He won't come. It doesn't matter that he loved Billy Bob. He loved me too.

She got down on her knees and crawled across the kitchen floor to the counter and sat with her back against the cabinet. "You can do this. You can do this," she said. She reached up and felt for the bananas, tried to remember exactly where they were. Over further, to the left? No, to the right. Yes, there they are. I can feel the ends of them. Now if I can only reach them. She pulled herself up onto one knee and grabbed for them. She missed. She tried again. They tumbled off the counter and onto the floor all spread out like a fan.

"I'll have to make banana bread," she said, edging toward them. "They'll be all bruised now." She clutched one in her trembling hand and bit the end off. Only a little banana pulp, but enough for a bite. She spit the peel out, "Just like John Wayne," she muttered out loud as she chewed and swallowed. There, let that sit a minute. Nausea washed over her. Don't eat too fast. She took another bite, chewed and swallowed, and then another. She ate not one whole banana but two and then lay her head down on the floor. As she drifted off, she heard Billy Bob whinny again and again.

Seconds passed in her mind, perhaps minutes, perhaps hours. She had no sense of time when she opened her eyes. She glanced at the sun shining through the kitchen window and heard someone knocking on the door.

"Lady? Lady, are you home?"

It was the little boy. She sat up tentatively and was surprised to be feeling rather well. When she pulled herself to her feet, the room was no longer spinning. "Thank heaven."

"Lady?"

"Just a minute. I'll be right there." She hurried to the bathroom, peed forever, then splashed water on her face and toweled dry. The little boy was still waiting when she opened the front door. Bessie's puppy sat at his side, drooling.

"I think there's something wrong with her. She won't stop doing that."

"Here, let me take a look." Hannah bent down and pried the puppy's mouth open. "It's a splinter." She examined it closer. It appeared as if it had been in there for some time, all red and inflamed. "Hold on, let me get my tweezers."

The little boy nodded.

"I'll be right back. Do you want to bring her inside?"

"No, I'm not allowed."

"Okay, stay put."

Hannah returned quickly and with the little boy's help, was able to extract the splinter. "Oh my, that had to hurt." She petted the puppy and fussed over it. "You are so brave. Yes you are, so brave. That's a good girl. That's a good girl."

The little boy laughed. "You talk funny."

Hannah smiled. "She should be fine now."

The little boy thanked her and took off running with the puppy bouncing alongside. Hannah thought about following them at a distance to see where he lived, but went to check on Billy Bob instead. As she started down over the hill, she could see that he was fine. He was grazing and looked up at her, happy as can be. She checked his water; one bucket was still full. The other one had a little left. She filled it, gave him some hay, and hurried back up to the house to get dressed for work.

"I'm late, I'm late," she sang. "I'm late for an important date. Go tell it on the mountain, over the hills and everyyyyy-wherrreeeee. Go tell it on the Mountain...."

She took a peanut butter and jelly sandwich with her and ate it on the way. It hit the spot. She made a promise to herself on Billy Bob's behalf to eat better from now on, to take care of herself, if for no other reason than his well-being. What if something *had* happened to him? What if something happened to me?

"Never again," she said, and went right back to singing, "You're not a kid anymore. When people ask me." She touched her chest. "What would you like to be? Now that you're not a kid anymore." She waved to an old neighbor at the stoplight and kept right on singing. "I know just what to say, I answer right away. I want to be Bobby's girl...." She paused. "No, I don't. I want to be Charlie's girl." To have and to hold, for richer or poorer.... "That's the most important thing to meeee."

Richard was out in the front yard of the funeral parlor when she pulled in and called to her. "Hey, Hannah! Come here a minute. Come take a look at this."

She walked over and stood next to him.

116

"I heard this tapping noise in my office, so I come out to look and...."

There on the window ledge sat the carrier pigeon, preening itself. "Well, hello!" Hannah said. "What are you doing here?"

Richard looked at her. "I can't believe I'm asking this, but do you know this bird?"

Hannah chuckled. "Yes, it's a carrier pigeon that's lost its way. It showed up at my house the other day. I've been feeding it." She gently stroked the pigeon's head. "The owner called it a rogue pigeon. I say he's just a wayward adventurer."

Richard stared at her as if she was from a different planet, newly arrived. "So..." he said. "What do we feed it?"

"Just bread and water so far. I have to go to the feed mill today anyway. I guess I'll pick up some birdseed."

"He's rather messy," Richard said. The window ledge was littered with bird doo.

Hannah smiled. "I'll feed him at home."

"Do you care to take him home now?"

"No." Hannah laughed. "He'll find his way. Hopefully," she added. "What do we have today?"

"A C-death with a wig."

"Did the family bring photos?"

"Yes. She's all ready for you."

Hannah spent hours thinning and shaping the wig so that it would appear more natural; more like the way the woman looked when she'd been healthy.

"I don't know how you do it, Hannah." Richard said, when she'd finished. "She looks like she's content as can be and just taking a nice little afternoon nap."

Chapter Twenty-One

A trip to the gas station for ten dollars worth of gas, a stop at the feed store, the hardware store, then the grocery store for a few things, and Hannah was home with fifty-three cents in her pocket. "A banner day!" When the phone rang, she hesitated before she answered. "Hello."

It was Colleen. "How are you doing?"

"I'm good. I just got home from work."

"And you're feeling okay?"

"Yes, though I did crash this morning. I don't know what came over me. I practically passed out."

"Why? What happened?"

"I don't know. I just got all fuzzy and weak. I think I might have been dehydrated."

"That's scary. The boys are going shooting tonight, so Lucinda and I thought we'd come over and hang out with you if that's all right?"

"That's fine with me, but you don't have to."

"Nobody said anything about having to. We want to. What else are we going to do, go to the Honky Tonk and listen to Dave whine?"

Hannah laughed. "He is a bit of a whiner, isn't he?"

"Yeah, and we heard it for at least an hour last night after you left."

Hannah laughed again. "I'm going to be making pies, so come after seven and they should be done. What kind do we want?"

"Apple?"

"Apple pie coming right up." Hannah had nine pies baked and cooling by the time Lucinda and Colleen arrived. Three apple, three boysenberry surprise, three peach. She'd also made some egg salad sandwiches. Colleen brought veggies and spinach dip. Lucinda brought a bottle of wine and Buffalo wings.

"A feast!" Lucinda opened the wine and poured each of them a glass.

"Out on the porch?"

"Sounds good to me."

"I love your desk."

"Me too."

They hauled the table and three chairs out onto the front porch again, set the food and drinks down and got comfortable. It was still relatively warm out, no sweaters needed. And, the wine added warmth. "Are we going to wave at all the cars?"

"Yep! Here comes one now," Hannah said. "Wave!" The three of them waved and then giggled like school girls when the driver honked and waved back. "We have too much fun."

"Speaking of which." Hannah told them all about everything that had happened the night before, all except for the part about the old man appearing and disappearing. She decided to keep that to herself. Besides, the more she thought about it, the more she figured it was delirium, just plain being too tired, and most definitely dehydrated. It had to be. She felt perfectly fine now. She'd felt fine all day.

Lucinda was fascinated with the tale of the carrier pigeon. "How did it know that you work at the funeral parlor?"

Hannah looked at her. "I don't know that it associated the two places with me, if that's what you mean. I think it's just stopping along the way everywhere. It's confused."

"I'll bet he followed you there one day. I hope he comes back while we're here."

"I put some birdseed out for him. We'll see."

After they ate, the three women headed down to the barn, wine glasses in hand. Billy Bob seemed happy to see them, but at the same time, preoccupied with something far, far away, from the look in his eyes.

"I don't know what it is. Last night he was okay because I was outside and he could see me."

All three women gazed off into the distance.

"I don't see anything," Lucinda said. "Do you?"

"Nope," Colleen said.

"Me neither."

Colleen and Lucinda picked handfuls of grass for Billy Bob and fed it to him while Hannah did his stall. "I'll have to go get some more hay tomorrow," Hannah said, as much to herself as them. "I've only got two bales left." She recalled the time years ago when three bales of hay fell off a huge truck going by their farm. The truck kept right on going. She was low on hay that day too and hurried to get the wheelbarrow. Too late. Before she could get down to the end of their driveway someone stopped in a pickup and threw them into the back and drove on. She'd felt like crying. It wouldn't have been charity. It was just chance, a stroke of good luck for a change. "Yeah, right," Charlie had said. "That's what you get for having hope."

Hannah put Billy Bob in his stall and the women walked back up to the house. "So what's on the agenda for tonight?" Lucinda asked.

"Well," Hannah hesitated. "I'm thinking about camping out in the pickup outside the barn for a while and seeing what shows up. I need to know if it's coyote. I don't hear them, but something gets him going."

"What if it is coyote? What are you going to do?"

"I don't know. Charlie always took care of these kinds of things." She looked at Colleen. "And no, I do not want DAVE to come help."

The three of them laughed.

"I first need to know what it is. I'll figure out how to deal with it once I know. I could shut the barn door. I'm going to have to shut it sooner or later, but with Billy Bob in there by himself and closed up, I don't know how he'll deal with that."

"Oh, look," Lucinda said, pointing. "Is that the pigeon?"

Hannah laughed. "No, that's a barn swallow. The pigeon's about three times that size."

"Do you remember the scarecrow we built that one Halloween?" The memory triggered a smile for all three of them. They'd dressed it up like Dolly Parton - wig, bangles, boobs and all.

"Love's like a butterfly," they all sang, laughing. As soon as they'd hung it on the post, the crows flocked to it and even crawled into the cleavage. They'd stuffed it with corn husks.

"That was my favorite shirt," Lucinda said.

It was getting dark. The women hurried and cleaned up the dishes, hauled the table and chairs back into the kitchen, and piled into Hannah's pickup. "No Baja-ing!" Lucinda insisted. "Let's take it nice and easy."

Hannah looked at her. She had her feet braced on the dashboard, wine glasses in hand. Colleen had what was left of the apple pie balanced on her lap along with three forks and a batch of napkins. Hannah drove slowly down over the hill toward the barn, checked on Billy Bob, and backed the truck up into the orchard under two apple trees.

"We'll have to be very quiet," Hannah said. "And don't put out any pheromones. Coyote can smell a bitch in heat five miles away."

"We're safe," Lucinda said. "I don't know what heat is anymore."

The three of them laughed.

"Shhh...."

Colleen motioned to the wine bottle. "Pour now before it gets too dark."

"What do we do if it's a bear?" Lucinda asked.

"Throw out the pie, roll up the windows as fast as you can, and start screaming," Hannah said, and that had them laughing again.

"Got it."

"Did I tell you coyote can hear a stomach growl a mile away? They'll even know what you ate for dinner. They smell it on our breath, so whatever you do, don't breathe." More laughing. "Okay, okay, now I mean it. We have to be quiet."

The three of them sat for a moment, perfectly silent as they sipped their wine under the soft light of the moon. Lucinda leaned her head back and sighed contentedly.

"What?" Hannah whispered.

Lucinda shook her head. "This is nice," she said. "That's all."

Colleen and Hannah nodded.

"Jason says this is what it's like hunting."

Hannah pretended to fire a rifle. "Until the bang." It was a sobering thought. Colleen helped herself to some pie.

Hannah leaned forward to look at Billy Bob. He was standing at the stall front and appeared to be dozing, his head hung low. He had one of those bottom lips that sagged when he was sleeping or resting. She imagined him wondering how that lip thing happened all the time. When he would wake, he seemed annoyed that he had to lift it back up.

"Look!" Lucinda gasped.

No sooner said, than Billy Bob whinnied.

"It's horses."

Hannah stared. It was dark, but even so, she counted five of them. "Well, that's explains that. He hasn't been scared. He's been excited."

Lucinda and Colleen agreed.

"Where do they come from?"

"Are they wild horses?"

Hannah shook her head. They didn't look like wild horses. "Probably not," she said. "But that's my property, so they're okay. I'll check for hoof prints in the daylight tomorrow and see if I can figure out what direction they came from."

"Cool," Lucinda said, helping herself to another forkful of pie. "Do we want to still wait and see if any coyote show up?"

"No," Hannah said. "Those horses don't look upset. If there were coyote around, they'd know it." Billy Bob whinnied and whinnied and turned round and round in his stall. "Besides, there's proof right there. Look at him." She reached for a fork and ate a couple of bites of pie and finished her wine. "Well, this has been fun."

Lucinda and Colleen smiled.

"We're going to grow up some day, you know that," Colleen said. "And then what?"

"It'll be a sad day. Let's not," Hannah said. "You two ready?"

"No, let's just sit here a little while longer," Lucinda said. "This is just so nice. No mosquitoes, the full moon."

Hannah leaned back. Billy Bob was settling down some, watching the horses, watching them. "Charlie and I staked out once, for bear actually now that I think about it. We fell asleep in the truck. I was sore for a week."

Lucinda raised her eyebrows. Hannah smacked her and laughed. "Ah, those were the days."

Colleen looked at her. "Don't you miss that? I mean, really. Charlie's not the only man on earth, you know."

"He is for me," Hannah said. "Look!" She pointed. "There, right there. It's the pigeon." He'd roosted on one of the pear trees.

"That is so cool," Lucinda said. "I read this story once about a woman who had a pet crow."

Hannah shook her head. "I don't like crows."

"Me neither, but this one was nice."

Lucinda drained the rest of the wine into their glasses, giving them each about an ounce. Hannah studied the grazing horses.

"What?" Colleen asked, from the look on her face.

"Nothing," Hannah said. "I'm just uh, glad that I found out what's been getting Billy Bob going." The horses were in the area where it always looked as if someone had mowed the grass. This explains that, but.... "Well, what do you say we call it a day?" Hannah started the truck and headed up the hill. When the old man appeared right in her path, she swerved.

"Whoa!" Lucinda yelled. "What the hell? I said no Baja-ing. What did you do, hit a bump?"

"Uh...." Hannah glanced in her rearview mirror and looked at her. "I must have. I guess I didn't see it. Did you see anything?"

Lucinda and Colleen shook their heads.

"So, it's Chili Night at the Honky Tonk tomorrow. You're coming, right?"

Hannah nodded. She couldn't dodge Dave forever. Besides, the chili was great and it was cheap. "I'll see you there."

Chapter Twenty-Two

Hank, the fellow from the phone company was right on time in the morning to pick up his pies and even tipped Hannah two dollars. "I'll be here same time next week," he said. As soon as he left, Hannah headed out to the field to look for evidence of the horses from the night before.

Nothing. No tracks, no hoof prints, no manure. "Where's the old man when I need him?" she said out loud. "Old man, are you here?"

Billy Bob nickered.

"I wasn't talking to you," she said. "But I'm glad you're paying attention." They'd come a long way over the years. When she and Charlie first bought Billy Bob, the horse wanted nothing to do with her. He'd snub her every chance he got, but would follow Charlie anywhere. Today, Billy Bob stood in the pasture with his neck and head over the fence, watching her every move.

"Where are your horse friends?" she called to him.

Billy Bob just looked at her.

"And where's Charlie?" Her voice echoed in the trees. "Call for him. Say, Charlie, where are you?"

Billy Bob lowered his head and went back to grazing.

"I saw that."

She walked back up to the orchard and stood assessing the trees. Now that all the brush was burned and the logs and timber stacked, the orchard had a whole different feel to it. It almost looked happy. She stood, thinking, "I'll bet it was pretty in its day." Someone had put a lot of planning into the placement of the trees, and the choices of what kinds of trees to plant.

Hannah glanced up the hill to where she saw the old man last night, or thought she saw him. It was a relief to see he wasn't splayed out in the grass. She smiled, watching the sun glisten on the dew. "It's diamonds, Momma," she remembered saying as a child. "We're rich. It's diamonds."

Her Momma wasn't much for nonsense and told her to get ideas like that out of her head. "There ain't no diamonds here, Baby. Just dirt and cow patties."

"I really need a lawn mower," Hannah said, heading back toward the barn. "Cheap." First things first. She filled Billy Bob's water buckets in the pasture and gave him some hay. "I won't be long," she said. "You won't even have a chance to miss me."

She stopped by the junk store on the way to work.

"You and me have to stop meeting like this, Hannah," Big Jim said. "People are gonna start talking."

Hannah laughed. "I need a mower."

"Riding or push?"

"Push." She followed him through the shop and out back.

"That one there is twenty-five dollars. That one's fifty. And that one I can let you have for seventy-five bucks."

Hannah shook her head. "I want one that will start with one or two or three pulls." The mowers he'd just pointed out looked like they hadn't started in years, maybe even decades.

"I thought you said you wanted something cheap."

Hannah laughed. "I did. I do. But if it doesn't run, what good will it do me? It doesn't have to run forever. I'll probably only have to mow once or twice before…." Her eyes fell upon a pretty little neon green mower with a bagger. "How much for that one?"

"Well, that one's mine," he said. "It ain't for sale."

Hannah ignored that minor detail and walked over to get a closer look at it. She checked the gas, it was half full. "Does it have oil in it?"

He nodded. "It ain't for sale, Hannah."

"Well, then rent it to me." She held in the choke button, pulled the cord, and it started right up. "Twenty dollars every time I use it, how's that? And I'll bring it back each time with a full tank of gas."

"I don't know." He rubbed the back of his neck. "How much do you have to mow?"

"Just a little bit around the house and down by the road. I'll bring it back tomorrow. I promise. Here." She fished into her pocket for the twenty dollar bill and two dollar tip the pie man had given her this morning. "See," she said, "I even have the gas money all ready right here."

"I might want to cut my own grass tomorrow," Big Jim said, trailing along behind her and the mower.

"I'll be here bright and early. What time do you open?"

"Eight."

"I'll see you then."

Work at the funeral parlor kept Hannah busy for the rest of the day. Two cremation services were scheduled for tomorrow and both families requested meals afterwards. The first service was to take place at eleven in the morning, the second one at three. As customary, Hannah placed orders for the groceries and they were delivered within the hour. The first family was expecting approximately fifty people. The second one estimated that around thirty-five would attend. Both families were supplying desserts.

Over the years, Hannah had acquired an ability to gauge the spiciness of the meals based on the deceased's age. If someone in their twenties and thirties had passed, she would season the food for the meal without restrictions. This group of attendees usually was slow to start eating. Perhaps it seemed ludicrous to eat at such an occasion, with one of their best friends now gone. Hannah always put out plenty of snack foods for this age group, the most popular being salsa and corn chips. Finally, one person would start eating and the rest would follow. The more jalapeno in the salsa, the better.

She used slightly less seasonings for the families of a person who passed in their forties and fifties. It seemed that group in general were all watching their diets and taking antacids. They weren't sure what to eat anymore. Food scares flew into their faces like swarms of mosquitoes. Bacon causes cancer, red meat – heart disease, dairy is a no-no, don't consume alcohol, no – drink a glass a red wine a day.

She used more seasonings for the family members of a person in their sixties, as this age group appeared to be back into enjoying food. They wanted a variety of foods and lots of it. "Pile it on."

She used very little to no seasonings for family members of the elderly, particularly if there were only a few people expected. For the most part, those in attendance were all of the same advanced age and had very little appetite. A light meal, coffee, and sweets were more to their liking.

Rigatoni and meatballs pleased all ages, as did scalloped potatoes. Corn pudding was another favorite as well as tossed salad, and potato salad. Hannah prepared what could be made ahead of time, set the table for the lunch, and called it a day. She hurried home, hayed and watered Billy Bob, and started mowing.

It took a lot longer than she'd anticipated using the bagger on the mower, but it looked so nice. She kept telling herself next time would go easier doing it this way, and that kept her going. She mowed all around the house and the front and sides of the barn. She mowed down both sides of the driveway, and mowed a wide path to the orchard. All the bagged clippings, she piled just this side of the orchard. She stopped often and made sure to drink plenty of water and even made a point of eating two snacks, albeit on the go.

She hurried and cleaned Billy Bob's stall, put him back in the barn, fed him, washed up, and headed for the Honky Tonk by way of her young neighbors Douglas' and Patty's farm, with pies in tow.

Patty's face lit up. "Oh, it smells so good. Thank you! Would you like to come inside for some coffee?"

"Not tonight," Hannah said. "But soon, thank you. You two have a good evening." She waved over her shoulder and headed back down the road with a smile on her face. This was probably the first time she'd driven past her farm without turning into the drive. If she had to say so herself, the place looked pretty damn good. It looked like home. Even the barn roof appealed to her.

"I'll be back," she called to Billy Bob and honked the horn. "Keep an eye out for the old man." Her good mood spilled over into the Honky Tonk. Jason and George seemed quite entertained with her story about how she'd rented Big Jim's lawnmower.

"That's flat amazing," Jason said. "Jim don't part with anything he says is his."

Hannah laughed. "Well, I didn't give him much choice. Besides, I felt like twenty dollars was fair."

"I'd say so." George downed the rest of his beer and motioned for another round. "Maybe old Jim's got a crush on you."

Dave showed up at the table with their drinks. "Who?"

"Big Jim. Hannah got the best of him today."

Dave met Hannah's eyes for a brief second. "I'm going to go kick his ass."

Hannah laughed. "I've got pies to sell. I think he's going to buy them all."

Dave shook his head. "How many?"

"Five. They were baked yesterday."

Dave turned around. "Who wants the best, uh...?" He looked at Hannah. "What kind are they?"

"Two boysenberry, two peach, and one apple."

"The best boysenberry, peach, and apple pies in the county!" Dave sounded like an auctioneer. "Ten dollars a piece. Any takers?"

All five pies sold in less that a minute. Some people started eating them right then and there at their tables.

"I'm charging for forks," Dave kidded. "Napkins too."

"My phone number's on the bottom of the pie pans," Hannah told each and every buyer. "I bake on Thursdays for the weekend." She marveled to hear herself, because it came right off the top of her head. Equally amazing was her sense of pride. This wasn't charity; this was selling some damned good pies.

Chili Special nights at the bar were boisterous events: lots of laughter, shouting, telling jokes, loud music on the jukebox and singing and dancing. Whenever the Texas Two Step was played, the dance floor was packed. Hannah found herself partnered up with a cowboy from Macon County, a handsome blue-eyed gray-haired specimen in creased jeans, boots, flannel shirt, Stetson hat, and a huge longhorn belt buckle.

He made for a pleasant addition to the party atmosphere, particularly when she talked him into joining their table. He had stories to tell a mile long. The fact that he was happily married and waiting for his wife to join him any minute now, made him all the more likeable to Hannah. It was such fun for her to talk to a man who didn't have any ulterior motives.

"You do what, darlin'?"

Hannah laughed. She was used to this reaction. "I work in a funeral parlor. I do dead people's hair."

"Holy sheet," he said, with a drawl. "I'll bet you don't get many complaints."

"Nope, none!" Everyone laughed. "I also make pies. Did you buy one of my pies?"

"I did rightly," he said. "It's out in my truck. I figure me and the wife can enjoy it at the motel."

"Why are you here?" Jason asked, equally taken with the guy. He was a man's man, a real charmer.

"I'm fixing to buy me a tractor."

"An antique?" Hannah asked, thinking of the one she had sitting in the barn.

"No," the man said. "This here one I'm lookin' at is only a few years old. A fella by the name of Cal Able...."

"To put you in a car today!" the group chorused.

The man laughed. "That'd be him. I saw the advertisement on TV and phoned him. He said it's good as new. I'm meeting him in the morning."

Hannah smiled. "Well, I know Cal, so you tell him tomorrow that Hannah said he's an honest man and to give you a good deal."

"I'll do that, Ma'am." He nodded and then waved to a woman entering the bar. "Over here, Honey."

His wife had been shopping at Peeble's Department Store and had victory written all over her face. She'd apparently found what she came looking for. Hannah grew quiet for a moment. It was buying a tractor, a tractor and a combine actually, that sealed her and Charlie's fate with losing the farm. Charlie thought upgrading their equipment would make them more competitive in the long run. What it actually did, was dig them a hole they could and never would climb out of, or ever recover from.

"Come on, Hannah, don't you want to see it?" Lucinda tugged at her arm.

"What?"

"The bedspread. Come on."

The four of them went outside to the woman's car and oohed and aahed over the chenille spread. "It's just like my mother's," she declared. They all took turns pressing their faces to the tufted fabric. "It's so soft."

With the long day facing her tomorrow, Hannah gazed up at the stars and decided to head on home. She went back inside to say good-bye to everybody and even made a point of going over to talk to Dave.

"I'll walk you out," he said.

"That's not necessary."

"I know. But I want to, okay?"

Hannah smiled.

Dave slipped his hand over hers as they walked to her truck. "I don't know what came over me the other night," he said. "I'm sorry. And I want you to know I'll wait for you forever."

Hannah looked at him. "Why? Why me?"

"I don't know." He shrugged. "Because you *are* you."

"Thank you." Hannah kissed him on the cheek. "Now go back in there and sell some beer."

Though the night was cool, Hannah drove home with her window open. If felt refreshing on the warmth of her skin. How long had it been? Two and a half years: a long time for a woman to not be loved. As she approached her driveway, she turned her blinker on out of habit. She was the only vehicle on the road. She pulled down over the hill and around to the back of the barn and kept her lights on to check on Billy Bob. He nickered.

"How're you doing?" She stroked his neck and gave him a hug. "I'm going to hang out with you for a little while and see if the horses come back." Billy Bob sighed. "Do you think they're for real?"

She threw him some hay and picked his stall, then drew some water and topped off his water buckets. She gazed in at him. "I don't know what I'd do without you, Billy Bob. And don't you worry. I'll take good care of myself and you too. No more fainting for me. I ate good tonight and had fun, had a couple of beers. I feel good."

She sat down on the remaining bale of hay and drew a deep breath and sighed. "I have quite a bit to do tomorrow, but I'll make sure you're okay. It's going to be nice so you can stay out all day."

The horse looked at her.

"That's right, it's fall. The night's are getting longer. That's why I need to figure out what's going on with those horses and if that's what's been getting you worked up at night all the time. I'm sorry you're here by yourself. I wish I could afford another horse. Some day."

She pulled a blade of hay from the bale and ran it between her fingers. "There was a guy at the Honky Tonk tonight that reminded me of Charlie. He didn't really look like him, but had a lot of his mannerisms." She stood up and walked over to the barn door, thinking, remembering, longing....

"Charlie? Charlie, are you out there? I hope you're okay. I hope you're eating right. Because I am," she said, chuckling. "The last couple of days at least." She turned her face up toward the moon and drank in the cool light. "Tell Charlie I love him," she whispered. "Make sure he knows."

She stood counting the stars. One for each bill we need to pay, Charlie once said. She smiled. Charlie hadn't left until every last bill *was* paid. Looking back, she was glad he didn't tell her he was leaving, but surely he must have had it planned for some time.

"Did you stop loving me, Charlie?"

"No," she heard in the whisper of the wind. "No."

What was it he said the night before he left? "Don't look at me like that."

"Like what?"

"That. Look at how you're looking at me."

She remembered turning away and then his arms around her. "I've got nothing left in me, Hannah. You'd be better off without me."

She shook her head.

"Go on to bed. I'll be up in a little while."

She was exhausted. They both were. Did he come to bed that night? She'd never know. She'd fallen sound asleep, and in the morning he was gone.

Hannah stared past the orchard, looking hard, and brightened. The horses had appeared. She walked softly past the truck, debated whether or not to turn off the lights and just kept right on walking. She couldn't tell which direction they'd come from, but there they were, all grazing and seemingly content. She stopped short of the orchard and noticed one had a pronounced limp. And two were thin, very thin.

"They're not really here," she heard someone say. Was it the old man? She turned to look for him and recalled something he'd said once about this farm housing sale horses. She crept closer.

"If they're not really here, how is that Lucinda and Colleen saw them? How am I seeing them now?" Billy Bob whinnied. "How are you seeing them? You're seeing them too, aren't you?"

Hannah got down on her hands and knees and crawled the rest of the way ever so slowly. "It's all right," she kept saying softly. "It's all right." She sat down close to the one horse, the one that was limping and it grazed right around her. She resisted the temptation to reach out and touch the horse. She didn't want to frighten it. She didn't want to find out if it was real or not. She just sat quietly, reassuring them with her presence that all was well. When she glanced back at the barn, Billy Bob was watching intently, calm as could be. Something moving over by the orchard caught her eye. It was the old man. She didn't dare wave; she didn't dare move. Bessie sat at his side.

"They're happy," she said in her mind. And the old man nodded. Somehow she knew that these were horses that had died here, perhaps horrible deaths, hungry, starving, in pain.... "But they're happy now." She smiled a sad but contented smile. "They're happy now."

Chapter Twenty-Three

Hannah woke extra early, ate a quick breakfast, took care of Billy Bob, loaded up the lawnmower and was on her way. Big Jim was waiting for her and glanced at his watch when she pulled in. "Right on time," she responded to his grumbling. "I really appreciate this, Jim." She drove to the feed store next and picked up five bales of hay. Since it was going to be a long day, she didn't want to chance not getting there before they closed and having to wait until Monday. "If it's done now, it's done."

She parked in the back of the funeral parlor parking lot. Richard was very big on appearances. He'd frown on her parking a truck with hay out front. She let herself in the back door, thinking about last night, the horses, the old man, and for some odd reason, Dave.

He really could be nice when he wanted to be. Actually he was nice most of the time, and the times that he wasn't, "Probably has more to do with me than him."

"What?" Richard said.

"Nothing. I was talking to myself again."

Richard laughed. "It goes with the territory. It's Showtime!"

Hannah knew some of the first deceased's family members and was chatting with one of the nieces after the meal when she saw the old man looking in the window. She excused herself and went outside, but he was gone. "You know, I wonder about you sometimes," she said to herself. "You see things. You talk to yourself." She drew a deep breath and sighed. "You turn down a perfectly good man for a phantom husband." As she started back inside, she noticed a car pulling out of the parking lot.

It was she same old car she'd seen the day she'd ridden Billy Bob home through town. She squinted, couldn't see who was driving the car, but could make out a large dog in the back seat. A German Shepherd.

The bereaved from the first service all pretty much left together, except for two of the women Hannah knew who insisted on helping clean up. "It's the least we can do, you doing this all by yourself." They helped stack the dishwasher, changed tablecloths, and then wanted to set the table. Hannah smiled. These two women were of the same mindset as hers. At times like this, keep busy.

"Thank you," Hannah said, hugging them both. "You've been a big help." No sooner had they gone, family members for the second service arrived.

"The immediate family," Richard liked to say. It was his way of venerating them, honoring them. "But we have a problem."

Hannah looked up from putting the finishing touches on the salads, adding thinly-sliced tomatoes and red onion last. "What?"

"The widow won't attend the service."

"Family issues?"

"No. Alzheimer's."

Hannah stepped past him to open the refrigerator. "Does she not think he passed?"

"No, that's not it." Richard rubbed his eyes and pinched the bridge of his nose, a habit of his when a migraine was coming on. "Apparently she doesn't want the 'old biddies' at the nursing home to see her with her hair a mess."

"Old biddies?"

"Her words, not mine." Richard looked at her. "Do you think you could come talk to her?"

"Me? Why me?"

"Because you're a hairdresser."

"Yes, for dead people."

Richard smiled. "It's a sad scene. I don't know what to do."

Hannah washed her hands, took her time drying them, and followed him upstairs. The woman had been seated in his office and had two distraught daughters in tears at her side.

"Momma, please."

The woman appeared to be in her nineties and couldn't have weighed more than eighty pounds, but could still wield power. Hannah liked that.

"Mrs. Maketty," Richard said. "This is Hann-ah. She's a hair-dresser." He dragged each word out loud as can be with exaggerated enunciation. "Mrs. Mak-etty, your hus-band's serv-ice is in twenty-five minutes."

The two daughters looked at Hannah. The old woman looked at Hannah. "I don't know you," the old woman said. "Do I know you?"

"Well," Hannah said. "You might remember me. I uh...." She glanced at the daughters, both about her age. "When you came to the...."

"Nursing home," the one daughter said, filling in the blanks.

"Yes, at the nursing home," Hannah said. "I think I may have done your hair once."

The old woman scowled.

"Maybe twice. I told you how pretty your hair was."

The old woman puzzled and then smiled. "I remember."

"Good." Hannah nodded to the daughters. "Do you mind if I work on it now? I can see why you're upset. They didn't do your hair the way you like it."

The old woman put a hand to her head. "Yes, please...." Tears moistened her eyes. "My husband has never seen me without my hair done."

"Well, we'll take care of that," Hannah said. "I think it's too chilly to wash it, but I can make it look pretty. I can fix it."

The woman's hair was perfectly fine the way it was, it was already pretty. She had snow white hair and a nice cut with a little curl. "Do you have your comb and brush with you?"

"Yes. In my purse." She looked at her daughters, snapping orders with a glance. One materialized a comb, the other a brush.

"I can't remember. Do you like hairspray?"

"No, no hairspray."

Hannah started combing her hair. "I remember now. You don't need hairspray. Your hair lays so nice without it. I'll bet your husband liked your hair."

The old woman smiled. "He loved my hair. When I met him, I had hair down to here." She touched her shoulder, her eyes wistful, and then started rocking gently in the chair. "He loved my hair."

Hannah styled it exactly the way she'd had it and then motioned for a mirror. One of the daughters had one in her purse. Hannah looked from one to the other, all three holding their breath as Hannah placed it in front of their mother.

"Thank you," the old woman said. "Thank you."

Everyone heaved a silent sigh of relief, even Richard, who stood frozen just inside the door. "Don't forget to tip her," the old woman said, rising to her feet and standing as tall as she could.

Hannah shook her head at the daughters and watched as they walked with their mother out into the hall, past Richard, and up the stairs. Hannah and her mother had walked up those stairs, the exact same way the day her father died. Hannah remembered supporting her those last few steps. "I'm so tired," her mother had said.

"I know, Mother. I know."

One of the daughters looked back over her shoulder and smiled. Hannah nodded.

"Good-bye, Daddy."

Hannah had to rush to get the dinner onto the buffet table then stood catching her breath for a moment. She could hear the guests milling about upstairs. The service had ended. "A perfectionist," Richard called her. She scanned the room, everything in place. She adjusted the volume on the music. Too loud and no one would talk, too low - and no one would talk. It had to be just right. She looked up and smiled when the people started filing in. The sadness had passed. They were talking and laughing. They were eager to eat.

Chapter Twenty-Four

It was after six before Hannah had the funeral parlor kitchen and dining area cleaned up, and was able to leave. She'd have to unload the dishwasher first thing Monday, but aside from that the place was "Ship Shape" as her mother liked to say. She locked the back door behind her and was stretching her arms and shoulders as she walked to her truck when something caught her eye. She stared ahead. There was an envelope on her dashboard. It was from Dave.

"I was going to put this in your mailbox, but saw your truck here," he'd written on the outside. She opened the envelope with trepidation. "I'm going to take a half hour break for dinner at 8:00." It read. "Please come join me. No strings attached. Dave."

\Hannah shook her head and sighed. She'd so looked forward to just going home and staying home. But he was being so nice, so careful. How she could she say no? "I hate rushing." She sat in the truck as she debated and agonized. "If I go, will this encourage him? I don't want to do that. But I don't want to hurt his feelings either. I can go home, take care of Billy Bob, wash up, go have dinner with him, and still be home by nine. I have tomorrow off and probably most of Monday. I can get a lot done then. I need to get some wood stacked on the porch. I need to call and get the chimney done. I need to go to the laundromat. I need to fine-prune the fruit trees...."

She had a plan, at least for the moment. When she walked into the Honky Tonk right on time, Dave met her eyes and smiled. He didn't say, "I didn't think you'd show," but it was written all over his face, that and tremendous relief.

"Thank you. I saved us a table over there."

Hannah sat down. "Oh, so this is how the other half lives."

Dave laughed.

Hannah and her friends, particularly when husbands, fiancés and the likes were there, all sat closer to the bar. "I'll be right back," Dave said. "Cheeseburgers and fries okay? Beer?"

Hannah nodded. "That'd be great."

She purposely didn't watch him walk away for fear someone was watching. She felt eyes on her from all over the room. When she drew a deep breath and glanced around, she returned some smiles and a couple of waves…all the while thinking, what am I doing here, what am I doing here? You're having dinner with a friend, she told herself, nothing more and nothing less. He *is* a friend after all.

Dave came back with their meals and beer, and sat down across from her.

"Thank you." Hannah busied herself with putting ketchup and mustard on her burger, ketchup on her fries. "I am so hungry."

"You don't eat when you're there?" he asked, referring to the funeral parlor.

Hannah shook her head. "I taste along the way to make sure everything's good. But I don't like to eat, because it seems…." She took a big bite of her burger and rolled her eyes in ecstasy. "Ooh, you put garlic on it."

"I remember," he said, taking some big bites out of his burger as well. "Garlic on the burgers, cheddar cheese if we have it. American will do, but under no circumstance, Swiss."

Hannah chuckled. "I like Swiss cheese, just not melted."

"Not even on a Reuben?"

"Only if it has Thousand Island dressing on it."

Dave smiled. "I'll have to remember that next St. Patty's day."

Hannah ate a couple of fries. "Real fries," as she called them. Cut fresh daily and with the skins on. "This is very nice of you, Dave."

He nodded. "Thank you."

"So how are the sheep?"

Dave paused, as if he had to think about it. "They're all good. This time of year, they don't require a lot of care. I fuss over them, but hey, that's just me."

Hannah smiled. "I like that about you."

He blushed, but in a pleased way. "Eat...I only have a half hour."

Hannah laughed.

"Hey, Dave!" someone called from the other side of the room. "I need another beer!"

"Tell Romeo. Bring two more over here too."

Romeo was a regular and apparently Dave's cover for his break.

"I've never known you to take a dinner break," Hannah said.

He smiled. "There's a first time for everything."

The two of them ate their meal, with some idle chit-chat thrown in along the way, and before Hannah knew it, it was time for Dave to go back to work.

"Thank you," she said, leaning back as he reached for her empty plate.

"Do you want another beer?"

"No, I'm fine. Thank you."

Dave pulled out her chair. "And thank you. You're free to go now."

Hannah laughed.

"I said no strings attached. Go!"

Hannah kissed him on the cheek and waved over her shoulder. "Thanks again." She didn't glance back at the door. She just walked right on out and found herself singing along with the radio on the way home. When she belched, she said, "Excuse me, such a Piggy!" She shook her head, feeling rather content. "Okay, so this was fun. I can handle this, particularly if he's not going to pressure me."

"Yes, but how long will that last?" she could hear her mother say, always one to ask questions like that. "Hmmm."

She drove down to the barn, shone the lights on the inside, and checked on Billy Bob. "You're going to be on your own tonight," she told him, as she picked out his stall. "I'm going to get up early, so...." She patted him on the neck. "Remember those horses are your friends. Think of them as pasture buddies. Talk to them." She climbed into the truck. "But no messing with your stall gate. You hear me?"

Hannah slept like a baby and woke on top of the world. "Yes, Mom, you heard me, on top of the world." She was excited about her day. She made a breakfast of fried potatoes and over-easy eggs, mopped up the yolk with a piece of toast and had a big glass of orange juice. "No bottoming out today, no sirree. I have too much to do."

She headed down over the hill to the barn to feed Billy Bob and while he was eating, she cleaned his stall. "I have a treat for you today," she said. "And you'd better behave." She sat down on a bucket outside his stall and started tying strings of baling twine together. When they were all done, she put Billy Bob's halter and lead rope on him and led him up to the orchard. "This is where we're going to haul your manure, but in the meantime...."

She wound the baling twine around several of the fruit trees where she'd be working and made a makeshift pasture for him. "Look at all this grass." Billy Bob had his head down and was already grazing. "And it's all just for you." Her plan was to just keep moving the twine, and eventually he will have eaten all the grass down. This time of year the grass was still good, so it would help her save on hay.

She parked her truck to the side of the trees and started stacking the fireplace-sized wood in the back. She was careful to separate what looked like dead wood over the green that had been downed in the storm. Most was dead. Even so, "I'm going to have to line up more wood if I'm going to make it through the winter."

She hoped to supplement heating the house with the fireplace, though admittedly, a fireplace wasn't the most efficient heating method. She planned out loud. "If I set the thermostat at fifty, I won't have to worry about the pipes freezing when I'm not here." She tossed a few more logs into the pickup bed.

She knew several people who sold wood, Jim Gaskin being one of them, but buying wood would defeat the purpose. Besides, Jim would feel bad charging her full price, and it wouldn't be right to put him in that position. After all, he sold wood to make a living.

Hannah stood up and wiped her brow. "The only thing I have to barter with at the moment is pies, and there aren't enough days in the year to make as many as I would need. Next year I'll have jam, and apple butter, and chutney, and maybe even some pear butter." She counted five trees on her property line that looked dead or near dying. "Probably elm." There was a blight that was killing all the elm trees.

She'd never dropped a tree that size, but figured there was a first time for everything.

She wondered what they did with the hardwood "spoils" at the lumber yard. She'd have to check with Cal Able. When Billy Bob nickered, she turned, and there stood the old man and Bessie.

"Aren't you afraid your horse'll get loose?"

"Not while I'm here. He has no reason to leave."

The old man looked at her. "Why'd your husband leave?"

Hannah stared. "Don't ruin my day, old man. Okay?" She petted Bessie on the head and then shook her paw.

He shrugged. "Just wondering."

"Well don't. I've been doing enough wondering about that for ten people." She tossed a log past him. "What were you doing at the funeral home?"

"They have ashes that belong to me."

She tossed another log.

"I've been there several times. They won't give them to me."

"Why not? Did you pay for them?" Two more logs, three, four.

"Yes, I think so. I'm not sure. My son was supposed to pay."

"I can check for you tomorrow if you want." She climbed into her truck and moved it forward. "What's the name?"

The old man hesitated. "I don't know what name they're under."

Hannah glanced at him. "What are the possibilities?"

"Uh...."

"Whose ashes are they?"

"Mine," he said.

Hannah sat staring at him.

"I want them here where they belong."

Hannah drew a breath and sighed. "You used to live here, so you are...?"

"A man shouldn't have to leave his land. My son doesn't care. I left enough money."

Hannah nodded. "Are you a Brubaker?"

"I don't have a name. Not until I get my ashes back."

"Did it ever occur to you to just get buried?"

The old man looked at her and then shook his head. "My wife's everywhere here. That's where I want to be."

Hannah watched him walk away and went back to stacking wood. "Did you see that old man, Billy Bob?"

Her horse never even looked up.

"City girl," she heard the old man say.

"City girl or a country girl, you're still a ghost, old man." She tossed a log so hard it sailed over the bed of the truck and landed on the other side. "And for the last time, I'm not a city girl. I'm a fifty-four year old woman talking to an extremely rude ghost."

She heard a dog barking off in the distance.

"Have a nice day," she called to the wind. By lunchtime she had the back of the pickup full of dry dead logs, a good start. She led Billy Bob back to his pasture and drove the truck up to the front of the house to unload the wood. "Lunch first." She made herself an onion and mayonnaise sandwich and when she was still hungry, made another. She liked lots of salt and pepper on the onion. Charlie did too.

"Why *did* you leave me, Charlie?" The onion was good and sweet and crunchy. "Why?"

She remembered she hadn't checked the mail yesterday and took a walk down to the end of the driveway. There were eight letters in the box; all but one was junk mail. She stared at the return address, the Courthouse, same as the other one. "What did I do with that letter?" She walked back up the drive, debating whether or not to open the letter. "Not on a Sunday. What's the point? Whatever it is, I can't do anything about it, but worry." She tossed it on the table, glanced down and saw the other one on the floor. She picked it up and stacked the two of them together, nice and neat. "I know. I'll put them on my kitchen desk. There."

"Freedom," she sang. "Freedom. Freedom, ohhhh freedom. Freedom."

When a car pulled in, she looked out the front door. It was Lucinda and Colleen. "We're going to a movie. Do you want to go?"

"Nope. Thanks though."

"What are you doing?"

"I'm working on the orchard."

"Do you need help?"

"Not today."

"What about dinner? Do you want to do something for dinner?"

"Where are the guys?"

"Hunting."

Hannah paused. "You know what I have a taste for? Spinach dip. I'll make some and you two come back after the movie."

"I'll bring veggies," Colleen said.

"I'll bring Pumpernickel bread."

"Ooh," Hannah said. "That sounds good."

"Wine or beer?"

"Wine."

"Beer."

"Both."

"Make it late, say around seven or so."

Hannah spent the rest of the afternoon working in the orchard, with Billy Bob her constant companion. By the time Lucinda and Colleen returned, Billy Bob was in the barn for the night, all content, and Hannah had the dip made, had showered, and lit some candles. The three of them set the food out on the coffee table, and Hannah sat on the floor.

"So how was your date last night?"

"Date?"

"We heard."

Hannah nodded. "Figures."

"So was it nice?"

"Yes."

"See, we told you it would be."

"I'd rather not talk about it if I don't have to," Hannah said. "I'm still *processing* it."

The three of them laughed. Last year when Lucinda and George were having a bit of a tough time getting along, "processing it" had become Lucinda's favorite expression. She'd been watching that Dr. Phil TV show regularly.

"How are the grandkids?"

"Wonderful. By the way, before I forget, Raven wants three pies for this Saturday. She's having a get-together and we're all invited. Dave included."

Hannah hesitated. "Did she say what kind?"

"No, but you need an answering machine. She said she tried phoning you several times."

Hannah shrugged. "I've never had one before."

"Yes, but you've never had your own pie business before," Lucinda said.

"Good point." Hannah smiled. "I wonder how much they cost."

"Not much. I saw one at the drug store the other day for only nineteen dollars."

Only nineteen dollars? "I'll check tomorrow. I have to run some errands in the morning."

"Are you done with the orchard?" Lucinda asked, twirling a broccoli floret through the dip.

"Pretty much. The dead stumps will have to stay, but I've pruned the trees way back. I hope they make it."

"You'll have more fruit than you know what to do with next year. You've always had a green thumb."

"Hope so. I'd like to set up a stand. I've always thought that would be fun."

"I'll man it, I mean *woman* it," Colleen said. "And wave at everyone!" The three of them laughed.

"First thing tomorrow, I'm going to look into getting the chimney cleaned."

"Good idea."

"And then depending on how long I have to work, I'm going to close off the upstairs. I want to sterilize it first with some bleach. That one bedroom is full of bird poop."

"Has the pigeon been back?"

"No. I haven't seen him. Or her, if that's the case," Hannah added.

"We can come help with the cleaning."

"It's going to be an icky job."

"We'll bring gloves and masks."

Hannah smiled. "Thank you. I'd appreciate it."

When it came time to leave, the three of them walked down to check on Billy Bob. "I wish I could get power run down here," Hannah said.

"It's going to be the pits in the winter."

"I can't believe they never had lights in the barn."

"Once upon a time they did," Hannah said. "You can see parts of what used to be a hook-up from the outside."

"Well then how does the water work?"

"It's works on a vacuum. Lifting the handle primes the pump."

Lucinda chuckled. "How do you know so much?"

"I don't. But what I do know is from always living on a farm."

Since Hannah had to work for at least a little while in the morning at the funeral parlor, they made plans to meet at the farm at three. This would give her time to run errands, gather what supplies she needed, and get the barn done.

"You're life is so exciting," Colleen said, giving her a good-night hug. "I'm so happy for you. And I'm actually a little envious. You're so independent."

Hannah drew a breath and sighed. "I don't know what I'd do without you two. You both make it all possible."

Lucinda wiped an instant tear from her eye. "All right, that's enough. No more mixing beer and wine." They laughed. "See you tomorrow."

Hannah slept straight through the night and woke to a persistent tapping sound on her front door window pane. Probably the carrier pigeon, she thought. "There's food out back, you little rogue."

Tap-tap.

She propped herself up in bed and focused. It wasn't yet daylight. "Go away," she said, and marveled at herself. "Talk about being hospitable." She reached for her jeans. "Hold your horses."

It wasn't the carrier pigeon, it was the old man. "I'm just making sure you get my ashes today."

Hannah looked at him. "I was sleeping up a storm, you know."

The old man shook his head. "The sun's up, city girl."

"Not quite. And I swear if you call me that one more time...." Hannah stepped back to close the door. "I'm going to have friends here later, so...."

The old man held up his hands. "I need my ashes."

Hannah looked long and hard at him. He appeared to be getting smaller. "How long have you been waiting for them?"

"Too long." With that, he turned and left.

Hannah made a pot of coffee and went down to feed Billy Bob. He was happy to see her and seemed to have had a restful night also. His stall was in relatively good shape. "I love you, Billy Bob," she said, petting him. "Do you know that?"

He sighed.

"I've got a big day today. Lots to do. So you best behave. Okay? I'll be down before I leave to turn you out."

First thing on her list, once she got going, was a stop at Cal Able's.

"What can I do for you, darlin'?"

"Well, I'm wondering if you know of anyone in the scrap metal business."

"You're kidding me, right?" He flashed his toothy grin. "If it's for sale, I'm buying. What's your pleasure?"

"Well." She ran through a mental list of items in the barn. "I've got a lot of old tools, old farm implements, antiques more or less, and an old tractor."

Cal Able's eyes lit up. "Does it run?"

Hannah shook her head. "I don't think so."

"Too bad," he said, and noted how her shoulders slumped in disappointment. "But I'll come take a look anyway, long as you're not trying to get rich off of it."

"No, I'm mainly wanting more space. I need to get some hay put up before winter."

"I can stop by later today."

"Thanks," Hannah said, shaking his hand. "I'll be home after three. By the way...." She stopped at the door. "If I made you a sugar-free pie, would you eat it?"

"Will it taste good?"

"It'll be delicious. I promise."

Next stop was the chimney sweep's. Hannah knew the secretary vaguely but couldn't remember her name. She used to have a horse where Hannah boarded Billy Bob. "How's Carmen?" Hannah never forgot a horse's name.

"Good, good. I don't ride him much anymore. He's twenty-seven this year."

Hannah smiled. The horse was a buckskin with gaskins the size of Sherman tanks. Hannah rode him for her a couple of times when he was acting up on her. Hannah straightened him right out. All he needed was a little more rein.

"We actually have a cancellation for the last call today, say around five."

Hannah paused. "That should work out good." She gave the address and was just about to leave, but then stuck her head back in the door. "By the way, I make pies for the weekends - ten dollars a pie, all different kinds. If you ever want one, you have my phone number. I'll need to know by Thursdays."

Wow, I'm really into this marketing, she thought, as she climbed into her truck. "It gets easier as I go along."

Richard was out back dumping trash when she pulled into the funeral parlor parking lot. "We have a live one," he said.

Hannah shook her head and chuckled at his standard report. "When's the service?"

"Tomorrow."

"Lunch?"

"No." Richard sighed. He liked it when they included lunch with the service since it meant more money for him as well. "I tried."

"I know." Hannah followed him inside. With a little luck, she'd still be on schedule. The deceased was a man eighty-five years old with coal black, dyed hair. "He looks like an Elvis impersonator."

"He *was* an Elvis impersonator," Richard said. "He died doing a gig."

"You're kidding."

"Nope."

"And the sneer?"

"It's permanent. He had it done by a plastic surgeon. Old people, they amaze me."

Hannah studied the deceased's "permanent" expression. "Which reminds me," she said, rubbing her dye-stained fingertips together. "Do you remember a Brubaker? We might have ashes here for him."

Richard stared. "I remember the son. Not a happy camper."

"How long ago?"

"I don't know. Ten, maybe fifteen years ago."

"And we still have the ashes?"

"The kid never picked them up."

"The kid?"

"Well, maybe I shouldn't have said "kid." He was in his forties maybe."

"Can I see them?"

"Sure, but what for?"

"I don't know. I just...." Hannah scrambled for a reasonable explanation. "Did an old man ever come trying to get them?"

"Not that I know of."

Hannah followed him down the hall and into the room Richard called the "Barbeque Pit." There were at least thirty unclaimed urns, which amazed Hannah when she first started working here. "How does a family just not come get their loved ones' ashes?"

"Easy," Richard had said. "Out of sight, out of mind."

144

Hannah reached for the plain metal urn with the name Brubaker on it. "Is it paid for?"

Richard nodded.

"Can I have them?"

"Why? Why would you want them?"

"Well." Hannah still couldn't come up with a good reason, one that wouldn't cause Richard to think she'd taken leave of her senses. "I bought the old Brubaker Homestead, remember?"

"And you want the ashes to…?"

"Well, I thought it would be nice to have them on the farm. There's all sorts of uh, places where I can almost see the old man there."

"What made you think they'd still be here?"

"I don't know," Hannah said. "That's a good question."

"I'll check into it and let you know."

Hannah was tempted to say, "Quickly please," but refrained. She opened the lid and stared at the contents. "Who's a city girl now?"

"What?"

Hannah smiled. "Nothing, I'm just talking to the old man."

Chapter Twenty-Five

Next stop was the Army surplus store on the other side of town. With a little luck, they'd have wool blankets in stock. Hannah figured to layer two of them, maybe three, depending on their size and thickness, to seal off the stairs. They had plenty although they cost a little more than she'd hoped, but she needed them to help save on heat. She bought three.

Next, she stopped at Big Jim's to see if he had a TV antenna. If she could get one cheap enough, maybe she could pay the chimney sweep a little extra to install it for her. She didn't really mind not having a television, but sooner or later, come winter….

He had two, one that went right on top of the television and one for the rooftop. "Which one's the best?" Hannah asked.

"Well." Big Jim appeared to be wrestling with his integrity. "Probably this one." It was the one that went right on the television. "This other one's missing a few rods."

"Thank you, Jim. I appreciate your honesty. I'll take the little one. How much?"

"Ten bucks."

Hannah reached into both pockets and counted what loose dollars and change she had on her. "How's nine dollars and sixty three cents?"

"That'll do. You see this wire here, just wind it around the connection on your television, and you should be able to get at least channels three, five, and eight."

"Thank you." Hannah started out the door but then noticed a set of old fireplace andirons sitting next to a hearth screen and fireplace tools.

"They're antiques," Big Jim said.

"Ah, that's too bad. I need a set but I just need old 'cause that's all I can afford."

Big Jim shook his head. "Five bucks."

"Sold." Hannah went out to her truck and came back with the five dollars. From there, she went to the grocery store, bought a pound of boloney, a small jar of sweet gherkin pickles, a jar of mayonnaise and a loaf of wheat bread. "Time for some ham salad."

Last stop was the discount drug store, where she picked up bleach, ammonia, and a gallon of vinegar. When she arrived home, Lucinda and Colleen were already there waiting for her. While Hannah made the ham salad, using her mom's old grinder to chop up the boloney and pickles, Colleen hooked up the antennae on the television and Lucinda made a batch of iced tea.

"I have a bit of a headache," Lucinda said.

"Oh wonderful. You're going to feel great once you smell all that bleach."

"I brought masks. I wasn't kidding."

They were all set. They each tackled a bedroom. Hannah insisted on cleaning the one with the bird poop, and within an hour, all the bedrooms were done. They stood in masks and gloves staring at the bathroom.

"I wonder how we can drain the toilet," Hannah said. "I don't want the pipes to freeze."

Everyone cringed, all thinking the same thing: scoop it out. "No thank you."

"Call Jason," Lucinda suggested. "See what he thinks."

Colleen came back upstairs a few minutes later. "He says to just turn off the water at the base and to put anti-freeze in the toilet and down the sink and tub drain."

"Did he say how much?" Hannah had about half a gallon behind her seat in the truck.

"He said it wouldn't take a lot."

Hannah scrubbed everything down first and then went to get the anti-freeze. Colleen had some in the trunk of her car as well. They decided to use as much as it would take to make the water a solid green color. That task completed, they wiped down the hallway, then closed all the registers and doors and worked their way back downstairs.

"How are you going to hang the blankets?"

Hannah motioned to the ceiling on the first landing. Hanging the blankets there wouldn't be seen from the living room. One would have to climb the first rung of stairs and turn the corner to see them. "There's a stud right here on each side. It means pounding holes into the wall, but I don't have much choice. I want to stop the heat going up any further than here." They stretched the blankets out. "Perfect." Hannah went to get her hammer and some nails, poked the nails through all three blanket layers, and pounded the nails into the side walls and ceiling. She repeated the process on the bottom and secured the blankets to the step above the landing.

"I'm happy! Is everybody happy?"

The three of them gave each other high-fives and laughed. Just then, Cal Able pulled into the driveway right behind the chimney sweep.

Cal Able flashed the 'ladies' his dazzling smile. "Lead the way, darlin'."

Hannah chuckled. To look at Cal Able's face, the contents of the barn was a treasure trove. He all but had cartoon dollar signs in his eyes. Hannah encouraged him to look around and went and topped off Billy Bob's water buckets and gave him some hay. The grass in his tiny pasture was getting pretty well eaten down.

"You have a lot of junk in here, Hannah," Cal Able said.

"Well, don't look at the junk. Just look at the good stuff. The rest of it can just stay here."

"No need for that. I know you want to get it out of the way."

Hannah crossed her arms and paid extra attention to anything he touched. It was as if he was making a tally of sorts. He was. "Two hundred for the tractor, and the rest I'll have hauled away."

"You mean all the iron and the aluminum over there, and that little batch of copper...."

Cal Able blushed. "Old habits are hard to break."

"I can see that."

How about seventy-five for whatever you want to get rid of?"

"And two hundred for the tractor?"

"Yes."

Hannah stood considering the offer and was just about to say, "Okay, it's a deal," when she saw the old man standing off in the corner, clutching his heart. You're already dead, old man, she thought, spare me the theatrics.

He appeared now to be gasping for breath.

"Well?" Cal Able said.

"Uh...."

The old man shook his head vehemently.

"I'm not so sure about the tractor," she said. "Let me think about it."

"Think long, think wrong, is what I always say."

The old man went down on his knees.

"I know," Hannah said, trying not to laugh. "I tend to agree. But I am going to have to think about it. Charlie and I used to have a tractor just like this one, and...." She shook her head and pointed. "You see that right there?"

"What?" Cal Able said.

"Oh nothing, I thought I saw something. I'll take the offer of seventy-five dollars for the scrap metal. I'll let you know about the tractor Friday when I bring you your pie."

Cal Able smiled. "It had better be good."

The chimney sweep was just finishing up as they started up the hill. Cal Able gave the man his card, then climbed into his Cadillac, waved, and honked as he barreled out the drive.

"You're going to need some mortar repair on that chimney soon," the man said, handing her the bill. "And, the damper's closed. Make sure you open it when you use it."

Hannah nodded. "Thank you. I'll go get a check and be right out."

Lucinda and Colleen were setting the kitchen table. "It's going to rain tonight," Colleen said. "I just heard it on the news."

"Oh good, I'll light us a fire." Hannah brought the fireplace andirons, screen, and tools inside. There was no sense trying to clean the andirons; they were so rusty. "I'll let the fire do it." By the time she cleaned the fireplace poker, broom, and hand shovel, and they all washed up and sat down to eat, it was close to seven.

Lucinda sighed. "This is so good. I can't remember the last time I had a ham salad sandwich."

"Me neither," Hannah said. "I used to make it all the time. Charlie loved...." She took a big bite. "I love it too."

"So what's on the agenda for tomorrow?" Colleen asked. "By golly, I'm getting fit. We keep this up and I'll have Jason chasing my firm behind all over the house."

They laughed. "Actually, tomorrow after work I was going to tackle the root cellar. I want to get rid of the old preserves, and...."

"What are you going to do with them?"

"I'm going to compost them and wash up the jars. I want to clean it out good and then lock it up for the winter."

"Daylight Savings Time is this Saturday."

"Oh no. Think we can hold it off for a week?" Hannah laughed. "I need more daylight when I get home."

Lucinda made herself another sandwich. "I wonder why they call this ham salad. Why don't they call it boloney salad?"

Colleen shrugged. "I'll bet some people make it with ham."

"I tried it once," Hannah said. "I didn't like it as much. I made it once with beef boloney too and didn't like that either. This is my favorite, just plain old boloney."

"Mine too," Lucinda and Colleen echoed. Hannah opened the damper and lit a fire in the fireplace, using twigs, some newspaper and apple wood. They moved the coffee table and sat on the floor, backs against the couch and legs stretched out, warming their feet. Soon they were all yawning. The living room was nice and cozy with the sound of the crackling fire. Lucinda closed her eyes and dozed for a few minutes. When she woke herself snoring, they all laughed.

"Time to go home," she said.

After they left, Hannah headed back down to the barn to bed Billy Bob down for the night. It was already getting dark. The old man was still in the barn.

"You can't sell this tractor," he said. "I bought this tractor new."

Hannah glanced at him. "And how many years ago was that?"

"I can't remember," he said. "A farm is not a farm without a tractor."

"All right, all right." She walked past him.

"Did you get my ashes?"

"I'm working on it."

The old man started to say something but hesitated. Hannah looked at him. "Do you sleep?"

He shook his head. Hannah was about to inform him that he'd better not wake her up before dawn, but suddenly felt sorry for him. "How long have you been, uh…you know, waiting for your ashes?"

"I don't know." He glanced at her. "It feels like yesterday when I bought this tractor. I died here on this property."

"I figured as much."

"I'll be going now," he said.

Hannah marveled. No insults, no accusations.

"Don't sell the tractor," he said, and was gone.

Hannah stayed in the barn until the stars appeared, and smiled at the herd of grazing horses. The one that had the most pronounced limp, seemed to be limping less. It raised its head and looked at her.

"You've nothing to fear," she said. "Right, Billy Bob?"

Billy Bob went back to eating his hay.

She looked at him. "We have a big day tomorrow. If you behave, I'll let you graze over by the root cellar. I should be able to make you a nice little turnout with the trees there." She gave him a big hug and walked back up to the house.

The phone was ringing when she came inside, but she didn't get to it quickly enough. Whoever it was, hung up. "Well, you'll just have to call back," she said. She wondered how many times it rang in a day. Sales people probably. She put two more logs on the fire and sat gazing at the flames for a moment. Since it was still early, she decided she might as well clean the bathroom. She wiped the walls down, scoured the toilet, sink, and tub, and scrubbed the floor.

"This old house might be old, but by golly, it's going to be clean." She could almost hear her mother's voice of approval. She drew herself a hot bath and climbed in and settled back. "Ahh…." When she closed her eyes, she imagined Charlie standing at the sink, shaving. He smiled

at her through his reflection in the mirror. "It's been a good day, Babe."
She sighed.

Chapter Twenty-Six

The first thought Hannah had upon waking was about needing drapes. She made a pot of coffee and sat down at her kitchen desk to go over her list. She decided she'd like to find four pairs of those old-fashioned insulated drapes that were so popular in the 70's. They were heavy and didn't let much light in, but because they were insulated, they also kept the heat in and the cold out. "I can always tie them back during the day to let the sun shine in."

She added Annie's Consignment Store to her list, crossed off the items and tasks she accomplished yesterday, and walked down to feed Billy Bob. He nickered at the rustling sound her boots made in the grass and stood bobbing his head up and down in greeting. He was adjusting to their new home and so was she. She fed him and did his stall, filled his water buckets, hung them on the fence posts, and when he was done eating, put him out in the pasture.

"Be good," she told him. No response. She laughed. She went back up to the house, ate breakfast, straightened up the kitchen, and headed for work. As she pulled out the drive, she saw the little boy walking alongside the road. She rolled her window down. "Are you going to school?"

"Yep."

He had his books held together with an old leather belt.

"Where's the bus stop? Do you want a ride?"

"No thank you, Miss."

"Okay. Have a good day!" Hannah watched him in her rearview mirror until she drove around the bend and he vanished from sight, then turned on the radio and caught the weather. A heavy frost was forecast for tonight. When she saw a flock of birds overhead, she wondered about the carrier pigeon, wondered how he or she was doing. Do carrier pigeons fly South? What if he really had lost his way?

She stopped at the lumberyard to ask about the sawed-off hardwood lumber, was told they sell it, and climbed back into the truck and drove on. The idea is to *not* pay for the wood she burns. When she got to work, she touched up the Elvis impersonator's hair and make-up.

She made him look perfect, even if she had to say so herself, and stood back and smiled. "I hope you had a good life," she told him.

The man's wife and son came early with their own CD's to be played – Elvis's ballads, and then more people arrived. Hannah couldn't remember the last time a deceased at Davidson's had this many visitors. They were lined up all the way out into the parking lot. The man's wife, a pretty little woman looking to be in her mid to upper 70's, spoke with each person that came in, their hands clasped gently in hers. "Thank you for coming."

Hannah made four thirty-cup pots of coffee throughout the afternoon and refreshed the sugar and creamer numerous times, as well as the cookie trays. People milled about as if it were a cocktail party. Hannah heard snippets of stories about the man, affectionate stories, compassionate stories, silly stories. He was well-liked. He was loved.

Richard kept the doors open until the last visitor had paid their respects and then left to join the family at the local VFW for dinner. Hannah cleaned up, put everything away, and before leaving, went to check on the Brubaker ashes. "I don't know why I'm looking in here," she told the urn. "It's not as if anything would have happened to you. You've been here for years."

She stared at the contents. It was mostly all ash, with an occasional, she cringed, piece of bone. She closed the container carefully and put it back on the shelf. When she heard a noise behind her, she turned around.

There was no one there, no one that she could see at least. Time to leave. It was not unusual to hear noises at the funeral parlor. For the most part, she ignored them. It *was* rare though for her to be alone. Richard was usually here. She turned out the lights, locked the door behind her, and laughed as she walked towards her truck. The old man was sitting in the passenger seat.

"Are you for real?" she said, climbing in behind the wheel.

He nodded. "Did you get them?"

"No, I don't have permission. They're fine though, I just checked on them."

The old man stared at her. He was not much bigger than a child. "What if someone else takes them?"

"Like who?"

"My son."

"Well, then...."

152

The old man crossed his arms, pouting. "He won't bring them home."

Hannah started the truck and drove down through the parking lot. "I have an errand to run. You're welcome to...."

"I don't like shopping."

"Neither do I, but I need drapes, so...."

The old man sighed.

Hannah glanced at him from time to time as they rode down the highway and at times, she could literally see right through him. "Are you okay?"

He nodded.

Hannah parked in front of the consignment store, debated whether to leave the keys in the ignition, or.... She imagined the conversation she would have with the sheriff. "Well, I think the old man took it. I'm not sure. What old man? Well...."

She took the keys with her. "I'll be right back. I'll only be a minute." Annie, owner and sole sales clerk was happy to see her.

"Where have you been, Hannah?"

"Oh, around. Keeping busy."

"Are you here to sell something?"

"No. Actually, I'm here to buy." Hannah described the drapes she was looking for.

"Does it matter what color?"

"Uh." Hannah thought of all the colors in the fabric on her couch. "Not really, I guess. I think I have them all covered."

"Well, I have two sets of two pair. And they're in pretty good shape. They're in the back. Come look; they're heavy."

"Heavy. I like the sound of that."

They were indeed heavy and smelled like cigarette smoke. One set was forest green and the other a dusty shade of lime. "Hmmm." Hannah looked them over for holes and tears. They were in remarkably good shape but for the dirt and stench. "How much are you selling them for?"

"Ten dollars a pair."

Forty dollars.

"They came with hooks and the rods."

Hannah smiled. That would be a bargain, but forty dollars is forty dollars. "Let me think about it. Maybe if they were all the same color."

"I hear ya," Annie said. "How about five dollars a pair? They'll need washed. I was going to wash them, but...."

"And that's with the hooks and rods?"

The woman nodded.

"Okay, it's a deal."

Hannah gave her twenty dollars and loaded the drapes and rods and bag of hooks into the back of her pickup. She half expected the old man to have vanished, but he was still sitting there waiting for her.

"Women shop too much," he said, as she climbed in behind the wheel.

Hannah waved to Annie standing in the store doorway and rolled down the window. "By the way, Annie, I'm making fruit pies and custard pies, ten dollars a pie. Wait, I'll give you my phone number." She wrote the number down on the back of an old envelope that had been in the glove compartment and walked back to hand it to her. "They're all natural and they're really good. I make them on Thursdays, so people can have them on the weekend. I'll need to know if anyone wants one by late Wednesday. Tell them to put their order in soon, 'cause they go fast. Thanks much."

Hannah laughed at herself as she pulled out onto the highway. "Listen to me. I sound like Cal Able."

"You really do talk too much."

Hannah laughed again. "I never used to."

"Maybe you talking too much is why your husband left."

Hannah looked at the old man and shook her head. "You know, I was in a good mood up until now." They rode in silence for a few minutes. "My husband was a farmer," Hannah finally said. "He couldn't stand losing the farm. I'm thinking when he decided to buy all that new equipment, I *should* have spoken up."

"Do you blame him for losing the farm?"

Hannah shook her head. "No, I don't think anyone is to blame. But...." She pushed her hair off her face and drew a deep breath.

"You do blame him, don't you?"

Hannah hesitated. "I don't know. I didn't realize it, but I guess I do."

"That's why he left then," the old man said. "I would."

Hannah turned into her driveway and put the truck into park. "What do you mean? He doesn't know I blame him. I never...."

The old man shook his head. "I've had enough talking for one day." He opened the door, got out of the truck, and walked off. "I'll be back for my ashes tomorrow."

154

"Oh yeah? Well that's if I have them."

Hannah unloaded the drapes and hauled them into the utility room. "It would be nice to have a washer and dryer," she told herself. "Some day." She really didn't mind going to the laundromat, but not for this job. She was afraid, as old as the drapes obviously were, that they'd fall apart if "agitated." She chuckled. "I like that word - agitated." She opened the back door and stuck her head out. "You agitate me, old man, you hear me?"

When an unassociated gust of wind kicked up, she laughed. "Just kidding." She dumped the rest of the bleach and what little Pinesol she had left, evenly into both tubs, put two pair of drapes into each one and using a broom handle, swished them around and around. The smell was overwhelming. She propped the back door open and walked down the hill to take care of Billy Bob.

He nickered and trotted up to the fence, happy to see her. "You ate all your hay." She checked his water buckets: one was empty, the other two-thirds full. "We'll graze tonight," she told him. She gave him some hay and grain, dumped the one water bucket, and filled them both. "Did you have a good day?"

Billy Bob munched on his hay, as good an answer as any. "I'll be back down in a while," she said. She wasn't sure what she was going to have for dinner, but was getting hungry. She smiled as she started up over the hill. The carrier pigeon sat perched on the open back door.

"Well hello, you little rogue." He'd brought a friend. "And you too." She watched them both fly to the bird feeder and eat. They pushed at one another and ruffled their feathers. The rogue bird's friend didn't have a band on its leg. Apparently the little rogue pigeon was indeed a rogue after all.

Hannah left them to eat and went inside to fix herself dinner. She fried two eggs and made a sandwich, mayonnaise on one piece of bread, mustard on the other, and ate it standing at the back door, so she could see the pigeons. They'd finished feeding and were perched in the oak tree on a low branch. One of them was cooing softly.

When the phone rang, it startled her. It was Lucinda. "What's the plan for tonight?"

"Well, I'm still thinking of tackling that root cellar."

"Okay, we'll be there in a few minutes."

"Wait, you don't have to...."

Click.

Hannah drained the wash water on the drapes, refilled the laundry tubs and stirred the drapes round and round, not once but twice. The second batch of rinse water was almost as murky as the first. After the third rinse, which was fairly clear, she filled the tubs with soapy water.

She gathered up the broom and some cleaning rags and was going to go down and get started on the cellar, but decided to wait and show Lucinda and Colleen the carrier pigeon. When they pulled into the driveway, she motioned for them to come in the front door. "The pigeon's here and he or she brought a friend."

The two birds sat perched in the tree, preening themselves. The little rogue pecked at its leg band. "Well, look at that," Lucinda said. "They look just like pigeons." The three of them laughed.

"They are pigeons," Hannah said. "What did you expect?"

"I don't know. I thought they'd look like pigeons, but not be actual pigeon-pigeons."

"What are you washing?"

"Oh, drapes. I bought them at Annie's. The former owner was a smoker."

Lucinda sloshed the drapes around and examined the color. "Green?"

"I know," Hannah said. "It's all she had. They'll do."

The three women gathered up their cleaning supplies and headed down to the root cellar. "Here," Colleen said, handing them each a babushka. "Remember the spider webs?"

Lucinda cringed. "Who could forget?"

They donned their babushkas at the door to the cellar and pulled down their sleeves to cover as much skin as possible. "We look like studda bubbas." They laughed. The door was held shut with the hickory stick, but Hannah could tell someone had been inside. The chair was moved clear across the room.

"Here, we can use this." She handed an old bushel basket to Lucinda. "We'll load it up with the jars and I'll go dump them by the orchard. I want to get Billy Bob out anyway. This way he'll see us coming and going and behave."

She tied the baling twine around a different group of trees and led Billy Bob over so he could graze, then doubled back to the barn to get the pitchfork. She figured when they dumped the contents of the preserve jars, it'd be a good idea to pile some manure on top to start the breaking down process. That and she didn't want to cause an unsuspecting critter to become sick. "Lord only knows how old these things are."

Since the cellar was so small, the largest part of the job was emptying the jars. It wasn't long before all the shelves were emptied and dusted, the floor swept, and the ceiling de-cobwebbed. "Are you going to store anything in here?"

"Not this year. I'm hoping to put up a lot of fruit next fall. Vegetables too." They stuffed the trash in an old feed sack, which Hannah hauled up to the truck. Then they hauled all the jars up to the house and washed them. Lucinda washed, Colleen rinsed, and Hannah dried. There was plenty of room on the top shelves of the kitchen cupboards to store them. In no time, they were done.

Hannah walked down to put Billy Bob away. He nickered when he saw her coming, but put his head right back down to eating grass. "Wow." Hannah felt a chill in the air. Apparently so did Billy Bob; his hair got all puffed up. "I'll have to check the weather." It didn't feel like rain, there was no humidity at all, and it was too early for snow. There were still some leaves on the trees, not that it hadn't ever snowed this early before.

By the time Hannah put Billy Bob in his stall and bedded him down for the night, Lucinda and Colleen had laid out a shrimp cocktail platter, a tray of cheese and crackers and olives, sliced apples, and....a birthday cake.

"You're kidding me," Hannah said, laughing. "I have never, I mean never ever, forgotten my own birthday before. This is amazing."

Lucinda popped the cork on a bottle of champagne and poured three frothy glasses. "To Hannah! The best friend a gal ever had!"

"Cheers!"

Chapter Twenty-Seven

Hannah cleaned the fireplace out first thing in the morning and dumped the warm ashes on the compost pile. The heavy frost on the ground looked almost like snow. Hannah actually liked snow. She loved how everything looked so clean, fresh as a new white blanket, but hoped it would hold off for at least another month or so. Even as it was with just the frost, the grass would soon be affected. Billy Bob could still graze on it, but the nutritional value would be diminished. She definitely needed to get a load of hay in for the winter. There was no telling how much snow they'd get and how she'd get the truck down to the back of the barn once it hit.

Hannah fed Billy Bob and did his stall, then turned him out. She made a mental note to check at Big Jim's for a plastic sled. She still figured that would be the best way to haul manure come winter, with or without Billy Bob's help. She also wanted to stop at the used tack store to look for something that could serve as a harness.

She'd drained and rinsed the drapes one more time after Lucinda and Colleen left last night and was hoping to get them out on the fence to dry before she left for work. The phone rang while she was hauling one pair outside, so she didn't get to it in time. She'd definitely have to seriously consider getting an answering machine.

She hauled out the other three pairs of drapes, slung them over the fence rails, and glanced up at some chattering squirrels in the trees. She looked to see if the carrier pigeon and its friend were still hanging around and smiled when she saw them huddled together on a high branch with their feathers all ruffled.

"It's coming," she said. "Winter's coming early."

When the phone rang again, she rushed inside and got to it in time. "Hello."

"Hello, you don't know me, but I got your number from Raven, and I'd like to order three pies for tomorrow. I'd like a peach, an apple, and the one that's called Boysenberry Surprise.

"Good choices." Hannah wrote the woman's name and phone number down. "Do you want me to deliver them or would you like to pick them up?"

"Do you charge for delivery?"

Hannah was just about to say no, no charge, but changed her mind. "It's five dollars for delivery."

"Super! Deliver them, please."

Hannah figured it cost her about four dollars for the pie ingredients, so essentially she was making about six dollars a pie and would be driving into town anyway, so this would make her at least another dollar a pie, gasoline excluded. She preferred selling multiple pies to one person. Even so, single order or multiple orders: it made sense to charge for delivery. "I'm certainly not going to get rich, but at least it's cash flow." She laughed. "Oh, listen to me, 'cash flow.' Lah de dah!"

She checked her flour supply; it was getting low. She needed to buy some aluminum foil pie pans too, as she'd already used all the ones she'd accumulated over the last couple of years. She sat down at her kitchen desk and looked over her to-do list. She crossed off drapes. "Making progress," she noted.

She checked on Billy Bob before she left for work and stopped at Big Jim's to ask about a sled. He didn't have one. "By the way, did I tell you I make pies? All kinds," she said. "Ten dollars a pie."

"Wow, that's expensive."

"You wouldn't say that if you had one of my pies."

"I'll think about it," he said.

"Okay." She waved over her shoulder. "I make them for the weekends, so if you want one tomorrow you need to order it today, otherwise it'll be next weekend."

"Wait a minute," he said. "What kind did you say you make?"

"All kinds, fruit and custard. The most popular is the Boysenberry Surprise."

"Boysenberry?"

"It goes real good with vanilla ice cream or milk."

"Okay, I'll take a boysenberry one."

"I'll deliver it tomorrow. And if you come across a sled in the meantime, let me know." She stopped next at the grocery store, then the Dollar Store for the pie pans, and on to work. Richard had a transport order waiting for her.

"The body is at the morgue in Columbia Stanton."

"Where's Jeb?"

"I've got him headed in the opposite direction."

"Does he have the hearse?"

"Yes."

"Which means...?"

Richard nodded. "The station wagon. I tried getting Jeb to take it, but he said it gives him the creeps."

The station wagon, being smaller, put the body virtually right at the driver's back. It did have a nice radio, but Hannah thought it disrespectful to "jam" with the newly departed practically resting on her shoulder. "Okay. Well, I'd better get going." It was a two-hour drive at least.

She listened to the radio on the way there and sang along with the *Oldies But Goodies.* "Soldier boy, oh my little soldier boy. I'll be true to you." She recalled the day Charlie left for Viet Nam. It was raining and she was shivering. "Wherever you go, my heart will follow...."

She wiped her eyes and when traffic slowed, glanced at the printout of directions Richard gave her. With a little luck, she'd get to Columbia Stanton right around lunch time. "It's my party and I'll cry if I want to, cry if I want to. You would cry too if it happened to you."

She saw the flashing lights up ahead and sighed. Beyond it was a jack-knifed semi truck and trailer. She turned the radio off and crept along with the rest of the traffic. As she neared the accident scene, it became evident that the pile-up had happened quite a while ago. There were no emergency vehicles on the scene, just the Highway Patrol and a clean-up crew. Hannah stared straight ahead in passing; she didn't want to see any evidence of death. Having lost her appetite, she drove straight to the morgue instead of stopping to eat, and stood waiting at the loading center for the transport body.

She signed the paperwork and opened the back hatch. Though it was a typical-looking station wagon from the outside, albeit with heavily-tinted side and rear windows, the inside had a sliding ramp and three seat-belt-like straps to hold the gurney in place.

Two men wheeled the body out, lifted, and slid it onto the ramp. Hannah crawled up into the back, secured it with the straps, and closed the back hatch. "Thank you," she said to the men.

The one fellow nodded. The other walked away. "I'm surprised they didn't get you an escort."

"What?" Hannah looked at him. "Why? No, never mind," she said. "I'd rather not know."

"I hear ya," the man said.

Hannah got in behind the wheel and backed the station wagon out of the dock. Richard had a knack for getting criminals. She had no idea if this was a man or a woman. As usual, she preferred knowing as little as possible about the person. Richard probably had the details, but had spared her.

She drove for about half an hour with her stomach growling and decided she needed to eat, no matter what, and pulled into a diner. She parked off to the side, but in a spot where she figured she could still see the station wagon, got out, and locked the doors. A bright-eyed young woman behind the counter greeted her with a smile.

"Table or the counter?"

"The counter's fine," Hannah said. She sat down and picked up a menu. The prices were good. "I'll have the cheeseburger and fries."

"Coffee good?"

Coffee, a dollar and a quarter for just one cup. "No, just water. Thank you."

Three teenagers parked next to the station wagon, got out, and for whatever reason, tried looking through the tinted windows. Hannah shook her head. They came in laughing. Hannah drank half a glass of water. It was so cold and tasted so good. "Is this well water?" she asked.

The waitress nodded and refilled her glass. "It's our claim to fame here in Hobuk, good well water."

Hannah smiled. "Well, I'm hoping you're known for your cheeseburgers and fries too. Are they real fries?"

"You betcha."

One of the teenagers made a point of talking loudly. "Whatever's in the station wagon looks like a body."

Hannah sighed. "Yeah, right. That's my car. It's nothing but drapes."

"Shit."

Hannah ate her lunch, which she deemed most tasty, paid and left a tip. "Thank you. I'll stop again next time I'm in town." The ride from there to the funeral parlor was quiet, no accidents and no incidents. Hannah hummed softly as she drove along. At times, she almost forgot she had a dead person camped out practically on her shoulders, and perhaps a notorious criminal at that.

"Everyone deserves a decent burial," Richard always said.

Hannah wondered: if she knew the crime and the person was indeed guilty, would she refuse to work on them? Would she say no on principle? "That's why I *don't* want to know," she said out loud.

Richard had the loading dock doors open when she pulled in. She backed the station wagon down the ramp and he and Jeb unloaded the body. "You're dismissed," Richard said, and smiled, meaning she was done for the day. "I'll need you early tomorrow. We have calling hours at two, and a private service for this one here at eleven. Both need your expertise."

Hannah nodded.

"Oh, by the way, the Gingrich family sent this for you." When he handed her an envelope, she looked at him. "Go ahead, I already opened it. It's okay. They insisted."

Inside was a crisp fifty-dollar bill.

"Remember the widow woman's hair you did, the one that...."

Hannah remembered. It was the woman with Alzheimer's. "Um, how do I thank them?"

"I already did. They said they'd never forget your kindness. Consider it a bonus and enjoy!"

Hannah climbed into her truck and fought back tears. She'd never gotten money handed to her before when she needed it, nor did she expect it. "We've got a hay fund going, Billy Bob," she said to herself, and waved to Richard. "One more errand to run, the tack store."

Her good luck continued. There were pieces of an old harness that had been there forever. "The owner said he'd take anything. He doesn't want them back and they're drying out. He said if anyone looks at them, get an offer."

The price marked on them was seventy-five dollars. "Will he take ten?"

"Maybe, probably."

"Do you have to call him?"

"No, ten dollars is fine."

Hannah went back to the truck and got two five dollar bills out of her wallet and change out of her ashtray for tax. "How much for the calendars?"

"Oh, you can have one. Next year's will be in soon."

Hannah lugged all the harness pieces out to the truck and was on her way. As she passed the neighbor's farm, the young woman was sitting on the porch and waved. Hannah waved back and then shook her head. The girl looked so sad. "If I had more time, I'd stop. But I've got pies to bake."

Lucinda and Colleen had offered to help, even though they knew better. "I'm a lone baker," Hannah said, laughing. When it came to baking, help got in her way.

Hannah stopped the truck and backed into the neighbor's drive. "How are you doing?"

"Oh, okay. Just sitting out here."

"Where's Douglas?"

"Working late."

Hannah nodded.

"We loved your pie."

"Thank you." Hannah hesitated. "I'm baking some more tonight. Do you want to come help?"

"Really? Yes! Let me get my jacket."

Chapter Twenty-Eight

Not surprisingly, Patty grew up in the city, and welcomed the opportunity to talk, to tell her story, so to speak. Hannah drove down to the barn so this very pregnant young woman would not have to forge the hill. Patty sat with the door open, chatting, while Hannah brought Billy Bob in and fed him.

"He's so pretty!"

"I know. Thank you." She gave Billy Bob a pat on his shoulder. "Behave. I'll be back down later to check on you. Watch for your friends."

"Friends?" Patty asked.

"Oh, you know, uh, critters. They come by and seem to entertain him, his being alone and all."

"Is it hard him being alone?"

Hannah sighed. "In a perfect world, he'd have a stable buddy and pasture mate. Maybe someday, it's hard being alone period."

"Are you divorced?"

Hannah smiled sadly. "No, just abandoned. But let's not go there." She brightened her smile. "I have to haul in the drapes, then it is pie baking time!" The drapes were almost completely dry. Only the bottoms where they'd been hemmed were damp. Hannah liked the colors. The dark green had become a lot lighter in color and the lime green were a lot darker. They almost matched. She laid them out in the living room across the couch.

Her earlier plan had been to bake ten pies. "Let's do eleven. You watch me and then you're going to make your own," she told Patty.

"Cool."

Hannah chuckled. "What kind do you want? Apple, peach, or Boysenberry Surprise?"

"I don't know if Douglas would like Boysenberry Surprise. How about peach?"

They made the pie dough first. Hannah showed Patty how to cut in the shortening using two knives. "I've always done it this way," Hannah said. "Don't cut the shortening too small. You want it pea size." They rolled out the dough and cut eleven bottom crusts. Using the pie pans for measuring, Hannah cut the dough about half an inch from the edge all around. "We'll roll out the tops once we get them filled."

They set pie pans all over the kitchen counters, on top of the little fridge, and the kitchen desk, and sat down to peel the apples and peaches. "What goes in the Boysenberry Surprise besides boysenberry?"

"Usually whatever I have," Hannah said. "Raisins, nuts, any leftover fruit. I actually put shredded carrots in one once. Charlie liked it, but I didn't. All I tasted was carrots. Maybe if I'd cooked them first. I thought an hour in the oven would be enough. Do you want to call Douglas to let him know you're here?"

"I called him on my cell phone. He's going to pick me up." Patty watched how Hannah peeled the apples, slicing the skins so thin, and tried doing the same. "What kind of apples are these?"

"Those are Winesap and these are Rome. I like mixing them. Those ones right there are Gala. I'm going to use them for the sugarless pie I'm making for Cal Able. They're sweeter naturally."

"You mean, 'Cal Able, to put you in a car today?'"

"Yep, that's him."

"How'd you get started making pies for people?"

"Well, actually, I'm just getting started. Did you want some tea?"

"Is it decaf?"

"Yes." Hannah put on the kettle and sat back down to peeling.

"You say your husband left. Where did he go?"

Hannah shrugged. "I don't know."

"Do you ever hear from him?"

"No." Hannah picked up another apple, peeled it within seconds, and reached for another.

"So, you've been a farmer all your life. What kind of farming did you do?"

"Well, we grew all our own vegetables. And we did beef cows and dairy cows. Raised pigs, chickens, grew our own hay and corn. I loved it when we filled the corn crib every fall. It was a good feeling, like having a full pantry. And then...." She hesitated. "And then we got talked into growing soybeans, *nothing* but soybeans."

Patty looked at her, noting her sudden change in tone.

164

"Let me just say, if I never see another soybean for the rest of my life it would be too soon."

"They didn't grow?"

"Oh, they grew, and so did the demand for equipment to harvest them. Then we had to buy in corn and hay, and...."

The phone rang and Hannah excused herself to answer it. "Hello." It was Lucinda.

"It is too late to order another pie?"

"Um...." Hannah assessed the dough, the fruit. "Maybe an apple one. Why, who wants it?"

"Dave. We're down at the Honky Tonk. He said he tried phoning you to order one but there was no answer."

"Tell him I'll deliver it tomorrow."

"Here, he wants to talk to you."

"No, don't. Wait. Oh hi, Dave."

"How are you?"

"I'm good. Thank you. How about you?"

"Great, now that I'm talking to you."

Hannah stared out the window. "Lucinda says you want a pie."

"Yes, if it's not too late."

"I should be able to. I'll drop it off tomorrow. I'd better get going."

"Have a good evening."

"You too." Click.

She sat back down and sighed.

"Boyfriend?"

Hannah smiled. "Keep peeling."

Patty laughed. When the tea kettle whistled, Hannah made them both a cup of tea, then mixed up the dry ingredients for the pies. "Are you hungry? Do you want something to eat?"

"I'm always hungry." Patty tapped her pregnant belly.

Hannah looked into the fridge and then the cupboards. "Fried egg sandwich or peanut butter and jelly?"

"Fried egg sandwich? I don't think I've ever had one."

"Well, then you're in for a treat," Hannah said, and made them each one. Hannah ate hers while filling the pie shells. Patty devoured hers.

"How do you know how much sugar to add?"

"I use about three-quarters of a cup."

"And the flour for on top of the apples?"

"I wing it." She sprinkled cinnamon next. "Use lots of cinnamon." She put a crust-sized dough ball down in front of Patty and had her roll it out. "Very good. Make it just a little thinner though."

Hannah finished her tea, then set the oven to preheat. Every time she turned the oven on, she said a silent prayer that it would light. Who knew how old this stove was? It lit.

"We'll bake yours with the first batch. That way it'll be done in time. If it's not, I'll run it down in the morning." Hannah had her roll out a top crust and then showed her how to place it gently on top, folded in half and then unfolded. "Be very careful. You don't want the crust to tear." It tore. "That's okay, we can fix it." Hannah had her dip her fingers in water and pat and pinch the crust back together. "See, good as new."

Patty sat back proudly.

Hannah demonstrated how to cut around the edge and fold the top crust under to join the bottom crust. "Now here's the fun part." Using the blunt end of a bread knife, Hannah demonstrated how to hold her fingers on each side, pressing down softly while peeling back the crust to form a perfect fluted edge. "Now you just need to make some air holes. What's your last name?"

"Jamison."

"Then make a big "J"."

Hannah rolled out the next batch of top crusts for the peach pies. Patty put them on, cut the excess off, and Hannah made the fluted edges. The oven fit six pies, but Hannah figured since she had to do three batches anyway, she'd just do four, four, and four. With room to breathe, they'd cook more evenly. She set the timer and started cleaning up. Patty got up to help. "No, sit," Hannah told her. "Rest."

"You sound like Douglas."

Hannah smiled.

"Do you have children, Hannah?"

"No." Hannah looked at her. "We tried. It just wasn't meant to be."

"I'm sorry."

Hannah smiled. "I think I'll officially adopt you."

"Okay." When Patty yawned, Hannah insisted she go lie down on the bed in the living room, and covered her up with an afghan. It was too warm for a fire in the fireplace with the oven going, but covering her up, just felt right.

"Go to sleep, take a nap."

Hannah finished rolling out the top crusts for the Boysenberry Surprise pies. She stretched the filling with the rest of the apples and peaches, added some raisins, and set the pies aside. She washed up all the bowls, put all the peelings into the compost bucket, and wiped down the table. Half hour into the pies baking, the house smelled heavenly.

She checked on Patty, who was sound asleep and snoring softly, glanced at the clock, and decided to go bed Billy Bob down for the night. He was happy to see her and nickered. She gave him a big hug, smiling, then turned and sobered. There stood the old man.

"Did you get my ashes?"

Hannah's blood drained from her face. She'd forgotten. She'd never given it a thought today, what with hurrying to run errands and then going for the body in the station wagon, and then....

The old man shook his head. "I knew I couldn't count on you."

"Now that's not true."

The old man threw up his hands in disgust and walked away. "Probably too busy and forgot."

Hannah stared at his back as he disappeared. "I'm sorry," she said, and sat down woefully on a bale of hay. How could I forget? She drew a deep breath and sighed. When she turned back to Billy Bob he seemed to be looking at her in the same accusing, disappointed way. "Where have you been?" he seemed to say. "I've been home by myself all day."

Tears welled up in her eyes. "Just when I thought I was having a good day." She sat there for a while, staring at the floor, then picked herself up and cleaned Billy Bob's stall and gave him a quick grooming. "I'm sorry," she said. "Once I get everything done, we'll have more time." She topped off his water buckets and gave him hay for the night, then started back up the hill. The old man was standing underneath one of the fruit trees with Bessie at his side.

"I'll get them tomorrow," she said.

He shook his head.

Patty was still sleeping when Hannah got back up to the house. The timer went off for the pies. Hannah took them out and put the next batch in. A knock on the front door woke Patty and startled Hannah. Thinking about the old man, she'd forgotten that Douglas would be coming by to pick up Patty.

Hannah opened the door and let him in. He was surprised at the bed in the living room, but not that Patty had been napping. He gave her a hug. "How's my girl?" he asked.

Hannah smiled. They looked so in love, so attentive to one another. She turned and bit at her bottom lip, willing herself not to well up in tears again. "I've got a box in the back. I'll put your pie in it."

Douglas raved about how pretty the pie was, how delicious it smelled, and even stuck his finger into the center to taste it. "Thank you, Hannah," Patty said.

Douglas helped her out to the truck and came back for the pie. "I want to thank you too. Patty gets awfully lonely out here."

"I know," Hannah said. "I know the life."

Douglas nodded. "I hear you don't have a husband, Hannah. Are you a widow? I want you to know that if you ever need help around here, you just let me know."

Hannah managed to shake her head and smile, and then to nod, to thank him, but all she could think about was the term widow. Why would he ask that? She stood on the porch and waved as they backed out the driveway. A *widow*?

Wouldn't she know if Charlie was dead? Wouldn't someone notify her? Wouldn't she sense it? Is that why I haven't heard from him? She stared up at the North Star and made a wish. "Please don't be dead, Charlie. Please. I don't know where you're at or what you're doing or who you're with. But please, don't be dead."

Chapter Twenty-Nine

Hannah went to bed thinking about Charlie dead, and woke up thinking about Charlie dead. "Maybe that's why I've never heard from him but that one time from Fresno. Maybe he's been dead all along." She made a pot of coffee and bundled up to go down to the barn. They'd had another killing frost. "Well, at least I won't have to mow again." Her boots crunched into the grass.

Billy Bob nickered, his breath swirling in puffy clouds. Weather was going to be a mystery since Hannah hadn't watched the news. For all she knew, it could rain or snow today, though to look at the sky she'd bet it was going to be a sunny day. She hoped the fella for the pies came on time.

168

She needn't worry. Hank's truck was sitting in the drive when she walked back up the hill. "Morning!" He was a man of few words. No sooner had he paid for the pies and laid them on his passenger seat, he whipped out a fork and started eating one. "Damn, these are good."

"I'm going to make some custard ones next week."

"Put me down for one."

"One custard and one fruit."

"No, one custard and two fruit."

Hannah thanked him and smiled. "I'll see you Friday." She loaded up Raven's friend's pies and the ones for Dave and Big Jim, figuring she'd drop them off on the way to work. This way she wouldn't have to worry about making lame excuses to Dave about needing to leave right away. She could keep her truck door open and the engine running. Dave worked into the wee hours of the morning at the bar, so maybe he was the type to sleep in. Maybe she could just knock on the door and leave the pie on his porch.

Before she left, she turned Billy Bob out into his pasture, gave him hay and water, and picked his stall. She was well ahead of schedule. She hadn't given much thought to the "gangster" at work or what kind of haircut he would need, but thought about him now for some reason. "It's probably a good thing I don't watch the news. I'd have known."

She dropped Big Jim's pie off first, knowing he'd be open at eight. He paid her with a crisp ten dollar bill. "I just minted them," he said.

Hannah chuckled. "Have a great day. If you want more, let me know." She left him a piece of paper with her name and phone number on it and headed for Dave's farm. It was a nice drive. The sun was bright, the sky blue. Dave's place was well cared for. When she got out of the truck, she saw him coming from the barn and waved.

"I brought you your pie."

"Thank you," he said, and kissed her on the cheek. "Good morning! Do you want some breakfast?"

"No, thank you, I ate already. I'm on my way to work." The truck was running as planned, the door was open....

He paid her.

"I'll see you at Raven and Tom's tomorrow night."

When he smiled, Hannah hesitated leaving. He hadn't shaved yet this morning and had a whole different look; more rugged, more hard-working farmer and less bartender-like.

"What?" he said, in response to her expression.

169

"Nothing." She waved and got into her truck.

Dave smiled. "This *is* the way to a man's heart you know," he said, holding up the pie. "Though you already have my heart, Hannah."

"Enjoy the pie." Next stop was at Raven's friend's house. She wasn't awake yet, but the house maid was there and expecting her.

"Thank you, Miss." She handed Hannah an envelope.

"Gracias."

Hannah had thought about bringing Cal Able's pie too, but figured the car dealership wouldn't be open yet. She wished now that she had, as his big Cadillac was sitting out front. She honked in passing. Not that there was enough room anyway since she didn't want to put a pie on the floor.

There were two cars in the funeral parlor parking lot when she arrived for work; one had "unmarked cop car" written all over it. When she walked inside, she was greeted by two men in dark suits.

"Hello," she said.

Both men nodded and said in unison, "Ma'am."

She looked at Richard, standing between them.

"Hannah, do you have identification with you?"

She nodded and produced her driver's license. Both men examined it. "All right, let's get this done," the one said.

Hannah was ushered into the work room where the "gangster" lay. She'd expected him to be older. He appeared to be in his forties. He did not die under good circumstances. There was a permanent grimace on his face.

The two men watched her. "He has nice hair," she said, for lack of anything better to say. "Is he to be done up completely."

"Yes." Both men nodded, arms folded, legs spread military style.

"Okay." Hannah rubbed her hands together for effect. "Then let's do it."

The table had a drop-down head support, which made washing hair over the basin a quick and easy process, the gurney on wheels. She was shown a photo. The man's hair was slightly longer now, probably prison time. "It'll need to be cut."

Both men nodded again. Hannah cut it the way it had been cut before, same style, same length, and gave the man a shave. He was rather handsome. Because of his good looks, Hannah imagined him having a pretty-boy gangster-like name. So sad, she thought, to have taken the path you took, the lifestyle you chose. There was an indentation on his ring finger.

Do you have a wife? Children? No, I don't want to know, she kept telling herself. His fingernails were accustomed to being manicured. They needed only to be buffed. Hannah glanced at the clock. The man's service was set for eleven. No one milled about upstairs.

"All done," she said, and stepped back.

"Thank you."

Apparently the two men were going to stay with the body; when Hannah left the room, they remained in their on-guard position. Richard was in his office. "I don't want to know," she said, when he looked up, her mantra.

"I figured as much. As soon as the service is over...."

"What service? No one's here."

"The priest is coming."

"Ah."

Hannah had another body to attend to, but first things first. "Richard, remember when I asked you about the Brubaker ashes?"

"Yes." He sat back, shaking his head. "I phoned the guy, the son. Talk about a flaming asshole. According to him, he is out of the country and did not appreciate being contacted. I told him I didn't appreciate him storing his father's ashes here all these years, free of charge, that if he didn't want them, he should put them in a mausoleum, and he started swearing at me. I should send him a bill."

"No, you should just let me take the ashes. That way...."

"I can't. He says he wants them."

Hannah stared.

"I doubt I'll ever actually see him or any money to pay for storing them here, but...."

Hannah sat down, imagining the conversation she'd be having with the old man, his disappointment.

"I told him I would hold them a month. He's supposed to be back in the states in a couple of weeks."

A month? Hannah sighed. "And if he doesn't come, then what? What would you do with them then, after the month I mean?"

Richard shrugged. "Nothing. They'd just sit there."

Hannah stared out the window, half expecting the old man to be outside looking in and shaking his head at her. "I want those ashes,

Richard. They belong on the farm. His son's not going to take them there. He doesn't even own the place now. I do."

Richard held up his hands. "What do you want me to do?"

"I don't know. Nothing illegal or unethical," Hannah said, motioning to the back room. "Can we substitute the ashes with…?" They both turned, as a priest in full regalia appeared in the doorway. Apparently the gangster was going out in style.

"Father," Richard said.

Hannah lowered her head in respect, but stopped Richard from leaving. "What you don't know, you don't know, right? Then you don't know. Actually, no one would know. You know. I might not do anything, right?"

Richard looked at her. "Okay…?" She wasn't making any sense.

"Just say right."

Richard hesitated and nodded. "Right."

"Thank you."

Chapter Thirty

As soon as Hannah got home, she checked on Billy Bob. His hay was gone, but he'd hardly drunk any water. "Are you okay, big guy?" She gave him some more hay and walked inside the pasture to check for fresh manure piles. There were plenty, and of healthy standards. She looked up at the sky. "At some point, I'm really going to have to start listening to the weather." There were dark billowing clouds overhead. In a downpour, she would have trouble driving the truck down here again, for fear of getting stuck or tearing up the drive. Once upon a time it was a gravel path, now it was just grass.

"I'll be back in half an hour," she told him and headed for Cal Able's and Raven's to deliver the rest of the pies. Cal Able was with a customer, but excused himself and rushed over to Hannah. He took a big whiff of the pie.

"If it's as good as it smells, I'm hooked."

Hannah smiled. "I'll leave it on your desk. I'll be home tomorrow if your men want to come by for the scrap."

"What about the tractor?"

Hannah shook her head. "I'm thinking I'll hang on to it for a while."

Cal Able flashed her a big grin and hurried back to his customer. Raven's delivery was next. She answered the door in her Pilates workout outfit.

"You're coming tomorrow, right?"

"Yep, I'll see you then. I thought I'd bring some corn pudding. Will that go with what you're having?"

"You don't have to bring anything. But yes, it would go perfectly."

"How many people are you having?"

"Fifteen or so."

"I'll see you then. Dress up or regular?"

"In between."

Billy Bob seemed reluctant to come in when she got home. There was still some daylight, so Hannah put his bridle on him, climbed on bareback, and took him for a walk around the property. It was nice when passing the root cellar to know that it was all cleaned out. "Yes, Mom, Spic-n-Span." It was nice when passing the orchard to see all the trees pruned in anticipation of next year. Everywhere she looked, it was nice.

She looked for the carrier pigeon and his friend, but they were nowhere to be seen. It was too early for the spirit horses to appear, so it was just Billy Bob and her. She stroked his mane. "You're a good boy." She let him graze off and on in low grass areas and when the sun started to go down, headed back toward the barn.

Even though she didn't have to work tomorrow, she wanted to come up with some ashes by morning and swap them out for the old man's. One thing she noticed when she'd opened the container at the funeral parlor and looked inside, in addition to their being small bone fragments, it did not have a wood-fire scent. "That makes sense." Bodies were cremated using gas furnaces. There would be no wood smell at all, or wood ash period, for that matter.

She gave Billy Bob a good grooming and walked up to the house in darkness. "I'll have to get a second flashlight and leave one in the barn, batteries too." It was so dark; she practically stepped on the old man.

"Did you get my ashes?"

"I'll have them tomorrow," Hannah said, and just like that he disappeared. "Bones, I need bones," she said to herself. "It's a shame I don't know anyone in the restaurant business. Some chewed off T-Bones would be great."

She walked inside her house and sat down at her kitchen desk. "Soup bones would be cheap. That's an idea. I can even make some stock with them first." That became the plan. Back out she went and into town to the grocery store. "It's a good thing I don't live far, I'd be spending a fortune in gas."

She ran into her old neighbors from the apartments at the grocery store and chatted with them for a few minutes, then took off in search of bones. She only had two large pots, which would each hold about four big soup bones each. She figured while she was at the store, she'd buy what she needed to make the corn pudding. She also bought two cans of tuna, a fresh loaf of bread, a box of corn flakes, and a half gallon of milk.

"No milk with fish," her mom used to say. "It's not a good mix."

But I'm not mixing them, Mom, Hannah thought, and smiled. How many of those old wives tales did her mom pass on over the years? Old wives tales - such an odd expression. Old wives and widows.... She listened to the radio on the way home and heard the weather forecast for the first time in days. They were in for partly cloudy skies this weekend, mid fifties for the highs, and frost tonight, Saturday, and Sunday nights. There was a forty-percent chance of rain Sunday afternoon.

She thought about what to wear to Raven and Tom's. Maybe she'd wear her hair up. She tried to remember where she'd put her hair clip. Since she was going to be busy cooking and burning bones, she decided to drive down and around to the barn now to check on Billy Bob and bed him down for the night. She left the truck lights on so she could see and while she was there, grabbed an old barrel lid. She didn't want to be burning bones in the fireplace, figuring it would leave a godawful smell in the house.

She made tuna fish salad; she still had some mayo and sweet pickles, a tiny piece of onion. It tasted good on the fresh bread. "It'll taste even better tomorrow." She wished she had baked an extra pie. She put the soup bones on to cook, seasoned them with salt and pepper for good stock, and went into the living room and felt the hems of the drapes. They were totally dry.

She debated whether or not to put the dark pairs on the front windows and the two light pairs on the side windows, or the other way around. She held them up to the different windows. The west window would get the most light, the most wind, the windows were not airtight. This side would also get the most snow buildup. Color wouldn't matter from outside. The insulation thickness on the drapes was all the same. She sat down on the couch, drapes in hand, and had an idea.

"I'll cut each panel down the center and sew the light panel on the insides. That way they'll all match." She folded two panels back to see how they'd look and smiled. "That's pretty." She thought about what she could use for the tie-backs. "Now where's my sewing kit? Where did I put it?"

She didn't recall seeing it upstairs. "Thank heaven." She didn't want to have to undo the heat barrier. She phoned Colleen? "Do you remember seeing my sewing kit?"

"Yes, I put it in the cupboard over the stove in the kitchen. By the way, Jason said to let you know we'd pick you up tomorrow night if you want."

Hannah laughed. "What, does he think I'm going to get tipsy?"

"No," Colleen chuckled, and then lowered her voice. "I think he thinks you'd let Dave take you home then."

"Oh... I see." Hannah sighed, and lowered her voice in the same whispering way. "Thanks for telling me, girlfriend. I think I'll drive."

The two of them laughed.

"So what do you have planned tonight?"

"Well, I'm going to work on the drapes." Hannah told her about her idea and when they hung up, located her sewing kit and checked to see how much white thread she had. She decided she probably had enough to do two sets, and there was enough beige to do the other two. "Who'll know?" The insulation side was off white, both would work. She's use white for the front two windows, where people could see in from the porch, and the beige for the side windows.

She had a taste for another tuna fish sandwich, so she had that first, then gathered some twigs and started a fire in the barrel lid out in her front yard, nearby, but not too close, so she could tend to it. She made a mental note to pick up some more newspapers from the laundromat. She was getting low.

When she had the little fire burning good and hot she went inside for the soup bones, drained them well, and wished herself luck. "Odds are they should burn." She placed one of the bones smack in the middle of the fire. It sizzled and hissed. Then she put some more twigs around it. She hoped by using twigs and not logs that there would be no wood scent. All she could smell at the moment was the night.

"What are you doing?" the old man asked, appearing out of nowhere.

"Well." She placed another bone on the fire and then another.

"Don't you have anything better to do?"

"Actually." She looked at him. "I'm doing this to help out a friend."

"Burning bones?"

"Yes, see I'm doing it out here in front of the house and not in the backyard, because I don't want the spirit horses to be frightened by the fire. I don't want them to smell the smoke either, so I picked this here spot because it only catches the wind coming out of the west, which is away from them and away from the barn. I'm using twigs instead of logs, even though logs would burn hotter. I had to use newspaper to get it started, but I don't think there will be any paper residue when it's all said and done. It's burning nice. This should work."

"You sure do talk a lot."

Hannah smiled. "I can't get your ashes unless I replace them with something."

The old man looked at her, letting this all sink in. She'd called him a friend. He motioned to the fire. "That's what you're going to replace them with?"

"Yep."

He nodded and smiled. "City girl."

"Old ghost."

The two of them sat on the porch step and watched the fire burn.

Chapter Thirty-One

Hannah awoke bright and early, bundled up, and headed down over the hill to feed Billy Bob. "It's going to be a great day!" she told him. "It's just you and me, big guy!" Since she didn't have to go to work there was no rush, so she left him to eat in his stall and went back up to the house. With coffee cup in hand, she walked out to check on the bone ash. When the fire had all but burned down last night, she turned the barrel lid over to cover it. She was sure it wouldn't entice critters, the bones having "burned to death" but wanted to be sure.

There was a nice little pile, probably just enough to suffice. She decided to scoop it up now, to be safe, and went in search of a container. An old candy tin looked to be the right size. The ash had no smell, thanks to the frost, but was damp. She took the container inside and spread the ash onto a cookie sheet and put it in the oven on low.

"I can just see it all now, the kid opens the container and it's all moldy and mildewy." The kid? She laughed. "He's probably my age."

She thought about the old man, how he sat with her last night for the longest time, not saying anything, not moving, just watching the flames. And then, after a while, how he just disappeared.

She heard some chatter outside the window and took a look. The carrier pigeon and his friend were having words with a red squirrel. The squirrel looked like a boxer, up on his hind legs ready to throw a punch, jaws full. She clapped her hands, shooing all of them.

Cal Able phoned, raving about the pie. "I've eaten half of it already."

"Well, let's not defeat the purpose. It still has natural sugar from the fruit in it."

"How much do you sell these for, darlin'?"

"Ten dollars, but that one was on the house. If I'm going by, there's no charge for delivery. If I have to make a special trip, it's an additional five dollars, regardless of how many pies."

"You drive a hard bargain. Now, you sure I can't talk you into selling me that old tractor?"

"Yes, positive. I'm going to hang onto it, I think, at least for a little while."

"My men will be by for the scrap around ten. Is that a good time?"

"Perfect." Hannah made her bed and cleaned up the kitchen, then went down to turn Billy Bob out and do his stall. He bucked and played in the pasture for a few minutes, feeling his oats and the cool morning air, then took to grazing on the little nubbins of grass that were left. "I'll stake you out later," she said, throwing him some hay.

She hauled the manure to the compost pile on her makeshift sled and gazed out over the spirit horses' still frosty pasture. No one would ever believe her, as there wasn't a hoof print in site, but she knew they'd been there last night. She could sense it. She hauled the sled back to the barn and stood looking around.

She took a deep breath. She loved the smell of a barn. "I'd like it even better if I had a winter's stock of hay." Once the scrap was all

177

removed, she planned to.... When a thought crossed her mind, she hurried up to the house and phoned Cal Able back.

"Do you have any old wood pallets I can have?"

"For free?"

"Yes, for free." Hannah laughed. "They don't have to be perfect. I'll need about six of them. They're just for stacking hay up off the cement."

"I'll see what I can do. If they come from the mill, I'll have to charge you a delivery fee you know."

Hannah laughed. "Then I'll pick them up."

"Have a good day, darlin'!"

"You too."

Hannah hung up the phone and paused. She had so many things she wanted to accomplish; she didn't know where to start. "Put one foot in front of the other," her mom used to say. Hannah stepped her way across the kitchen tile, almost as if she was dancing, playing hopscotch, and sat down at her kitchen desk.

"Hello, desk," she said, and laughed at herself. "Hello, lamp." She looked at her to-do list. She looked at her calendar. Her first mortgage payment was due in three days. She took out her checkbook and looked at her balance. She was okay. When she deposited her next paycheck on Monday, there'd be enough with a few dollars left over. It would be a lean week for her, but she was used to lean weeks. Her main concern now was raising enough money to put up hay for now through the winter.

Billy Bob was an easy keeper. But even so and with his getting some grass now, he was being fed better than a third to a half a bale a day. And he wasn't wasting any. The hay she'd been buying was three-fifty a bale. They were big bales and she liked the quality. Better yet, Billy Bob liked it. Half a bale a day for five months, and if she could swing buying seventy- five bales, she could get a price break of twenty-five cents a bale. That would get her through March.

Charlie used to be able to load fifty-two bales on the truck. She wouldn't attempt that. "But I can certainly get it done in two trips, that's for sure." If delivered, it would cost more. She chuckled. "It's all about delivery." They'd help her load it there. She'd just have to unload and stack it herself when she got home. She pictured Billy Bob eagerly watching her unload each and every bale, licking his chops and grabbing a mouthful each time she passed by.

She had the fifty dollars she'd gotten as a tip, plus the seventy-five she'd get from Cal Able's men today. When she heard someone pull into the driveway, she walked out onto the front porch. It was her neighbor Patty.

Hannah smiled. She looked so cute driving her husband's pickup, all pregnant and sitting behind the wheel.

"I'm going to town. Do you need anything?"

"No, thank you."

"The pie was delicious."

"I knew it would be. You made it with love."

Patty waved. "Thanks again."

Hannah caught sight of the little boy way off in the distance, playing ball with Bessie's puppy. Who could ask for a nicer day, she thought. "Not me, I'll take it." She glanced around the living room, thinking again about the drapes and decided to start cutting them now. If the weather forecast held out, she'd sew them together tomorrow afternoon when the rain hit. She had two cut evenly down the middle when Cal Able's men arrived. She went out onto the porch and motioned for them to go down and around the barn. They had a huge dump truck. She was glad the drive behind the barn was still dry and hard.

As they started past her on the porch, she saw the six wood pallets in the back of the dump truck and smiled. They were rickety-looking, but they'd do. Hannah turned off the oven and walked down over the hill. The two men had unloaded the pallets and were already inside the barn. They had a list. Hannah looked it over. "Yep, that's it."

One of the men gave her seventy-five dollars while the other started loading up. "Wow, look at this!"

His partner frowned at him.

"Never appear to be too interested in an item," Hannah said, jokingly.

The two men laughed. "You got that right." They stood examining an old wood-spoked steel-rimmed wagon wheel. "Are you interested in selling it?"

Hannah shrugged. "Could be."

The man phoned Cal, described the wagon wheel, and pressed the phone to his chest. "Twenty-five dollars."

Hannah held her hand out. "Sold."

The men loaded up the rest of the scrap metal, didn't find anything else of interest, and were on their way. Hannah topped off Billy Bob's water buckets, gave him some hay, and walked up to the house. It was almost lunch time, so she made herself a tuna sandwich and looking into the container at what little that was left, finished it off with another half sandwich.

Viewing hours were scheduled at the funeral parlor, so this would be a good time for her to swap the ashes. She'd be in and out the back door in the blink of an eye. She took the ashes out of the oven, pleased with how dry they were, and put them into the candy container. There were even bone fragments to be seen. No one would ever know.

She washed up and was headed for the truck, container in hand, when she glanced ahead and saw the old man sitting in the truck "What, don't you trust me?" she said.

"I just want to make sure we get the right ashes. I don't want to scatter any soup bones."

Hannah laughed. "Here, hold these."

The container went right through him. In fact, at times along the way, the old man was there, and then he wasn't. The funeral parlor parking lot was full. "Did anyone here see you before?"

The old man shook his head. "I don't know. No one would talk to me."

"Good," Hannah thought. She led the way, carrying the container under her arm. When she entered the building, Richard was standing at the other end of the hall. He looked at her. She motioned to the container and he nodded.

"Does he know?" the old man asked.

"Yes, in a way."

"Guess I misjudged him too."

The old man seemed fascinated with all the urns. Some were quite fancy. His was plain. Hannah hadn't given thought to needing a container to put the burned bones in so she could make the switch. She looked around. A wastebasket seemed somewhat sacrilegious, but would have to do.

She dumped the phantom contents into the bottom, slowly and carefully, so as not to lose any of it to stirred-up dust, and opened the old man's urn. He looked inside.

"You ready?"

He shrugged.

Hannah dumped the ashes into the candy can a little at a time. It filled to the rim. She put the lid on tight. Then she filled the urn with the burned bones and put the urn back onto the shelf. The old man stood at her side.

"You okay?"

"I guess."

She hadn't given thought to this being traumatic for him, but apparently it was. "Do you want to sit down?"

He shook his head.

Right, dumb idea. "Let's go."

As they were walking out the back door, someone called Hannah's name. She glanced back. It was Jeb.

"Do you have a minute?"

"Not really," she said. "Why? What's up?"

"I need a favor."

Hannah paused. Last time he needed a favor he wanted to borrow money. "I really have to go, Jeb."

"Can you drop me off at Bill's garage? My car's ready."

"Uh...." The garage was only about a mile away, but....

"Come on. Richard won't even know I'm gone."

Hannah shook her head. He obviously couldn't see the old man standing at her side. "All right, let's go. I don't have much time." She walked to the truck, wondering how this was going to play out. Where would the old man sit?

"Was that thunder?"

"I didn't hear anything," Jeb said.

By the time they reached the truck, the old man had disappeared. Hannah hesitated. She couldn't just leave without him, could she? She glanced all around. He was nowhere to be seen.

"It's not supposed to rain until tomorrow," Jeb said, plopping himself into the passenger seat.

Hannah hesitated. The old man had appeared at the funeral home before on his own. He obviously knew how to get there, so he should be able to get himself home. "Right?" she said out loud.

"Right, what?" Jeb said. "Are you okay? Are those cookies?"

Hannah batted his hand away. "They're not for you."

Jeb laughed. "Let's go, come on. Like I said, I don't want Richard to know I'm gone."

"Then you'd better duck, 'cause...." Richard was standing at the front door, greeting visitors.

Jeb hit the floor.

Hannah waved in passing and pulled out onto the highway. It was then that she glanced in the rearview mirror and saw the old man sitting in the truck bed, his back to the window and arms spread wide, gripping the sides.

She laughed.

"Can I sit up now?" Jeb asked.

"Yes."

She glanced in her mirror again. Okay, silly question, she thought, can I drive fast, or will I lose him? She crept along at twenty miles an hour.

"What's wrong with you?"

"Nothing, the truck's missing. I think I need new sparkplugs."

"It sounds fine."

"What, so you're a mechanic now? What are we doing going to Bill's then?"

Jeb laughed. The mile ride to the garage took more than five minutes. He got out shaking his head.

"I'll see you Monday," Hannah said, relieved the old man was still with them.

"Can you wait? I want to make sure it's ready."

"I thought you said it was."

"I did. Just wait, I'll be right back."

Hannah sighed. The old man appeared in the passenger seat next to her, looking none the worse for wear. "You need to learn how to say no."

Hannah looked at him. "I know how to say no."

"Yeah, right." He stared out the window.

Jeb was back in a flash. "Problem."

Hannah's shoulders slumped. "Now what?"

"He won't let me take it unless I pay the whole bill."

"And I take it you're short?"

He nodded. "Twenty two dollars and four cents."

Hannah sighed and reached into her pocket. "Here." She gave him two tens and two ones and fished into her ashtray for four pennies.

"Uh...."

Hannah looked at him.

"Can I have another ten? I need to pick up milk and bread for the kids."

Hannah gave him the additional ten. "I need you to pay me back this time, Jeb. I'm counting on this money, okay?"

He nodded. "Thanks, Hannah. You're the best."

Hannah watched him jog back inside the garage, and put her truck into gear. She looked at the old man. "Not one word out of you, you hear me. Not one."

Chapter Thirty-Two

There was a notice from the mailman posted on Hannah's front door when they arrived home. It was for a certified letter that she would have to pick up during post office hours. All it gave as a return address was a zip code; the same as her own.

"Well, it's a cinch it's not someone ordering pies."

Hannah shoved the piece of paper in her pocket and turned to the old man. "Well, how do we want to do this? Where do you want to...?"

He looked around. "I think I'd like to be out back."

"Do you mind if I check on my horse first?"

He shook his head. When she started down over the hill, the candy container of his ashes in hand, the old man lagged behind. Billy Bob nickered.

"Why, you little porker, you." He'd eaten all his hay and drained one of the water buckets. Hannah gave him a little more hay, filled his water bucket, and glanced at the blue sky. She waited for the old man.

"It's a nice day," she said.

"Yep."

Hannah paused. He seemed to need time.

"There's an old oak tree out back," he said. "I'm thinking I'd like to be there."

Hannah nodded.

"I'm also thinking I'd like to be over by the root cellar. That little shanty has brought a lot of comfort to me all these years here alone."

"We can do both," Hannah suggested.

"I also like the pasture where the horses graze."

"There's lots of ashes. We can put them all around. Do you want up by the house?"

"No, it was too lonely after Maggie died. I'd rather be outside."

"Okay."

"I'd like to be in the orchard too. I'll keep you company next harvest."

"All right." Hannah chuckled. "I promise not to talk too much."

The old man smiled.

"Where to first?"

"The oak tree."

He showed the way. The tree had to be over two hundred years old, with strong sprawling arms and a gnarly trunk. Hannah could see why it meant so much to the old man. She took the lid off the container and the two of them just stood there for a moment.

"Do you want to say anything?" she asked.

"Like what?"

"I don't know, like a eulogy or something."

"I had me a funeral."

"Okay. It just seems like we should say something though."

The old man shook his head. "I'll leave that up to you."

"All right." Hannah drew a deep breath, thinking, and then began. "Mr. Brubaker was…."

"Earl," he said. "My name is Earl."

"Okay." Hannah started over. "Earl Brubaker was a hard-working man. He was an honest man."

The old man nodded.

"He loved this farm and he worked it year after year."

"That I did."

"He loved his wife and he treated her good."

The old man wiped a tear from his eye.

"May he rest in peace."

"Amen."

Hannah sprinkled ash all around the perimeter of the tree and stood back and smiled. It felt good, her bringing him home. It felt right. The old man bent down and sifted some of the ashes through his fingers.

When he stood up, they walked to the pasture. "A little here and there," he said. Hannah dusted the pasture and watched as the breeze scattered the ash. It was as if it was taking it everywhere.

"Do you want some inside the root cellar or just around it?"

"Outside, don't want no dirt in there after all your cleaning."

Hannah smiled. She scattered ashes all around the root cellar and even some on the steps. The old man liked that. The orchard was next. "Any particular tree?"

He looked inside the container to see how much was left and shrugged. "The cherry trees are my favorite."

"Mine too." After Hannah scattered the rest of the ashes around the cherry trees there was just a little bit remaining. "Do you want to put the rest by the barn?"

"That's a good idea," he said, and walked slowly at her side. Billy Bob watched their every move.

Hannah emptied the rest at the barn entrance, and stood back.

"Thank you," the old man said. "I think I can rest in peace now. Thank you."

Chapter Thirty-Three

Hannah felt a little like Paul Bunyan as she approached the stand of dead elm trees on the side of her property. She'd dropped trees before, but Charlie was always somewhere nearby, taking down trees of his own. "What's the difference?" she said. "At least this way I won't have to yell, 'Oh no, look out!'" She laughed at herself, and from a safe clearance distance, the old man laughed too.

She started with the smallest tree. She'd chosen to leave Billy Bob out in his pasture during all this, figuring he'd be happier seeing what was going on and not just hear a huge thud from inside his stall. She revved up the chainsaw and planted her feet wide apart. The tree hit the ground after about twenty seconds. "Timber!!!"

Billy Bob barely raised his head. The second tree dropped just about the same way. It took a little more sawing, but not that much more work. She decided to saw the two trees into logs before going on and was just about done with the first tree when she caught sight of someone walking toward her. It was her neighbor Douglas.

"Holy crap, Hannah. All you had to do is say you needed help and I'd be here."

Hannah smiled. "Well, that's just it. I don't need help."

"I can see that."

Hannah sat down on one of the logs to take a break. "So what's up?"

"One of our cows is ailing."

"How so?"

"Well, it acts like it has a belly ache."

"Probably colic."

"So what do I do?"

"Well, what have you done so far?"

"Nothing, just watching him. I've heard that farmers don't call vets for every little thing, so…."

Hannah studied him for a moment. "Well, let's go take a look." The two of them trudged up the hill, into his pick-up, and down the road. The cow didn't show any signs of bloat. He'd passed manure from the time Douglas left to come get Hannah and the two of them returned. The steer also belched upon their arrival, was chewing his cud, and seemed relatively happy.

"Maybe it was the other one," Douglas said.

Hannah looked at him. "And how long have you had these cows?"

Douglas blushed. "A couple of months now."

"Well, that one right there has a big huge half-moon on his shoulder, that's unique. And this one, look right here, doesn't that spot look like the state of Texas."

"I know. I should be able to tell them apart by now." The Guernsey let out a big moo. "Now, her I know."

Hannah and he laughed.

"So, you're saying I should pay more attention."

"Yes, that way you know what's normal and what's not normal for each one. There's no two cows alike. Don't sell them short."

Douglas thanked her and drove her home. "Can I help you with the trees?"

"I appreciate that, Douglas," she said. "And don't take this personally, but I kinda want to do it myself. For the first time in my life, I'm on my own. I went from my daddy's farm to my husband Charlie's farm. They were both home to me, but it wasn't *my* farm. You know what I mean?"

Douglas smiled. "I'm glad you're our neighbor, Hannah."

"Me too."

Hannah spent the next couple of hours dropping the remaining dead trees and cut them into pieces. They weren't overly large trees, but Hannah felt a great sense of accomplishment as she cut them down and sawed them into manageable lengths. Being realistic, she didn't think she had it in her to hand-split them and hoped to be able to rent a log splitter before the first snow. Either way, at least this part was done.

She walked up the hill, "Whistling a happy tune," as her mom would say, gas can in one hand and chainsaw in the other. She planned to return the chainsaw this weekend, figuring she'd had it long enough and took it into the barn to clean it, then hauled it up to the house and put it in the utility room.

She hesitated, standing there thinking. Since she didn't have a washer and dryer and no prospects of getting any real soon, this utility room would make the perfect place to stack wood. She could use up what she had on the front porch first. Even though it was closer to the fireplace, once the bad weather hit it wouldn't make sense to keep opening and shutting the front door all the time and lose heat when this room was sitting back here perfectly empty. She could stack the wood in here whenever there was good spells in the weather and not have it all snow covered.

"Yep, that's what I'll do."

It was a little after five. She'd accomplished a lot in one day. She sat at her kitchen desk, tired but happy, and proud to be able to mark "drop trees" off her list. She checked the cupboard to see if she had enough peanut butter left, and made herself a peanut butter and banana sandwich. It tasted good with a glass of milk.

She made a grocery list of items that would have to get her through a week from Monday, including what she'd need for pies, and sat back. She didn't have to be at Raven's until around eight. She didn't want to be the first one to arrive and planned to get there around eight-thirty or so. Time to make the corn pudding.

When she had it in the oven, she walked down the hill to bring Billy Bob into the barn and gave him a good grooming. She eventually wanted to set up crossties for grooming, but couldn't decide exactly where yet. She brushed and brushed and brushed. He leaned, he turned, he contorted his head and neck. He loved being groomed. She picked out his feet, thankful for the Appy trait he had of slow growing feet. In a couple of weeks, she'd have to have the blacksmith come by. She kept Billy Bob barefoot, but he'd be ready for a trimming by then. She fed him and gave him a big hug and walked back up to the house, again, in the dark.

"It's a good thing I know the way by heart," she said. It was a cloudy night, not a star in sight. The kitchen light was like a beacon on the high seas. Better yet, was the aroma of the corn pudding when she opened the back door.

She turned the oven off and set the pudding on the counter, leaving the oven door open to warm the kitchen. "Waste not, want not," her mom used to say. Then she took a shower and washed her hair. It's not as if she could dress out in the living room, not yet at least without the drapes hung. So she'd taken what she planned to wear into the bathroom with her and dressed there. She blew dry her hair, working in some styling gel with her fingertips while it was still damp, not something she normally took the time to do, and her hair brushed out fuller, fluffier. She went in search of her hairclip, found it in her jewelry box, and pinned her hair up. She tried on a pair of earrings she'd owned for about twenty years, liked the look and the memories, and put on the necklace to match. She applied some eye shadow, mascara and lipstick, dabbed on a little perfume.

Raven said somewhere between casual and formal. "I think this works." The peach earrings and necklace complimented the multi-colored silky blouse with grey slacks. Hannah slipped on a pair of gray flats and was ready. She placed a sheet of aluminum foil over the corn pudding, took it out to the truck along with her purse, checked on Billy Bob, and left for the party.

She didn't have to knock as the door was partially open, and entered with corn pudding in hand. It was one of those entrances where people in the room all of a sudden stop talking, first one, and then another, and then another. Everybody turned to look at her.

"Hannah?" Tom, Raven's husband, said. "Is that you?"

"Yes." Hannah chuckled.

Dave came around the corner from the kitchen. "Wow!" He took the corn pudding and stole a quick kiss on her lips before she could even think of pulling back.

Lucinda and Colleen hurried across the room. "You look beautiful, Hannah! What did you do, go to a spa?"

Hannah laughed, flattered by the compliments but rather uncomfortable being the center of attention. "Yes, I spent hours there."

Raven brought Hannah a daiquiri. "Everyone's having one! It's how we're starting the evening! Drink!"

Hannah took a sip, thanked her, and glanced around the elaborately decorated living room. There were huge paintings showcased on every wall, soft lighting, and candles. Priceless-looking figurines adorned every table. A huge fresh flower arrangement with sparkle lights twinkled in the fireplace. Music played an upbeat tune. Appetizers were being served by the housemaid. There was a bartender on duty. And from the back wall of the living room which was all glass - floor to ceiling, the guests were treated to a dazzling lighting display reminiscent of Christmas's past, present, and future combined for all eternity.

Lucinda rolled her eyes. "You know Raven. She never does anything half way."

Hannah smiled. "It's very pretty." She glanced at Raven and raised her glass. "Everything looks beautiful."

"Thank you. I hope you came hungry. Maria's been cooking all day."

Colleen pulled Hannah close. "Were having Prime rib and lobster tail, green beans almondine, stuffed manicotti, Jello fruit salad and baby greens salad with feta cheese, Ciabatta and baguettes, and for dessert, Hannah's Famous Pies a la mode."

Hannah blushed and took another sip of her drink. "It sounds like you read the menu."

"I did. It's posted in the kitchen. Come see."

Raven's gourmet kitchen was as large as most people's entire first floors. It could easily be a television chef's dream classroom. And sure enough, there on the blackboard in Raven's distinctive script was the dinner menu.

"Amazing!" all three women said as one.

Hannah smiled at the billing her pies received.

Dave was standing by the back door leading out onto the deck talking with Jason and George. There was a woman standing at Dave's side that Hannah had never met before but she looked familiar. "Who is that?" she asked in a low voice.

"Your competition. She's been glued to Dave all evening."

Hannah smiled. "All evening. The party just started."

"You know what I mean." Lucinda shrugged.

"Her name is Faith," Colleen said. "She's a horse friend of Raven's. She came *alone*."

"So did I," Hannah whispered, and the three of them chuckled. Dave looked over at Hannah just then and did the most endearing thing; it almost took Hannah's breath away. He touched his chest and then pointed to her and pressed his hands together as if praying. Such a simple gesture, and yet so…. She smiled and shook her head.

"Why does he care about me? What does he see in me?" Hannah asked, turning and speaking to Lucinda and Colleen in a low voice. "Why?"

"Because. Look at you, Hannah. More importantly, look how you are. You're awesome. If I were a guy, I'd go after you," Lucinda said.

Colleen nodded. "Me too."

"You're fearless. Dead people don't even scare you," Lucinda said.

"Oh yes they do." Hannah nodded. "I just don't let them know it."

The three of them laughed. For a moment, it was High School again: guys across the room and is he looking at me? What's he doing? What's his name? Isn't he cute! Look at the size of his arms!

Hannah finished the rest of her daiquiri and looked around for a place to put the glass. It was whisked away instantly by the bartender who'd been watching her from across the room, and replaced with another.

"Thank you."

When he walked away, grinning, Lucinda and Colleen leaned close.

"See?"

Hannah laughed; the daiquiri was going to her head. "Let's go find the appetizers." They ended up in the den and were soon joined by the woman who'd been hanging on Dave's every word.

"So you're Hannah," she said. "I'm Faith."

Hannah shook her hand. "It's nice to meet you."

Raven appeared at her side. "Oh, I'm glad you've met. You two have a lot in common."

"Oh?" Hannah said.

"Yes, Faith's horse won't load either."

Hannah smiled. "Well, misery loves company."

Faith nodded. "I don't know what I'm going to do with him."

"I solved my problem," Hannah said. "I'm never taking him anywhere again." The two of them chuckled. "He's perfect in every other way and my showing days are over, so…."

"See, now that's the beauty of dressage," Raven said. "Those days are never over. What's that saying? Old dressage riders never die, they just…."

"Piaffe away," Faith said.

Hannah laughed and helped herself to some Brie.

"So how long have you been riding, Hannah?" Faith asked.

"All my life."

"I got started late," Faith said. "It was shortly after my second divorce settlement."

Lucinda, Colleen, and Raven glanced from one to the other. "Dinner's in about five minutes," Raven said. "Mark your territory at the table."

Raven and Tom had to be the only couple Hannah knew that could seat fifteen people at their dining room table comfortably. When Raven said, "Mark your territory," she wasn't kidding. Drinks marked the spots. Hannah placed her daiquiri at the place setting next to Lucinda's and across from Colleen's. Dave was just about to put his drink next to Hannah's, but Faith put her drink down ahead of him. He ended up setting his drink down next to Faith's. She either had no idea that he was pursuing Hannah, or didn't care.

One of the guests kept looking across the table at Hannah in the buffet line. Finally he said, "I know you from somewhere. Where do I know you from?"

Hannah smiled amiably. Probably the funeral parlor, she thought, but figured there was no sense in saying so. The mere mention of the word *funeral* could really put a damper on a party.

"Wait a minute, I know!"

Hannah looked up from dishing herself a serving of green beans almondine.

"You're Hannah Martin, aren't you?"

Hannah smiled. Martin was her maiden name. She started showing horses as Hannah Martin and continued even after she and Charlie got married.

"Yes, I'd know that smug look anywhere! I'll be damned!"

Everyone laughed, even his wife, who was standing at his side, then asked for an explanation. "We used to show together," he said. "Well, not together, I was always trailing behind."

Everyone laughed again and then, all looked at Hannah; her turn to say something. "And your horse's name was...?"

"Big Pete."

"Big Pete? Oh my God!" Hannah smiled. "Gosh, he was a nice horse." She thought for a second. "Big Pete, ridden by....Jordan Miller. Jordan?"

"That'd be me." He reached across the table and shook her hand. "I can't tell you how many times this woman beat me out of High Point," he said, glancing around the table and back at Hannah. "God, I hated you!"

Hannah laughed, along with everyone else. "So, are you still in the horse business?" She took her plate to the table and sat down. Jordan Miller was still piling on the food.

"No, I'm a financial consultant."

Hannah smiled.

"What kind of showing?" Raven asked. "Jordan, I didn't know you showed horses."

He nodded. "Hunter – Jumpers. I did it for years."

"Why'd you quit?" Faith asked.

"Life."

"Why'd you quit, Hannah?"

"Farming." She didn't say I quit so Charlie and I could try and get pregnant, but that was the biggest reason. They'd tried for years.

"Ma'am," the bartender said. "Can I get you another drink?"

Hannah handed him her glass. "Thank you. Just ice water with lemon, please."

He smiled and gave a little bow.

Faith sat down and reached for the salt and pepper. "So what kind of horse was this Big Pete?"

Jordan was still filling his plate and also had his mouth full.

Hannah answered. "Well, if I remember correctly, he was a Thoroughbred Trekaner cross, stood about 16.3 and was a bay with one white hind sock."

Jordan swallowed his food, challenging her. "Oh yeah? What leg?"

Hannah hesitated, thinking, remembering...picturing him going over a jump. "The right hind."

"Damn, you're good!" Jordan said. "No frigging wonder you kept beating me."

Everyone laughed.

Jordan sat down and started eating. "So your horse, uh...?"

"Buggaloo."

"Ooh, Buggaloo," Faith said. "I like that."

It was not Hannah's imagination that right about then, Dave sighed. He was either tired of the conversation or tired of being left out. She looked at him and smiled. He smiled back. "Buggaloo lived to be twenty-nine. He's buried on the farm. The old farm I mean," she said, correcting herself.

Conversation turned to the food, the prime rib so rare and tender it melted in your mouth. The corn pudding complemented the taste wonderfully, the manicotti; the perfect combination with the fruit-filled Jello salad which was ice cold, crisp and tart. "Delicious."

"You outdid yourself, Hon," Tom said.

Raven shrugged proudly. "Thank you."

Hannah took her glass of water from the bartender and smiled. "Thank you."

Another handsome bow.

Another tale-tell sigh from Dave.

Hannah glanced at Lucinda and Colleen. The three of them had a way of speaking volumes without uttering a word. Their eyes locked on one another's briefly.

When they'd finished eating dinner, Raven suggested they retire to the living room. "Maria will be bringing out the dessert cart in a moment. Hannah, can I see you in the kitchen a second?"

Hannah nodded and excused herself. Raven stood staring down at the pies. "Should we warm them or serve them cold? How many pieces should we cut for each pie?"

"Warming them would be good, about a minute each in the microwave. You don't want them too warm."

"And cutting them?"

"Probably eight to a pie." They were nine-inch pies. "That way if someone wants two different kinds, they can have a sliver of both, with the ice cream in between.

"Perfect." Raven looked at Maria. "You got that?"

The woman nodded.

"I can help," Hannah said. "Let's cut them first, they'll ooze less that way."

Raven frowned at Hannah having to help, but then raised her hands. "Okay."

"Do you have caramel sauce?" Hannah asked.

"Yes."

"Good, we'll heat that too and drizzle it."

Raven nodded happily, then went back to make sure everyone had gone into the living room and closed the sliding mahogany doors so no one would have to see the messy dining room table. Most of the men and some of the women were in line at the bar. Lucinda had gone to the ladies room. Colleen was at Jason's side, trying discreetly to warn him about slowing down on the drinks.

Faith had her arm wrapped around Dave's elbow. "You didn't say. Are you into horses too?"

"No, sheep," he said.

"You're kidding, right?"

"Nope."

Faith paused, taken aback, but recovered quickly. "A lot of sheep?"

"Eighty three of them," he said, looking past her into the kitchen, watching Hannah.

"Wow, that's a lot. How large is your farm?"

"I have sixty-two acres."

Faith smiled. The size of his property apparently put him back into good stead. "Are there different kinds of sheep? Or are they all just sheep-sheep?"

His response was interrupted by Maria's grand entrance with the dessert cart, complete with espresso, decaf coffee and a pot of green tea. The guests converged upon it and oohed and awed. "These are 'Hannah's Famous Pies,'" Raven said. "And trust me, you have never had a better pie in your life."

Hannah blushed, and then shrugged when everyone looked at her. Maria served each person to their liking, and even Hannah had to admit, it was damned good pie. "Delicious," she said, of the Boysenberry Surprise. "I may be onto something here."

Everyone laughed.

Hannah sat with Lucinda and Colleen on the couch, listening to the advice of Jordan, the financial advisor, and a woman named Ricky, who was a marketing executive.

"Do you have a website?"

"No."

"All right, that's okay, it's not like you're going national. You're local. What's your e-mail address?"

"Uh, my computer's out of commission." Hannah sold it last year to pay for Billy Bob's vet bill when he'd colicked.

"No computer, no e-mail." Ricky stroked her chin. "Do you have business cards?"

Hannah shook her head.

"At the very least, Hannah, you have to get some business cards. Word of mouth is one thing, but you need to be able to hand out contact information. Put an emblem of a pie on it with steam coming out the top. It sounds simple, but trust me, one look and you're making them hungry. Don't just have the pie sitting there."

Hannah thanked her for the advice and sipped her coffee. Business cards, answering machine. She yawned, relieved when the conversation centered on one of the other guests; a woman who'd just returned from a business trip in China. She listened as intently as she could, but could hardly stay awake.

George looked at her from across the room, imitated her starting up a chainsaw and she nodded. "How many?" he asked, in a whisper so as not to interrupt the conversation.

Hannah discreetly held up one hand. Five.

He shook his head and smiled.

At the first possible opportunity, when most everyone was going for another round of drinks, Hannah thanked Raven and Tom and got ready to leave.

"Call me tomorrow," Lucinda said.

"I will." Hannah stopped in the kitchen to retrieve her baking dish. Maria had just about everything all cleaned up. "Thank you," she told her. "You do a wonderful job."

"I try," she said. "Thank you."

Hannah lost sight of Dave, and in fact, hadn't even given him a thought as she started out the front door. He called after her.

"That's it, you're leaving?"

"I'm beat," she said. "And I need to go home and check on my horse."

"I'm sorry we didn't get to spend time together tonight."

Hannah nodded, yawning again, and when he just stood there looking at her, she gave him a hug and a kiss on the cheek and turned to walk away. "Good night."

"Hannah."

She looked back.

"I love you."

She shook her head.

"I'm sorry, but I do. You don't need to make pies. I'll take care of you."

Hannah sighed. She just sighed. That's all she could do.

"Good night," he said.

"Good night."

Chapter Thirty-Four

Hannah woke early looking forward to her day, Sunday; a day all to herself. She made a pot of coffee, then bundled up and headed down over the hill to feed Billy Bob. He looked half asleep. "I know, it seems like I was just here," she said. It was after midnight when she came home last night and checked on him. "We're going to have a great day today, so you'd better behave." She laughed at herself. She wished she had a dollar for every time she told him to behave. For the most part, he always behaved. But maybe her reminding him all the time was why. She fed him, cleaned and filled his water buckets, then picked his stall and since there was still a heavy frost on the ground, left him in the barn. "I'll be back down in a little while."

Up at the house, she poured herself a cup of coffee and sat down at her kitchen desk. She wasn't really hungry after eating so much last night, but figured she'd better eat something. She had a long day ahead of her. She made herself a peanut butter and jelly sandwich, using the last of the peanut butter.

Since today would be the best day to go get hay, she gathered up her money. In addition to the fifty-dollar tip plus the sixty-five dollars left over from what Cal Able gave her for the scrap metal and the ninety-five dollars from the pies, she had a total of $210.00. "Damn!" She needed $243.75 to get seventy-five bales of hay at the discounted price of $3.25 a bale.

She sat back and crossed her arms. It didn't take a mathematical genius to figure out if she still had the thirty-two dollars she gave Jeb, she'd almost have enough. Then again, his kids wouldn't have milk and bread either. That's if in fact that is what he was using the money for. "Guess it'll have to wait until tomorrow." She set aside twenty dollars for groceries and put the rest of the money in a mason jar in the back of one of the kitchen cabinets.

She checked her to-do list. At some point today she wanted to drop off the chainsaw. She could do that on the way to the grocery store. If it was going to rain later, she wanted to get Billy Bob out now, and on grass. She downed the rest of her coffee and went back outside. The carrier pigeon and his friend were eating the birdseed.

"You little rogue," she said.

Billy Bob was eager to get outside. He danced and pranced. Hannah decided to put him in his pasture for a few minutes, then stood there watching him rolling, bucking, and running back and forth. When he settled down, she tied her makeshift baling twine rope around four trees near the ones she cut down yesterday, made sure it fit and could be tied tight, and then led him over to graze while she worked on cleaning up the branches and brush. The frost had melted and it was still cold, though not unbearable in the sun. At some point she was going to have to get a real pair of gloves. She worked up a sweat.

Because the trees had been dead for so long, probably years, there were very few branches. It was mostly all tree trunks. She rolled the logs into piles, heaviest ones on the bottom, and raked up what little branches and twigs there were. Billy Bob grazed contentedly all the while.

"I'm going for a drink of water," she said. "And you'd better behave." She laughed at herself saying that. "There I go again."

When she was almost to the house she caught a glimpse of something out of the corner of her eye moving fast, and got tumbled to the ground by Bessie's puppy. She laughed. The puppy was all over her, licking her face, jumping up and down, barking. Hannah rolled her onto her side and lay in the grass facing her. "Look at you, you silly girl. Look at those ears." One ear stood up, the other lay bent in the middle. "Look at you, look at you."

When she heard someone giggling, she glanced up to the see the little boy standing there watching them. "I'm sorry, Miss. She doesn't mean to be bad, she just can't help herself."

"Oh, she's not bad. She's just a puppy. Aren't you? Aren't you just a widdle puppy?" Hannah rubbed the puppy's belly. She was so soft and so cuddly. "That's a good girl. Yeah, that's a good girl. You're so sweet." When the puppy settled down, Hannah sat up and dusted herself off.

"You've been a big help to us, Miss," the little boy said. "Thank you."

Hannah gazed up at him. There was something familiar about the way he said that, the wording, the inflection. She looked into his little boy's eyes and saw the old man. He *was* the old man. She looked at the puppy and realized this wasn't Bessie's puppy; this was Bessie. Time held no boundary for either one of them. This was the dog the young boy grew up with. And the dog the old man never forgot.

"You're welcome," she said. "I've enjoyed getting to know you both."

The little boy nodded. "I'd better get goin' now."

Hannah watched them disappear into the brush and shook her head. "I don't know what I did to deserve any of this, but thank you," she said. "I am so blessed."

As if to agree, out of seemingly nowhere the carrier pigeon swooped down onto the ground and waddled up next to her. "Hello," she said, and stroked its head. "I bet you're wondering what I'm doing down here on the ground."

He looked at her with one eye and then the other, then flew up onto the feeder and started squawking. Hannah laughed. The feeder was empty. "All right, all right. I'll fill it."

Done, she drew herself a glass of water and drank every last drop. That "spell" she had when she was so weak and decided it was dehydration would not be quickly forgotten. She watched Billy Bob from the back door. "I see you," she said, as if he could hear her. She went to the bathroom real quick, had another glass of water, and headed back out. It was warming up.

"Okay, we're moving on," she told Billy Bob. She took down the baling twine rope and led him toward the barn. There was a lot of tall grass right around the back door that would keep him busy for at least an hour. If only she could just turn him loose. She put him in the pasture and went about trying to figure out how to rope that area off. She didn't want to pound any nails into the side of the barn for fear if he pulled on the rope and popped the nail loose, it would be where he could step on it. Chances are the rope would give way first, but she didn't want to take that chance.

There were two rickety old sawhorses over in the corner in the barn. They were barely holding together, but, "It's not as if I'm going to leave him alone." She hauled the sawhorses outside, placed them up against each end of the barn, cut the bailing twine rope in half, and tied it from each sawhorse to a pasture rail.

"Okay, and I really mean it this time," she said, turning Billy Bob loose. "Behave."

He put his head down and started eating grass.

"I'm going to clean out the rest of the barn now and make room for hay. Yes, hay, a bunch of it, and all for you." The first thing she did was take down all the cobwebs. Every time she walked outside to shake out the broom, Billy Bob looked up at her and sighed. Next was sorting through all the remaining contents of the barn. She dragged one of the old cow stanchions over to the empty stall, the best of the bunch, and then stacked the rest near the barn door. She sorted through old wood piles; most of the planks had rotted, so she stacked them near the door too. Any other items that looked worthless were added to the piles by the door. She swept the floor, concrete for the most part, except where it wore through to the dirt, and stood back to admire her work. Aside from the tractor, workbench, and what little hay and bedding she had left, it was nearly empty.

Billy Bob was right outside the door now and grazed watching her. "Looks pretty good, huh?" she said. Fortunately the junk yard was open seven days a week. She figured she should be able to get it all loaded and make one trip. She walked around outside the barn, looking for any debris left behind from the storm that she might have missed, and gathered it all up.

"You're a homegrown weed-eater, Billy Bob." He was eating the grass all the way up to the barn wall. Clumps of dirt and roots lay scattered here and there. She picked them up and flung them into the woods on the other side of the barn. She debated whether to leave him on his own while she went up to the house to get something for lunch. He seemed contented enough, but she wouldn't be able to see him. "I don't know." He had another ten feet of grass to eat, he should be all right. She could shut the barn door. No. With the grass out here, he won't go inside, and even if he did.... "I'll be right back," she said. "Behave."

She opened the other can of tuna, mixed it quickly with mayonnaise and pickles, grabbed a fork and what was left of the loaf of bread, a big glass of water, and back down to the barn she went. As she rounded the corner, her heart dropped. The horse was gone.

"Billy Bob?" She ducked under the rope and ran to the open barn door and heaved a sigh of relief. There he was - halfway in his stall, getting a drink of water. When he was done, he turned and walked back outside nonchalantly and continued grazing.

Hannah sat down on the tractor seat and made herself a sandwich. "I think I need to learn to trust you more. I'm buying carrots today, I'll bring you some." She planned to make some soup, using the stock from the bones. It would be a meal or two. The rest of the tuna would be one. She planned ahead, Chili Night at the Honky Tonk, maybe a can of tomato soup one night. No, she'd need crackers. Tomato soup wasn't the same without Saltines. She'd see if they were on sale. "Maybe I'll make stuffed cabbage soup, that's cheap and good for at least two dinners."

She walked up to the house to put the rest of the tuna in the fridge, and drove the truck back down. "I see you've literally reached the end of your rope," she said, to Billy Bob and laughed. He was cleaning up the last of the grass at the far end of the barn. She glanced at the clouds in the sky. She'd best hurry.

She put Billy Bob in his stall, took down the rope fence, and backed the truck in so she could load it from the side. It was easier for her that way, up and over, and thunk, let it land where it may. No pushing and shoving or tugging it forward from the tailgate. She stopped up at the house before leaving and picked up the chainsaw.

Colleen was still in her housecoat and nursing a throbbing headache. "Don't ask. The bartender started making zombies."

"Ooh…" Hannah said, sympathizing with her. "Tell Jason I put the chainsaw in the garage. Thank him for me."

He came down the stairs right about then and looked worse than Colleen. He held up a hand, his greeting, his good-bye, his wishing he could die.

"I'll talk to you later," Hannah whispered.

Colleen nodded and then cringed, holding her head still. "You set your clock back, right?"

Hannah stared. "Oh no, I forgot." Less daylight left. She stopped at the grocery store next, picked up peanut butter, a pound of ground round, a small head of cabbage, a can of stewed tomatoes, a bag of rice, a bag of carrots, a potato, an onion, and a loaf of bread. While she was standing in line, she leafed through one of the Home Decorating magazines and marveled at the picture on the front. It was of a country home with a cottage garden. With a glimmer of imagination, it looked just like her place, or how it could look, faded clapboard and all.

"That'll be $19.92," the cashier said.

Hannah smiled, paid, and hauled her groceries outside. Looking ahead at her truck piled high with junk, she had to laugh. "Oh, Charlie, if you could only see me now. I'm puttin' on the Ritz."

There were two cars and a van ahead of her at the junkyard. Although she had enough room to pull around them, she didn't want to chance driving over something sharp. She leaned out the window and glanced up at the sky. The clouds were getting thicker, darker.

The van was apparently a work truck for a painter. Some of the cans of paint he was flinging weren't closed tightly and splattered paint everywhere. Hannah got out of her truck. "Do you have any worth saving?" she asked. "I could use about a pint to paint an old door."

He smiled. "What color?"

"Uh, whatever you've got."

He reached inside his van and slid out a five-gallon bucket. "There's about a gallon, maybe a gallon and a half left in here. It's white. Latex."

"White's perfect, Latex is perfect." Hannah smiled when it handed it to her. "Thank you."

"You need a brush?"

"You're kidding? Tell me I'm going to get a brush too."

"You bet." He handed her three of them, all sizes. "People pay for the job, what's left over is left over. I've got nowhere to store it."

"Thank you."

Hannah put the paint and brushes on the floor of her truck and walked back around to drive forward when the painter finished. He waved.

"Thank you again!" Hannah said.

"No problem."

Hannah drove ahead and parked at an angle, climbed into the back of her pickup, and starting heaving the rubble over the side. It came off easier than it went on, even the old stanchions. She was on her way home in no time.

Chapter Thirty-Five

Hannah started a pot of soup and headed down over the hill with some carrots for Billy Bob. She'd cut them up into small pieces so he would eat them nice and slow. He'd practically choked once when someone gave him a carrot whole. She'd never forget that. He just kept coughing and coughing, looked as if he would choke to death, and finally a big chunk of carrot came flying out of his mouth.

She topped off his water buckets then gave him some hay and was headed back up to the house when it started to rain. She ran the rest of the way. Eager to cross another chore off her to-do list, she dried off and sat down at her kitchen desk. Clean barn. Done. Sewing the drapes was next, her rainy-day project. She glanced at the clock on the stove. It was four-fifteen. She set it back an hour. It clicked on the minute, three-sixteen. "Time's a wastin'."

She changed the clock radio in the living room and turned it on. LeAnn Rimes was belting out, "How do I live without you?"

"One day at a time," Hannah said, and sang along with her. "How do I get through one night without you?"

The phone rang. Hannah put the drapes down and answered it. "Hello."

It was Dave. "Hi, Hannah."

"Hi."

"I was wondering if you wanted to go to dinner."

Hannah hesitated. "Not tonight, I have a project I'm working on. Thanks for asking though." There was a tension between them. It was hard acting as if nothing monumental happened last night, his saying "I love you."

"Oh, what are you working on?"

"Drapes," Hannah said. "I've been looking forward to it." No sooner said she cringed. It was the truth, but it sounded like the old, being busy tonight - I'm planning to wash my hair, joke. "It's a big project and I need to get it done. Once it's out of the way…."

"Are you coming up for Chili Night?"

"Yep, wouldn't miss it."

"I'll see you then."

When Hannah hung up, she felt a pang of guilt, but it passed quickly. She really *was* looking forward to tackling the drapes, and if it

202

took all afternoon, all evening, all night, so be it. The soup was simmering, she had fresh bread. "It just doesn't get any better than this."

She sat down on the couch and finished cutting all the drapes down the middle, then started pinning them together. "I think this is going to look nice, very nice." She still didn't know what she was going to use for tie-backs. "I can't buy anything. It's got to be something I already have." One thought led to another.

With what was left over from her paycheck after the house payment tomorrow, she just might have enough to get the seventy-five bales of hay. She couldn't count on Jeb paying her back, but if he did, then she wouldn't have to....

The phone rang again. She debated letting it just ring. She thought about the suggestions that she get an answering machine. She wondered if you could program it to pick up before the actual ring. That would be nice. No noise, no interruptions. She thought about business cards, wondered how much they cost.

"Hello."

It was Lucinda. "Colleen and I are going to the mall to do the Chinese Buffet. Do you want to go? We figured with it raining and all."

"No, I'm working on my drapes."

"Do you need help?"

"No, I'm okay."

"Do you need anything?"

Hannah hesitated, thinking, some tie-back hooks and loops would be nice. "No, but thank you. How's Colleen's headache?"

"She's feeling better. My God, can that woman put 'em away. By the way, what did you think of that woman Faith?"

"She seemed nice."

"I kept wanting to smack her, the way she was all over Dave. Raven should have told her."

Hannah chuckled. There was nothing to tell.

"So what are you doing tomorrow night?"

"Well, if I can get the drapes done, I think I'm going to paint."

"Paint what?"

"The kitchen desk, and if I have enough paint left over maybe the front door."

"Do you want us to come help?"

Hannah paused. "Well, I do have three brushes. And I made some vegetable soup."

"Alrighty then, what time?"

"I don't know, how's four? I hate that it's going to get dark so early."

"Four's good. We'll bring something to go with the soup."

Hannah bundled up, put on a rain slicker and went down to the barn to feed Billy Bob. The rain on the roof had such a nice soothing sound to it. While he was eating his grain, she gave him a good brushing and picked his feet. "This is a good life, isn't it?" she said. "We're doing fine."

She had a small bowl of soup for dinner with a tuna sandwich, and went back to sewing the drape panels. She checked on Billy Bob again around eight-thirty, showing the way with her dim flashlight, and heard distant thunder as she started back up the hill. As heavy as it was raining, there was no way she was going to be able to get hay tomorrow and get it unloaded. Even if it stopped right now, the ground would have to dry out considerably.

She wondered about backing the truck onto the roof of the barn and dropping them down by the back door. That would work well for a few but not seventy-five, not with having to handle each bale twice. She wished now that she hadn't sealed off the hatch. There was still a gravel path of sorts going up the ramp to where the loft doors used to be. She could have pulled right up to it.

"If nothing else, I'll get a few bales tomorrow to get through till the weekend." She'd need bedding soon too. She only had one bag left. She gathered some wood off the porch, lit a fire in the fireplace, and finished sewing the last of the drapes.

The first set she hung brought a big smile to her face. When she'd hung the other three, "pleased as punch," as her mom liked to say, she sat down on the edge of the bed in front of the chest of drawers to try and find something that could serve as tie-backs.

The chest of drawers had been for Charlie's clothes and now held household items like tablecloths, curtains, and knickknacks. She took out two pairs of curtains; one set for the bathroom and one for the kitchen. They were the same pattern, but that didn't bother her. They would do. Both windows already had curtain rods, thanks to the previous owner or renter. She put up her ironing board and pressed them, then hung them, and glanced from room to room with another big smile on her face. "I'm liking it!" The curtains were a pale yellow. They looked good.

She moved the two bedside tables over to the living room side, one on each end of the couch, the one butting up to the loveseat, and placed the bedside lamps on them. Then she moved the end table over by the bed. She didn't like the looks of it so close to the front door, so she moved the bed away from the far wall and put the table in the corner. She placed the living room lamp on it and stood back.

"That looks nice. I'll just have to get used to sleeping away from the wall. It's going to be ice cold soon anyway." She doubted the house had much insulation.

She took out a table runner and put it on the coffee table, then placed her mother's Bible on the end table along with a photo of her mother and father on their wedding day. She found silk flowers in the second drawer that she'd been saving forever and in the third drawer found a vase wrapped in newspaper. She thought she'd sold it at the garage sale. "Apparently not." She arranged the silk flowers in the vase and searched for a yellow table cloth for the kitchen table. She didn't have one large enough, but had a small round one with a yellow, green and lavender print. She positioned it in the middle of the table and set the vase in the center. She put one of the chairs in the bathroom, and pulled the table away from the wall. She placed the remaining four chairs at each side of the table. It looked nice in the middle of the kitchen, especially with the matching chair over at her desk.

The bottom drawer of the chest of drawers held two horse-head bookends and five books, her favorites over the years, the ones she couldn't part with. She placed them on the mantle, moved them from one side to the other, then in the middle, then back to the one side. On the other end, she set a framed photo of Billy Bob. Next to that, she placed a photo of her and Charlie that had been taken at the County Fair. It seemed so natural putting it there. They looked so happy. She stood gazing at it for a moment, then changed her mind and was going to put it back in the drawer, but hesitated.

"Get on with your life," she could hear everyone saying. "Forget him."

"But this *is* my life."

She placed the photo back on the mantle and straightened it just so, then went back to searching for something to serve as tie-backs. She found an old scarf big enough to probably make two sets, but not four.

"I wish I had more baling twine. I could braid it." She sat back. "Or a clothesline. Wait, I have a clothesline."

She searched the kitchen drawers and found it. It had seen its better day. She remembered cutting it down at the farm the night they moved. "I'm not leaving it, I'm not leaving anything," she told Charlie.

"I wonder if I could dye it." She looked in the cupboard for food dye. "Please be some green left." There was only half a bottle of green; she'd used most of it on the St. Patty's day sheet cake. "It'll have to do."

She measured the size clothesline pieces she'd need, cut them, and put them into the sink with as little water as possible and all the dye she could shake out of the bottle. "Wow!" Hannah marveled. The rope turned green in an instant. She added salt to the water so it would hold its color.

While the rope soaked, she put the soup in the fridge, then put another log on the fire and went back to looking through the chest of drawers. She needed something for the center of the coffee table and the middle of the fireplace mantle. She used to have a clock that sat on their mantle at the farm, but it too got sold. She found her keepsake box, which held nothing now. She ran her fingertip across the brass buckle and glanced at the coffee table. It would look perfect there. "I'll just have to collect more keepsakes."

She placed it on the coffee table, then took out her jewelry box and put it on the dresser. She looked for the doilies she'd always kept on the dresser and chest of drawers, found them way in the bottom of the second drawer, and ironed them. She took out every figurine and knickknack she'd saved, and played with positioning them on the dresser, then the chest of drawers, some here, some there, and found an arrangement to her liking. The sight of them placed all around brought back so many good memories.

She checked on the clothesline pieces. They were still green, very green - maybe too green. She drained the sink, rinsed them thoroughly, and was pleased. They'd have to dry first to see the exact shade, but held promise. They were a medium color green, not the color of either of the dark panels or the lighter panels of the drapes, but somewhere in between. After she rung them out, she took them outside onto the front porch and twirled them around and around to get rid of as much water as possible, then laid them on the floor in front of the fireplace. She woke in the night to put more logs on the fire and turned the tie-backs over. By morning, they were dry.

Chapter Thirty-Six

Hannah woke in her little cocoon of a combined living room and bedroom, and stretched. She couldn't remember the last time she slept so well. She closed her eyes and almost dozed off again but then rolled over, looked at the clock radio, and gasped. It was a quarter after eight.

"Oh no!" She hurried, washed up and got dressed, went down over the hill to feed Billy Bob and left for work. Somehow managing to get there on time, albeit hungry and still feeling half asleep, she did something she'd never done at work before. She made herself a pot of coffee.

Richard smelled it brewing and came downstairs. "Good morning!"

She smiled. "I slept in."

"You?"

She nodded. "Me."

He shook his head. "If you start slacking off too, I don't know what I'll do."

She sipped her coffee and looked at him. "Jeb?"

"He called off."

"Everything okay?"

"He says the kids are sick."

Hannah took another sip of coffee. "So what do we have going on today?"

"Oh, it's so sad," he said, pouring himself a cup of coffee and sitting down next to her. "An old couple."

"Car accident?"

"No." He made a motion as if taking something by mouth. "They were found together by their neighbor, holding hands. They'd left a note."

Hannah sighed. She and Charlie used to talk about doing that. "When the time comes," he'd say, "and we can't take care of ourselves anymore...."

"When's the service?" she asked.

"Tomorrow."

Hannah finished her coffee and went to tend to the old couple. "They look peaceful enough," she said reverently, as she glanced from one to the other. Their wedding bands had embossed silver crosses on them. The man's hands were calloused.

"They were married for sixty-eight years. No children. Here, the neighbor brought photos."

Hannah liked one in particular, taken probably in the last couple of years. The couple looked similar to the way they looked now, but were smiling. "Is there going to be a lunch?"

"A light one. I'll order the food in the morning. The neighbor thinks only about twenty people."

Hannah brushed a soft curl off the woman's forehead. "Order a container of vanilla pudding. "

"Why?"

"I don't know. Just a feeling."

Hannah would bet that the old man was clean shaven when he'd laid down that final time with his wife of sixty-eight years. And she'd bet the woman had on perfume. "Let me guess. Jasmine," she said. She checked the cabinet to see if they had any and found it.

Hannah drove to the bank after work, deposited her check, made her house payment, and stopped at the grocery store to pick up some ginger ale and cola, several large cans of chicken noodle soup, a loaf of bread, a gallon of milk and a dozen eggs. She knocked on Jeb's door. There was no way he'd be lying, not on payday.

He answered the door looking as if hadn't slept all weekend. He hadn't. "The kids have been so sick," he said. "They're feeling a little better now."

"I'm not coming in. I don't want it." Hannah smiled "Here, if you need anything, call me. I wrote my number on the egg carton."

"Thanks, Hannah, I really appreciate this."

Hannah stopped at the dollar store and bought eight big plastic tie-back hooks for $2.56 and drove home. It was getting close to four o'clock. She headed down over the hill to the barn first, put Billy Bob out in the pasture, and gave him fresh water and hay. The pasture was muddy, but most of the grass was gone anyway, so there was no worry about his tearing it up. Billy Bob rolled in a big soupy mud puddle.

"Oh wonderful," Hannah said. "Nothing like mud on a white horse."

She went up to the house, anxious to get the drapes pulled back before Lucinda and Colleen arrived. She wanted them to be able to see the whole picture. She hammered the hooks into the window trim, just a little lower than halfway down, then tied looped knots on the ends of each clothesline piece. The first loop would stay in place on the hook; the other end would be used to pull the drapes back or when unfastened, to let them hang. When she had all the windows done she stepped back and shook her head in awe.

"Now *that's* pretty."

If only she had something to put in the center of the mantle. She looked through the kitchen cupboards. She looked in the chest of drawers again. She even looked in the bathroom cupboards. Nothing. She put her coat on and hurried down to the barn and stood looking around. Since it was practically empty, there wasn't a whole lot to choose from.

"Behave," she told Billy Bob in passing, and headed for the root cellar. They'd emptied it out, but left a few things. She removed the hickory stick from the latch, opened the door, turned on the Christmas lights, and stepped inside. There was an old two-handed saw. Too big. She picked up a kerosene lamp. Too small. She stood with her hands on her hips, disappointed, and then saw something with possibilities - the top half of an old cider press. It was clean, it was the right size. It would do.

She rushed it up to the house, placed it in the center of the mantle, turned it one way and then the other, closer to the back, closer to the front, adjust, adjust, adjust, and stepped back. Placed a little bit off center and angled slightly was simply, "Perfect." She was washing her hands when Lucinda and Colleen arrived.

Both stood just inside the front door with their mouths open. "Oh my God," Lucinda said.

Colleen marveled. "This is beautiful."

"I know," Hannah said, and couldn't believe she said that. "I know!"

Colleen sat down on the bed, shaking her head. "This is unbelievable. It's not the same house."

"There's more," Hannah said. "I only did curtains in the bathroom, so just glance there."

"Very pretty."

"And now the kitchen." Hannah stepped aside.

"Wow!" both Lucinda and Colleen said.

Hannah repeated herself. "I know. It's amazing. It's home."

209

Lucinda and Colleen put their bags down on the counter and emptied what needed to go into the fridge. Hannah went out to her truck to get the paint and brushes. When she came back inside, Lucinda and Colleen were standing in front of the fireplace looking at the photo of Hannah and Charlie.

"Are you sure this is a good idea?" Lucinda asked.

Hannah nodded. "He's a part of me, Luce. That's a part of me."

Colleen picked the photo up and examined it closer. "I remember this. We were all at the fair. That's the day I found out I was lactose intolerant."

The three of them laughed.

"Come on," Hannah said. "Let's get to work." She divvied up the paint.

"I'll do the desk," Lucinda said.

"Okay, I'll do the front of the door," Hannah said.

Colleen smiled. "Well, I guess I'll do the back."

As they put newspaper down, Hannah reminded herself again that she'd have to get more paper from the laundromat soon. The desk and door took hardly any paint. "Let's do the windows," Hannah said. "Let's paint till we run out of paint or daylight. Whichever comes first."

While Lucinda and Colleen painted the trim on the front windows and then continued on to the porch posts and railings, Hannah tackled the side windows. "Don't worry about the crumbling calking, just paint over it." She finished both living room side-windows, then the bathroom window, and walked around to the other side of the house and painted the kitchen window. The three women gathered at the back door, pooled their paint, and while Colleen and Lucinda got dinner ready, Hannah painted the back door, inside and out. She glanced at the sky. It was probably getting close to six, it'd be dark soon. She put the lid on the paint can and headed down to the barn. Billy Bob nickered when he saw her. He was ready to go inside.

"I'm glad you're adjusting to this time change, 'cause I'm not." She put him in his stall and fed him. "There's no way I'm brushing you tonight." She patted his dried muddy neck. "I'll be back down later."

She wished she had a good ladder. There were only three windows upstairs; one on the front of the house, two on the back. "It doesn't matter," Lucinda said. "You're almost out of paint."

"There might be enough for the front window upstairs."

"How will you get up there?"

"I'll climb."

"What?" Both women shook their head.

"Come on, we're running out of time." Hannah took her boots off and climbed up onto the porch railing. "Don't worry. We'll touch it up when I'm done." She tried pulling herself onto the roof. "Give me a push," she said, when she got one leg up and over.

"No! You're going to kill yourself."

"Don't be silly. Come on, give me a push," Hannah insisted.

Lucinda and Colleen gave her a big push and she rolled onto the porch roof and sat up. " See? Okay, now hand me the paint." She reached down. "This'll only take a minute."

"Yeah, and then how are you going to get down?"

Hannah stared. "I don't know." There was nothing to hold onto. What was she thinking? "I'm up here now though, so let me get the window painted first. Throw me my boots."

Painting the window took about fifteen minutes and by then it was dark. Lucinda and Colleen stood out in front of the porch, looking up at her. "Why don't I go upstairs and let you in the window?" Colleen suggested.

Hannah gave that some thought. She didn't want to undo the blanket barrier, but she didn't have any other ideas. "Wait." She handed the paint can down. It was all but empty. "Pull my truck around and I'll climb onto the cab."

"You'll break your neck," Colleen said.

Lucinda agreed with her. "You'll fall for sure."

"No, I won't. Come on." She sat down to wait while Colleen went for the truck. "Don't pump it," she yelled. "You'll flood it."

Colleen pulled the truck around, put it into park, and got out. "I don't want to be held responsible if it moves when you land."

Hannah laughed. The truck cab was only about four feet below her. All she had to do was dangle her legs and jump. "Now if I fall, one of you have to take care of Billy Bob for me. Okay?" Before they could answer, she jumped down, landing square on the cab of her truck. She then slid down onto the hood and onto the ground. "There now," she said, dusting her hands off. "That wasn't so bad."

Lucinda scraped the bottom of the paint can and touched up the porch railing. "You worry me, you know. You really do. Now come on, let's eat." She'd brought homemade corn bread to go with the soup, along with a tossed salad. Colleen made an upside-down pineapple cake for dessert and brought a bottle of red wine. Hannah turned the radio on low.

"Welcome to my home." They clinked glasses, all smiles.

"I am so proud of you, Hannah," Lucinda said. "Even though you scare me half to death sometimes."

"Me too," Colleen said.

"Thank you." Hannah took a sip of wine. "Now no talking about Dave tonight. Okay? Please."

Her friends nodded.

"I don't want to ruin the mood."

Lucinda passed her the corn bread.

"He told me he loved me last night. I can't believe that."

Colleen hesitated. "I thought you didn't want to talk about him."

"I don't. But can you believe that? He doesn't even know me."

"Hannah, he's known you most of your life," Lucinda said.

"Yes, as Charlie's girlfriend, as Charlie's wife. That's freaky."

"He's seen you practically every week since Charlie left."

Hannah took a bite of cornbread. "I don't want to talk about it."

"Oh? And do you really mean it this time?"

Hannah laughed. "Yes. Pass the salad."

Chapter Thirty-Seven

Hannah wasn't taken any chances of sleeping in again and set the alarm. She fell asleep to a crackling fire and woke to the sound of Jimmy Buffet singing Margaritaville and belted out, "Searching for my lost shaker of salt."

"Oh no, sing before breakfast, you'll cry before dinner," her mother used to say. Would Hannah ever forget that? "I wasn't singing, Mom, honest," she said, in a non-sing-song like voice. "I was just remarking about how I was looking for my lost shaker of salt. Oh look, there it is." She laughed and picked it up and tossed salt over her shoulder for good measure.

She dressed, bundled up, and headed down to the barn. "I'll be home early," she told Billy Bob, while picking out his stall as he ate. "The service is at eleven and the lunch right after. I'll be back down before I leave to turn you out." As she started up the hill, she was amazed at how good the back door looked painted white. It was the perfect contrast to the faded brown clapboard. She walked around front and shook her head. The front door and windows and porch posts and railing looked so nice. It was as if the wood on the house had been sanded down to bare wood and weathered on purpose. She walked all the way down to the end of the driveway to get a full view and loved it. It wasn't too much, it wasn't too little. It was a Goldilocks, "Just right."

She ate the leftover cornbread for breakfast with her coffee and sat in the living room admiring the mantle. It was nice having all her things out, especially accompanied by the old cider press which was obviously a part of this farm's past. She thought about the old couple that would be laid to rest today. Sixty-eight years as husband and wife. "That's longer than I've been alive."

When she arrived at the funeral parlor she went right to work preparing the luncheon. Soft music played overhead. She heard the shuffling of feet. Richard came down and stuck his head through the doorway.

"Fifteen people."

Hannah nodded. Since she had a few minutes to spare, she went ahead and made up sandwiches and cut them in quarters and arranged them on platters for each table. She cut the cake and put the slices on small plates, poured the coffee into carafes and placed them on the three tables, along with cream pitchers and sugar bowls. She made a pot of tea for each table, put water glasses and a pitcher of ice water on each table along with slices of lemon, and placed a bowl of vanilla pudding on each table.

When the guests came in, all they had to do was sit down. Most looked to be the age of the departed, frail and with canes and walkers. A buffet would have been too difficult for many of them. Hannah poured water for those who needed help, served the coffee and the tea, and remained near the tables as if she were each and every person's own personal assistant.

The guests were delighted with the meal. They particularly liked the butter on the sandwiches, and not mayonnaise or mustard. They loved the vanilla pudding. The lunch was over and done in less than an hour. Hannah got hugs and kisses. Upstairs, she helped two of the women use the bathroom. She helped them wash up.

Richard sang her praises again. "Hannah, you're a wonder."

She shrugged. "Thank you. It was a nice tribute," she said, putting the last of the dishes away. "There was no sadness, just acceptance. It was as if the couple weren't even gone. They just happened to be out of the room at the moment."

From work, she headed for Big Jim's in search of an ash pail. If she was going to speed up the breaking-down process of the manure pile, she needed to be dumping hot ash on a regular basis. He didn't have one, but was happy to report he'd found her a sled; a big long red plastic one with a rope handle. "How much?"

"For you, three dollars."

Hannah smiled. Three dollars, aside from what she'd set aside for Chili Night at the Honky Tonk, was about all she had left. "I'll take it." She paid the man and drove home. She still had enough daylight to give Billy Bob's pulling it a try. When she brought out the harness, he was leery. He kept looking at it and snorting. She put on his halter, hooked his lead rope to it and ground tied him. Then she put the harness girth on him. He didn't mind that; he was used to a lunging surcingle. What concerned him were the long lines *attached* to the harness girth. His eyes grew big and wide watching them. It was as if he was saying, "Snakes! Are those snakes?"

Hannah led him outside, the long lines dragging behind him, and let him graze wherever wasn't mowed or grazed down already. He soon forgot about the long lines. She alternated putting one across his back, then both. She wanted him totally used to the feel. When he seemed perfectly okay with that, she looped the long lines around the rope on the sled and walked along next to him with the sled slung over her shoulder. When she put it down on the ground and he spooked, she picked it up again. This went on for about an hour. When he seemed totally bored with this little "game," she untied the sled and dragged it along behind her. He was soon bored with that too and paid no attention.

"All right, tomorrow's the real thing."

She put him back in the barn, picked out his stall, flinging the manure onto the sled, then went up to the house for a quick snack. It was time to go buy some hay. She got the money out of the mason jar and was on her way out the door when the phone rang.

"Just making sure you're coming to the Honky Tonk tonight," Colleen said.

"Yep, I'll see you guys in a bit."

214

The hay man was in a good mood. "How many do you want, Hannah?"

"Five today, but I'm going to want seventy-five total. I can pay you a hundred and ninety today, and I'll come back in a few days and pick up the rest. I can't get my truck back to the barn after all the rain we got Sunday."

"Okay, sounds good to me." He took her money and put it in his pocket. "I'm going to be just about out of hay here shortly. Some fella took over the old Rickshaw boarding place and was by here today. No one's going to beat my price. He'll be back."

"But you'll hold my other seventy bales, right?"

He nodded. "You betcha."

Hannah shook his hand. It was something Charlie would always do to seal a deal. She wasn't going to take any chances. The man only dealt in cash and didn't give receipts. She questioned the decision to give him the hundred and ninety today, but was just going to have to trust him.

When she got home, she backed the truck onto the old hayloft - now barn roof, and tossed the hay bales down the other side. She glanced at the sky: she was running late. She parked the truck by the house, hurried down and around the barn to put the hay inside, fed Billy Bob his dinner, and jogged back up to the house to wash up. She thought about starting a fire in the fireplace before she left, that way the house would be warm when she returned, but didn't have any time and she didn't have any paper or fire starters.

She stopped at the laundromat on the way to the Honkey Tonk, ran inside to get some newspapers, and was headed back out when she saw a familiar face. "Susie?"

The woman smiled. "How long's it been?"

Susie was their neighbor from when she and Charlie lived on the farm.

"Years."

They gave each other a hug.

"Are you still at the...?"

The woman shook her head. "Bill and I split."

"Oh, Susie, I'm so sorry."

"I know," she said. Tears sprang to her eyes. She wiped them away. "Do you hear anything from Charlie?"

Hannah shook her head. "Listen, I have to go, but...." She motioned over her shoulder, the truck engine running. "I'm meeting Lucinda and Colleen at the Honky Tonk. Do you want to join us?"

"Maybe some other time."

"Well, if you change your mind, we'll be there."

The woman glanced at the clothes dryers. "Maybe."

Lucinda and Colleen were seated and had a beer waiting for Hannah. "Dave said this one's on the house."

Hannah sat down and raised the bottle to thank him. He waved. "God, this is so awkward," she said to Lucinda and Colleen. "Did he buy your beers too?"

When they said yes, she felt somewhat better. "Guess who I just ran into? Susie Jones."

Both women sighed. "That's so sad, them splitting up," Lucinda said.

"So you knew?"

"Everybody knows."

Having been on the receiving end of that same grapevine, Hannah could relate. "I asked her to join us, but...." No sooner said and in walked Susie, looking lost. Colleen waved her over and there were lots of hugs and kisses. "Beer?"

Susie nodded and sat down. "When you left, Hannah, I thought, what am I doing here all by myself? I'll hang my clothes to dry in the friggin' bathroom, my pantyhose too. I'll hang them everywhere."

They all laughed.

Colleen went to the bar and came back with a beer for her. "Are you going to have some chili?"

"Yes."

Colleen motioned to Dave to add another chili and soon they were all eating and getting caught up. "He left me for a younger woman," Susie said. "It's as simple as that. I should have realized with all the miles he was putting on the truck. She lives over in Hitchcock County." She laid the whole story out. Lucinda ordered another round of beers.

When they were done eating, Dave came over to the table and cleared their dishes. "Excuse me. Hannah, can I talk to you a minute?"

Hannah hesitated. "Okay." She walked with him to the bar and sat on the end stool. "How are you doing?" she said, to the man sitting next to her.

"Not so good," he said.

Hannah smiled. "Maybe it was the chili?"

He shook his head. "Maybe it was my wife."

Hannah looked at Dave. "Just kidding, the chili was delicious, as always. So what's up?" She glanced over her shoulder at her friends, clearly wishing she was back at the table with them.

"I was wondering if we could go out for a real date. You know, like to a restaurant, maybe Pittinger's? Get a nice steak."

"Sure, um…I'm still getting settled in, but maybe in a couple of weeks."

"I was thinking of this Friday?" He took her hand in his. "I'm not trying to pressure you or anything."

She glanced at their hands. "All right."

"Good, I'll pick you up around seven-thirty."

"That's not necessary. I can meet you there."

"It's a date, remember. I'll pick you up." He smiled. "Just don't look as good as you did at Raven's, or I won't be responsible for my actions."

"I'll see what I can do," Hannah said, easing her hand free.

All three women looked up when she retuned to the table. "Well?"

She shook her head. "We're going out Friday night to Pittinger's."

"Fancy schmantzy," Colleen said.

Hannah held up her hand, palm open.

"What's that mean?" Susie asked.

"It means she doesn't want to talk about it," Lucinda said.

They all laughed, Hannah included.

Jason and George were over at the barn. George called to them. "Another round?"

Hannah shook her head no, but everyone else said yes, and here came four more beers. Hannah nursed hers.

"Are you still at the funeral parlor, Hannah?" Susie asked.

She nodded.

"I don't know how you do it."

"Me neither." Hannah paused, staring at her beer. "I think I'm meant to do it though. I think I'm supposed to be there."

Lucinda gave her a hug. Hannah rarely talked about her job in a serious way. But whatever Hannah did, she did one hundred per cent. For her to say this…. Tears filled Lucinda's eyes. "You deserve the best, Hannah. I want you to have the best."

217

Hannah looked at her. "I have the best. I have the best friends in the world." She looked at each one of them. "I have the best house. I have the best horse."

Susie started crying now, and then Colleen. "Oh, God!" they all said.

George looked over at them. "That's it! You're all cut off!"

Lucinda, Colleen, Susie, and Hannah laughed.

Chapter Thirty-Eight

Hannah browned the pound of ground beef, put it into her crock-pot with chopped up cabbage, added two cans of stewed tomatoes, a half a cup of rice, a little water and seasoning, then headed down over the hill to the barn. Though she preferred more daylight at the end of the day, she was getting used to the time change. No frost last night and there was a glorious sunrise.

She fed Billy Bob and cleaned his stall, piling the manure onto the sled, then turned him out in his pasture with hay and two buckets of water. "It should be a short day," she told him. "When I come home, we'll work on hooking you up to the sled. And you'd better behave," she added.

The crock-pot already smelled good by the time she got back up to the house. She turned it on low and left for work. Jeb had been there and gone, but left money for her.

"He went to the bank and came back," Richard said. "He said to tell you his kids are feeling much better."

Hannah smiled and put the thirty-two dollars in her pocket. "So what do we have going on today?"

"Not much," Richard said. "This town's too healthy. We need an epidemic."

Hannah chuckled.

"If you don't mind though, I've got some errands to run. Watch the phones for me. I'll only be a couple of hours."

Hannah looked around the office. She wasn't one to just hang out for hours waiting for the phone to ring.

"I've got some filing to do if you want."

Hannah tackled the small stack of papers and had them filed in no time. Now what to do? The cleaning crew that came in once a week was just here yesterday. The place was clean, all neat and tidy, even the kitchen. She sat down at Richard's desk and rocked back and forth in his swivel chair.

"I'm going on a date," she said, "a real live date." She was more apprehensive than excited, dreading it more than looking forward to it. "And yet I'm going. Why didn't I just say no?" She turned the chair and looked out the window. "Well, for one I didn't want to hurt his feelings. So that must mean I care for him a little." She shrugged that off. "I don't know, maybe if he would just take things a little slower."

When the phone rang, she took a message and then put her head down on the desk. She studied the wood grain, her mind wandering. I wish I had some grapevines. I need a wreath for the front door. She used to have a really nice wreath at her and Charlie's farm. She'd made it herself from vines off their property. She soaked them in warm water to make them pliable, wove a patchwork ribbon through the branches. She closed her eyes and could see it, could see their front porch, her favorite rocker. "Where do you want the hook?" Charlie had asked. "Higher, no lower."

Get on with your life.

Get on with your life.

Get on with your life.

"Hannah?"

She opened her eyes and looked up. Richard smiled at her.

"What time is it?"

"One thirty," he said.

Hannah yawned and stretched. "Wow, I can't believe I slept that long." She handed him the message. It was from a John Mason.

Richard blushed. "Is this all he said?"

"Yes, just that he'd call you back tomorrow."

Richard nodded. "Okay, Hannah, but just so you know, and this is between you and me, I'm not saying I'm selling."

Hannah stared.

"I'm just entertaining my options."

What? Selling? Hannah lowered her eyes to the floor.

"And it's not to say that the new owners wouldn't keep you and Jeb on. Come on, Hannah, don't do this to me. You look like you've been hit by a bus. You know this time of year I always get the itch to go South. Nothing ever came of it before. Don't worry." He laid the phone message down on his desk. "Besides, I promise you, you'll be the first to know."

Hannah nodded. "Do you need me for anything else today?"

"No," he said. "Get outta here."

Hannah forced a smile. "I'll see you tomorrow."

"Okay. And I mean it. Don't worry. All right?"

Hannah walked to her truck in a fog and just sat behind the wheel for a moment. "Don't think too far ahead," she told herself. "Take this a step at a time. He's right. He does think about this every year this time. Don't panic."

She drove to the grocery store, bought what she needed to make pies, and stopped at the drug store to price an answering machine. The cheapest one was $14.98. "I wouldn't buy that one though," the clerk said. "It's junk. People bring them back all the time." She showed her one on sale for $23.49. "This is the one you want." There were only two left. What would be the odds of both selling by Friday?

"Can you hold one for me?"

"Sure. Can you give me your credit card number?"

Hannah smiled. "No, I don't have one."

"Well, then let me check with my manager."

When the young lady picked up the paging microphone, Hannah shook her head. "That's okay. I'll just take my chances." This was already embarrassing enough. "I'll see you Friday." She stopped at the printer's next to price business cards.

"Custom designed are $27.00 for a box of a thousand."

"I don't need a thousand and I don't need them custom designed."

"If you want your pie on it, then it's custom designed."

Hannah sighed. "How much for just plain, for just the lettering?"

"We're running a special." The man pointed to a sign over her shoulder. "$10.99 for five hundred of them."

Hannah thanked him for his time and drove home. She checked on Billy Bob, gave him hay and topped off his water, then walked back up toward the house. The newly-painted window trim looked so pretty. She went around front and stood gazing at the freshly-painted door. "Yep, I need a wreath," she said, and inhaled deeply. The house's old lack of insulation lent itself to aromas coming from inside. Cabbage roll soup.

She sat down at the kitchen table with a big steaming bowl of it and a glass of milk. "Oh, this is good, very good," she said, dipping buttered bread into the broth. "Oh, yeah." As soon as she was done eating, she headed back down to the barn.

"All right, Billy Bob, it's time to go to work."

He still had mud all over him, dried and crusty, so she brushed him and combed his mane and tail. She looked as if she'd been in a dust storm. She wiped him down with a damp towel to get the rest of the dust off, then ground tied him in the middle of the barn and reached for the harness.

"Hannah? Hannah, are you down there?"

She didn't recognize the female voice. "Yes, I'm in the barn."

It was Raven and Faith, both dressed from riding. "We came to see 'John Boy,'" Raven said.

Hannah chuckled and stepped back as Billy Bob lowered his head watching them.

"Oh, Hannah, he is so pretty," Faith said. "When Raven said Leopard Appy, I didn't picture this."

"You should have seen him a few minutes ago. He was mud from head to toe." That dried-up mud lay on the floor everywhere at his feet.

Faith reached up to pet Billy Bob's face. "Wow, he has such a keen look in his eyes."

Hannah smiled. "He's pretty level-headed."

Raven stood next to him at the shoulder. "How tall is he?"

"Fifteen-three."

"I didn't know Appy's even came this big."

"I think his size was why Charlie took a liking to him at the sale."

"Charlie?" Faith said. "The infamous runaway husband?"

Hannah nodded. "That'd be him." She put the harness girth over Billy Bob's back and buckled it.

"What are you going to do?"

"I'm going to see if I can get him to pull this sled. I want to be able to haul the manure to the orchard this winter in the snow the easiest way possible. Besides," she said, patting him on the shoulder. "He needs to earn his keep. Don't you, big guy?" Billy Bob looked at her.

"Is this your first time trying it?" Raven asked.

"Yep. We worked a little yesterday with him just getting used to the sight of it."

The two women looked at the sled, piled high with manure. "Shouldn't you do a dry run with it first?" Raven asked.

Hannah shook her head. "With no weight in it, it'll flop all over the place and it's liable to scare him. He can come unglued on occasion."

Hannah pulled the sled out of the barn and positioned it facing the orchard. "All right, let's give this a shot." She walked Billy Bob up to sled, let him take a good look, a good sniff, then positioned him in front of it and ground tied him again. She wrapped both long lines around the sled rope and tied them in some semblance of a loose slip knot for quick release.

"Do you want us to help?" Faith asked. "Do you want us to move away? What do you want us to do?"

Hannah picked up his lead rope. "He's probably going to balk from the weight. So just click to him. Don't get too close." She chuckled. "This'll either work or it won't. We could have horse shit flying everywhere."

Raven and Faith laughed.

"All right, Billy Bob," Hannah said. "You're not afraid of that big old sled. Not you." She led him forward to pick up the slack in the long lines and rubbed his ears. "See, it's nothing." She led him forward another step, the weight of the sled pulling on the girth. He backed up. "Nope, forward, come on."

She looked at Raven and Faith and nodded. They both clicked softly to him. He took a step forward, the long lines taut again. "Come on," Hannah said, and started walking. He pulled the sled forward about a foot and bucked. "That's all right, that's all right."

Another step forward, another buck.

"Come on, you can do it."

Raven and Faith clicked to him again.

"Come on...."

Billy Bob dug in and started pulling. "Look at you, big man," Hannah said. "Look at you."

Raven and Faith followed from a distance, shaking their heads and smiling.

Pull, pull, pull.

Hannah almost tripped herself, walking backwards.

Pull, pull, pull....

Before she knew it, they were in the orchard. "Good boy, good boy."

Faith and Raven pretended to clap, no noise so as not to spook him.

Hannah let him stand for a moment, ground tied again, and then walking all around him - untied the sled, removed the harness, and dumped the manure.

"Yeah! Victory!"

When a truck went by just then and backfired, Billy Bob took to standing in place and bucking. Hannah laughed. He was still ground tied, but bucking up a storm. When he stopped, Hannah looped the lead rope around his neck and tied it like reins. "Okay, who's riding?"

"Bareback?" Faith shook her head. "Another truck goes by, he'll buck me off."

"No, he won't. It's a different mindset with a rider on his back. Come on." She gave her a leg up. "How long did you say you've been riding?"

"A couple of years."

Raven and Hannah trailed along behind them with the sled and harness. Billy Bob walked as calm as can be. "He leg yields," Hannah said.

Faith leg yielded him to the left, then the right.

"Turn on the forehand."

Billy Bob worked his hind end around in a perfect turn on the forehand and stopped, facing them, from Faith's leg commands.

"Turn on the haunches."

She turned him back around and he walked on.

"Does he piaffe?" Raven asked.

"No." Hannah laughed. "At least, not on command."

Faith took Billy Bob into the pasture and trotted around the fence line. "This is so much fun, having faith in a horse." She laughed at herself saying this. "You know what I mean."

Hannah nodded.

"Should I canter?"

"Sure."

Billy Bob went right into his rocking horse canter when asked, and Faith was all smiles. "This is too much fun."

"I want a turn," Raven said. "Me next."

When Faith brought him around and slid off, Hannah gave Raven a leg up. First a trot, then a canter. "Does he leg yield at a canter."

"Yep, but be ready. He gives you a lot more action."

Sure enough, he put more weight on his hind end. Raven laughed out loud when he almost unseated her. "Oh my God! This is too cool!"

"Are you up for a lead change?"

"I don't know."

"Bring him down the diagonal."

"I'm scared."

"Come on, trust him."

Raven turned him down the diagonal, asked for a lead change with her legs and seat and sat beaming from ear to ear. She asked for another lead change. "Too cool! Too too cool!" She brought him back to a trot and then a walk and sighed. "There's a lot to be said for a backyard horse."

Hannah nodded. A couple of weeks ago, she'd have taken that as a dig. Today, no.

"I have to pee," Raven said. "He got me all excited."

The three of them laughed. Billy Bob hadn't worked up a sweat, so Hannah took off the lead rope and turned him loose in the pasture. She gave him hay and checked his water, then the women walked up to the house.

"Oh, wow, Hannah, this is so darling," Raven said, of the living room. "It's like an oasis."

Hannah thanked her and looked around. "I know. I really like how it turned out."

"I like it too," Faith said, emerging from the bathroom. "When Raven told me you bought an old rundown farm house, I had no idea how darling it would be."

Raven looked at her.

"Well, I'm sorry, but that *is* what you said."

Raven glanced at her watch. "Come on, we have to go. Come to the car with us though, I have something for you."

Hannah followed them out.

"Do you remember Ricky from the other night?"

Hannah shook her head.

"She's the one that was telling you about the business cards. Well, she made one up for you."

One, Hannah thought.

"It's on disk." Raven handed her a CD. "She said get some card stock and you can print them off anywhere."

Hannah thanked her and stood smiling as they got into Raven's BMW and pulled out. "Thanks for the ride, Hannah!"

She waved back and when they'd vanished, turned and stood looking at her front door. "That does it," she said. She took the CD inside and put it on her kitchen desk, grabbed a big pair of scissors, and went in search of a vine, any kind of vine. Not another night was going to go by without a "Welcome" wreath on her front door, and that's all there was to it.

There was a tree line at the back of her property which would be her best bet. She had about an hour of daylight left and headed straight for it. She knew from the past to be wary of vines growing up oak trees. Ideally she wanted wild grape vines. The closer she got to the stand of trees, the more encouraged she became. There were definitely vines of some sort hanging.

"Wow!" They were everywhere. Since she'd only brought scissors, she couldn't tackle the thick vines, but she didn't want too big a wreath anyway. She searched and searched for just the right vine, chose one that narrowed about three feet off the ground, and started bending it back and forth in hopes it would break off. "It would probably be easier to rip it with my teeth," she said, and laughed. When she finally got it bent enough and then cut, she leaned back, bracing herself, and yanked on it. It was wound around the tree and took a lot of tugging. Finally, it came crashing down on her.

"Yes!" It was thin and pliable at the top and had plenty of length to work with. She thought about trying to cut down another one, but was running out of daylight. "I can always come back tomorrow."

As she walked along, she started winding the vine around her arm, elbow bent. Billy Bob nickered to her. "I'm coming." She laid the vine down outside the barn and put him in his stall and fed him and fussed over him. "You're such a good boy, you old showoff. I'm so proud of you."

She continued winding the vine around her arm on her way up to the house, and inside, got nylon thread out of her sewing box and secured it. It was just the right size. She sat at the kitchen table wishing she had ribbon. "Wait a minute, what about the scarves."

The two were complementary colors of brown and greens with a touch of blue. "Okay," she said. "We can do this." She tied two ends together in a little knot, then made four streamer-like cuts on each scarf. She placed the knot on top at the back of the vine then pulled the

225

lengths of scarf through and started threading the material in and out, matching one side to the other in color and thickness. She took her time, so as not to break any of the tendrils on the vine. At the middle top part of the bottom, she took all the pieces of scarf left hanging and tied them in a big bow. They hung perfectly.

She hammered a nail into the door, hung the wreath, and stepped back.

"Now that says 'Welcome.'"

Chapter Thirty-Nine

The phone rang all evening. Hannah was amazed. No sooner would she sit down, than it rang again. She had orders for fifteen pies, including the three for Hank. She checked her supplies. "I just may have enough. Just to be sure I'll pick up more flour and sugar tomorrow. I'm thanking my lucky stars, Mom," she said, "that I didn't buy that answering machine. I'd have no money then."

She lit a fire in the fireplace and sat on the couch eating another bowl of soup. She made sure to save enough to have for dinner tomorrow. She thought about turning the television on, but didn't. She glanced at the radio, maybe some music. It was too far away. When she was done eating, she set the bowl on the coffee table and curled up in the corner of the couch. The possibility of losing her job was far, far away. The thought hadn't even crossed her mind since she came home. She was happy, she was content. She was home.

When the phone rang yet again, she glanced at the clock. It was nine-thirty. An order for ten pies? "I'm sorry," Hannah said. "I can probably take that order for next week, particularly if I can deliver them on Saturday, but...."

The woman was calling from a restaurant in Crawford County. They were unhappy with their current baker and heard about Hannah's pies through the "grape vine."

Hannah chuckled, glancing at the backside of her front door.

"Are you sure we can't get them this week?"

"Yes, I'm positive. I can probably make one or two for you, but that would be it."

"We'll take 'em. We'd like to try the Boysenberry Surprise."

Hannah took down the contact information and address, thanked her, and hung up the phone. Ten pies from one customer, exciting, yes. But for the life of her, at the moment all the she could think about was "soybeans." That first big order; the beginning of the end.

"Hold your horses and think twice," she said. "You can't even read the manufacturer's name on your stove, that's how old it is. You can't make twenty or twenty-five pies a week."

"Be careful what you wish for."

"I hear you, Mom," she said. "I hear you." She grabbed her dim flashlight and headed down to the barn, shaking her head. "You can't even buy batteries. Look at you. You're walking in the dark."

Billy Bob nickered. "Hey, my man," she said. She picked out his stall, gave him hay and topped off his water buckets. As she was about to leave and head back up to the house, her flashlight went dead. She stood in the doorway of the barn in almost complete darkness. No moon, no stars, no distant planets, just clouds. "So this is what you see, huh?"

Billy Bob sighed.

"Are the spirit horses grazing?" She looked hard and couldn't make them out at first, but as her eyes adjusted to the night, one by one, they slowly began to appear. "In a perfect world, I'd make pies every day. Oh, if only life were that simple. We'd never have to worry, you, me, them." She glanced in the direction of the Douglas' farm, their whole lives ahead of them, baby on the way. "I want to crochet an afghan for them. I'll make it in pastels, yellow, pink, blue and green. Patty didn't say if it's a boy or girl, maybe they don't know."

Billy Bob stood chewing his hay.

"Good night, big guy."

She walked up to the house in the dark and took a warm shower. Tomorrow was going to be a busy day. She closed the drapes, set the clock alarm, and climbed into bed. Try as she might, she couldn't fall asleep. "I'm going on a date, Charlie," she said. "I can't believe it, but I am." She hugged his pillow close with tears welling up in her eyes. "Some people marry for life, Charlie. I think I'm one of them. I always thought you were too. I guess I was wrong." She wiped her eyes. "I think it's time I let you go."

Chapter Forty

Hannah woke to the phone ringing and Cal Able's southern drawl on the other end of the line. "Is it too late to order a pie, darlin'?"

"Um...." She looked at the clock, two minutes to seven. "I don't think you should eat a pie every week."

"But it's sugarless. Can you make a sugarless peach pie?"

"I can try. How about if I make it Saturday morning and drop it off?"

"Are you going to town anyway Saturday? I don't want to have to pay for delivery."

Hannah chuckled. "I'll make sure to be on my way somewhere." As was her morning routine, she made a pot of coffee, washed up, bundled up, and headed down to the barn to feed Billy Bob.

"I'll put you out before I leave," she told him. "And if you behave, I'll bring you an apple." Billy Bob had his head in the feed tub and never even looked up. "I get the feeling you take me for granted," she said, laughing.

For breakfast she made herself some scrambled eggs and toast, packed a peanut butter and jelly sandwich for lunch, and went back over her list of pie orders and supplies. "I need four more pie pans." She glanced at the stove. If it weren't so old, she might try making three racks of pies. But chances are they wouldn't cook evenly and she'd end up with sides of them having burnt crust. They baked okay four at a time. But three at a time would actually be best, she thought. Two on the top rack, spread out and one on the bottom rack. It would take longer that way, but they'd bake better. It would also make it easier to move them around for even baking. She had to keep turning them that night when Patty was here. "Hmmm." Five hours straight of pies baking in the oven.

"I'll stop by the library and pick up a couple of books."

There were two bodies waiting for her when she arrived at work. The first one was a woman age eighty-six with long white hair that she wore piled loosely in a bun on the top of her head; wisps of curls framing her face. Hannah placed her pearled hairpins on each side of the bun, the way the woman had them in a photo taken recently. There were several photos of her, some dating back to before her hair turned gray and then white. She'd worn her hair the same way all these years. It looked pretty on her.

The second person was a man of sixty-two who had died of cardiac arrest. He had a full head of blonde hair, gray at the temples, and groomed eyebrows. He was not happy to have died, it took him by surprise. Both were to be cremated after their funeral. Both families were having a reception elsewhere.

Hannah checked in with Richard before leaving. He looked up from his desk with a worried expression on his face. "All done?"

She nodded. "Are you okay?"

"I guess." He sat back. "Don't panic, but I've had an offer."

Hannah stared.

"It's not exactly the deal I wanted, but...."

"When will you decide?"

"I have a few days, but I told them I'd let them know tomorrow. I can't stand this hanging over my head."

Hannah sympathized with those sentiments. "I'll see you tomorrow."

Richard smiled. "Someone said you're making pies to sell."

"Yes," Hannah said.

"Good." Richard nodded. "Good."

Hannah walked out with a sigh. She could probably make enough pies to live on, but not to pay a mortgage. She stopped at the grocery store, picked up a few more apples, flour, and sugar. She'd have to wait until tomorrow to buy Cal Able's peaches.

She stopped at the Dollar Store next to pick up the pie pans, and headed for the library. When she took her book choices to the counter, two autobiographies, the librarian looked up and smiled.

"Hannah, I haven't seen you in so long. How are you?"

"I'm fine, fine, thank you. And you?"

"I'm good. Everything is good. The grandkids are in college. My husband's retired." She ran the books through the scanner. "How's Charlie? Do you hear anything from him?"

"No," Hannah said, adding before the woman could. "But I'm getting on with my life."

"Good. You have a good day now."

Hannah tossed the books onto the passenger seat of her truck and walked across the street to the hardware store. "What can I do for you, Hannah?"

Hannah smiled. "Hey, Ralph. How are you?"

"I'm fine."

"Good, me too." She glanced around. "Paint is...?"

"Aisle four. What are you looking for?"

"White trim paint. I only need about a pint. I'm not buying today, I'm just checking?"

"I heard your place is looking pretty good."

"Thank you."

A pint of white trim paint was $6.42. That seemed extravagant to Hannah but it was nagging at her that the back two windows on the house weren't painted. She was basically the only one that could see them, but they weren't done, and she liked things done. "I'll be back tomorrow."

She checked on Billy Bob when she got home, gave him some hay and topped off his water buckets. Both were practically empty. The sun was out and it was warm. He looked as if he'd been dozing.

"Did I wake you? I'm sorry. Go back to sleep. I'll be back down later."

She put the rest of the cabbage roll soup on to heat and started on the pies. She got into a rhythm and soon had pies everywhere. She held her breath when she turned on the oven and smiled when it lit up. While the first batch baked, she ate dinner and then washed all the dishes and did a general clean up of the kitchen. She wasn't an obsessive housekeeper, but did like things nice and neat.

When the second batch of pies was baking, she took an apple down to Billy Bob and bedded him down for the night. She was getting used to walking in the dark, though it was a bit challenging picking out his stall.

"I'll get batteries tomorrow," she told him. Everything rested on tomorrow. Pie deliveries first, then business cards, hay, paint. "I'll see you in the morning."

She thought about the old man as she walked back up to the house. She hadn't seen him for a couple of days, the little boy either, or the pigeon. "They've all deserted me."

During the third batch of pies baking, she curled up on the couch with an afghan and started reading the Catherine Dewhurst biography. It had started out as an autobiography but Catherine died before it was done and her friends finished writing it for her. Hannah liked that. She smiled, thinking about the book Lucinda and Colleen would write about her. She could see the first line. "She was stubborn and relentless...."

When she phone rang, she knew it would be one of them.

"How's it going?" Lucinda asked.

"Great, I'm about to take the third batch out and put the fourth one in."

"Are you all ready for your date?"

"It's tomorrow. And no."

"What are you going to wear?"

"I don't know," she said, and changed the subject. "Raven's friend Ricky, do you remember her, she made a card design for me. I'm going to get card stock tomorrow and print some at work."

"Did you look at it?"

"No, I was busy all day. A lot going on." She let it go at that. No sense talking about losing her job until it happens. "I gotta go, the timer went off."

"Okay, do you want to do breakfast Saturday?"

"I'll let you know."

Fourth batch of pies, Hannah took a shower and put on a pair of pajamas. It was the first time she'd worn pajamas since she'd moved here. She was definitely settling in. She closed the drapes and picked the book back up. "Catherine Dewhurst was a hellion." She laughed reading that line. "She was a drinker and a smoker. She liked the company of men." Married six times, when she passed, she was engaged to wed number seven. "Oh, she was a looker," her intended said. "She worked hard and she played hard."

Hannah studied the photos in the center of the book. Catherine was smiling in each one. "Apparently she was never sad," Hannah said. She particularly liked the one of Catherine during a refreshment break at a fox hunt. She was riding a big gray, dressed in a scarlet coat, and was reaching down for a cocktail.

Fifth batch of pies, Hannah had to fight falling asleep; her eyes were tired, her mind was tired, her body was tired. When the timer went off, she heaved a tremendous sigh of relief. She took the pies out, turned the oven off, and left the oven door open.

"Done." She slid into bed and covered herself up to her chin. The kitchen was nice and warm all evening, but the living room had chilled off. It was too late to light a fire. She'd have to tend to it to get it going. "If I wake up as a Popsicle, so be it."

She woke to the first snow of the season. It was just a dusting, but snow nonetheless. She was thankful for the insulated drapes, as the windows were frosted on the outside. She turned the news on and was happy to hear it was going up into the mid-fifties and would be sunny all afternoon. "That's good to know, Mr. Weatherman, 'cause I've got a busy day ahead of me. Thank you!"

She took care of Billy Bob. "No, that's not a joke, that's snow," she said. "But don't worry, it's going to warm up nice. I'll be back down before I leave."

Hank was right on time for his pies and dove right into the custard one. "Oh, baby, I've been waiting for this all week. Oh, this is delicious," he said, with his mouth full. "Just like my grandmother used to make."

Hannah smiled and glanced from the living room to the kitchen. "Hank, would there be a way I could move the phone into the kitchen without it costing a fortune? I'd like it at my desk."

"Well, that makes sense," he said. "I'll be right back." He took the custard pie with him and ate it all the way to the truck. He came back with a roll of cord and in five minutes had the phone moved. Hannah sat at her desk and picked it up. "Hello."

Hank laughed. "I'll see you next week. Two fruit, one custard." When he paid her she started to give some of it back.

"How much do I owe you for moving the phone?"

"Oh, nothing," he said. "It never happened."

Hannah smiled. "I'll see you next week."

She hurried down to the barn to turn Billy Bob out, filled his water buckets and gave him extra hay, then grabbed the CD off her desk, loaded up some pies, and left for work. "If I'm lucky, it'll be a light day. Oh listen to you, next week you'll be crying you have no job."

She stopped at the office supply store to pick up card stock. The drug store was right next to it; she went in and bought batteries. Then she stopped at the gas station and got ten dollars worth of gas. "Thank heaven you get good mileage."

"What?" a man standing at the next gas pump said.

Hannah chuckled. "Nothing, I was talking to my truck."

"I hear ya," the man said. "If gas prices keep going up, I'm gonna to be talking to a Volkswagen."

Hannah drove to work in a good mood, positive attitude. "Live for the moment, live for the day."

"Bullshit," her mother would say to such "cockeyed optimism."
Hannah laughed.

"What's so funny?" Richard asked, greeting her at the door with
his "Mortician Face" on.

"Nothing. Do you have good news or bad?"

"Neither," he said, rubbing his forehead and pinching the bridge of
his nose. Migraine time. "I can't decide."

Hannah nodded sympathetically. "I'm sure it's not an easy
decision."

He shook his head. "You got that right."

"So what's going on today?"

"Oh, not much. The two showings. You'll just need to set up
coffee and…." He trailed off, preoccupied with his pending decision.

"Do you mind if I use the computer for a minute." Hannah held up
the CD. "My business cards."

"No, go right ahead," he said, and followed her. He leaned over
her shoulder as she pulled it up on the computer. "Wow, those are nice,
Hannah."

She smiled. Raven's friend Ricky had followed through with her
suggestion to use a steaming pie as the logo. "She's right, it grabs ya! I
like it, I really do." But what caught her attention mostly, was the title
of her business. "Hannah's Famous Pies."

She sat back and crossed her arms.

Richard picked up the envelope of card stock and loaded several
sheets into the printer. "Let's see what they look like in person."

Hannah chuckled, then hit Print and waited.

"Wow!" they both said.

"Very professional," Richard added.

Hannah nodded. "I guess I'm in business." No sooner said, she
wondered out loud. "Do I need a permit?" That thought instantly led to
another; oh no, that certified letter. "How did I forget that?"

"What?" Richard said.

"Nothing; it's nothing." While Hannah ran off another sheet of
cards, Richard separated the first two sheets at the perforated edges. He
stacked them nice and neat. When they were done with all of them, he
drew a breath and sighed.

"If only I could decide."

Hannah put the cards in her purse and so she wouldn't forget, took
the CD and the rest of the card stock out to the truck. "Well, hello

there," she said. The carrier pigeon was perched on the driver's side mirror. "I was wondering about you." She stroked its little head. "How are you? Where's your friend?" She looked around and found her, him, in one of the trees near the back door. She smiled. "I see you two are still together. Good for you." When she opened her truck door, the carrier pigeon hopped up onto the cab and started preening. "You'd better go on home now. I've got work to do."

She went back inside and prepared the coffee and tea and put out cookies for the guests. She gave the bathrooms a quick check, straightened the hangers in the cloak room, organized the cards, brochures, and handouts. She glanced in at the flowers around the coffins, knew better than to touch them, that was Richard's department. He always spread them out too far apart in her opinion, but.... She lined up the chairs, turned on all the lamps, and switched on the music.

So somber, so sad.

She checked on both of the deceased, said a silent prayer for each and went looking for Richard. He was at his desk, still fretting.

"You're all set," she said. "Thanks for letting me print out the cards."

"Anytime," he said. "Well, for as long as I'm here, that is."

Hannah shook her head. "If you need me before Monday, give me a call." She hesitated at the door, and walked back, smiling. "Here. Here's my card."

She delivered six pies on the far side of town and gave each person a card, then drove home, checked on Billy Bob, and picked up the other six pies, delivered them, handed out more cards. She stopped at the hardware store to pick up the paint, gave them a card too, and then it was on to the drugstore for the answering machine. She bought a can of root beer, a treat – it was ice cold, and ate her peanut butter and jelly sandwich on the way to get hay.

The young man at the loading dock told her they were sold out. "We should be getting some more in next week."

"What? I've already paid."

"Oh, you're Hannah? Oh, don't worry. We have yours. Pull around to the other side."

Hannah sighed. Thank heaven. "I'll take forty now and come back for the other thirty in about an hour." She gave the kid the rest of the money and went inside to use the ladies room. They had a bulletin board next to the exit door. Hannah tacked a business card to it.

Billy Bob looked up and nickered when he saw her coming down over the hill with a load of hay. She backed the truck up between the barn entrance and his pasture, and he helped himself. He took a bite out of one and then another, and then another.

Hannah laughed. "What are you doing, a taste test?"

She lowered the tailgate and climbed up, untied the rope holding the hay in place, and started throwing them into the barn aisle way. When her arms got tired of tossing, she hopped down off the truck and started stacking the hay. She already had the wood pallets in place where she wanted them. Being an old hand at this and as fit as they come, she had the rest of the hay unloaded and stacked in no time. She took a breather, checked Billy Bob's water, gave him some hay, and headed back to the feed mill. While the young man loaded the remaining thirty bales, Hannah went inside and bought a bag of sweet feed and two bags of wood shavings. The clerk wheeled it out on a dolly and Hannah stacked them onto the passenger seat of her truck. "We be loaded now," she said.

When the hay was tied down and secure, Hannah pulled out and drove home, smiling and singing along with Melissa Manchester on the radio. "I'm going back someday, come what may, to Blue Bayou. Where the fishing boats and the sails afloat on Blue Bayou." She had her arm propped out the window, her hand loose on the wheel, and couldn't have been happier. "That familiar sunrise through sleepy eyes, on Blue Bayou." But then all of a sudden a thought crossed her mind. "Oh shit! That damned certified letter." She turned around and headed back into town.

"I'm sorry, Hannah," the postmaster said. "It's out on the truck. Your carrier was going to attempt to deliver it again today." There was a notice in her mailbox when she got home.

"Final attempt at delivery. Pick up your certified letter at the post office."

"Guess it'll just have to wait till tomorrow." Hannah leafed through days of mail: the electric bill, the gas bill, three offers for a credit card, more junk mail. She stuffed the mail in her visor and started down over the hill to unload the rest of the hay.

"Wait a minute."

She turned the truck around and parked it at the back door, then went inside to get a paintbrush and a screw driver. She opened the can of paint and climbed up onto the tailgate. From there she set the paint

235

and brush onto the roof and climbed up onto the hay and stepped right onto the roof. She still had plenty of daylight, got both windows painted in about a half hour, climbed back down, walked to the end of the driveway and painted the mailbox and post.

She unloaded the rest of the hay, brought Billy Bob inside, and fed him his dinner. "I have a date," she told him. "But don't worry, I won't be too late." She petted his neck and mane. "You're all set for the winter now, big guy. You have enough hay now through March. Isn't it a good feeling knowing that?"

Billy Bob munched his grain.

"I'll see you later."

She pulled the truck back up and around and admired the newly painted windows on the back of the house. "It's all done, all of it. Let it snow, let it snow, let is snow."

Chapter Forty-One

Hannah looked in the mirror and for a moment didn't recognize the woman she saw gazing back at her. But then the hurt appeared in her eyes, the uncertainty...the fear. "I'd much rather just stay home," she said. "I'm not ready for this."

"When *will* you be ready?" a voice in her head asked.

"I don't know, probably never."

She'd decided to wear her hair up again. It was a fancy restaurant, why not? She wore her gray dress slacks, but with a different blouse. This one was pink and purple with a swirly pattern. She liked this blouse. She remembered the day she bought it. Where were she and Charlie going? Someplace special? Was it someone's anniversary? She slipped on her gray shoes and took her gray sweater out of the drawer. She glanced at the clock. Seven twenty-two. Dave would be here any minute.

She put a couple more logs on the fire and turned when there was a knock on the door. The drapes were open. She couldn't run, she couldn't hide, though both of those thoughts did cross her mind. She drew a deep breath and exhaled slowly, then walked across the room feeling slightly lightheaded.

She opened the door. "Hello, come in."

Dave smiled and entered. It was obvious from the flush on his face that he too was nervous and perhaps had doubts. Hannah smiled. "Have you dated since your wife passed?"

He shook his head and changed the subject. "The living room looks nice. What's wrong with the upstairs?" he asked, motioning to the bed.

"Well, I decided to shut it off for the winter. There's no sense heating it if I don't have to." She picked up her sweater and purse and motioned to the door. "We'd better get going. What time is our reservation?"

"Eight," he said.

As they walked out to his truck, Dave glanced back over his shoulder. "The trim looks nice."

Hannah nodded. "I know. I like it."

"Are you going to paint the siding?"

Hannah shook her head. "Not this year."

"Because I can help you if you want," he said, opening the door for her.

"Thank you," she said, implying both, the offer to help, and his gentlemanly act of opening the door for her. "I'll keep that in mind."

He had the radio playing softly in the truck. It saved them from what could have been an entirely awkward silence. Hannah gazed out her window and smiled when she saw the old man standing in the side yard with Bessie. "It's going to be cold tonight," she said.

"What?"

She looked at Dave. "Um, I was just saying that it's going to be cold tonight. I think I heard on the news that we're going down to twenty-five."

"Are you heating with just wood?"

"So far. The furnace was serviced recently, there's a sticker on it. I kicked it on and it works. I just don't want to use it until I need to. Charlie and I used to..." She paused. "I'm sorry."

"No, that's okay. You were saying?"

"I was saying, we used to heat entirely with wood. It's a different kind of heat. It somehow seems warmer to me."

"I used to have oil. Then when they put gas lines down our road I switched. I like it, it's nice and clean."

Hannah smiled. Talk about idle conversation. They bypassed the line at the restaurant and were seated off in a corner by a window. A soft candle lit their table in contrast to the rather lively music playing. A waiter took their drink order.

"A gimlet sounds good," Hannah said.

"Vodka on the rocks," Dave said.

Hannah opened the menu. She could eat for a week on what the entrée's cost.

Dave leaned forward. "Do you want an appetizer?"

"I don't know. I don't want to spoil my dinner. Do you want to split one?"

"Sure."

They settled on the artichoke spinach dip. It arrived within minutes, steaming hot and served with tortilla chips and pita bread. "This is delicious," Hannah said. It tasted especially good with the gimlet.

"So what are your plans, Hannah?" Dave said, out of the blue.

"Um...." She pointed to the menu, as if that's what he meant. "I'm leaning toward the petit filet and stuffed scampi."

He smiled. "I'm going to have the porterhouse. But I was asking more along the lines of your future, tomorrow, next week, next month, next year."

Hannah wondered if holding up her hand would get her off the hook. Probably not. "Well...." She sat back. "If there's one thing I've learned over the years, it's to not plan too far ahead and don't count on anything. Jobs come and go, people come and go, husbands come and go." She chuckled and picked up the menu again.

"What? That's it?" he said.

Hannah shrugged. "Listen, here's the way I look at it. I can plan things and sometimes I get lucky and they happen, but sometimes they don't. I've got myself to look out for and Billy Bob. It's a good feeling knowing I've got the barn stacked with hay and a lot of pasture for next year when I can get it fenced in. I've got the beginnings of the pie business. Oh, which reminds me." She fished a business card out of her purse and handed it to him. "It's official. It says so right there."

Dave smiled. "Can I keep this?"

"Yes." She sipped her drink. "So what about you? What are your plans?"

"I'm not quite sure," he said, falling silent when the waiter returned to the table. The music started playing even louder right about then.

"So…?" Hannah said, leaning forward when they'd placed their orders and were technically alone again. "You were saying?"

Dave hesitated. "Well, my future plans depend a lot on you, Hannah."

"Me?" Hannah frowned, thinking, I'm struggling with the concept of first dates and relationships, and he's planning our future?

"I've been thinking," he said.

Hannah nodded. "Apparently so."

He smiled. "I know I said I wasn't going to push you and that there was no pressure. And that's true, but."

Hannah chuckled. "Tell me now before I eat, I don't want to be beholden for my dinner if I don't like where this is headed."

Dave laughed. "You're fun to be with, Hannah."

"I'm a laugh a minute," she said, and finished her gimlet.

"Would you like another one?"

"No." She pointed to her glass of water. "This'll do. Maybe later."

The waiter brought their Caesar salads to the table and took away the empty artichoke bowl. "That was delicious," Hannah said.

"Do you know how to make it?" Dave asked, when the man walked away.

"Of course, it's simple."

"Is yours better, the same, or not as good?"

Hannah looked at him. "Better."

Dave laughed again. "See, that's another thing I like about you, Hannah. You say what you think. You don't mince words."

Hannah took a bite of her salad and shrugged. "I haven't mastered pizza. Mine's good, but not as good as pizza parlor pizza. I think it's their ovens."

"Hannah?" Someone being seated at the table next to them called her name.

She turned. "Oh, Louise! Hello, how are you?" The two women stood up and hugged one another. "It's so good to see you!"

"How are *you*? You look great!"

"You too!"

"Wow, it's been a long time!"

."We'll have to get together soon. There's a show in a couple of weeks at Danbury. Do you want to go?"

"Sure, sounds good," Hannah said. "I moved so I'll have to give you my new phone number. Wait. I just so happen to have a card."

When Hannah sat back down, Dave sighed and leaned forward. "You'd better finish your salad," he said. "They'll be bringing our meals soon."

Hannah just looked at him for a moment and then picked up her fork. "I know I asked you this before, but you didn't really answer me. What was your wife like?" It was Hannah's guess that she must have been rather subservient.

Dave downed the rest of his vodka. "She was a good woman. She took good care of me. I took good care of her."

Hannah smiled. "I see." She didn't really know any more now than she did before and was about to ask something more specific when he stopped her.

"Just so you know, Hannah, I would take good care of you too."

Hannah almost choked on the salad. She reached for her glass of water to wash the vinegar down.

"Hear me out," he said. "I'm going to lay it on the line here. I'll wait, but these are my intentions, my thoughts. You don't need to make pies, I've said that before. You don't need to fix up that old house, or that barn. My farm is paid for, I earn a good living."

Hannah looked at him. Did he actually make a face when he said, "that barn?"

"I have plenty of room for your horse. He'd have a big six-acre pasture with good fencing and a sturdy barn."

"Dave, in all due respects," Hannah said, still trying to discreetly clear her throat of the vinegar. She coughed several times. "I'm not even comfortable with this dating process yet. This is my first date in say, oh about, forty years. You are *way* ahead of me."

He smiled. "I'm just letting you know my intentions. They are honorable."

"Duly noted." Hannah nodded.

The waiter appeared at her side just then. "Your petit filet and stuffed scampi, Ma'am."

"Thank you," she said, for more reasons than one. "It looks delicious."

Oddly enough, as soon as they'd started eating, Dave became more relaxed, more personable and less man-on-a mission-ish. Now that he'd stated his intentions and got that out of the way, he was rather charming. Somehow they got onto the subject of High School, favorite teachers, teachers they hated, the state championship football game their senior year.

"I didn't know you even played," Hannah said.

"Yep, I was the backup quarterback."

"Good for you."

"I warmed the bench a lot. They put me in that day at the two-minute warning. I threw three short passes and then I took a knee and ran out the clock."

Hannah smiled. "Isn't it amazing the things we never forget."

When they were done eating, the waiter appeared immediately at their side to take their dishes away. "I'll be back with the dessert menu."

Dave looked up at him. "No thanks. I think we're okay."

The waiter turned to Hannah. "Ma'am?"

She smiled. "Yes, I'd like to see the menu."

Dave sat back. "I also wrestled in High School. I guess I'm still making weight."

Hannah studied the dessert menu. "Wow, everything looks good. What do you suggest?" she asked the waiter. "What's the crowd favorite?"

"The Banana's Foster. It's to die for," he said.

"Then that's what I'll have."

"Would you care for a cocktail, brandy, or a glass of wine to go with that?"

"A glass of merlot would be nice."

When the waiter bowed and backed away smiling, Dave shook his head. "What is it with you and waiters and bartenders?"

Hannah laughed. "I am a server. We are kindred spirits. Look at you!"

"Thank you." He reached for her hand and kissed the back of it. "It's nice to be included in your "stable" of admirers."

"You old charmer, you," Hannah said.

Dave blushed.

"So tell me about your children," she said, sliding her hand away and taking another drink of water.

"Well, as you know I have two sons. They're both married and live in Franklin County. The one is a mechanic and the other one is an accountant." He told her all about where they lived. One had just built a new home, the other, lived in an apartment over the shop where he worked. "They're a lot alike in some ways," he said. "And complete opposites in others."

"Do you have any grandchildren?"

"Just one so far, a little girl, Nancy. She's going to start school next year and I hardly know her."

"Why's that?"

"Well." He shrugged. "The boys are busy, and so am I."

Hannah nodded. She found it interesting that he'd referred to his sons as boys, and no mention of the wives. "Are your two sons close?"

"Oh yeah," he said. "They're best friends."

Hannah sat back and smiled. Here came the Banana's Foster. The waiter placed it in front of her and lit it. "Ooh...." When the flame went out, she ventured a taste. "Oh my goodness," she said to the waiter. "You were right."

She offered some to Dave. He declined. "Go ahead," he said. "Enjoy yourself."

"Thank you."

Dave looked up at the waiter. "The check?"

"I'll bring it right out."

Hannah let nothing of the Banana's Foster go to waste, and sipped her wine in between. "It really does go well together."

Dave sat back and crossed his arms. "Did you want to go for a night cap somewhere? There's a blues bar just around the corner."

"Thank you," she said. "But I think I'm comfortably done for the night. This has been a very nice first date. I don't want to overdo it."

"Okay," he said. "That's fine with me."

Hannah smiled. "I really do need to take this slow, Dave. I hope you understand."

He nodded and glanced away.

It was rather quiet in the truck, even with the radio playing. Hannah was deep in her own thoughts, and Dave, his. At the intersection in town, Hannah looked at him. "Would you mind stopping at the supermarket? I need to pick up a few things for the pies tomorrow and this'll save me coming back out."

He shrugged and pulled into the parking lot. "Do you want me to come in with you?"

"No, I'll only be a second. Thanks."

He'd turned the radio off while she was in the store. It made for an even quieter ride the rest of the way home. He obviously had something more on his mind he wanted to say, his goal perhaps for this first date, but Hannah didn't make it easy for him. Whatever it was, she would rather it wait. She hummed the tune "Amazing Grace."

"It's early, Hannah," he finally said.

It was close to ten. "I know, but I've got some pies to bake, and one is an experiment. It might take me a couple of tries."

"Do you need help?" he asked, as they pulled into her driveway.

"No," she said, and squeezed his hand. "This was really nice, Dave. Thank you." When she leaned over to kiss him on the cheek he turned and kissed her on the mouth.

"I love you," he said.

She shook her head.

"And I'm going to say it as many times as it takes till you believe me."

She touched his face gently. "Good night."

"Good night."

He waited until she'd gotten safely inside her house before he backed out of the drive. Hannah waved and he dimmed his lights, blinking them twice.

"Oh God," she said. "Why me?"

Chapter Forty-Two

Hannah changed into jeans and a sweatshirt, slipped on her boots, grabbed her flashlight, and headed down to the barn to check on Billy Bob. The old man was in the barn, apparently watching over him. He startled Hannah.

"What's going on?"

"Your horse is acting funny."

"Why, because he's seeing a ghost?"

The old man smiled. "No. He's just not himself."

Hannah looked in at him. He was just standing there at the back of the stall, and appeared fine at first glance, but the old man was right. He wasn't himself. "Billy Bob, what's going on?" She opened his stall gate, went in, and checked him over. He had lots of good sounds in his gut, his hay had been eaten, he'd drank a good amount of water.

"He looks sad," the old man said.

Hannah handed him the flashlight and shook her head when it dropped right down through his hands to the floor. She picked it up. Fortunately, it still worked. She propped it in between two bales of hay, aimed so she could see to pick out the stall. There was plenty of manure, two wet spots. His stall wasn't torn up, he didn't appear restless.

"I tell you, he's depressed."

Hannah looked at the old man. "About what?"

"I don't know. He's your horse."

Hannah shook her head and smiled, so much for his pleasant mood of late.

"Billy Bob, are you depressed?"

Her horse sighed.

"Are the spirit horses out?"

The old man shook his head. "Not yet. Maybe they're depressed too."

Hannah chuckled.

"It's not funny."

"I know," she said. "But I just had a dinner date and a couple of drinks. I guess I'm feeling a little mellow."

"Women should not drink," the old man said.

Hannah looked at him. "Yeah, right, and men should not say things like that."

The old man shook his head. "You need to figure out what's wrong with your horse and take care of him. I have to go."

Hannah waved; good-bye, good riddance.

The old man looked back from the door. "You went on a date?"

"Yes, not that it's any of your business."

"I thought you were still married."

"I am, technically."

The old man shook his head again and disappeared.

Hannah gave Billy Bob hay and topped off his water and stood looking in at him. Though indeed he did look depressed, he'd seemed fine before she left for dinner. "I'll come check on you again in a little while. I've got to bake some pies. Wish me luck on the peach one." She hesitated, about to say, "You, behave now," but didn't. "Okay, you can be bad, just not too bad, only mildly bad, nothing dangerous bad. Kick the wall or something, just not the gate."

Rather than waste a whole pie, she decided to cook sample peaches on the stovetop. The first batch she sweetened with orange juice, too tart. The second batch, she sweetened with pear juice. "Nothing to brag about." The third batch, she sweetened with a little boysenberry juice. "Now we're getting somewhere." She didn't want to use too much, for fear the peaches would taste more like the boysenberry than peaches, and on a whim, she mixed the three batches together. They tasted good. "Almost as good as the Banana's Foster." She pureed the mix, added lots of cinnamon and cloves, a little corn starch and butter, and used it as a dressing for the peach pie.

Before long, she had it and the two Boysenberry Surprise pies in the oven. Though it had only been an hour or so since she'd checked on Billy Bob, she was concerned, so back down to the barn she went. He seemed fine, was eating, and had another pile of manure in the back of his stall. She'd brought the thermometer down and checked his temperature. It was normal.

"You do still seem a little down though, big guy."

He sighed.

"I'll see you in the morning. I'm going to be home mostly all day. I just have to deliver the pies and that's it. You and me'll go for a ride." She gave him a big hug. "Don't be depressed. I love you," she said.

As she walked back up the hill to the house, the thought occurred to her that love just isn't enough sometimes. She looked over her shoulder from the back door and could make out the silhouettes of the spirit horses.

"But sometimes love is the only thing you have to give."

She checked on the pies and while they finished baking, closed the living room drapes and put on her pajamas. She lit a fire in the fireplace and curled up on the couch. "Let's see what Catherine Dewhurst is up to."

She'd been to a cocktail party, one of her friends wrote, and had too much to drink. She got into a fight with her escort, a man she hardly knew, and walked home two miles in high heels, champagne glass in one hand and bottle in the other.

The phone rang. Hannah answered it, expecting it to be either Lucinda or Colleen, wanting details of the date. It was Dave.

"I figured you'd still be up."

"Yep," Hannah said. "The pies are almost done."

"I wanted to thank you again for going out with me tonight. It means a lot."

"It was fun. Thank *you*."

"Anytime. Good night, Hannah."

"Good night."

Hannah sat back and sighed. He was such a nice guy.

When the timer for the pies went off, she welcomed the diversion from her thoughts. She placed the pies on a towel on the counter to cool, turned the oven off, left the over door open for heat, and went to bed. Halfway through the night, she got up to add more logs to the fire in the fireplace. It sparked and crackled.

"Apple wood," she muttered. She pulled the drape back and gazed out into the night. It was snowing. She thought about the carrier pigeon. Is he or she used to being outside when it's this cold? Do they become dependent on shelter when they're domesticated?

She climbed back into bed, lay watching the fire, and recalled all the nights on the farm when she and Charlie slept on the sofa bed in front of the fireplace to stay warm. How they warmed one another. "Remember that night we got two feet of snow." She closed her eyes, could feel his arms around her, could hear his voice, and drifted off to sleep.

When she woke in the morning, there were still warm embers in the fireplace. She looked outside. They'd gotten a couple of inches of snow. She made a pot of coffee, sniffed the pies, then bundled up and headed down to the barn.

Billy Bob nickered as the sound of her boots crunching along. He seemed happy to see her, but hadn't eaten all of his hay. That was unusual for him. She checked his stall for manure; there were several healthy-looking piles and a fresh wet spot.

"I don't know about you, Billy Bob. Don't you dare get sick on me."

He dove right into his grain, which was a good sign.

"It's Saturday," she told him. "It's just you and me, big guy. Well, aside from those errands I mentioned. Did you know I'm starting my own business? Yep, I am." She gave him a little more hay, dumped his water buckets, scrubbed them and filled them, and brushed him while he nibbled at his hay.

"It's the same hay as before, Billy Bob."

She picked it up and smelled it. "It smells yummy! If I had some salad dressing, I'd join you." She checked his mouth; he slobbered all over her arm. His mouth looked good. She checked his legs. She ran her fingers down his back. He didn't dip, flinch, nothing.

"Okay, I have deemed you are fine. You're just 'not yourself.' Who are you, Billy Bob?" she teased. "Are you a ringer?" She scratched the back of his ears and he turned his head, the way he always did when she scratched his ears.

"Yep, you're Billy Bob. No doubt about it." She gave him a pat on the shoulder and walked out of the stall and closed the stall gate. "I'll be back down after I deliver the pies. And you had better snap out of it!" she added, smiling. "You and me are connected at the hip. You keep this up and *I'll* get depressed." She paused. "Who am I kidding, I am depressed."

Back up at the house, she poured herself a cup of coffee and scrambled up the last of the eggs, used what was left of the butter, and had some "jelly toast," as her mom would say. It tasted good. She did up the dishes, left them in the strainer to dry, and washed up and headed out to deliver the pies. She drove to the restaurant in Crawford County first.

The woman seemed pleased with the looks of the pies, but said she wanted to taste them. She cut herself a slice of one. "I've heard a lot about this Boysenberry Surprise."

Hannah watched her eyes as she took a bite and smiled.

"The texture is good, the crust is delicious, nice and flaky, the boysenberry isn't too sweet, it's not tart. I definitely want ten each week."

"All Boysenberry Surprise?"

"No, mix them up." She reached into the cash register and handed Hannah a twenty-dollar bill plus a five for delivery. Hannah glanced at the handwritten menu above the counter. A piece of pie sold for $2.99.

Hannah thanked her, and felt good about the deal. She'd made a profit and so would the restaurant.

"Can you deliver them every Saturday morning right around this time?"

"Yep, I'll see you next week." Hannah handed her one of her business cards. "I'm going to look into getting plastic containers for the pies."

From there she drove to Cal Able's and smiled at the sight of that huge sign of his above the building, "CAL ABLE - TO PUT YOU IN A CAR TODAY!" It had to be twenty-feet tall. His big shiny Cadillac was parked out front.

He looked up and grinned when she walked in. "Hey, darlin'!"

"Your pie, sir," Hannah said.

"I've been looking forward to this." He dug into his pocket for money to pay her. "Were you just passing by?"

"Yes." Hannah laughed. "But before you pay me, I want you to taste it first."

He reached for one of several forks lined up on his desk. "Drum roll, please," he said, and piled the fork high.

Hannah watched his expression. As soon as the pie made it to his mouth, it was as if his face lit up. "Is it good?"

"Better than good." He ate another forkful. "I don't know which one I like best, the apple or this."

Hannah gave him her card and held her hand out for the money. "Enjoy," she said. "And don't eat it all in one day."

She stopped at the grocery store and picked up a pound of butter. She figured with what food she still had at home, that was all she needed to get her through until payday Monday. Since she hadn't heard from Richard, she decided to stop at the funeral parlor to check in on him, and was surprised to find he wasn't there.

"Hmmm...."

By the time she arrived back home, the snow was all but melted. The sun was out and the sky was blue. She put Billy Bob out into his pasture, cleaned his stall, gave him some hay and water, and promised she'd be right back down. She expected him to buck and play a little when she'd turned him out, but he didn't. He was eating his hay though, which was a positive sign.

She sat down at the kitchen desk and opened the answering machine container. "I hope this isn't too complicated." It wasn't. All she had to do was plug one end of the little cord into the wall and the other into the phone. Done. She read the message instructions. Then she got all ready, took a deep breath and pushed down on the recording button.

"Hello, you have reached...." She stopped the recording. Don't just say Hannah, they'll know you're a woman alone. She tried again. "Hello, you have the...."

"Reached, silly," she told herself. "Reached." Maybe if I write it down. "Hello, you have reached the Shaw residence." Wait a minute, do I want to say residence? Am I really still a Shaw?

She pushed the button. "Hello, you have reached Hannah's Famous Pies. If you leave your name and number...." She stopped it again. "Do I want to say, I'll call you back, or *we'll* call you back?"

"Last time," she said. She pushed the button. "Hello, you have reached Hannah's Famous Pies. We can't take your call right now, but if you leave your name and phone number, Hannah will call you back. Thank you and have a great day!" She pushed Stop and sat back. "I'm sweating," she said, and wiped her brow. "I'd have never made it as an actress."

She played the message over, was happy with it, and headed back outside. The carrier pigeon and his friend were at the bird feeder. As Hannah watched, the two of them flew from one side to the other, flapping their wings and squawking. She smiled.

"Are we having a disagreement?" She checked the feeder; there was plenty of birdseed left. "What's going on?"

The carrier pigeon's friend flew up into the tree, squawked some more, and then took flight. Hannah and the carrier pigeon watched as it circled round and round and then landed on the feeder again and nudged its mate.

Hannah saddened. "I think she's telling you it's time to fly to warmer weather." Hannah swallowed hard. "I think I agree with her. The nights are getting too cold." When she reached up for the carrier pigeon, his mate squawked and squawked at her. She held the carrier pigeon close. "Come back in the spring, little one. It's time for you to go." She pressed her cheek to the side of his face. "It's time."

When she turned him loose, he and his mate flew high, circling above her again and again, soaring, and then finally the two of them flew away, headed South. Hannah wiped her eyes. "You came when I needed you, little one. Thank you."

Chapter Forty-Three

No sooner had Hannah started back down over the hill, she heard the mail truck. "Oh no." She'd forgotten to stop at the post office again.

How can I keep forgetting, she wondered, and decided that she'd better go now. She went inside the house for her purse and the certified letter notice and saw that she had a message on the answering machine. "Already?" She pressed the Play button.

"Hi, Hannah, it's Richard. I wanted to let you know I haven't made up my mind yet. This is such a difficult decision. I'll let Jeb know too. My head is killing me. I'll see you Monday."

At the post office, she went through the formality of signing for the letter and walked to the truck with the dreaded certified letter in hand. Part of her didn't want to open it, ever, let alone now. She used her keychain to open the letter and started reading.

"What?" She glanced at everything around her. It was Twilight Zone time again. "I just bought the house. How can this be?" The letter stated that she owed $3,205.63 in back taxes. Legal action would take place if the taxes were not paid in full within ten days from the date on the letter, seven days ago. She scanned down the page, various words leaping up at her along the way. Lien, garnishment, attachment, attorney, sheriff's sale....

"You've got to be kidding me." Her first instinct was to go straight to the Courthouse. But then she remembered it was Saturday. She laid the letter down and stared out the window, then picked the letter back up and read it again. The taxes on the property hadn't been paid for the last eighteen months. She shook her head and tried putting the truck into gear, but it wouldn't budge. The motor wasn't running.

"Breathe," she said to herself. "Just calm down and breathe. There has to be an explanation for this. I'll have to try and get ahold of the landlord." Her heart dropped. The old man's son; E.J. Riley. "Out of the country." She started the truck and drove down the road in a haze.

Her first thoughts were not about how being homeless was going to affect *her*. All she could think about was Billy Bob. "I promised him he'd never have to leave home again."

"Promises, promises," she could hear her mother say.

She saw a package on the porch when she pulled into her driveway. She parked the truck at the back door and walked around to the front of the house. The package was from the local Chamber of Commerce Welcome Wagon. It was full of discount coupons for local businesses, samples of cleaning products, a granola bar, diet lemonade-flavored powder straws, a bar of soap, and a mini-sized deodorant.

"They got me covered," she said, and walked down over the hill to feed the granola bar to Billy Bob. "I have some bad news, big guy," she said. "There's some back taxes owed on this property."

Billy Bob licked her hand of every last morsel.

"I don't understand how they could have sold me this farm if that was the case. Then again, it's not like I went through a bank or a realtor. Of course it's Saturday and I can't find anything out."

Billy Bob sighed and went back to eating what was left of his hay. "Wait a minute. You're almost out of hay." That was a good sign. She threw him some more hay and stood watching him for a moment. "I'll bet you're just tired of being in the barn by yourself in the dark. If I could bring you up into the house, Billy Bob, I would. I'm lonely too."

There was another message on the answering machine. It was from Colleen. "Okay, so we're obviously not doing breakfast. How about dinner? Call me."

Hannah picked up the phone and dialed her number. She answered on the second ring. "We are so wanting to know how the date went."

"Well," Hannah said. "It was nice."

"Are you okay? You sound sad."

"No, I'm fine. I just didn't get much sleep last night."

"Oh…?"

Hannah chuckled. "I baked some more pies."

"So, you want to do something?"

Not really, she thought. "Well, I don't want to go to the Honky Tonk, that's for sure."

"Why not? Dave's off tonight. He won't be there."

"Oh really? Okay."

"Do you want to meet around seven?"

"Make it eight and I'll see you all there." As she was about to hang up, a thought crossed her mind. "This isn't a setup, is it?"

"No. I wouldn't do that to you, girlfriend."

Hannah chuckled. "You have in the past."

"Not anymore."

Hannah hung up and sat staring at the other two Courthouse envelopes on her desk. "They probably say the same thing as this one or worse," she said, laying the certified letter down next to them. She propped her elbows on the desk and put her head in her hands. "Everything was going so good. I should have known better." She picked her head up and looked around. "I love this house. How could this happen?"

"It'll take six months to get you out," she recalled their attorney saying when she and Charlie were first served papers on their farm. "And that's when we had an actual deed. I've only been here one month. One month," she repeated. "I don't have a leg to stand on." She figured she'd be lucky if she had a couple of weeks. "What am I going to do? I don't even know if I still have a job."

Tears welled up in her eyes and trickled down her cheeks. "Damn it! How much more can I take?" she said, and shook her head. When the phone rang again, she let it ring. It was a woman in Portsmouth wanting to order two pies. She left a number.

Hannah thought about her date last night. "I'll take good care of you," Dave said. That seemed so tempting at the moment, more than tempting. Things would be good for Billy Bob there too. She looked at her left hand and traced the indentation where her wedding band used to be.

"Charlie left you. What part of that don't you understand? He left you to fend for yourself. He left you knowing you had to take care of Billy Bob. He left you, plain and simple. Deal with it." All those voices.

"I am dealing with it."

"No, you're not."

"I drove him away."

"No, you didn't. And you've mourned enough. Look at you now. In a week, you're going to be homeless, no job, no nothing. You need to make a decision."

"Oh my God," she said, replaying over and over again Dave's comments at dinner last night. "That's it. That's why? That's why he loves me."

She shook her head and grabbed her keys. "Why didn't I see this earlier? It's as plain as day. 'I love you. I'll take care of you. I'll be good to you.'" How many times did he say that? And he means it. He means every word. *He* would never leave you.

Hannah hesitated before getting into her truck and looked around at everything she had here, everything she stood to lose, everything she would have to leave behind. Do you know what you're doing? Do you know what you're going to say? "No, but I have to make this right. I have to make him understand. I've hurt him enough already. And if anybody knows what hurt is, it's me." With that resolve, she climbed into her truck and drove across town to Dave's.

Chapter Forty-Four

With each stop sign, each traffic light, each turn, Hannah became more and more convinced this was the right thing to do. "I should have realized this sooner."

Dave was surprised when he opened his front door and saw her standing there, looking anxious. "Hannah? Are you all right?"

She nodded and gave him a hug, hugged him tight, and then drew a deep breath looking up at him. "You are the nicest man," she said. "And you have been so kind to me. I can't thank you enough for making me feel good about myself. But I'm sorry, Dave. We need to talk."

He stepped out of the way and motioned for her to come in. "This isn't good, is it? I pushed you too hard last night. I know that now."

Hannah sat down on the chair near the sofa and waited for him to sit down facing her. "It's about me. I keep asking you, why me? I think I know the answer to that now. You don't love me, Dave. You love the idea of taking care of me."

He shook his head.

"No, listen. I think you see me as, I don't know, wounded somehow. I'm that injured lamb you picked up and carried. You see me broken. You want to fix me and you want to fix everything around me - my barn, my gate, my house."

He sat back.

"I'm not saying that it's wrong and that you don't have good intentions. You've got such a good heart. But Dave, I'm not broken. At least, not in a way anyone can fix. I'm on my own in this. I'm on my own in everything I do. Charlie probably never gave it a thought: poor Hannah, how will she get along without me. He'd laugh if he heard someone say that. And yet, you don't see that side of me. I keep saying, you don't even know me, and you don't."

He crossed his arms.

"And look at you," she said. "You're sitting there and you're still thinking, what, that I'm only saying this because I'm hurting, that I don't really know what I need. Be honest, right? Isn't that what you're thinking?"

He tipped his head slightly and shrugged.

Hannah fell silent for a moment, just looking at him. "You're a good man, Dave. No, I don't know you inside and out, but from what I've seen...." She bit at her bottom lip. "There's a woman out there for you, one that you can take care of, and that'll stand at your side." She shook her head. "But it's not me. I'm sorry. It's not me."

When she rose to her feet, he stood also.

"Do you think with some time...?" he started to say.

Hannah shook her head and kissed him gently. "But I do plan to spend some time fixing you up with the perfect woman." She laughed and wiped her eyes. "I hope we can still be friends. You're a good friend to have."

He nodded, with big tears trickling down his face.

Hannah wiped them away with her sleeve. "Oh, and about last night." She reached into her pocket for her pie money. "This is for my share of the bill. That was awfully expensive."

"Hannah, that's not necessary."

"Oh, but it is," she said. "Because this," she took his hand and folded his fingers around the money. "Is who I am, Dave. This is the Hannah I've always been."

He smiled.

"So I'll see you Tuesday?"

Chili Night. "I'll see you Tuesday," he said.

As Hannah drove through town, she felt as if the weight of the world had been lifted from her shoulders. Then she passed the post office and after that the funeral parlor, and the certified letter, back taxes, and her job hanging in the balance came rushing to the forefront.

Instead of turning left at the main intersection, she turned right and drove exactly seven-point-two miles to her and Charlie's old farm. It wasn't a working farm anymore. It was a country estate. The couple that now owned it "Poured a ton of money into it," she'd heard on more than one occasion. "You should see it, Hannah."

"No thanks."

This would be the first time. It was pretty, but held no charm for her now. She found comfort in the fact that it hadn't been sold to a developer, but such a waste of all that good farmland, she thought. She remembered lying in bed and hearing the snowplows go down the road in the middle of the night. She remembered the sound of the rooster every morning at five. She remembered the cows, the warm milk. "Here, kitty-kitty." She remembered old Blue.

She didn't stop; she drove right on by, and took the next side-road home, her home for however long she had left there. When she rounded the bend and could see the house, she smiled. But then....

There was a semi-tractor trailer in her driveway. She pulled in slowly past it and parked. "What? Is somebody here to move me out already?" She got out, figuring to go talk to the driver to find out what was going on, and stared ahead.

"Charlie?"

He was sitting behind the wheel, with his arm propped on the open window.

"Charlie, is that you?"

He smiled.

"Oh my God," Hannah said, tears filling her eyes instantly. "Oh my God...." She climbed onto the footboard and touched his arm, his face. "What are you doing here, Charlie? What are you doing here?"

"I missed you, Babe," he said. "I'm so sorry."

Hannah kissed him, and then kissed him again. "Oh, God, please be real," she said. "You're not dead and a ghost, are you?"

"No."

She lowered her eyes to the name "Hannah" painted on his door, and touched it.

Charlie pulled her close and kissed her. "Please forgive me."

She nodded. "You forgive me too, right?"

He kissed her again. And then Hannah stepped down and turned around, and then turned around again. "Please, please, please, God, please. Please...."

Charlie climbed down out of the truck and took her into his arms. "I'm so sorry, Hannah. I'm so sorry."

Hannah nodded and held him tight. "Are you home now, Charlie?"

"If you'll have me?"

"I have you," she said, and laughed. "I mean..." she wiped her eyes. "I mean...."

Charlie laughed too, both wiping their eyes, laughing and hugging one another.

"Where have you been?"

"Everywhere," he said. "Everywhere."

Hannah pressed her hands to her face in an effort to compose herself. "I talk to you, you know. I talk to you all the time."

"I know. I talk to you too. You should hear some of the things I say, and the longer I'm on the road...."

Hannah laughed and took his hands in hers. There was *so much* to say, so much she wanted to know. So many things she couldn't think. "Um, when did you get the truck?"

"A little over a year ago," he said. "She's not paid for yet, not entirely, but the money's good and the work's steady. It won't be long."

Hannah looked at her name again, written on the door, and started crying all the more.

"Shhh..." he said. "It's all right. I'll never leave again, ever."

Hannah nodded, trembling.

"Except," he added, "three or four days at a time each week."

"I can handle that," Hannah said. "I think. As long as you *are* coming home."

Charlie kissed her and smiled. "So this is home?"

Hannah nodded and looked around. "At least for a little while."

He studied her eyes.

"Never mind. I'll tell you later," she said. "Did you see Billy Bob?"

"Yes, I gave him some hay."

"Was he happy to see you?"

"Oh, yeah. He tried to bite me."

Hannah laughed and slipped her hand in his. "Come on, I want to show you the house. You're going to love it."

Chapter Forty-Five

Hannah and Charlie spent the afternoon as if they were on a honeymoon. They made love, they showered, and they made love again. They even took a nap. "This is nice," Charlie said. "Laying here in bed and you next to me."

Hannah was right. He loved the house. She cuddled closer. "It has issues," she said. "I'll tell you all about it, but right now, I'm thinking I should figure out what we're going to eat for dinner."

"I'm really not all that hungry," Charlie said. "We can go get a burger or something."

Hannah glanced at the clock. "Well, I *was* supposed to meet the gang at the Honky Tonk in a little while."

"Sounds good to me," Charlie said. "Do you want to warn them first?"

"No, I'm thinking I'll surprise them, and if they don't see you standing next to me, I'll know I'm hallucinating."

Charlie laughed. "God, I've missed you." He smiled and pointed to their picture on the mantle. "I remember that day."

Hannah closed her eyes. If this is a dream, please don't let me wake up. "You've lost weight," she said.

He nodded. "You too."

Hannah propped herself up onto her elbow and looked at him. "So what kind of work did you do before you got the semi-truck?"

"Well, just about everything," he said. "Anything I could get. I didn't stay in one place too long. I drove a delivery truck for awhile. I worked on a horse farm for a couple of months. I worked on a digging crew. They were installing culvert pipe. I worked a cattle drive. I rode an unridable bull for ten seconds one day and made a hundred bucks. Good thing, because I had about five cents to my name at the time."

"I wish you would've come home sooner."

Charlie shook his head. "I wasn't coming home broke."

Hannah rested her head on his chest and relished the familiar beat of his heart.

"Oh, and I worked in a bowling alley for a while. I've got one hell of an average."

Hannah laughed. She'd already told him she was still working at the funeral parlor, and about baking the pies. She'd told him about Richard's decision-making dilemma. She'd told him about Dave.

"I'm going to go bring Billy Bob in and feed him," she said.

He rubbed his chin. "I need to shave." He was at his truck when she came back up over the hill, and had two satchels tucked under his arm. "I'm going to leave some papers here, and you'll need to go through them."

The two of them walked to the house together. "What are they?"

"Life insurance papers, hospitalization, my pension plan." He put his arm around her. "I was on a six-month trial with the company. This all just came into play. We have a big deductible, but we're insured." When they were inside, he laid the one satchel on the kitchen counter and went into the bathroom to shave.

"Wow, Charlie," Hannah said. "If you die, I get twenty thousand dollars?"

He laughed. "Don't make me cut my throat."

When he came out of the bathroom, ready for them to go get something to eat, he sat down at the kitchen desk to wait for Hannah. He looked at the certified letter. "Hannah, what's this?"

She looked around the corner at him. "Oh, that. I was going to get around to telling you. I got that today."

He motioned, was it okay for him to read it?

She nodded and disappeared.

"How'd you buy this place? What kind of contract?"

"I bought it directly from the owner, no money down."

"How long ago?"

"A month."

Charlie sat back for a moment and then leaned forward. "What're these other two letters?"

"I don't know," she said, from inside the bathroom. "I've kinda been avoiding opening them."

"Do you mind?"

"No, go ahead."

Charlie opened the letters and glanced from one to the other. "They're all the same letter."

"Good thing I didn't open them then," Hannah said.

"Do you have your purchase agreement?"

"Yep." It was in her top dresser drawer. She got it and handed it to him. He looked it over. "Are we doomed?" she asked.

Charlie shook his head and laughed. How many times had she asked him that over the years?

"I mean, can they do that?"

"We'll look into it Monday. I don't have to be on the road till Tuesday. If we need to pay it, we'll pay it."

She looked at him.

"I said I wasn't coming home broke."

"Oh that's good, because I'm not leaving, Charlie. I've got plans for this place. Did you see the orchard? I want a garden again. I want a huge garden. I want berries, I want currants, I want grapes."

Charlie looked at her. "I'm not a farmer anymore, Hannah. I don't think I ever was."

Hannah smiled. "Well, that's okay. Because I am."

When the two of them walked through the door at the Honky Tonk, Lucinda and Colleen screamed! They rushed over and hugged Hannah, hugged Charlie. "What's going on? When did you get home? What's happening? Are you home? Are you home for good?" George and Jason appeared at their sides, shaking Charlie's hand, patting him on the back, smacking him. "Where have you been? Damn you! What the hell?" Their voices all blended together. "Beers! Beers!" Jason said, and pointed to a table. "Come on, everybody sit!"

It was party time! A celebration! A homecoming! "I'm going to call Jim," George said. Within ten minutes, Charlie's best friend Jim and his wife Sara showed up.

"I ought to kick your ass," Jim said, shaking Charlie's hand. "You old son of a bitch."

Charlie laughed. "Well, if you think you're up to it."

Jim gave Charlie a big bear hug. "I've missed you, buddy."

"You too," Charlie said.

They made room at the table for two more, and way too many people sent over rounds of drinks. Way too much laughing. Way too much dancing. Every time the Texas Two-Step played, they all packed the dance floor, Charlie included. They even did the "Electric Slide." It was after midnight before everyone left to go home.

Charlie woke up bright and early in the morning. Hannah stirred. "Where are you going?"

"I've got a taste for Ditz's Harvey Ballbangers. He still makes them, right?"

"Uh huh," Hannah mumbled.

"How many do you want?"

Hannah had to think. "Two. I'll make coffee."

"No, don't. I'll pick us up some." He planted a kiss on her forehead. "How much grain do you give Billy Bob?"

"Half a scoop."

He kissed her again. "Go back to sleep."

She woke about forty-five minutes later when she heard her truck pulling back in. She got dressed, figuring Charlie would be coming into the kitchen any second now, and looked out the back door. She couldn't see her truck anywhere. "He's probably down by the barn."

She bundled up and walked down over the hill. The truck was half in and half out the barn doorway. He must have fed before he left, she

259

figured, as Billy Bob had almost finished eating his hay. Charlie was draining oil out of the old tractor.

"What are you doing?"

"I have a feeling I can get it running." He'd bought a bunch of items he needed at the service station to work on it. "Do you remember the one we had just like it?"

Hannah nodded and looked in at Billy Bob. "Daddy's home," she said.

"Your donuts and coffee are in the truck."

Hannah got them out and climbed up onto the tractor seat. She took a sip of coffee, then a big bite of donut, and another sip of coffee. "I could get used to this. Yep, I could."

Charlie smiled, and it was then that Hannah saw the old man. "Good morning."

Charlie looked at her. "Good morning."

Hannah laughed from his expression. "No, I was speaking to...." She took another bite of donut. "Charlie, do you believe in ghosts?"

He shrugged and leaned down to unclog the oil valve. It was draining slowly because of the sludge. "Ditz told me he heard this place was haunted."

"Humph." Hannah finished off her first donut and dug into the bag for the other one. "Well, it is, but in a good way."

When the old man looked at her, she could almost read his mind. "You talk too much," she imagined him saying.

The old man smiled.

"Earl Brubaker died and is still here, so to speak."

Charlie looked up at her.

"I'm serious. He's standing right next to you."

Charlie chuckled and looked around. "Oh yeah? Well, if that's the case, ask him if they were having trouble with the starter when they parked this tractor?"

The old man shook his head.

"He says no."

Charlie chuckled again. "Somebody was beating on the starter at some point." He showed her the nick marks.

"My son," the old man said.

"It was his son," Hannah said. "I don't think he was very handy."

Hannah finished eating and drank the rest of her coffee. The sun was out and it was nice and warm. She turned Billy Bob out into the pasture, dumped his water buckets and refilled them, threw him some hay, and cleaned his stall.

Charlie looked up from working on the tractor.

"I taught Billy Bob to pull it," she said, of the sled. "I'm hauling the manure to the orchard every day."

Charlie nodded and went back to what he was doing. "I'm going up to the house," Hannah said. The old man was still hovering over Charlie's shoulder, supervising, and looking happy as can be. "Uh, what time is everybody coming?"

"Around one," Charlie said.

In the midst of all the excitement and celebrating last night, an indoor-outdoor picnic got planned. The details swirled in Hannah's head. Someone was bringing a gas grill. "Jason, I think," she said to herself. "George is bringing beer and pop. Lucinda is making potato salad. Sara's baking a cake." She paused. "Oh, and Colleen's making baked beans. We're doing the chicken and spoon bread, right?"

"Yep." Charlie motioned for her to get his wallet out of his pants' pocket. Hannah took out twenty dollars. "We're going to need paper plates and napkins too." She took out another ten. "Are you sure you don't see the old man?"

Charlie looked around. "No, but things are going much too smoothly here. I'm a believer."

Hannah laughed. She went to the store and came back, and was unloading the groceries when she heard the tractor engine fire up. It spit and sputtered, snuffed itself out, then spit and sputtered again and rumbled to an almost smooth roar.

"Billy Bob's probably clapping his hands!" Hannah said.

Charlie came up to the house with a big grin on his face and washed up at the kitchen sink. Hannah handed him a towel. He sat down at the kitchen desk and just watched her for a moment. She was prepping the chicken for barbequing.

"You're as pretty as the day I met you, Hannah."

She smiled.

"So." He glanced at her to-do list laying on the desk. "Do you want help with any of this?"

She shook her head. "No, I think I can get all that done by myself. It just might take awhile." She walked over next to him. "But I *could* use some help with my wish list." She motioned for him to turn the page.

261

Charlie laughed. It was a sizable list and no small chores. He read them out loud. Lights in the barn. Move stumps to burn pile. Turn over garden bed. Fence in property. Gravel driveway to barn door. Get a pony for Billy Bob.

"Get a pony for Billy Bob?"

"Yes, I think he's going to get too lonely down there by himself this winter. I thought if I could get an easy keeper, you know, maybe an old pony that needs a home. I saved one of the cow stanchions for the stall next to his."

When he'd seen the stanchion leaning against the stall wall, Charlie figured she had another horse in mind. "Maybe we can go to the sale this weekend. If you're going to get one, you might as well get one big enough for me to ride," he said.

Hannah smiled. "And just when I didn't think I could love you any more than I already do."

Charlie laughed. "I'm going to go look at the electrical."

Hannah didn't see Charlie for hours after that, though her truck came and went several times. He appeared back up at the house only when everyone started arriving. Tom and Raven were first. Raven brought chips and dip and pretzels. "I didn't have time to cook anything on such short notice," she said.

Hannah smiled. "Chips and dip and pretzels are perfect. Thank you. You ready to take Billy Bob for another ride?"

Raven nodded. "Bareback? I just might. My trainer said I had an epiphany after that day."

One truck followed another into the drive and with equipment galore, chainsaws, log splitter, chipper. "What's this?" Hannah said.

Charlie motioned for Jim to back up over by the trees Hannah had cut down. "We're going to split the wood," he said. "It won't take us long. You have two more dead trees over there we're going to drop too."

No sooner said, she heard a tractor come down the driveway. She stared.

"Oh, that's the neighbor kid, Douglas. He stopped by earlier. Nice guy. I invited him for dinner, but he said they have an 'in-law' thing they have to do." Charlie motioned for him to drive on back to the orchard. "I'll be right there." He looked at Hannah. "Where do you want the stumps?"

Hannah stood, staring still. The old Charlie would never ask for help. "If I can't do it myself, it's not worth getting done," he would always say. That sometimes admirable quality of his, and hers too, was a downfall for them in many ways.

"Hannah?"

"Um...." She was standing on the back step. "I thought maybe over by where the um...." She wrapped her arms around his neck and hugged him tight.

"Hey, it's all right," he said. "It's all right? What's going on?"

Hannah wiped her eyes. In a flash, Lucinda and Colleen and Raven and Sara were at her side.

"Hannah?"

"Oh, just decisions, decisions," she said, and laughed. "I'm sorry, I'm okay. I'm okay."

"You sure?" Charlie asked.

"Yes." She looked at all of her friends. "Thank you," she said, pressing her hand to her heart. "Thank you." She wiped at her eyes and drew a deep breath, composing herself. "The stumps, um...."

She didn't want the fire seen by the spirit horses. She smiled at Charlie, figuring she'd save sharing that bit of information with him for another day. "Why not right over there to the side of the orchard? That's where we're going to put the garden. I want to have a big bonfire celebration in the spring to mark the planting season."

"Okay." Everyone just stood quietly for a moment, a benediction of sorts. Then they all went to work. Trees were dropped, tree trunks were sawed up, logs were split, wood was stacked, branches were ground up, stumps were moved, chicken was grilled and a feast was laid out. There were no speeches and no more tears, just some good old-fashioned hard work, fun, and good food. By nightfall, all the guests had gone and the farm was quiet.

Hannah checked on Billy Bob, and for the first time, had lights in the barn. "It's a temporary setup," Charlie said. "We'll get some florescent lights and you'll be able to turn the switch on up at the house."

Billy Bob looked up from eating his hay and sighed. Hannah smiled. She was exhausted. She'd insisted on helping load the wood into the utility room. It was stacked full. Charlie put his arm around her.

Hannah fell asleep that night without a care in the world, and at the same time, with all the cares in the world. Who knew what tomorrow would bring? She closed her eyes and recalled her and Charlie's wedding day. She could see her mother smiling. She could feel her father's hand on her arm as they walked down the aisle. She could see Charlie standing at the altar.

"For richer or for poorer, for better or for worse, till death do us part."

"Good night, Charlie," she whispered. "I love you."

"Good night, Hannah. I love you too."